Heart of the Hunter

Band of Bastards, Book 3

Lois Templin

DRAGONBLADE PUBLISHING, INC.

ARE YOU SIGNED UP FOR DRAGONBLADE'S BLOG?

You'll get the latest news and information on exclusive giveaways, exclusive excerpts, coming releases, sales, free books, cover reveals and more.

Check out our complete list of authors, too!

No spam, no junk. That's a promise!

Sign Up Here

www.dragonbladepublishing.com

Dearest Reader;

Thank you for your support of a small press. At Dragonblade Publishing, we strive to bring you the highest quality Historical Romance from some of the best authors in the business. Without your support, there is no 'us', so we sincerely hope you adore these stories and find some new favorite authors along the way.

Happy Reading!

CEO, Dragonblade Publishing

Additional Dragonblade books by Author Lois Templin

Band of Bastards Series
Heart of the Hawk (Book 1)
Heart of the Viking (Book 2)
Heart of the Hunter (Book 3)

Also from Lois Templin
The Knight, The Lady, and the Curse (Novella)

For Michelle, because she knew I would love Julie Garwood and goaded me into reading my first medieval romance. Without her persistence, my writing life would look very different.

For my parents, because they instilled in me the love of reading, stories, history, and the belief I could do anything I dreamed. And for letting me "tap, tap, tap" on my laptop in the corner of their living room when I visit but am still on deadline.

For Braden, because their creativity never ceases to inspire me, their encouragement gives me the confidence to continue when I'm convinced I should just throw the story out, and their insight and creative instincts make me a better writer.

And especially for Fritz, because he believes in me more than I believe in myself, he is my rock and knows when to push me, and because he will forever be my true hero. You are the inspiration for every hero I write.

Chapter One

England, Autumn 1286

K ENRIC "HUNTER" WARD watched the woman who had haunted his dreams for nigh on two years emerge from the bedchamber of a man he had every intention of putting in his grave.

He'd never harmed a woman in his life, but in this moment, his fingers itched to throttle the vixen. Anora had snuck through the shadows of the corridor to the man's chamber with about as much stealth as a goat.

What was she doing here, sneaking about a castle in the dead of night when she should be home, tucked into bed in her chamber above her father's goldsmith shop? He was well enough acquainted with Anora's father, Frode, to know that as much as he indulged Anora, he would be appalled of what his willful daughter was doing in the castle of a notoriously cruel baron.

The foolish woman was dressed in breeches and a tunic with a cap over her long tresses, but he'd know her anywhere. The disguise did nothing to hide the feminine movements of her tall, slender body, or the subtle curves that had relentlessly dogged his thoughts for the last two years. His anger flared at Anora's complete ignorance of the danger that she was in. He'd already had to knock out one guard—at least he was relatively certain that the guard was only knocked out. He may have smashed the man's head into the stone wall a bit harder than was necessary.

He watched her replace the heavy lock on the chamber door when she emerged from the room—the same lock she'd opened with a key from a ring full of them she'd pulled from a pouch on her belt—then slip down the spiraled stone steps toward the lower chambers. She hadn't bothered to look in the short corridor to the privy to see if anyone was lurking before she descended the stairs, and therefore didn't see Hunter where he stood in the shadows. Granted, he was known as "Hunter" for good reasons: one being his ability to prowl after unsuspecting prey, and another his ability to stalk his targets without making a sound.

Anora, on the other hand, was an accomplished goldsmith, like her father, and had no business playing at covert missions when the risks and consequences were far more horrifying than she could imagine. He knew her to be intelligent and witty from the sennight he'd spent living in their home as protector because of a dangerous mess her friend Galiena had unintentionally pulled the family into when she sought refuge at their shop from a dangerous situation. His friend Red had also been dragged into it, and somewhere along the way, Red convinced her to fall in love with him and now the big Viking was living an easy life as a husband, father, and trainer of warhorses.

He felt an unexpected pang in his conscience, as if he'd just told a lie and he knew it. He didn't know what bothered him more, the fact that Red had surrendered and settled into a life that seemed to lack challenge and adventure, or the realization that he might be envious of his friend. He pushed the thought aside, because even if he wanted a different life, a different life didn't want him. What he knew how to do was hunt his prey, fight, and kill. He did have some morals—he didn't kill haphazardly or without reason—but having morals didn't mean there was anything left of his soul other than a charred stump. And he didn't know how to do anything but else, which meant he had nothing of value to offer anyone foolish enough to want to share his life.

Tainted as he was, he was not immune to Anora. Within the first hour in her presence, he had been completely enchanted by her exuberance and wit. She saw everything as an adventure, laughed easily, and radiated warmth and acceptance of those around her. Everything she was, he was the opposite. She was good and bathed in light while he was tainted and cloaked in darkness. During his stay as protector, and during the meals he'd shared with the family since, he'd memorized every expression on her face, the contour of her cheeks and lips, the way her eyes shone when she was about to say something witty, and the gentle easy curl of her lips when she looked at the people fortunate enough to have her affection. All of it had been burned into his mind as clearly as an insignia stamped on wax. But his admiration for her was his secret.

His appreciation of her skills and courage did *not* extend to her clumsily sneaking through a castle in the dark dressed in men's clothing. He couldn't even begin to fathom why she was here or what she hoped to accomplish. Did she realize what would happen to her if she was discovered by the guards? They would not hesitate to humiliate her in every way possible, believing she deserved every degradation they would bestow upon her. And they would not care one whit that the old baron—dead and gone for more than a year—had been a trusted friend of Anora's father.

He glided quietly behind her down the winding stairs. When she reached the baron's solar at the bottom of the staircase, she pushed the door open with hasty force and the hinges squeaked loudly as it swung wide and hit against the stone wall with a low thud. She flinched, looked quickly over her shoulder, then slipped inside the chamber and pushed the door closed behind her with more care.

Hunter waited until he saw the flicker of light dance along the gap between the door and the floor before he silently entered the chamber. Anora was stooped over a chest in the rear of the baron's solar, her back to the door as she fiddled with the lock, oblivious to his presence. He crossed his arms over his chest and waited as he watched her work her keys in the lock.

He knew Anora to be headstrong and determined, even obstinate, but to rifle through possessions in locked chests in the private chambers of a stone fortress belonging to a noble was beyond reason. The fact that she was independent, assertive, and completely unapologetic was a benefit to her in the field of goldsmithing, and, in truth, they were qualities he greatly admired about her. She was a woman who had learned how to function in a field typically dominated by men; there were very few women goldsmiths in the whole of Britain, and he doubted any were as accomplished as Anora had become at the craft. Skilled as she was, she was not adequately trained to sneak in the night around the castle of a baron with a history of nefarious dealings, no scruples, and a taste for being cruel. If she were a man, he would leave her to her own consequences. He hadn't failed a mission for years because he worked under his own rules, one of which was to not let anyone jeopardize his cover or his objective.

Damn the devil! He was about to break that rule.

In truth, for Anora, he would break all of his rules if it meant protecting even the wispiest strand of hair on her beautiful head. In the two years since he had come to know Anora and Frode, he had often found reasons to pay a visit anytime he was within a day's ride of Oswestry. He had placed orders for more daggers than one man needed with their close friend Sumayl, who was not only one of the most revered blacksmiths in the region, but practically family to Anora and her father. He had come to like and admire Frode and Sumayl and enjoyed hearing their stories, but the truth was he frequented the shop mostly to be in the Anora's presence for an hour or two.

Of late, he had forced himself to limit his visits to the goldsmith shop. She had started to occupy too much of his mind and his thoughts drifted to her far too often. When she was out of his sight, he could sometimes keep her from invading his every waking thought and fitful dream. But as soon as she was near, he lost all sense of who he was, and each time it took longer than the last to put her from his mind and right himself again.

"Success," she proclaimed in an elated whisper as she removed the lock and opened the lid to the smallest of the wooden chests situated along the wall. She picked through the contents of the wooden cask, then stood straight as she pressed her fisted hands to her waist in frustration and cursed in a harsh whisper, "Hell and damnation!"

He almost laughed out loud at her uttered curse words—so unladylike but also so unsurprising coming from her lips. She may be the most enchanting woman ever to grace the earth, but she was also one of the most uninhibited when it came to expressing the thoughts in her fascinating mind. Still, Hunter was annoyed as he watched her fiddle with the ring of keys in her hand, knowing the longer she lingered, the more likely she would be caught.

She moved to the next chest, worked at the lock until it opened, then lifted the lid to peer inside. She shuffled through what sounded to him like rolls and bits of parchment, then let out an exasperated huff as she closed the lid and started to replace the lock. At least she'd done some of his work for him by opening the chests.

He silently crossed the room to stand behind her. "Not so fast," he whispered in her ear as he slipped an arm around her body, then captured her arms at her side and pressed a hand over her mouth before she could scream.

"Mph," she said against his hand as she squirmed. To her credit, her first reaction was to throw her head back in an attempt to smash his nose with her skull as she lifted her knee in preparation of slamming her foot down onto his. To *his* credit, he was prepared and deftly avoided her head as he hooked her ankle with his before she could follow through.

"Is that any way to greet an old friend?"

Chapter Two

A NORA SMITH RECOGNIZED the voice of the most irritating and perplexing man she had the misfortune to know. She supposed she should be relieved it was Hunter and not one of the baron's guards, but it still pricked her ire.

Slowly, she turned her face toward him and waited for him to remove his hand. "What the hell are you doing here?" she hissed at him as soon as her mouth was uncovered.

"I would ask you the same but now is not the time. Stand here. Do not move," he ordered and pointed to the floor next to him.

Her mouth dropped open involuntarily. How dare he try to give her orders?

She shouldn't be surprised that he rudely commanded her as though she were nothing more than an errant child. For reasons unknown to her, Hunter's disdain for her had grown during the two years of their acquaintance, and he glared at her now in a way she assumed was meant to intimidate her. That might work on other people, but she was too angry to back down from him. "I don't know what you are here for, but whatever it is, get it done and be on your way and leave me to my business."

He narrowed his eyes and leveled a fierce glare at her. "Re-gardless of what my business was, now it has become getting you out of here before you are discovered and thrown in the dungeon. Or worse."

"You need not concern yourself with me. I found my way in, and I will find my way out." She'd been terrified every step of the way, but she'd also been exhilarated. She'd managed to get past the guards at the gate, hide until darkness fell, and then steal through the castle undetected. It had been easier than she even dared hope. Getting out would be more of a challenge, but she had a plan for that.

"Do you know what will happen to you if you are caught?" Was that fear she saw in Hunter's eyes?

"I am aware of the risks." She wasn't a fool. But she also had an advantage that Hunter wasn't aware of, one that she would use if the situation became desperate. Granted, the advantage required her to lie, and the consequences could alter the course of her life in the most undesirable way, but she wouldn't think about that unless she was forced. She tucked a loose lock of hair back into her cap and met Hunter's critical gaze.

"God above, woman!" Hunter stepped uncomfortably close and glared own at her, their noses nearly touching as she watched his pupils dilate to pinpoints. "Do really think a cap and a pair of breeches will fool anyone into thinking you are a man? You will be the death of us both. It is only a matter of time before the guard lying on the privy floor above stairs comes around."

"What guard? I didn't see anyone." She'd been careful and waited until the great hall and tower were abandoned and quiet before she tiptoed up the stairs to the baron's chamber. "You are making that up to scare me."

"I know you didn't see him," he drawled. "But he saw you. And he followed you up the stairs."

He turned away from her and reached into one of the chests *she* had opened with her keys. After a moment of picking up and scanning various missives, he tucked one into his boot. She hadn't opened the chests for his convenience. She'd opened them looking for any of the pendants or jewels stolen from her father's shop so many years ago.

Or the brooch stolen merely a fortnight past, lifted from a locked chest inside the locked shop while she, her father, and the blacksmith—who was like family to them and lived in a room of the manor above the shop—had attended the Lammas Day Festival in the churchyard.

The stolen pendants had been used to pay a debt at a bawdy house in Shrewsbury. She knew this because the proprietress of the establishment, Madam Ruby, had brought it to her father's shop to exchange for coin, as she'd done many times over the years when clients paid her in jewels, trinkets, or scraps of precious metals. With her father above stairs, Anora conducted the transaction—which was not unusual—and feigned idle curiosity about the piece. Madam Ruby couldn't be sure who had used the pendants to pay her, but she thought it may have been Baron Payne of Castle Whyte.

The revelation surprised her momentarily, but she wasn't completely shocked by the idea of Baron Payne's involvement in questionable activities—at a brothel or with stolen goods. She'd known the Baron Payne of Castle Whyte for as long as she could remember. His father had been a trusted friend of her father since boyhood. She remembered the old man as a kind and good, though stern, but his son was nothing like him. Edmund Payne had been a ghastly pest when they were children, but he'd become downright cruel since assuming his father's title when the old baron died two years prior. His inherited title and elevated position had made him even more arrogant and callous. He'd become a man who used his power to intimidate because he did not understand the difference between fear and respect. She would not put it above him to consider stealing from others as his right, as a means of taking what he felt he was duly owed. but so far, she'd found nothing damning.

Despite that, she wasn't convinced that it proved he was innocent. Rather, she felt it was merely because she had not yet looked in the right place. There had been nothing of value in his bedchamber, and the chests she found in his solar had yielded nothing more than a small trove of gold coins in one, and a collection of parchments in the other.

Hunter closed the lid and replaced the lock on the larger chest of parchments, then moved to the smaller chest, lifted a handful of the coins to let them run through his fingers as they sparkled in the candlelight. He turned to Anora and arched one brow, "Not what you were looking for?"

"That is not your concern," she said as she lifted her chin. "But apparently you found something useful."

He shrugged in answer as he turned to the table in the middle of the room and shuffled through the scrolls and bits of parchment strewn across it.

"Are you almost finished?" She fisted her hands and set them on her hips as her irritation grew.

"Almost. And then I'm escorting you out of here before you get yourself killed."

"I've not found what I am looking for as of yet, so I'd appreciate it if you would be on your way and leave me to my work." Hunter was a complication for which she did not have the time nor the tolerance. What was he doing here anyway?

He turned to her, his eyes wide as though what she said astonished him. "Your *work*?"

Her confidence waned slightly under his scrutiny, but she answered in a steady voice. "Yes, Hunter. And I do not require your presence. In fact, I would prefer to continue it alone."

"Is that so?" he drawled in a patronizing tone that grated on her nerves.

"Did I not speak clearly?" Her anger had replenished her confidence. She was not about to allow this man to treat her like a child when she neither asked for nor wanted his assistance.

He moved to stand in front of her again and pushed close as though he meant to force her to back away from him, but she refused. Which meant that when he spoke, she felt the warmth of his breath on her cheeks. "Then perhaps I should go above stairs and wake the guard I knocked unconscious for you, since you think you do not need me."

"I'm surprised you didn't kill him. It's not like you to be so merciful." She softened her face into an angelic expression as she spoke, which was in complete contrast to the intentionally snide tone of her words. "That is if the brazen tales about you are true."

His eye twitched almost imperceptibly, and she wondered if she'd actually offended him.

"As of now, we are only guilty of trespassing. I'd prefer we not add murder to the list of offenses." He tilted his head slightly to the side and gave her a bored look. "But I can go finish the job, if you'd like."

"No!" She did not want anyone killed because of her.

Hunter nodded once, then grabbed a handful of the coins from the small chest and put it in the pouch at his waist before he closed the lid and replaced the lock.

"What are you doing?" Anora's eyes went wide with disapproval as she looked from the pouch at his waist to the wooden chest of riches and back to the pouch again.

"Not your concern," he said in a low grumble, echoing her earlier dismissal of his question.

"Now you've added theft to the list of offenses," Anora said. She couldn't condone stealing, even from Edmund—unless it was to steal back something that didn't belong to him to begin with.

"That's rich, coming from you, lady-thief. You were just elbow-deep in that same chest." He hooked a hand around her wrist to pull her away from the chests. "Let's go before more guards come looking for the one in the privy."

"Not until I find what I came for," she protested as she planted her feet in resistance.

"Not so loud," he bit out between clenched teeth as he pressed a finger to her lips as though she were a misbehaving child, "lest you wish to attract more guards. In which case, I'll have to decide who to kill first, them or you."

She narrowed her eyes at him in what she hoped was a withering glare as she reluctantly pinched her lips shut. Though she did not believe Hunter would truly hurt her, he had a reputation as a dangerous man with skills that made him lethal and very useful to his lord.

"Later, you will tell me why you are here." The stern set of his lips indicated he was not in the mood for discussion. "But for now you are going to do exactly as I say, unless you prefer to spend the night chained to a dungeon wall."

Chapter Three

A S HE LED her across the room, he stopped at the table in the center, licked his thumb and forefinger, then pressed them to the wick of the candle to snuff the flame and douse the light. With her wrist still clutched in his hand, he kept her close to him as he moved through the darkness to the tapestry concealing the entry to a long corridor that ran the length of the castle wall behind the great hall.

"Two steps up," he whispered to her as he held the tapestry away from the wall. He heard a faint grunt as her toe scuffed against the stone step, but she did not trip. With his hand on the damp stones, he retraced his steps from earlier in the night when he'd come this way to search for incriminating documents. Fortunately, he found something of use among the parchments; unfortunately, he'd left with more than he planned when he found Anora in the castle. But he'd get her safely away from here even if it meant he had to kill every guard in the castle to do it.

She was sure-footed despite the blackness of the corridor, and unexpectedly deft on her feet. The moon was hidden behind clouds when he first entered the castle, which was his preference, but that meant that not even the dimmest of light shone through the narrow openings in the outer wall to guide them. There were a few small windows that looked down into the great hall below, but with only one sconce lit at the far end of that room, it was not enough to be of any significance inside the narrow corridor.

As they reached the far end of the passageway and turned to the right, the dim light from the spiraling stairwell of the north tower could be seen. He stopped to listen for guards on patrol and was about to take a step forward when he heard the soft thuds of footsteps as someone ascended the stairs. He turned and guided Anora back along the passageway they had just come through until he reached an alcove and tucked her into it. He leaned close and commanded in a low whisper, "Stay here until I come back for you."

He returned to the staircase and pressed himself against the wall, just out of the reach of the dim light and waited. The head of a man appeared, his faced turned down toward his midsection. He stopped on the landing as he fumbled with the belt at his waist. Hunter recognized the tabard the man wore, emblazoned with a simple green-and-white herald, as that worn by the baron's guardsmen. If the man continued straight, he would walk directly into Hunter hidden in the shadows. But to Hunter's good fortune, the guard rounded the corner into the other opening as he pulled his belt and sword free, then disappeared into the alcove. He heard a faint shuffle of clothing, then a thud as the man's bare arse dropped onto the wood plank seat of the privy.

Hunter contemplated whether to rid himself of the threat of the guard while he was vulnerable, or to retrieve Anora to slip down the stairs while the guard was occupied and otherwise indisposed. He heard a long groan and a muttered curse and decided it was best to take advantage of the man's distressed state to make their escape. He returned to Anora in a few quick steps, whispered to her to remain absolutely silent, and pulled her along behind him toward the stairwell. There was a wretched smell in the air and the man emitted miserable moans from the privy as they entered the spiraling staircase of the tower and started their descent.

At the bottom of the stairs, he paused at the open door out to the bailey. The doorway was tucked into a corner where the castle wall joined the tower, out of sight from most of the castle yard, but visible to the patrols on the wall walk across the bailey. He was not surprised to see another guard leaned against the stone wall as he gazed out onto the castle yard and awaited the return of his mate from the privy above stairs.

Hunter regretted his choice to pass by the first guard without putting him out of commission. The likelihood of him stumbling from the tower before Hunter could immobilize his partner was greater than he cared for when he had Anora to think about. He couldn't leave her in the tower while he made quick work of the man outside for fear the first guard would come upon her before he was done. He didn't relish the thought of killing more men, but he hoped Anora wouldn't protest when he did what was necessary for their escape.

He turned to her and crooked his finger at her to follow him from the tower. Once clear of the door, he quietly pushed her back into the dark cleft between the tower and the curtainwall, out of sight if the first guard exited the doorway before he could return for her.

Dread washed over Hunter when he heard the guard by the wall speak to someone out of sight from his vantage point, but he breathed a sigh of relief when it became apparent the man merely sang raunchy limericks to pass the time. He moved as quickly as he dared along the wall as he sneaked up behind the man and wrapped an arm around his neck, then forcefully bumped the back of his knees to make his legs give out. The guard fell back into him and Hunter shoved his head forward as he crumbled and quickly snapped his neck to the side. He'd wanted to avoid leaving a trail of bodies on their way out of the castle, but that was now impossible.

After the guard's body went limp against him, he hooked him under the arms and dragged his corpse back toward the dark corner next to the tower. Anora was staring at him with her mouth hanging open in shock, but thankfully she stayed silent.

He motioned with his chin for her to step out of the way then leaned the guard against the corner and pushed his legs as far as possible into the shadows.

The other guard had yet to make an appearance. Hunter stuck his head in the door to the tower and listened, determined the guard in the privy was still indisposed, then took Anora by the hand and led her along in the shadow of the castle wall. When they reached the corner, Hunter peered around the edge of the wall, made a quick calculation as to whether or not they could cross the yard to the southernmost tower before the guards on the wall noticed them.

He spied a pair of guards patrolling the parapets above as they made their way to the tower closest to them. When they crossed over the tower and started their trek south on the wall walk, Hunter took the opportunity to edge along in the shadows below where the guards could not see them unless they bent over the parapets and looked straight down. He'd not seen any other patrols and guessed that the light guard duty was a result of the baron and most of his men being absent from the castle. They reached the southern tower without incident and slipped inside.

"Tell me you didn't kill that man," Anora whispered to his back.

"The list of offenses is growing," he drawled at her as he took a small torch from the wall sconce and turned to her. To his relief, she didn't protest despite the way her face paled. He hitched his chin in a silent command to follow him and led her through the first doorway into a narrow corridor. After a few steps, it widened into a larger sitting area with cushioned benches facing a long, narrow gap in the opposite wall that looked into a chapel. He peered through the opening to assure himself no one lingered in the nave.

"What is this?" she asked.

"Private viewing room of the chapel for the lord of the castle. He can redeem his soul without mingling with those he deems beneath him. That door there," he said with a tip of his head toward the far end of the room, "leads to the confessional inside the chapel."

"How do you know this?" she asked. "Do you come here often to confess?"

He turned his head to face her, the smirk on her lips clearly visible in the light from the torch in his hand. He liked it more than he should when she teased him, though he never knew how to respond without sounding like an arrogant dolt. And now was not really the time for banter considering they trespassed where they did not belong. "I'd have to feel guilt to confess."

"Or remorse. Have you any?" She looked at him with earnest curiosity, but he knew the innocent look was feigned by the twitch of her lips as she fought to keep the corners from turning up in a smirk he'd come to know well.

"Never," he growled with irritation meant for himself at his inability to stay focused when in her presence. "Stop talking."

Ignoring the immediate ire that flushed her face at being told what to do, he pulled open the door and motioned her to pass through into the confessional booth, which was larger than most due to the private entrance for the lord of the castle. She waited for him in the confined space as he closed the door behind them and held the small torch high enough to avoid starting their hair on fire. He had to grit his teeth together not to think about how near she was and the things he wanted to do to her behind the drapes of the intimately close space if circumstances were different. He let out a soft snort of laughter at the thought that God might strike him dead with a bolt of lightning for such sacrilege.

"Why do you laugh?" Anora whispered as she looked through a gap in the curtains into the small chapel. "And why are we in a confessional?"

"Don't dawdle while I have a flame in my hand." He ignored her questions and nudged her gently with a hand on her back into the chancel, then held the curtain wide as he passed through with the torch in his hand. The confessional was built of wood and consisted of three compartments with plank walls on three sides and curtains at the front. The center compartment belonged to the priest, and the other two compartments on each end were for the faithful to confess. Hunter drew back the curtain to the center area and Anora let out a gasp behind him.

"What are you doing?" she hissed as she stepped close to him. Her body lightly brushed against his back as she peered over his shoulder into the part of the confessional rarely seen by anyone outside of the church clergy. He could feel her breath on his cheek when he turned his face in her direction, and he had to swallow hard as he willed his composure to remain intact while she stood so near to him before he could answer.

"This is the way out," he said, then held out the torch in her direction. "Here. Take this, just don't start the curtain on fire."

She took the torch as she cocked her hip to the side and gave him a scornful glare. "I'm not a halfwit."

"That's questionable," he muttered. She was smart, he'd give her that, but she lacked common sense, as evidenced by the fact she was prowling around a castle alone in the night dressed as a man. She gasped with indignation, but before she could say anything more, he turned his attention back to the task at hand. Now was not the time to chat. Or argue.

He entered the priest's booth and picked up the ornately carved chair with its cushioned seat and skirted legs, then backed out of the cramped space and set it aside. The draped material at the base of the chair was more than just a lavish addition for the priest's comfort; it also served to conceal the removable panel in the floor beneath his seat. Most would never dare enter the priest's booth and thus would never know there was a hidden door and escape route directly under his feet. He pulled his dagger from its sheath on his belt, squatted, then slipped the tip of the blade into a notch of the panel to lift it.

"How did you know this was here?" she asked as though he'd just revealed a hidden treasure.

"Let me tell you the tale. It's a long one, but a good one." He didn't know why he responded the way he did, but something about Anora brought out the unexpected in him.

She narrowed her eyes and smirked. "No need to be a boorish ass. I merely expressed a curiosity. Continue on." She waved her hands as though she were shooing a child on their way.

At least she got the message. If he stopped to answer all of her questions along the way, they would never get out of the castle alive. Hunter removed the floor panel and leaned it against the confessional booth wall as the scratch and shuffle of countless scurrying little feet reached their ears.

"Are those rats?" Her voice hitched higher on the last word.

Hunter's gaze snapped to her face, startled by fear in her question. *She didn't have the sense to be afraid of guards, but rodents terrified her?* "Hand me the torch."

She did as he asked, then backed away as he climbed down the ladder a few rungs and swept his arm in a circle to light up the room below with the flame from the torch. "They've scattered now."

She did not look reassured, and her face paled as she shook her head vehemently from side to side. "I'd rather take my chances with the guards."

"Don't you have rats in Oswestry?" He'd not expected her to be fainthearted about rodents. They were everywhere.

"Aye," she said, her eyes wide as she stared at the opening in the floor, as though she expected rats to jump out at her despite his shoulders filling the space. "But not in my house. Or the shop. Or even the smithy."

"There is no need to be afraid," he said in a feeble attempt to reassure her.

Her focus sharpened as her gaze snapped to his face. "Have *you* been bitten by one? They have teeth like tiny knives that are as sharp as razors."

"When did a rat bite you?" There wasn't time for questions, and he'd just chastised her for doing the same, but he couldn't help himself. As common a sight as rats were, they did not often bite people who lived in homes as grand and tidy as Anora's father's manor.

"When my brother thought it would be humorous to hide one in my bed when I was a girl and it bit my toe, which swelled up the size and color of a plum and was painful to walk on for days." Her eyes were wide with remembered terror.

Hunter tried not to laugh at her indignant tone and disgruntled expression. Obviously, she was still aggrieved by the event. "I won't let the rats bite you," he promised as he dipped his chin to hide the smirk he felt tugging at his lips.

She shook her head again and started to turn on her heel as though she meant to leave. "There must be another way."

He needed to act quickly before she did something that would get them both captured. From experience, he knew that one thing that always spurred a woman into action was anger—and the implication she was not capable of doing something. He would bet his favorite dagger that Anora was no different than other women.

"This is why I work alone," he muttered loud enough for her to hear, "and never with a woman. They lack the skills and courage required. Especially a woman afraid of rats."

As intended, she spun around to face him, her lips set in a hard line. "I agree. You *are* better suited to working alone." She turned on her heel again, though more forcefully this time, and walked with determined strides toward the door at the end of the nave, which opened into the castle yard in full view of any guards on the wall above.

That did not go at all as he had planned.

Chapter Four

Anora attributed her stubborn nature to the fact that she had spent most of her life surrounded by men. Her mother had died when she was a young girl and Anora had grown into a woman without her, leaving her life to be influenced almost solely by men. Perhaps other women were just as willful as she was, but she didn't know enough of them to be certain. What she was certain of was that she would not let Hunter intimidate her, hence the reason she had turned her back on him and strode determinedly toward the door at the back of the chapel when he tried to shame her into getting over her fear of rats.

She'd spent enough time with men to know that they were often full of bluster, and the easiest way to find out was to challenge them on it. Her intention was to make it clear that his attempt to press her into action would not be tolerated, but she fully expected him to stop her before she reached the door. She could play the game of manipulation just as well as he did, and she refused to be coerced into cooperation by demeaning taunts. With men, if violence wasn't involved, then it was merely a game of will, and of that, she had an abundance.

She heard his frustrated grunt as he hefted himself up the ladder and out of the hole to follow her from the confines of the confessional. Her height matched that of most men, but he still caught up to her in only a few strides before he grasped her arm and swung her around to face him.

"Let me go, Hunter," she snapped through gritted teeth.

"Do not run away from me," he countered. "Your foolishness will get us both captured."

"You are to blame," she said as she pulled her arm free of his grip. "I didn't ask you to help me; you ordered me to come with you. I've followed your every request, despite your propensity for rudeness. You whinge about me being here when it was you who said I must come with you, and now you are whinging about me leaving after you said you prefer to work alone. Make up your mind and be done with it."

At least he had the wherewithal to look abashed by his arrogant behavior. "I thought that if I angered you, you would try to prove me wrong and forget about your fear of rats."

"And I thought you to be a better man, but you are as much of an ass as the rest of them." She'd meant the for the words to sting but she softened her rebuke at his unexpected confession.

"You thought wrong. I am the worst of men, and you would do well to remember that."

The words were said in an even tone, but he averted his eyes as he spoke, and she wondered what caused him to think so lowly of himself. She didn't really believe him to be a bad person; she'd only wanted to get his attention. He may be a man of the sword with blood on his hands, but he had always acted honorably toward her and her father. "Now it is I who must apologize because I just tried to bait you as you did me. I do not think you to be an ass."

His gaze snapped to her face as though startled by what she said, but whatever she saw in his eyes was unrecognizable to her and gone as quickly as it appeared. "High praise, indeed."

She rolled her eyes at him. "For a man of few words, the ones you do speak have the sharpest of edges."

He looked flustered by her response, as though it were unexpected. "You are baiting me again. Now is not the time."

"You are right. On both accounts."

His eyebrows arched high in disbelief at her response, which seemed to fuel his arrogance. "I am always right. And I will not let the rats near you."

She shook her head at his arrogance and sighed. "Then lead the way, Hunter, for if you are wrong about the rats and I get bitten, I will have the satisfaction of reminding you of it every day for the rest of your life."

Much to her satisfaction, his lips twitched in the barest of smiles and he ran a hand over his face to hide it. "Fair. Let's go." With that, he turned on his heel and headed back to the confessional. She took a deep breath to steel her nerves in preparation for what lay ahead and followed in his wake.

Before he entered the confined space, he stopped and handed her the torch. "You must go down first. I will return the chair to its place and replace the door in the floor behind us."

"I-I can do that, just tell me what to do." She heard the desperation in her voice and swallowed hard to put the thought out of her mind of the sharp-toothed rodents waiting below.

He handed her the torch and shook his head. "The rats run from the flame. You will have all the control."

It was not the answer nor the reassurance she'd hoped for, but she wrapped her fingers around the base of the torch and positioned herself at the edge of the opening in the floor. With her legs dangling, she stuck the flame through the hole and waved it around, then grabbed the top rung with her free hand as she found her footing on a lower rung and started the descent into what she was confident must be the bowels of hell.

She waved the torch in a wide arc when she reached the bottom to ensure the rats were scattered before she stepped down onto the dirt floor. She didn't dare look up as Hunter started his descent, preferring to keep her eye on the enemies she expected to emerge from the shadows if she let her guard down. Above, she could hear the scrape of wooden chair legs on the floorboards and the thud as he dropped the wood panel in place overhead. With her back to the ladder, she continued to wave the flame in front of her muttering threats to any rats who might be lurking nearby.

"Unless you move, I will step on your head." Hunter's voice carried down from above her, and she looked up to see his muscular thighs nicely accented by the stretch of his breeches as he descended the stairs.

Reluctantly, Anora took a small step forward. His back brushed along hers as he dropped to the floor and his shoulder bumped against her when he turned to stand behind her. She could feel the heat of his chest at her back, and the rhythm of his breathing was a comfort to her as proof she did not have to face the rats alone. It wasn't until he reached around her that she realized she was leaning into him. She should be mortified by her conduct and put a decent amount of space between them, but she preferred his reassuring presence at her back to keep her safe from any rats who might think to attack from behind.

"You are not going to let go of the torch, are you?" he asked as he closed his fingers around the base of the torch and gently tugged.

She shook her head and gripped the torch like it was her only means of survival. When he closed his fingers over hers and nudged her forward with the pressure of his chest against her back, she did not resist. The chamber around them was only about the width of a man's outstretched arms, but the length of it stretched out before her with no end in sight. His arm circled around her waist, and they slowly started moving forward. She bit her lip and tried to concentrate on walking, but she was distracted by the way his body felt pressed to hers as they progressed like a stumbling four-legged creature who couldn't keep its feet from getting entangled together.

"How far must we go before we are free of this place?" Her voice sounded breathless, even to her own ears, and she hoped that Hunter would assume it was from fear and wouldn't realize that it was because she had never been this close to a man before, or had her body meld with a man's as hers did now, or felt dizzy from the thrill of being held in the circle of a man's arm.

She'd had one man try to kiss her, but she'd felt nothing but repulsion as his fingers dug into her shoulders and dragged her toward him while the stale odor of his breath wafted over her. His lips had felt dry and the pressure of his mouth grinding against her mouth had convinced her she never wanted to kiss a man again.

A snort of laughter escaped his throat and brought her attention back to the present. "When traveling at a pace greater than a shuffle, the distance is not so far. But like this? We should be out of here by Mabon."

She gasped. "But the autumn equinox is still five days away!"

"Aye," he grunted from behind her.

"That will not do," she said with a sigh. As much as she hated to give up the safety of Hunter's body shielding her, she hated more the idea of being stuck in this horrible rats' nest any longer than absolutely necessary. The rodents had scattered when they dropped into the underground chamber, but she feared it was only a matter of time before they became comfortable with their presence and returned to investigate. She released the torch and ducked under his arm but kept one of her arms wrapped around his midsection. "You lead."

Saints above, but this feels nice. She almost stopped in her tracks as that thought flitted through her mind, and there was no denying she liked the feel of her arm pressed against the solid warmth of his torso. His stomach was flat, and she had the sudden urge to splay her fingers across the hard expanse and press her cheek to his back. He smelled of trees and leather and something wonderfully earthy that made her want to bury her nose in the locks of hair that brushed along the top of his back.

"You will have to release your death grip on me if we are to move any faster." When she hesitated, he added, "You can either climb on my back and I'll carry you, or you can hold onto the back of my tunic and follow me."

"I'll not have you carry me," she relented. "Just get us out of here as quickly as possible, please." She cleared her head of the errant thoughts and dug her fingers into the fabric of his tunic with the same intensity as a falcon sinking its talons into the leather of a handler's glove. Later, she would think on the longings that were making her feel jittery and uncomfortable but now was not the time.

Hunter continued to hold the torch low enough to scatter any rodents in their path as they progressed deeper into the underground tunnel. The rats stayed far enough away for her to regain confidence that they might actually escape this horrible chamber unscathed, but she remained close enough to Hunter's back that she could jump onto it in an instant should any rats try to charge at her.

The pungent aroma of moss and wet earth filled her nostrils, and the soles of her boots slipped as the dirt floor gave way to stones, which were slick underfoot from the damp, dank air. "Where does the tunnel lead?"

"Out of the castle and onto the lower slope of the hill below the castle wall, but we still need to get to the forest from there."

"Will the guards not see us emerge?"

"Not if we are careful."

"How careful?" she whispered as a chill shivered down her spine at the thought of being shot through with an arrow. She had assumed that if she encountered a guard, she would use her words and wit to talk her way out of a bad situation, but that required close proximity. If spotted as they ran from the castle, they would instantly be known as trespassers and fair targets, and she would have no opportunity to use her acquaintance with the baron to leverage their safety.

"Quite careful. Sound carries up." His words did not reassure her. "There is some tree cover where we come out, but there is a clearing at the bottom of the hill that will need to be crossed." They had covered only a short distance more when he said, "Don't be frightened but I must extinguish the torch."

Before she could protest, he jammed the end of the torch into the damp moss coating the tunnel wall. She watched in horrified fascination as he twisted it until the flame was completely extinguished and they were cloaked in darkness. Her heartbeat raced in her chest as she imagined rats swarming toward her in the pitch black to scamper up her legs and bite at her skin, and the fear of them trapped under her gown as she fought to get away from them took her breath away.

"Calm yourself," Hunter said in her ear as his arms closed around her waist. "Umph!"

She felt her elbow connect with his ribs as she flailed her limbs to keep the rats away. Her feet were no longer in contact with the ground, but she did not dare stop squirming for fear the rodents would overtake her. She kicked and churned her legs as the ominous chorus of chirps and squeaks of the furry little beasts circled closer. "Don't tell me to calm myself! They'll get under my gown. I won't be able to find them."

"You aren't wearing a gown." The words were a murmured drawl near her ear. "You are wearing breeches tucked into boots. Stop squirming so I can carry you out."

The words penetrated her brain slowly through the fog of fear that enshrouded it. She brushed her hands over the rough fabric covering her legs and remembered that she had donned her brother's clothing and there was no reason to panic. She wasn't wearing a gown, and her legs weren't trapped in a sea of material for the rats to hide in while they scampered up her body. *Pull yourself together.*

"I will not have you carry me out," Anora said through gritted teeth. In truth, she very much wanted him to carry her out, but it was foolish and selfish of her. "That would definitely hinder our chances of escape. Put me down. Please."

"True," Hunter said as he slowly placed her back on her feet, his hands still at her waist while she found her balance.

She put her hands to her chest as it heaved to soothe the hysteria that tried to grip her like a steel band tightening around her lungs. If she couldn't conquer her fears, then what was to become of her future? Her papa was getting older, and the day would come when she would have to find her way without him. The pressure to find a husband to protect and guide her increased with each passing season, and she feared what would happen if she did not prove herself capable. "If I want to do this on my own, then I must learn to resolve my own issues. This is just another problem, like all the others, that I am capable of solve without a man."

"What problems?"

The deep, slow drawl of Hunter's voice cut through the litany of worries and reassurances that filled her head every time she thought about her future. "What?"

"You said you want to prove you can solve your own problems. What are they?" His voice was hard and angry, and awareness suddenly dawned that she had said everything out loud and not in her head as she had meant.

"Nothing," she said through tight lips as she took a deep breath and smoothed her hands down her torso, then balled her hands into determined fists at her side. "Let us be on our way before the rats come back."

She couldn't see his face in the dark, but she felt his hesitation, sure that he regretted his insistence that she come with him to escape the castle. Not only was she afraid of rats, but she'd also had a fit of hysteria that he likely perceived as proof she was weak and incapable. She didn't bother to explain that the frantic outburst was actually helpful to her, that it forced her to focus on what was important to her so she could move forward. She assumed men did the same thing, but the voices in their heads were probably much more judgmental and unforgiving.

"Don't think about where you are," he finally said, his voice calm as he found her hand and took it in his. "Take deep breaths and think about the open air that awaits you."

In truth, it helped to focus on what was ahead of her instead of what was around her. With a deep breath, she imagined the furry little pests being left behind as she made her way toward freedom. She told herself her boots and breeches were like armor and would keep her protected from anything terrible, such as sharp little rodent teeth. And as far as surviving without the assistance of a man, she was still convinced she would have found her way out of the castle without Hunter.

And it wouldn't have involved wading through rats.

Chapter Five

"THE WAY OUT is around the next bend. Stay behind me and stay quiet until I am sure no one is near." The crisp tang of autumn leaves filled Hunter's nostrils as a gust of air cooled his face. The faint gray light of the moon shone through the gap in the stones that opened out onto the hill below the castle wall. The rocks were at such an angle that the opening blended into the contour of the terrain and was concealed by the tree trunks and leafy brush growing on the steep incline. The foliage on the hill would provide some cover as they descended, but once they reached the bottom, they would have to cross a wide swath of land that had been cleared specifically to make anyone trying to approach the castle more visible. Once they reached the far side of the clearing, they would then be in the safety of a thick forest and the rest of their escape would be less complicated.

He peered around the edge of the stones and listened for any sign of danger, then eased through the opening with Anora behind him, her hand still in his as he led her down the slope toward the clearing. The feel of his fingers wrapped around hers distracted him in a way that was wholly unexpected. He liked the possessiveness of the gesture, the way it made him feel like she was his to protect, and the sense of pride that swelled in his chest at the thought that he had a purpose that went beyond him.

The realization sent a shockwave through his body and his head buzzed in warning. He released his hold on her hand, his instinct to detach from anything or anyone who could become a hindrance to him. And Anora was certainly someone who could cloud his judgment if he wasn't careful. It was why he had avoided the goldsmith shop in recent weeks, because when he was in her presence, he seemed to forget the hazards of an infatuation. His mind had become susceptible to foolish thoughts about her; thoughts of things that did not fit into the life of a man like him; thoughts he had to keep at bay for her sake as much as his.

With a quick shake of his head, he sharpened his focus to the task at hand. If he didn't time their sprint across the clearing to the trees correctly, the guards on the wall above would see them. He looked overhead, gauging the cloud cover for the most opportune moment to be cloaked in darkness, then craned his neck to scan the parapets for immediate danger. Once he'd assured himself the risks were minimal and the moment optimal, he reached for her hand and guided her across the grassy meadow.

God above, but he wished Anora did not have to be subjected to this danger. If he knew a better way to get her away from here safely, he'd take it. *How the hell did she get in the castle, anyway?* He'd question her later about it, and probably want to ring her delicate neck again for the danger she put herself in.

As soon as they were well in the cover of the trees, he stopped and turned back to check for anyone watching from the wall. Thankfully, all was clear. "Are you all right?"

"Aye." She put her hands to her waist and stretched tall as she took several deep breaths. "Oh, no!"

He'd not heard anything save her heavy breathing but immediately moved to block her from whatever had caught her attention as he scanned the forest for danger. "What is it?" He scanned around them in the darkness, looking for men behind trees or sitting in branches. Despite the clouds that continued to block most of the light from the moon, he could see a fair distance and saw nothing out of the ordinary.

"I've dropped my pouch with the keys. The tie must have come loose."

He turned to face her, ready to tell her the pouch and keys would have to remain lost, but if she lost them in the tunnel and the baron found them, it would become considerably more difficult to sneak into the castle again, as any man with half a brain would seal the passage.

"Do you have any idea where you lost them?" he asked, rubbing his fingers over his forehead to sooth the pounding that had begun in his temples.

"I had them when we were in the chapel. I remember touching my hand to the pouch to ensure it was still there when I was of a mind to find my own way out of the castle."

He felt certain he would have heard the pouch drop on the wooden planks of the floor if it had been lost there. That meant the pouch was likely in the tunnel. He contemplated whether it was too much of a risk to go back for them. "What else was in the pouch?"

"The keys, a few coins, and a few small smithing picks in case I needed them for the locks."

He made a note to ask her later who had made her the pass keys and taught her to pick open locks, but there wasn't time to dwell on that now. "Are they the same picks you use in the shop?"

"Yes, but I can have more made."

"True, but if anyone with a discerning eye finds them, they will recognize them as the tools of a goldsmith. The baron will know they do not belong to anyone in his employ. And if they are in the tunnel, he will know someone has discovered his escape route." Hunter sighed. "I will have to go back for them."

"I think it will be where you picked me up when I thought rats to be crawling on me, but how will you ever find them in the pitch black of the tunnel?" He could hear the desperation in

Anora's voice. "'Tis too great a risk. Let's be on our way."

"No. The baron will find the pouch eventually and close off the access, which will make my work more difficult." He scanned the woods to assure himself they were still alone, then waited as a pair of guards passed by on the wall walk of the castle. He knew from earlier reconnaissance that the guards would pass by this stretch of the castle wall about every quarter of an hour. He nudged Anora in the direction of a large tree and said, "Stand against that tree trunk and wait for my return. I will not be gone long."

He waited until she had done as asked, made his way back across the meadow while he kept his gaze on the parapets of the castle, then climbed the hill to the opening of the tunnel. It was difficult enough to find the crevasse behind the rocks in the daylight, and in the dark even more of a challenge, but he had memorized the contour of the hillside and found his way back without difficulty.

The tunnel was pitch black as he made his way by feel to the point where Anora had had her panicked episode of terror over the rats. After a few moments of shuffling his feet along the tunnel floor, his toe connected with a soft mound that carried some heft. He was relieved when he reached down to pick it up that it wasn't a dead rat and was indeed the pouch of keys and other bits.

He'd exited the tunnel and was part way down the hill when he heard Anora's voice in the distance, along with another voice that most definitely belonged to a man. Fear like he'd not known since he was a boy punched him in the gut. If anything happened to her, he'd have failed another woman, and he'd never forgive himself.

At the bottom of the hill, he stopped and assessed the situation. An opening in the cloud cover afforded some moonlight and he could see two men dressed in tabards—likely patrols from Castle Whyte—standing at the edge of the clearing with Anora. Red-hot rage coursed through his veins and his vision blurred. His first instinct was to race across the clearing and kill both men with his bare hands before they could touch Anora. But that would attract the attention of the guards on the parapets, and they'd all end up dead.

How had this night gone so wrong? He'd expected to be in and out of the castle in less than an hour with his mission complete and none the wiser to his presence. If it hadn't been for Anora, he'd already be on his horse and riding toward Hawkspur and his bed.

This was why he worked alone.

He could pretend that he wasn't going to risk his life to save her hide, or that he was too calloused and wrecked to have room in his heart to care. There were very few people in the whole of the world that he would consider sacrificing the mission or himself to save. He'd learned a long time ago not to let emotions get in the way of the goal, which was why there was no one in the kingdom more lethal than him.

"Hell and damnation," he muttered to himself, repeating the curse Anora had used when she couldn't find what she wanted in the chest. He could recite a litany of more vulgar words, but none were more appropriate in the current situation because he'd crawl through the fires of hell and commit his soul to damnation before he'd let anything happen to Anora.

Chapter Six

"W HAT'VE WE GOT here?" The sneered taunt sent a ripple of gooseflesh over Anora's skin.

Not long after Hunter had disappeared into the darkness on the other side of the meadow, two guards rounded the bottom of the hill and walked along the edge of the clearing then stopped only a stone's throw from where she stood in the trees. She tried to inconspicuously move further behind the tree trunk, but despite her cautious effort to be quiet, she stepped on a twig, and it snapped with a pop under her foot. There was a break in the clouds and a beam of moonlight shone down directly on her at the same time and she swore under her breath.

She couldn't run now that they'd seen her, so she had to think quickly if she wanted to save her hide and Hunter's. If she could stall them until Hunter returned and keep them from attracting the attention of any other guards, they might still have a chance of escape. She was certain he could handle both the guards if he maintained the element of surprise and stayed out of sight of the guards walking the castle wall.

"Greetings, gentle sirs," Anora said in a sweet tone. Despite being dressed as a man, she decided it was safer in the current situation to reveal her identity as a woman. The first plausible story that came to her mind was to present herself as a lovelorn woman hidden in the dark, masqueraded in men's clothing while she waited for her lover rather than a man who lurked in places he didn't belong.

"Ye' don' look like a lass, but ye' sure sound like one," one of the men said as they started up the hill.

"I wasn't expecting you. I was expecting…William." It was the first name that came to her mind, and she prayed neither of these men was called by the same. "He assured me he'd meet me here. Said I should wait for him if he wasn't here when I arrived, that he'd be along presently."

Anora turned away from the tree and said a silent prayer that the guards would follow her as she moved a little deeper into the forest. Hunter would need to cross the clearing undetected, which meant she need to distract the men and turn their attention to the forest. *Hurry!* She prayed silently. She wasn't sure how long she could pretend she lurked in the shadows for a clandestine tryst before the men decided to have a taste of what "William" missed.

Looking up at the castle wall looming from the top of the hill and realizing they were still visible to any guards patrolling the wall, she decided to direct the men even farther into the cover of the trees. Hunter would need to do what he must for their escape without attracting more attention. She noticed a fallen tree a short distance away from where she stood that looked like a good perch and turned toward it.

"Why are you dressed like a man?" one of the guards asked suspiciously as he eyed her up and down. "Wearing breeches is dangerous for a woman."

The guard who spoke looked over his shoulder and scanned clearing, but his hesitation was short-lived before he followed the other guard into the trees closer to Anora. The second guard reached for her coif and pulled it off her head, freeing the long braid. "I had to know for certain, because ye' look too bonny to be a boy."

She leaned a hip against the felled tree trunk and willed her nerves to calm. "I don't know what I'll do if my William disappoints me. Will you keep me company while I wait?"

"Depends," one guard replied. He wasn't a particularly tall man, but he was broad across the shoulder with a thick neck. "Are ye gonna' tell us true what yer doin' lurkin' around outside the castle dressed like that? If yer after a tryst, 'at ain't the way to dress."

"What mischief are you up to, lady?" the first guard asked when Anora did not immediately respond. This man was taller and lankier than the other guard, with a long, sharp nose and a bald head that reflected the moonlight shining through the smattering of clouds.

"My William loves me, but my father will not let me marry him," she said with as much forlornness as she could muster, relieved that the men were focused on her with their backs to the hill and clearing. "But we have a secret: We are running away together."

"Dressed like that and carrying nothing?" The shorter guard said as he looked Anora up and down. The moon was hidden behind clouds again, and the forest had become considerably darker. The taller man turned in a circle and peered suspiciously into the inky night around them.

"I don' like secrets," the taller guard said. "An' I don' like lies. What are ya really doin' out 'ere?" He stepped around her as he looked into the woods behind them, his fingers wrapping around the hilt of his sword on his hip. Anora pivoted her body trying to keep both the men in her view.

"I don't know what I'll do if he doesn't show up again." She gave her best impression of a naïve yet hopeful woman in love as she slowly backed away from the shorter guard. With the taller man still in her sight, she willed Hunter to make his appearance quickly. She wracked her brain for what to say next to distract the men, especially the one who stared intently into the darkness of the forest, without getting herself into a more precarious position with these men. She knew well what men could do to a vulnerable woman alone. "I appreciate you both for being so nice to me and staying to protect me while I wait for William."

"What say ya put William from yer mind?" the shorter guard said as he fumbled with his belt. "What's 'e got we can't give ya?" He gave Anora a good look up and down and swaggered closer to her.

Anora feared Hunter might not show up in time to save her from this situation. If it were just the shorter man, she might be able to coax him near enough to smash a knee into his stones and make her escape. But with two of them, even if she succeeded to catch one unaware, the other guard would be on her before the first man fell to his knees.

It occurred to her that these oafs might be the very same men who used the stolen pendants to pay for services in the bawdy house in Shrewsbury. That knowledge renewed her determination to keep the men occupied until Hunter arrived and did his worst to them.

"I could never forget about my William," Anora simpered in an innocent voice with a hint of disbelief.

A fleeting thought crossed her mind that she may have annoyed Hunter beyond his limit. Maybe he had no intention to get her out of this situation. Maybe he wanted to prove a point, show her that what she was doing was dangerous, and that she was not as capable as she believed herself to be.

She prayed that wasn't the case as a tingle of fear slithered down her back. If Hunter thought to leave her to her own devices, her father would never know what had happened to her. Could he really be so heartless as to befriend her family, eat at her father's table and gain his trust, then abandon her without any remorse?

Chapter Seven

HUNTER HAD TO calm the beast inside him that wanted to rip the men apart, limb from limb. His blood boiled as he listened to the guards question her, certain that it was only a matter of time before one of them forced himself on Anora.

At least Anora had the good sense to come up with a plausible story as to why she lingered in the forest alone in the middle of the night. And she did her best to keep the men distracted, which allowed him to get close enough to them to do something about the situation. He knelt behind a thicket of underbrush and gently rustled the leaves, then intentionally snapped a twig underfoot. As expected, the guard whose attention was only partially on Anora stepped closer to the spot where Hunter was hidden behind the brush. He looked intently into the forest and slowly turned his ear toward the woods as he rested a hand on his sword hilt and listened for whatever lurked in the trees.

"Psst," Hunter hissed from his crouched position an arm's length from the man. When the guard looked down in his direction, he lunged forward and stabbed his dagger into the man's stomach and twisted. The man gasped as Hunter's blade cut through the flesh of his gut and stumbled backwards as his hand fell from the hilt of his sword to grasp at the blood that soaked through his tunic. Hunter punched him hard, withdrew his knife as he shoved him aside, and advanced on the other guard.

The second guard turned toward the commotion with Anora's cap still in his hands. His eyes went wide when he saw Hunter lunge toward him. Anora shoved him hard from behind as he dropped the cap to fumble for his sword. Hunter's fist connected with the man's nose as he lurched forward and it broke with a satisfying crunch before he could draw his weapon, then he delivered several more blows to the side of his head and jaw. As the guard fell to the ground, sword still sheathed, Hunter grabbed Anora by the hand and pulled her along behind him as he broke into a run.

The noise of the attack attracted the attention of more guards on the wall walk above them. He heard the raised voices from atop of the castle wall and the thud of an arrow hitting a tree at the edge of the forest. He darted through the forest with Anora in tow as he veered left and right to remain in the cover of the thickets and underbrush as they ran. Men yelled orders and he knew if he didn't get her to his horse quickly, they would soon be overtaken by the castle guards.

He pushed on through the forest, making his way toward the small clearing where he'd left his mount and let out a shrill whistle as they approached. Instantly, branches cracked and snapped as his horse broke through the thick underbrush to get to his master. Shadow appeared like an apparition in the gray cloak of night, his nostrils flared, and ears turned forward attentively as he barreled toward Hunter. The animal slid to a halt in front of him and huffed out a breath as he stomped a hoof anxiously. Shadow wouldn't be happy to have an extra rider for their hasty withdrawal from the castle, but there was no other option. Hunter swung up on Shadow's back then held out an arm for Anora to leverage herself on to the horse's back behind him. She clasped her hand around his forearm but fumbled as she tried to get her foot into the stirrup to gain purchase. He was about to get off the horse and throw her up into the saddle when she managed to secure her foot in the stirrup and sprung up to straddle Shadow behind him.

Hunter pivoted the mount and branches cracked with a pop as the animal's big body cleared a path through the dense undergrowth. He avoided the road as he pushed Shadow through the forest to put more distance between them and the castle.

They'd not ridden far when Anora tugged on his tunic. "We cannot leave Willow!"

"Who is Willow?"

"My horse."

He should have known she had a horse somewhere. His first instinct was to deny her request, but they would move faster if they each had a horse instead of doubled up on Shadow. "Where is she?"

"The road leading to the main gate."

He felt his jaw drop. "You left your horse on the main road?"

"Don't shout at me," she chided.

"How did you plan to get to her? Walk out the front gate of the castle you weren't supposed to be in to start with and ask the stable hand to bring it around?" Hunter took her silence to mean that she heard clearly the disdain in his voice. Had she been anyone else, he would have dumped her off his horse and let her retrieve the mount herself.

"Sarcasm? Now?" she asked, her tone loud with anger.

"Keep your voice down," he commanded. "We are not out of danger. I wager there are guards on horseback galloping out of the front gate now."

"Then we best hurry or they will get to Willow first. I will not leave her behind."

He sighed in resignation because he knew he would bend to her will regardless of how foolish her demands. "How far up the road did you leave her?" he grumbled. He'd already turned in the direction of the main road when she said that was where her horse was tied, despite the imminent danger that awaited them.

"Perhaps a furlong up the road, no more."

"Did you bother to hide her in the woods, or did you just leave her alongside the road?" The mare would likely whinny once she heard other horses in the vicinity and it wouldn't matter how far away from the road she was tied.

"I'm not a complete dolt. She is in a hidden meadow out of sight of the road."

He knew the place—as did everyone familiar with the area, who had even the slightest discerning eye. There was a visible break in the trees from how often riders used the small clearing to take a bit of respite if not a guest at the castle. "Prepare yourself for the probability they've already found her."

As they crested the hillock on the edge of the meadow, Hunter could hear horses as they approached on the main road. "We'll have to leave her," he declared. It was too much of a risk and the mare was not a trained warhorse—easy to replace in his mind.

"We will not!" Anora protested as he veered the horse away from the meadow.

Hunter groaned. He should have known she'd have a soft heart for her mare and would refuse to leave her pet behind. Not that any harm would come to the horse. She may not be a trained warhorse, but the mare still had value and would be added to the stable of horses at the castle. "I'll steal her back later, if she matters that much to you."

"Stop! I will not leave Willow behind."

Hunter could feel Anora shifting her weight to jump from Shadow's back. He pulled up on the reins because he feared she would not hesitate to do something so foolish, even as the garrison of guards swarmed the forest around the castle looking for them. Before she could dismount, he brought Shadow to a stop and swung a leg over the neck of the horse to jump to the ground "Get in the saddle and take the reins. I'll get your damned horse. Wait here and *don't* go anywhere until I return but be ready to ride."

She scooted over the back of the saddle and took the reins

from his hands. "What if you don't return?"

He didn't have time to answer the absurd question if he were going to retrieve the mare before the castle guards found her. Were it not for Anora, he'd have completed his mission and been gone with no one the wiser. As it was, he was breaking his hard-learned rules that made him the best at what he did: never get distracted from the mission; never let someone else jeopardize the mission; never get emotionally attached to the mission; leave no trace; never be afraid to sacrifice whatever necessary to avoid detection and capture. Yet here he was, risking his hide to save a replaceable horse for the woman who sabotaged his mission because she nosed around where she didn't belong.

If not for her, he would have done a more thorough search of the castle until he found solid evidence to prove the baron was creating alliances with Marcher lords known to be hostile to the king. The missive he found before their escape was helpful, but not the proof he needed.

The shouts of mounted guards carried over the meadow as orders were given for a small contingent to check the clearing for any sign of the intruders. Hunter spotted the mare tied to a tree on the far edge of the clearing, closest to the road, and broke into a full run. He cursed her inexperience for choosing an obvious place to leave her mare, for tying the horse instead of leaving it free and ready to escape—though in fairness, the mare was not trained to stay where left or come when beckoned—and for placing the horse on the end of the meadow nearest to the road instead of nearest to the escape route under the cover of the forest.

He broke the thin branch with the reins looped in a tangled mess around it, then threw the reins over the mare's neck, branch and all. He leapt up on her back as he turned her head sharply and nudged her hard in the flanks. The shouting increased as the guards entered the meadow just as Hunter and Willow were bounding into the trees on the other side. To his surprise, the mare was adequately agile and more fleet of foot than expected.

"Follow me." He slapped Shadow's rump as he passed by them to jolt the horse into a gallop. "Keep low to his back." Just as he said the last word, he heard the zing and thwack as an arrow lodged in the trunk of a tree to the side of them. It was too dangerous to leave Anora behind him; he'd have to trust Shadow to know where to go. Reining Willow in, he motioned for Anora to pass him and yelled. "Take the lead. Give Shadow his head and let him go."

Shadow was trained to ignore the lashing tree branches and scratches of the shrubs as he blazed his own path through thick forests, but the mare was built for easy riding on roads and travel-worn trails. He decided to heed his own advice and let Willow's head go as he clung to a shred of hope that she could keep up with the trained warhorse. Again, he had underestimated the mare. Relief flooded him as she bound through the heavily wooded forest, instinct driving her to dodge around trees and thickets in the same jagged pattern as Shadow to make them more difficult targets for the armed guards. Once the shouts of the soldiers and the thud of arrows as they hit trees faded behind them, he turned Willow onto a straighter course and dug his heels in hard to pass Anora, confident Shadow would follow without hesitation.

There was a little used road some distance from the main road to the castle. It was a more circuitous route and the journey to Oswestry would take several hours longer, but they were less likely to encounter anyone, and Hunter knew the terrain better than most if they were followed. They shook off the first contingent of guards that chased them, but it was only a matter of time before more joined the pursuit. When they finally came upon the narrow road, which was little more than a well-worn trail, he turned toward the east. After they'd ridden some distance, he veered off the path once more and stopped the horses behind the cover of a hedgerow.

"What are we doing?" Anora asked in a low voice.

"Giving Willow a chance to catch her breath. And making

certain we aren't being followed." He patted the mare's neck to soothe her, but her chest continued to heave from the exertion. He looked up at the treetops, still visible against the scattered clouds in the night sky. Raindrops pattered a steady beat on the leaves, and storm clouds moved across the night sky in their direction. They didn't have very long before they would be drenched to the skin and the light of the moon would be completely snuffed out.

"How far are we from home?" Anora asked as she lifted her face toward the sky.

"Too far," Hunter replied.

"I told Papa I would be back in time for the morning meal. If I'm not back by the time they break their fast, Papa and Sumayl will be sick with worry."

He didn't want to think about the assumptions they would make when she returned in the early hours before dawn with Hunter. As many times as he'd fantasized about stealing her away in the dark of night to seduce her, that wouldn't be what happened this night. Yet, he'd probably have to suffer the wrath of Frode and Sumayl as if it had.

He turned to look at the silhouette of her delicate face as the realization of what she said sank into his brain. "If you said you'd be back to break the morning fast, then they know where you are?"

"Not exactly," she said, looking away from him.

"Where do they think you are?" Hunter knew, when it came to Anora, Frode and Sumayl were softhearted and indulgent, and would never suspect her of anything devious or misleading.

"I told them I was staying with the widow Griswold to assist her with an ill child and would be back late."

Hunter wanted to clutch his forehead in frustration, but instead he breathed deeply through his nostrils to temper his response. "If something had happened to you, if you did not return, they would have no idea where to look for you."

"They have more faith in me than you," she said defensively.

"They will trust I can take care of myself."

"Aye, when it comes to helping a widow care for an ill child. But I can't believe they would be so flippant in their concern if they knew you were sneaking around Castle Whyte intent on stealing from the baron. And if they did, they are blind fools," Hunter said, clenching his fingers into fists over the reins to stop himself from grabbing Anora by the shoulders and shaking a measure of sense into her. Frode had already lost his wife and son. Could she not comprehend what it would do to her father if something happened to her? Even Sumayl would be shattered if anything horrible were to befall Anora. In the thirteen years the blacksmith had worked for Frode, he'd become like family and doted on Anora like an adoring—and very protective—uncle.

A hollow feeling settled into his own chest at the thought of anything happening to Anora. He'd felt an unwelcome jolt to his entire being the first time he saw her at the goldsmith shop, and from that time, she'd rarely been from his mind. She was exuberantly stubborn, opinionated, audacious, and completely beguiling to him. Even if he could not call her his own, his life was more tolerable because she was a part of it. Never in his life had he felt the same about anyone else, and he was not convinced it was a good thing. It made him vulnerable, gave him a weakness to be exploited by his enemies if anyone ever discovered the truth of his feelings for her, but if anything happened to Anora, the rage and regret would turn him inside out. He would die trying to protect her because losing her would kill him anyway—even if she wasn't truly his to lose. Which she never would be, because she deserved so much more than a man so tainted with death and destruction that his heart and soul were nearly shriveled to nothing but dust and ash.

"Did you hear me, Hunter?" Anora hissed at him in a loud whisper.

"No. What did you say?" It wasn't like him to lose himself in his own head. It was an affliction that plagued him only when she was near.

Anora huffed with an impatient sigh. "I said that despite your lack of respect or caring for me, I've never known you to be an ungrateful bastard toward my father, but it appears that is what has become of you."

Chapter Eight

"UNGRATEFUL BASTARD?" HUNTER'S displeasure was apparent in the deliberately slow way he enunciated each word, as though speaking to a halfwit.

"Aye, you are." This was not the Hunter she'd come to know in the two years since he'd followed his friend Red into the goldsmith shop. He'd shared countless meals at her father's board with the family, and in that time, she'd come to see him as a valued friend. In the beginning, he'd hardly spoken, typically only answering in one-word grunts. Her father and Sumayl had convinced her it was because he was shy. For some time, they even suspected he was sweet on her, but she didn't believe it. But after a few months, he'd blossomed, talking more and laughing often with all of them. Despite the change in his treatment of her in the recent months, the friendships he'd built with her father and Sumayl felt genuine.

Yet here he was saying they were fools for believing her more capable than a child.

"We embrace you like family when you are in our home. My father has told you stories of his life, of his time working as a decoder for King Henry, even of the pain he endured losing my mother and brother. Sumayl has taken the time to indulge your interest in blacksmithing. And you dare criticize them for thinking me a resourceful woman capable of more than just cooking the stew and sweeping the floors."

"That is *not* what I said."

"I believe you did."

"I am criticizing you for lying to them, and for thinking me foolish enough to believe they would not balk if they knew the truth of where you are tonight."

The truth of his words stung, because she *had* lied to her father and Sumayl about much more than just her whereabout this night. She'd not wanted them to know that thieves were targeting them again, likely believing them weak because of her father's and Sumayl's advancing age and her station as an unmarried woman without a brother for protection.

Thirteen years ago, they had been victims of a thief who'd mercilessly knocked her mother to the floor where her head hit a sharp corner, and she'd died of the injury. The stolen jewels, including a cherished ring and several pendants her father made for her mother, had never been recovered. Out of respect to her father, the old Baron Payne had offered a reward for the capture of the thieves and provided the protection of his soldiers whenever her father requested in the years since. When the baron died two years prior, Edmund inherited his title and assured her father he would continue to provide protection as his father had done. But to Anora, he made the disgusting insinuation that she should become his lover if she wanted the full benefit of his protection. She had refused, and the goldsmith shop was robbed not long after.

Their fathers had been lifelong friends, and Edmund had developed an infatuation with her as soon as she started to mature from a girl into a woman. He'd been a boisterous and mean boy who made her uneasy with his attention then, and her apprehension increased as he grew into an arrogant and conde-scending man. He'd even offered for her hand at one time, but she did not have any desire to be his wife, and she was sure he only wanted her because he thought her father to be a wealthy man. She'd successfully deterred every offer of marriage thus far, and only Baron Whyte had persisted after her father had declined on her behalf.

Since she'd not found a man as worthy as her father of being a husband, she'd chosen to establish herself as goldsmith and provide for herself. It wasn't an easy undertaking, and the likelihood of her succeeding was almost nonexistent, but she clung to the shred of hope that she would find a way. It was true, the women she knew who maintained their independence included the proprietress of unreputable business and vendors of goods that were less desirable to thieves than precious metals and gems, such as fish or bread. But if those other women could find a way, so could she.

The theft of an important piece of commissioned jewelry from a locked chest in the shop workroom had undermined her confidence. The culprit had boldly entered her father's goldsmith shop while the village was celebrating Lammas Day. Anora and her father had attended mass to witness the blessing of the first wheat harvest of the season, and Sumayl had joined them for the food and festivities held in the yard of the church. They had secured the shop door with a heavy metal lock, as was customary when they were all away from the goldsmith shop. The next day, when Anora sat down to finish the final details on the brooch, she discovered that her tools had been rearranged, but it was done neatly and deliberately, as though to ensure she would know someone had touched them. Then she discovered that the brooch she'd nearly finished was gone—and only the brooch. The heavy cask attached to the wall where it had been locked away for safety showed no signs of tampering, but someone had taken the brooch and left all the other gems and precious metals right where they were. She knew her father had not opened the cask because he had not been in the room without her since she last put it away in the locked chest.

It was the first commission completely of her own design, crafted solely by her own hands, with the cooperation of the merchant who requested the piece. It was an ornate brooch set with rubies intended as a gift for the merchant's daughter to wear on a new cloak being tailored specifically for her wedding. She'd been delighted to be commissioned for the piece because it could prove to be a great advance to her reputation as a goldsmith if the bride's father—a prominent and revered merchant—was pleased with the result.

It was of the utmost importance for her to succeed in the assignment, and she dared not tell the merchant or her father that the piece had been stolen, lest she want to be relegated to sweeping floors again. Instead, she'd used her own funds to purchase more rubies and crafted another brooch before anyone was the wiser. The coincidence of Baron Whyte visiting the shop the day after the theft had seemed inconsequential—until he paid for services in Madam Ruby's establishment with the stolen pendants. If she'd found the other pendants or the brooch at Castle Whyte, then…well, she wasn't sure exactly what she would have done, but it would have proved, at least to her, the baron's guilt.

The rain splattered on her face with increased consistency, and she wished she had brought extra clothing, but she had expected to be home in Oswestry, safe and snug in her bed by this time. She looked up at the cloud-filled night sky, then she peered through the darkness for a heavier canopy of leaves to use as cover while they waited out the storm.

"It is true I was not honest with my father, but I have my reasons, none of which are your concern," she said, some of the guilt tamped down by her belief that she only did what was necessary to secure her.

"Let us call a truce to get out of the rain," Hunter proposed, nudging Willow toward the trail. "Follow me."

She preferred to ride on, but the wind and rain were increasing steadily, so she acquiesced and followed him. By the time they turned off the road again and veered back into the shelter of the trees, the rain was a blinding downpour. Thankfully, Shadow stayed close to his master because Anora could hardly see Hunter and Willow through the solid sheets of rain. If they became separated, Anora would be lost and stuck in the thick of the woods until either the storm broke, or morning dawned.

Shadow halted and a heartbeat later she heard a muffled thud as Hunter's boots hit the rain-soaked earth. Anora slid from the saddle, her feet barely touching the ground before Hunter was there to steady her.

"This way," he called over the howl of the wind and rain as he took her horse's reins from her and walked into the darkness.

"Where?" Everything was pitch black because of the lack of moonlight shining through the dense clouds and she could hardly see her hand in front of her face. She caught up to Hunter and grabbed a fistful of his tunic to cling onto him as he navigated his way through the forest. The leaves were thicker here but they were not enough to hold back the heavy rain. She looked down to hide her already wet face from the downpour and shuffled along behind Hunter, squeezed between the horses he led at his sides.

"Are you sure you are not one of the *Tylwyth Teg*?" she asked, baffled by his ability to know where to go in the pitch dark. Above his head, a wall of black loomed and it appeared they were about to walk directly into the face of a cliff. The pungent scent of wet moss and rocks filled her nostrils, and she could almost believe he was about to lead her through a gateway into the fairy world.

He chuckled. "Are you afraid of the fairy folk?"

"Perhaps," she admitted as she remembered the stories her mother used to tell her of the little creatures and their mischievous ways.

He stopped and she bumped into the back of him before she realized raindrops no longer pelted the top of her head or splatted on the saddles. She didn't think it possible to get any darker than in the forest, but now she couldn't see her hand in front of her face at all. If Hunter abandoned her, she'd have no idea which way to go. She didn't dare move for fear that one wrong step could find her sprawled out flat on the ground. Or worse. "Where are we?"

"It's the horse shelter of a small hut belonging to the forest wardens." His voice had grown louder, and she sensed he'd turned in her direction as his hand brushed against hers. "Take Willow's reins."

She did as instructed, then ran her hand over the mare's neck in a soothing gesture, though she did it to comfort herself as much as the horse. Nothing had gone to plan. She had not found the pendants, the brooch, or any other proof the baron was involved in the thefts. She'd encountered Hunter and he'd forced her to leave the castle before she'd finished her search. And now, there was little hope of returning to her home before the sun rose and her father realized she was not at the widow Griswold's cottage.

It wasn't as though she'd gone into this venture completely unprepared. She'd crept out of the house each of the last three nights to sneak along the lanes of Oswestry as she practiced moving with stealth and passing unnoticed. She'd even prepared a story about seeking out the baron as an old friend of the family for assistance with a private matter if things had gone terribly wrong and she'd been caught in the castle. She knew Baron Whyte to be away from the castle, but she planned to feign ignorance of his whereabouts and use the long history between her father and the baron's to her advantage, if necessary.

The steady beat of the rain was reduced to a soft patter when under the roof of the stable. She heard the muffled scuffing of the saddle being slid over Shadow's back then the gentle thud as it was set on a surface nearby. Her eyes had adjusted somewhat to the conditions and she could discern the movement of dark shapes as Hunter and the horses moved about the small space.

She turned to her own mare and started to loosen the saddle but the squish of hooves as they sunk into the mud distracted her. Did she hear Hunter's horse leave the shelter? Her heart started to beat harder in her chest as she turned to look for Hunter. When she was safe in her bed under her father's roof, she didn't believe in fairy folk hiding in the woods, waiting to lure unsuspecting humans to their mysterious world. But in the eerie depths of the forest on a moonless night that shrouded everything in inky black, she wasn't so certain. She strained to see what was happening when a dark apparition appeared directly in front of her. Her good sense told her it was Hunter, but she still jolted at the feel of his damp skin brushing against her hand and let out a little exclamation.

"It's me," he assured her. "Give me Willow's reins."

"What did you do with Shadow?" she asked as she handed him the reins.

"Let him go into the forest."

"Will he not get lost? Should we not bring him in here? There is room."

Hunter snorted with what sounded like derision as he gently pushed her aside so he could get closer to the horse. "That is asking too much of even him."

Puzzled by his response, Anora asked, "What do you mean?"

She heard him rustling with her saddlebags, then he pushed them into her hands. "Hang on to these." He turned away from her and continued to unsaddle her horse. "With nothing to distract his attention from your mare, I'd spend the night keeping him away from her. He is better off outside on his own."

"He won't run away?"

"He wouldn't dare."

Anora believed him. Man or creature, not many would dare defy Hunter. He had the countenance of a marble statue with his sharp, hard features that seemed perpetually set in a disapproving frown. He was a rigid man who disliked almost everyone, from what she knew of him, though he seemed to harbor some respect for her father and Sumayl.

She heard the slide of the saddle over Willow's back and the soft, repeated smack of the horse's lips as she released the bit, then another muffled thud as the saddle was set over a plank somewhere in the darkness.

"This way," he said into her ear as he directed her by the elbow.

The man's ability to see in the sheer darkness of the little stable was uncanny. "How do you know where to go when I can hardly see my hand in front of my face?"

"You exaggerate." He gently tugged on her elbow to stop her and then the swoosh of a door swinging open whispered in the night. "I've been here before. Step over the row of low stones in front of the door, then move to the side."

"I do not exaggerate. You must have the eyes of an owl." She didn't step high enough, and her foot caught on a stone as he guided her through the doorway. She would have fallen if he hadn't caught her with an arm around her waist to steady her. When she righted herself, her back was pressed against the expanse of his chest, which crushed the rain sodden fabric of her tunic against her skin and sent a cold shiver down her spine.

"Are you all right?" Hunter's voice was low and soothing in her ear.

Despite the wet chill of her clothing, a warm tingle of awareness swirled low in her belly. She'd never been held this intimately by anyone. Her instinct should have been to step out of his hold, but instead she felt her body relax and she started to lean heavier into him before she realized what she was doing and stopped herself.

"I'm fine," she said, peeved by her own clumsiness stepping over a simple row of stones. If she were honest, also because of her reaction to his nearness. She stood straighter as she spoke to decrease the number of places where her body contacted his. "When you said stones, I thought you meant small ones."

"Is that your stomach?" he asked as he moved her away from the door, his arm still around her waist. She heard him drop his saddlebags to the floor and push the door closed. "Because if it isn't, there's something large and intimidating already inhabiting the hut."

She didn't appreciate the sarcasm in his tone, or the way his hold on her made her body hum with awareness. "It's been some time since I've eaten," she grumbled, pushing at his arm. "Do you not have a flint to start a fire?"

"Aye. Stand still until I have the fire lit." He released her, but his fingers seemed to linger as they trailed across her stomach. Her senses were heightened and the pressure of his fingers felt as though they warmed her skin through the layers of clothing shielding her. When he moved away from her, she felt exposed and unprotected. His absence had pushed her off kilter just as much as his nearness, and she couldn't seem to right herself.

What had come over her? This was Hunter, the man hardly spoke to her when he sat at her father's table and averted his eyes whenever she joined in the conversation. She'd thought he'd enjoyed her company and her opinions at the onset of their acquaintance, but the last months had suggested otherwise. How could she be attracted to him when he obviously thought so little of her? She shook her head in the darkness to clear it of the notion and convinced herself it was the cold and her grumbling stomach that muddled her senses and her emotions.

Within moments, a small flame danced in a pit in the middle of the dirt floor and Anora could see the inside of the hut from the light of the growing fire. The room was sparse, as to be expected, furnished with a small table and chair in one corner, two low stools by the fire, and a wide bench along the entire length of the opposite wall that appeared to serve as both an oversized bench and a bed. An iron pot hung on a hook suspended from a tripod centered over the small firepit, which was simply a ring of rocks in the dirt. There was one long shelf attached to a wall that held candles, what looked like a stack of platters or bowls covered with a cloth, and some other odds and ends. Beneath it was an abundant stack of logs and kindling. The layer of dust on everything suggested it had been some time since anyone had used the space.

Anora blinked as her eyes watered from the initial rush of

smoke, but then it lessened as the gray haze rose upward through a small gap in the ceiling of the hut. "Are you not afraid of discovery?" Anora asked, though she was grateful for the heat as she set her saddlebag on the floor and crouched on a stool close to the little fire.

Hunter shook his head. "Smoke will be impossible to see on a night like this, and the rain will tamp down the smell of it."

Her stomach rumbled and she hugged her arms over her midsection to quiet the noise.

"Did you not eat today?" Hunter was seated on the other stool as he broke a small stack of twigs into shorter pieces and fed them into the fire.

Anora glanced at him as she picked up her bag to unbuckle the top flap and said irritably, "Yes, but it was hours ago!" She had packed a bit of cheese and a heel of bread for the journey home, but she was much hungrier than she expected. Granted, the activities of the night had proven substantially more vigorous than she anticipated, between the rats and the harrowing escape, and now she felt ravenous.

She reached into the saddlebag, then groaned in dismay when she pulled out a small bundle wrapped in a cloth sodden with rainwater. Inside, the bread was a soggy mess, but the hard wedge of cheese looked salvageable. It wasn't much, but she would have to make do with it as it would be hours before she'd be home. She was about to take a bite out of the hard cheese when she remembered Hunter.

"Do you have anything in your bag for you to eat?" she asked, her voice laced with guilt that she secretly hoped not to divide her meager fare. She was ashamed of her selfish behavior, but she hadn't heard his stomach growling, and she was quite certain hers was about to turn inside out. "Or shall I share my cheese with you?"

"I have food." He looked at her with an expression that appeared to be a mixture of pity and amusement. "Do you have any soggy oats for Willow in that bag."

She shook her head and felt the heat of embarrassment on her face. "I thought she would be back in the stable by morning. Now I feel terrible for not thinking about her in my preparations."

"That was preparing?" he asked doubtfully as he tipped his chin toward her wet saddlebag, ruined bread, and soggy cheese.

She gritted her teeth together and pressed her lips into a thin line as she looked away from him. It was pitiful, even she had to admit that, but she couldn't bring herself to say it out loud. "I thought it better to travel light, and I am not so very far from home. If I have to go a night without food, it is not the worst that could happen."

Hunter's eyebrows arched high as her stomach rumbled loudly in direct contradiction to her words. He hooked a finger through the cracked leather strap that connected her saddlebags and picked it up, then held it near to the fire to see it better as he twisted it this way and that to get a better look at it. "This saddlebag has lived its life and should be burned."

"No!" she exclaimed pushing off the stool to grab it from Hunter's hands and almost dropped her precious piece of cheese in her haste.

His head jerked up at her vehement response, but he did not protest when she took it from him.

"I will give you that it is old, but it is perfectly suitable when it is dry." She found a hook on the wall and hung it up to dry, then returned to the stool. He studied her curiously as she sat and took a bite of the cheese, but she kept her thoughts to herself.

The saddlebag had belonged to her brother Baldwin, who was five years her elder. It had seen much use when he was alive, and then it had been packed into the chest with his other belongings when he was killed three years prior while trying to protect a small group of travelers from bandits. It would sound foolish if said aloud, but she felt emboldened and not so alone when she wore her brother's clothing and carried something of his with her, like the saddlebag. It felt like a part of him was with her.

"I have grain for Willow." Hunter pushed to his feet and went to his own saddlebags leaning against the wall by the door. He opened a flap and pulled out a small burlap sack tied off with a bit of string. As he opened the door, Willow stuck her head through the opening. "Out, girl," he chided softly, then set a gentle hand on her muzzle to push her back out of the hut.

The glow from the fire spilled through the doorway to cast the stable area in a dim light. She watched as he guided her horse to the far wall and poured oats into a small trough, then heard his low murmurs as he spoke to Willow in a soothing tone and rubbed his hand over her neck.

As she watched him, she chewed her cheese and thought about what her friend Galiena had told her about him. Her husband Red was one of Hunter's few friends in the world, and according to Galiena, Hunter was not a warrior in the traditional sense. He was trained to fight in battle, but his skills were better suited for stealth, and he was given the missions that required one person to find their way into a difficult place, get the task done, and be gone before anyone knew he was there. When Anora asked about the nature of the tasks, Galiena had grimaced and slowly dragged her finger across the front of her throat to mimic a knife.

"He's intimidating, doesn't speak often, and always looks angry," Galiena had said to her, "but Red respects him, so he must have some redeeming virtues."

Hunter had never intimidated her, at least not in a threatening way. She'd been annoyed by him at times, and often curious about him, but she'd never been afraid of him. Not even when he grumbled at her in exasperation. Galiena was right when she said he didn't speak much, but there were times when he would tell a story at the supper table with her, her father, and Sumayl, and everything about him changed for a short while. The tension would drop out of his shoulders, the lines in his forehead relaxed, and sometimes he even smiled.

That smile took her breath away the first time she saw it. His whole face changed, his eyes glittered, and there was a glow that radiated from him. His features eased and she thought she'd never known anyone as handsome as him in that moment.

But it had been months since she'd seen him smile with his whole face. He'd hardly smiled at all of late, he stayed for supper less often than he used to, and when he did, he listened to her father's and Sumayl's stories but did not offer any of his own.

She caught herself staring at him and looked away quickly when his eyes locked with hers as he ducked back through the door of the hut. From the corner of her eye, she saw him stoop to pick up his saddlebags and open them again. He pulled out several items wrapped in cloth and then busied himself at the sideboard. When he turned toward her with two bowls filled with food, her stomach growled loudly, and she felt herself blush with embarrassment. But that didn't stop her from taking the offered bowl, which contained salted meat, more cheese, and half an apple—a veritable feast compared to what she'd brought. And not soggy.

"Thank you, Hunter." Her gratitude was genuine.

"It is the least I can do in return for the meals you've shared with me."

"Is this…venison?" she asked, astonished as she savored a piece of the dried and salted meat.

"Aye," Hunter said evenly, but his eyes narrowed as he watched her response.

She'd only had venison once but remembered well the sharp, earthy taste of it. She had been invited to dine at Castle Whyte with her father, the old Baron Payne, and his son Edmund. She'd recently turned seventeen years of age and Edmund was of a mind that he wanted her for his wife. He'd convinced his father to let him court her and sought her father's permission, but Anora would not have him. He made her feel self-conscious and strangely ashamed in the way he leered at her, as though he could see her naked body through the layers of her gown and chemise. He would whisper vulgar and disturbing things in her ear when he stood near to her and trailed his fingers over her possessively, which made her skin crawl.

She shuddered at the memory, but what had made her think of it was the knowledge that only nobles were allowed to hunt venison. For everyone else it was a punishable offense. "Is it still against the laws of the king to hunt deer?"

"Aye," Hunter said as he popped a large piece of the meat in his mouth and licked his fingers.

She was momentarily distracted by the curve of his lips into a smirk and the slow, deliberate act as he stuck the tip of each finger in his mouth and pulled it out clean. Suddenly unable to sit still, she shifted on the tiny stool and lifted her gaze from his lips to his eyes, which were locked on her. She opened her mouth to say something witty to cut the tension, but her mind was blank, save for the provocative image of what he'd just done.

"Are you going to turn me in for the reward?" he drawled, then bit into his half of the apple.

"That wouldn't be very chivalrous of me, considering I have every intention of eating every bite of it." She popped a piece of the meat in her mouth and let her fingers slide slowly between her lips to lick them clean as he'd just done.

His eyes widened and his jaw froze in place as he watched the movement. She'd not expected the intense response, or how much it thrilled her that he was affected by it. After a few breaths, she saw his Adam's apple bob, then he closed his slackened jaw and focused his attention on this meal.

Anora did the same, but her head swirled in confusion. He didn't care for her and was annoyed by her presence—at least that was her conclusion from his actions of the past months. And the affection that she had developed for him, purely as a valued friend of the family, had diminished with his dismissal of her. She'd tried to tell herself that it mattered not how he felt about her, and it had no bearing on her everyday life. Except images of his smile, the one so full of true joy, continually crept into her mind at the most unexpected of times. And it seemed the more he ignored her, and the more she tried to push him from her mind, the more vivid the images became—images that extended beyond his smile and made her heart beat faster with the memory of them.

Chapter Nine

HE'D DONE EVERYTHING he could to get Anora out of his head in the last few months, but the more he tried to distance himself, the more she invaded his every thought with images of the way her lips curved into a smirk when she was about to say something witty, how she brushed the pale locks of hair from her forehead when she was concentrating, the glint that flashed in her brilliant-blue eyes when she was excited about something, and the way she focused her complete attention on him when he spoke, as though there were no one else in the room.

He prided himself on his discipline, his ability to focus on the task at hand and shut out everything else, yet he'd not been able to stop himself from trying to catch a glimpse of her whenever possible. He'd stay away for weeks. Then he'd find himself near to Oswestry and at Sumayl's blacksmith shop, which was connected to Frode's goldsmith shop, where he knew he would find Anora.

He told himself he needed to see Sumayl to learn more about blacksmithing—an interest developed recently with a mind of one day turning it into a vocation when he was too old to be stealing into forbidden places in the dark of night to do dangerous deeds. He'd assumed he would die doing his duty, but he had a growing fear that he may just get too old to continue—a fear fueled by recent close calls, one of which he still bore the evidence of as a thin scar along his jaw. Like most old warriors, he would welcome death on the battlefield—preferably a quick one—but his skills took him away from the field and put him into dark corners and hidden nooks where he didn't belong, gathering information not meant for him, and carrying out deeds that would solidify his place in hell when he left this world and went to the next. But if he should not be so fortunate as to die a warrior's death and be forced to endure a long life, he would need something to keep his hands and mind occupied. And after years of wielding blades, who better than he to know what made one superior to another.

He tried to deny the other reason for his frequent visits, which was that some disillusioned beat in his heart wanted Anora to be a part of his future. But how could she? *Why* would she? He was a heartless bastard who'd killed men he deemed deserving and not just in battle or a fair fight, but in the dead of night when they were least expecting it.

His soul was beyond redemption.

And unworthy of a woman like Anora.

They ate in silence, and when they were done, she held out her hand for his bowl and went to the sideboard with them, just as she'd done so many times in her own home after the meal was finished. She set them down, but looked flustered when she realized there were no cloths or water to wipe the bowls clean.

Hunter stood. "I'll take them to the stream to rinse them."

She looked up at the ceiling where the steady rhythm of the rain pattered on the rooftop and raised a questioning eyebrow at him just as thunder rumbled in the distance. "You will be soaked through. Wait until the storm subsides."

He sighed to himself as he bent down to pick up his saddle-bags and thought a good soaking was what he needed to douse the fire that had started in his gut when she licked her fingers with her eyes locked with his. The movement had been slow and sensual and immediately put fantasies into his head about what her tongue and lips would feel like against his skin. Her little sensual display brought his control to the edge of its limit, and he would snap if she locked eyes with him in the same way again.

Instead of going out in the rain, he pulled his wool blanket from his saddlebag and handed it to her with a tip of his head toward the wide bench along the wall, and said, "Rest. Sleep if you can. I'll wake you as soon as the rain stops or the darkness lifts."

She took the blanket and smiled her thanks, then sat on one end of the bench, leaned her back against the wall, and stretched her legs out on the planks. With a flick of her hands, she shook out the blanket and spread it over her as he put another log on the fire. He kept his gaze averted from her and found a clear spot on the floor to sit with his back to the wall.

"There is room enough on the bench for you to sit on the other end instead of in the dirt. It must be cold." She bent her knees and tucked her legs in close to her body to show there was ample space for him.

"This will do," he said. He closed his eyes and leaned his head back against the wall. The cold, damp discomfort of the dirt floor was exactly what he needed to keep his mind focused on more important matters than the pointless temptation to seduce Anora.

"I cannot take your blanket if you are going to allow me the comfort of the bench." He heard her feet touch the floor and the rustle of her clothing as she stood.

"It is nothing," he said, his tone brusquer than intended.

She settled back on the bench and was silent for a long while, but he could feel her gaze on him as heavily as if she poked him with two prods. "What?"

"I did not speak," Anora responded.

"But you are looking at me."

"How do you know that? Your eyes are closed."

"I don't need my eyes to know you are looking at me."

"Do you often sleep sitting up?"

"When required." He shrugged and opened his eyes to watch

her squirm as she sought to find a comfortable position. "You know you can lie flat on the bench if sitting up does not suit you."

"It hardly seems fair of me to get comfortable on the bench when you are uncomfortable on the floor."

The logic made no sense since whether or not she was comfortable on the bench would not change how he felt on the floor, but he decided not to point out that fact. "Who says I am uncomfortable?"

A mirthless laugh escaped her lips. "How can you *not* be?"

"A lifetime of practice." In truth, he felt vulnerable when he slept lying flat. He preferred to rest while sitting with his back to a solid object to keep him from sleeping too deeply. It was easier to defend himself if attacked if he wasn't completely reclined. The habit started when he lived in a brothel as a boy and slept in whatever dark corner he could find. One drunken attack by a patron of the brothel was all it took for him to learn the usefulness of sleeping light.

"Do you think the rain will stop soon? I would like to be underway as soon as it lets up." Just as she finished speaking a loud clap followed by a peel of thunder sounded overhead.

"No," he drawled, eyes lifted toward the rooftop. He wanted to be gone from here and have this ordeal over with just as much as Anora, but likely for different reasons.

"How did you know about this hut?"

"Been here before," he said with a sigh. Obviously, she could not sleep and wanted to talk, which meant no sleep for him either. Not that there was any chance he would with Anora close enough to hear the rhythm of her breathing, let alone the fact that there was bound to be contingent of guards searching for them.

"Are you often in these woods?"

He rested his arms over his bent knees and turned his head to look directly at her. "Are you often sneaking around castles where you don't belong?"

She turned her body to face him directly and curled her legs in at her side, repositioned the blanket to cover them, then returned his direct stare. "Before I answer your question, you must answer some of mine."

"There is nothing I *must* do, save getting you back to your father before the guards catch up to us." He leveled a narrowed gaze at her, but when she stared back at him just as determinedly stone-faced and tight-lipped, he relented and answered her question. "Aye, I am often in these woods."

"This is progress." She smiled triumphantly and her entire face lit up with pleasure. The happiness that radiated from her because of something he'd done, even as simple as answering a question, made his heart pound faster in his chest. God help him, but he would do anything to have her light radiate on him again.

"Do you know tonight is the most you've ever spoken to me?"

"That's not true." He averted his eyes, his protest feeble. "We've supped together many times."

"Aye, but you spend all your time talking to my father and Sumayl. I can't remember when you've ever had a conversation with me, and you've hardly even acknowledged my presence the last few times you were with us."

The warm glow from earlier dissipated, replaced by a stab of guilt. He had ignored her of late and he felt like a selfish dolt because he'd done it to protect himself from the longing felt when in her presence, longing that he carried with him even when he was away from her. He'd not thought his self-serving behavior might affect her. In truth, he'd assumed she wouldn't even notice the change.

Her gaze locked with his as she waited for his explanation. Her eyes were wide, expressive, glittering like sapphires in the firelight, and he was mesmerized. He didn't want to look away from her. He wanted to lose himself in the depths of the woman behind those eyes. And before he could stop himself, he answered honestly with words that were not meant to be said aloud.

"It is true that I do not acknowledge you, but I am constantly aware of you."

Chapter Ten

A NORA HAD LITTLE experience with men, but her gut told her that Hunter had just admitted to something uncharacteristically significant for such a stoic man. He suddenly looked pained, perhaps even ill. The color drained from his face, and he looked away from her to focus his attention on his hands.

"Yet, you continue to avoid me whenever you are under my father's roof." She said the words gently, as though trying not to scare him away.

He nodded slowly.

"Why, Hunter?" A crackle of awareness buzzed in her head. Perhaps all those times she'd told herself she was overthinking a look he'd directed her way or caught him watching her from the corner of his eyes, she'd actually been right and his attention to her was of a more intimate nature.

He stubbornly refused to look at her as he pressed his lips together, and a muscle in his jaw flexed as he clenched his teeth. "It is of no consequence."

"Am I a distraction?" She wanted to hear him admit it, wanted to know that he was as preoccupied with thoughts of her as she had been with him.

He turned his face toward her, and Anora could see that it had changed. She'd thought she'd broken through the thick wall he shielded himself behind, but it was back in place. His expression was stoic, his gaze was steady, and the hard set of his mouth was evidence that he'd fortified himself against revealing anything more about himself. "Distractions are dangerous to a man."

"But not to a woman?" She was bored of men who thought women's lives easy and inconsequential.

"There are other dangers for women."

"Is that so?" She eyed him with curious anticipation. Hunter was unusual, which is why he intrigued her. She would be gravely disappointed if he proved to be less than what she had built him up to be in her mind. "What would those be?"

"Men."

Of course, men were a danger—they were a danger to all living beings—but it was not the answer she'd expected. Nor did she expect the bitter bite to his tone. "Are not men just as much of a danger to other men as they are to women?"

"Not in the same way. They don't target men just because they are men." The light of the flames reflecting in his eyes added intensity to the look he leveled at her. She detected something more behind his eyes than just a warning, something sad and haunted. He looked away and rose to grab another log from under the sideboard and add it to the fire, then stood watching the flames. "A woman does not need to give reason to become the target of a man. Existing is enough."

Now they were having a conversation! Just the two of them, face to face, and he could not ignore her here. She pushed to her feet and stood across from him as she held her hands out to warm them by the fire. "And do you believe a woman existing is offense enough?"

He shook his head. "But what I believe does not matter and will not keep you or any other woman from the dangers of men."

"What will?" She was genuinely curious. Her future depended on finding an answer to that question. If she could not find a way to defend against the dangers of men who would take her business from her or force her into becoming a mistress in return for protection, then she what was left for her? Marriage did not suit her ambitions, and the thought of it made her want to bare her teeth like a caged animal.

"The very thing that is the most dangerous to you is also what will protect you."

"A man," she said, her tone flat. She was not willing to admit defeat as of yet, but the answer was always the same: find a husband. But every man who expressed interest in her had no care for what she wanted and viewed the union only from the standpoint of what she would bring to them. Not one had ever asked her what she wanted from a husband.

"Aye, a man. And having enough sense to stay out of places you don't belong."

She dramatically pressed her lips together, tipped her head to the side, and squinted her eyes at him as though considering what he said. Then, with as much sarcasm as she could muster, she replied, "I am not interested in the former and I am not very good at the latter."

He laughed and rolled his eyes. "That is obvious. Is there not a baker or butcher in the village with his eye on you?" He looked away after he asked the question as though he didn't truly want to hear the answer, and she wondered if it was because he feared her anger at the presumptiveness of the inquiry. Or if he didn't want to hear her admit to having a suitor.

"No suitors." It wasn't a complete lie. The men in the village had given up on pursuing her some time ago. And the baron's offer was no longer an honorable one of a suitor, but rather something sordid and unsavory.

He braced his legs apart and crossed his arms over his chest as he stared down at the flames. After a long moment he asked, "Why are you not married?"

There was no accusation in the question, and she decided to answer honestly. "There have been offers, but I have not fancied any of them. I have yet to find a man who does not want to change me."

He lifted his gaze from the fire to look at her. "What changes do they expect?"

"They expect me to give up goldsmithing, to do their bidding, and be contented as the assistant to their vocation—whatever that may be. I have no desire to bake, or farm, or sheer wool, or pluck poultry. The last suitor was a goldsmith from a village in the north, but he dismissed my skills and didn't believe me when I showed him the pieces I crafted. He commended me on the fine job of polishing my father's work." She decided not to mention that Baron Whyte had been one of the men to offer for her hand. Multiple times. In the beginning, she assumed it was out of some sense of obligation due to his father and her father having a history, but then she turned into a fixation for him. A prize to be won.

"You've had many proposals." He said it as though there was something distasteful in his mouth.

She copied his stance, legs braced apart, and arms crossed over her chest and met his gaze. "You think me not worthy?"

"I think you to be very worthy," he said in an appreciative drawl that sent a little shiver down Anora's spine. "I'm merely surprised you have had so many offers but not found one man to your liking."

She shrugged. "I can provide for myself with my skills and that is what I want to do. Is that so different from you or anyone else to want to have a say in one's own future? To not have to constantly rely on others to take care of you?"

"Do you plan to be alone for the rest of your life?"

"If I ever find a man like my father, who holds me in the same regard as he did my mother, I may consider taking him as husband." Their locked gazes suddenly felt very intimate, and she felt the heat rise up her neck and into her cheeks at the fleeting thought that Hunter might be that man. He was the only man to set all of her senses on alert whenever he was near. It was true that he piqued her ire more than anyone else, but only because she was already unsettled and on edge in his presence in a way that never happened with any other man.

Hunter was the first to look away. He rubbed the back of his neck and blew out a heavy breath. "Frode may be a good man, but that won't stop him from whipping my hide when I return his daughter to him in the wee hours of the morning after spending the night alone in a hut."

"He will believe me if I tell him you behaved with the utmost of decorum." Even as she said the words the thought crossed her mind that she would prefer that he *not* behave with decorum. "Which is what I will tell him…no matter what happens tonight."

His head snapped in her direction as she said the last, his eyes narrowed in warning. "Nothing will happen."

She really shouldn't get so much satisfaction from riling him up, but she did. There was something about seeing Hunter—the quiet, stoic man who was always in control—lose his tenuous grasp on his composure. She moved to the bench to sit. "If you insist on being chivalrous, then at least entertain me with stories. Tell me something I don't know about you."

She saw the corner of his mouth quirk as he lowered himself onto a stool by the fire. "There is not much to know."

That she did not believe. There had to be a reason for the fortress of stone he'd built around himself. Hunter had secrets, she could see it in his eyes, and she wanted to know what had made him so cautious around people. "Let's give it a try. Tell me just a little bit about yourself, like… do you only perform your duties for Lord Hawk, or are you a sword for hire?"

Sir Erik "Hawk" Grogan was Lord of Hawkspur Castle, commander of an elite force of knights and warriors, and a man to make women's hearts skip a beat anytime his name was mentioned. He'd fallen in love with the Lady of Hawkspur Castle when he was sent there to find a traitor, protected her when it was discovered her brother was the culprit, supported her when she became lady and commander of the castle—a rare position for a lady and even more rare for a man not to try to take it from her—and endured a flogging from the king for putting the love of a woman before duty.

Hawk was the type of man every woman dreamed would fall in love with her, but Anora was even more intrigued by Lady Alyce. She'd proven herself worthy of commanding a fortress and had done it alone before she married Hawk. Her friend Galiena knew her and said she was every bit as awe inspiring in person as she was in the stories about her, and Anora longed to meet the lady.

Hunter's lips remained in a straight line for some time and Anora thought he was going to ignore her question, but then he said in an even voice, "I report to Hawk now. I am no longer…for hire."

He didn't seem pleased to admit the last and she didn't pry. "Do you have a home?"

He gave her a wry smile. "Nowhere that matters."

"Hm," she hummed through closed lips as she contemplated her next question. She studied his profile in the flickering light, noticing for the first time a thin red line running along the edge of his jaw. He had a dark beard, always neatly trimmed, and the marring from the scar did not detract from his appeal. Surely other women found him handsome, and she wondered, not for the first time, if he had a lover. Or lovers.

A pang of jealousy bit at her stomach at the thought of him with another woman—holding her, touching her, looking at her with those pale-green eyes that shimmered with bits of gold. If there were a woman somewhere who knew Hunter's secrets, it would break her heart.

That thought startled her, and she almost laughed out loud at her own foolish hope that he didn't have lovers. *Of course he did!* It would be preposterous to think he didn't. It was one of the great advantages of being a man in this world, and another cruel fate of being a woman, having to bear all the risks of taking a lover. There was no tell-tale sign that a man lost his virginity, no fear for them of getting with child, no ridicule for lack of morals. In fact, the more feminine conquests a man had, the more he was lauded.

Never were they pressured to get married until they were old and needed an heir. Yet women were expected to marry as soon as their bodies showed signs of being able to produce an heir. It was a miserable plight for a woman.

Men may not be forced to marry young, but that didn't mean they were expected to stay celibate and alone, as was the expectation for women. "You must have somewhere—or someone—you call home. Do you have a ladylove? Friends, other than Red?"

She liked Red. His Viking friend was the complete opposite of Hunter: jovial, quick to smile, always laughing, his eyes twinkling with mischief. Hunter, on the other hand, was quiet, reserved, stoic, and avoided eye contact.

"Why do you want to know these things?" His brows drew together, and he looked truly puzzled, as though he could not understand her reasons for the questions.

"I'm curious about you," she pressed, feeling only a little bit guilty about how uncomfortable she was making him, but she really did want to know more about him. "You've listened to my father's and Sumayl's stories, and occasionally you offer a story of your own, but it is always sparse of detail. I want to know more about you."

The first time she'd met Hunter, after he'd followed Red and Galiena into her shop where they'd come to seek refuge from a possible assassin, she'd been intrigued by him. There had been a connection, a feeling of comradery, as they teased and cajoled Red and Galiena to explain why he referred to her as wife when they'd only just met. The attraction between the Viking and her friend Galiena had been visible from the start, despite Galiena's attempt to deny it, and Anora and Hunter had done nothing to ease the tension between them. In fact, they'd both reveled in making Red and Galiena as flustered as possible about their mutual fascination with each other. That was her first introduction to Hunter, and she'd been immediately drawn to his wit and charmed by the easy banter.

In the days that followed, she'd been touched by the way he'd taken Tommy Cutpurse under his wing when the young boy was forced to stay hidden in the smithy with them after he got entangled with the same assassin who threatened Galiena. Hunter had been kind to the wary little street urchin, and Tommy had brightened from his attention. When the danger had passed, Hunter took it upon himself to find a place for the boy to live that didn't require him to find shelter in dark alley corners or work as a thief. After he gained Tommy's trust, he brought him to Hawkspur and put him to work in the armory where he could put his fascination with shiny objects to good use.

She suspected he helped Tommy because he saw some of himself in the boy, which piqued her curiosity about him even more. "Where did you come from, Hunter? Why are you always traveling alone?"

He turned toward her as she leaned back against the wall and folded her legs in front of her on the deep bench. His lips parted slightly, and he turned away quickly as though he'd just been caught ogling something forbidden. She watched his throat bob uneasily—another small victory that shouldn't give her as much pleasure as it did—and decided she liked wearing breeches.

"There is naught worth knowing." He said with a faint hitch in his throat.

"For an arrogant cur, you don't hold yourself in very high esteem, do you?" She said the words with a smile, lest he think she seriously meant to be spiteful—which she didn't; she merely wanted to coax him into responding to her. He may not like conversation of a personal nature, but she knew he liked to banter.

His eyes widened and his brows bunched together disapprovingly. "Arrogant bastard?"

"Perhaps I worded that too strongly," she said with a tilt of her head as she feigned pondering her words.

"Perhaps," he mimicked, his voice thick with sarcasm. "Though, to be fair, arrogant bastard is exactly what I strive for."

"I should have suspected," she said with a smile, delighted that he had joined in the conversation with more than just grunts and short, uncomfortable answers. "Tell me one thing about you that only your closest friends know."

He laughed then, but the sound was sharp, like stepping on jagged rocks. "I would not call the men I know friends. They are fellow warriors, and they don't ask questions about things that are of no matter to them."

"Now I know you are lying to me. What about Red? You can't tell me he hasn't wheedled a secret or two from you. And I'd wager he'd not be happy to hear you don't consider him a friend."

"Red does think we are friends," Hunter admitted, "and he probably knows more about me than most. But don't tell him I said that."

He smirked as he said the last, but Anora sensed there was true affection in his response. "Tell me something he knows about you that I don't."

"He knows I hate questions." He looked directly at her and arched a dark eyebrow, as though he dared her to ask another, but he seemed more amused than annoyed.

She dared. "Do you have a sweetheart?"

"No," he said without hesitation.

Anora had to bite her lip to stop the unexpected smile that pulled at her lips as relief flooded her. She didn't want a husband, and no man had attracted her attention until she met Hunter. He did not seem to want a wife, but he'd admitted that she was a distraction to him. Perhaps they were perfect for each other.

She felt her face flush with the audacity of what she was about to ask, and her hands started to shake nervously. She'd already done so many fantastically outrageous—and highly exhilarating—things this night, why should she stop now? Other women took lovers. Granted, they were often widowed and beyond childbearing years, but she didn't want to wait until she was old to know the touch of a man. She wanted to know now.

And she wanted Hunter.

She clasped her hands in her lap to keep them from trembling, straightened her back, and lifted her chin. "I have something I want to ask you."

Hunter turned in the stool to face her directly. "I'm done answering questions. It's time you answered mine."

"I think you—"

"No," he said sharply. "The only thing I want to hear from you is an explanation for what you were doing at Castle Whyte prowling around in the baron's private chambers."

His commanding tone and stern expression definitely dampened her ardor. She studied him for a long moment, the flicker of the firelight dancing across his features as he waited for her to answer.

If she expected honesty from him and wanted to know the secretive man beneath the hard exterior, then she had to give him no less in return.

"Curiosity."

Just not yet.

Chapter Eleven

FEW PEOPLE COULD infuriate Hunter as thoroughly as Anora did.

"Curiosity?"

She lied to him, and he knew it. And she knew he knew it. Yet she stared at him with serene and earnest eyes and expected him to swallow it as though she hadn't just put herself in grave danger by stalking around in the night in the castle of a sadistic cur who reveled in the humiliation of women.

A heartbeat before, when she'd looked at him with the eyes of a woman ready to take on the world to get what she wanted, he'd almost pulled her off her bench and onto his lap. Her confession that she just wanted to take care of herself without having to rely on anyone else was something he understood. But it was a lonely place to be; he knew that from experience.

Loneliness was the reason people built walls around themselves, in the belief that it made them stronger. And he'd seen another layer of Anora's wall built before his eyes when she'd refused to trust him and chose to lie to him instead.

He recognized the withdrawing inward and closing down, but he didn't know what to do about it. Others had tried to break down his walls for as long as he could remember, but no one had succeeded. Anora was the only person he'd ever had the desire to allow past his barriers, but he quashed that notion immediately. Nothing good could come of it.

"You have no idea the peril you put yourself in at Castle Whyte, or what could have happened to you if you were discovered." It made his stomach churn to think about what the guards would have done had he not interfered.

"I was prepared if anyone stopped me or asked questions." She flipped her long, slender fingers in the air as though she thought being captured to be a trivial matter.

"Your preparations have proven to be lacking thus far," he drawled, "but tell me what you planned to do if caught."

She scowled at him and held her head high, baring her long neck and looking as regal as a queen. "*If* I were discovered, I planned to say I had come to the castle looking for the baron to get his counsel on a private matter. Once I explained our families' long history of friendship, and that I trusted the baron because of it, I don't believe anyone would have dared to detain me. I can feign innocence and helplessness when it serves my purpose. And as much as I do not care for the baron, I am willing to use our lifelong acquaintance to my advantage."

He released a long, exasperated breath through his nostrils. There were so many flaws in her plan, but he decided to start with the most obvious. "Then what was the purpose of dressing as a man?"

"It is safer to travel as a man, easier to get through the gates with very little notice, and easier to move without hindrance. I knew the baron to be away from the castle, and if I'd shown up in a gown requesting his audience, they would have turned me away." She spoke as though her reasons were obvious and sound. In truth, there was some sense to what she said, save that most men did not move as gracefully as she did. Or fill out their tunics with the same curves and hollows. Or have a face with such delicate features and lips so pink.

"You are naïve if you think that ruse would have worked, that they would have taken your explanation and let you go. The guards in the forest were proof of that. You were moments away from…" He couldn't say it out loud without shuttering. "And you greatly misjudge your vulnerability if you think the baron would have offered any protection after he found out you were sneaking around his castle dressed like that." Men like the baron would not care that she was the daughter of an old friend and respected merchant. He would see it as his right to do what he willed with her because she put herself in the position of being alone in his chambers.

"It was because of you that I ended up in that situation." She pushed to her feet, planted her hands on her hips, and stared down at him where he sat on the stool. "It was your idea to take the most difficult route out of the castle."

He pushed to his own feet to stand over her, but she was taller than most women—and many men—and his height did not intimidate her in the least. He had wanted to force her to tip her head back to look at him, but she almost looked him square in the eye and needed only to lift her gaze slightly to meet his. He reached for her wrist and pulled it forward as she looked at him wide-eyed, then dropped the pouch of keys into her outstretched hand. "I think you forgot about these. Had I not gone back for them, we would have been gone before the guards found you."

She looked down at the pouch in her hand, then closed her fingers over the leather and met his gaze with a slight tip of her head to the side. "Again, that wouldn't have happened if you hadn't made me go down into that tunnel with the rats."

He felt his eyes bulge at her dismissal of the seriousness of her predicament. "What was *your* plan for escape? Walk out the front gate?"

"There's no need to shout at me."

It took him a moment to realize he'd stepped forward to stand toe to toe with her. Both of them were breathing heavily, their exasperation at a breaking point. Her eyes flashed and her cheeks were stained red, but she did not back away from his looming presence. She looked as spitting mad as he felt, but he would wager that in this moment she felt more compelled to slap his face than be kissed senseless—which was his overwhelming urge at the moment. *Pull yourself together, man!*

"Why are you shaking your head at me?" she snapped when he shook it to clear his mind of the impulse to pull her against his chest to find out if she would resist. Never had he been rough with a woman, or forced his attentions on one, but every time he was near Anora it took all his willpower not to pull her into him to taste her lips.

He gritted his teeth and flexed his fingers to bring his focus back to where it belonged, which was saving the daft woman from herself. If he didn't convince her to quit sneaking around in the dark in places where she didn't belong, he'd go mad with worry. From what he knew of the baron, the friendship between their fathers would not stop him from violating and demeaning Anora if he found her alone in his chamber in the dead of night.

Hunter wanted to hurt the baron badly the first time he had seen the marks the man left on the harlots in the brothel in Shrewsbury, and he wanted to kill the man when cruelty toward the women became part of his routine. There was a time when Hunter would have found the man in the night and buried a knife in his chest in a dark alley for his deeds. But once he'd become a member of Hawk's elite force, he'd been forced to be more cautious about committing a crime for which the courts would see him hanged.

Men did not deem whores as deserving of justice. Even if Hunter murdered a man who maimed or killed a prostitute, he would still be at fault for taking the man's life and be the one to suffer the consequence. Thought it was a risk he was more than willing to take, Hawk had convinced him there were better ways to administer punishment to men like the baron.

But if the baron, or any of his guards, harmed even one strand of hair on Anora's beautiful head, he would tear the man limb from limb. And he would feel no remorse, even if the king had his head removed and put on a stake at the tower in London.

"What was your plan for getting out of the castle, Anora?" He'd managed to regain some of his composure. Enough to take a step back from her and lower his voice below a shout. "Wait. First tell me, how did you gain entrance into the castle?"

"I walked in the front gate," she said over her shoulder as she returned to the bench. Hunter watched her every move as she folded her long legs under her before covering them with his blanket again.

He waited for her to say more, but she just stared at him with a smug grin and innocent eyes. He'd spent less time questioning men who were trained to resist interrogation. She was waiting for him to respond, he knew that, but he wasn't going to let her bait him into losing his control over the idiocy of her actions. Instead, he crossed his arms over his chest, clenched his teeth, and continued to look down at her while he waited for her to explain.

They remained locked in an unblinking stare until Anora finally rolled her eyes and relented. "I carried a basket of eggs and muttered 'For the kitchen' in a grumpy tone." She shrugged. "And I was in. Then I ducked into secluded alcove and waited until nightfall."

The sagacity of the direct and simple approach was often overlooked, and as much as he wanted to fault her it, he couldn't. That didn't stop him from glaring at her with immense disapproval or wanting to shake her until she saw the folly in what she tried to do. Her instincts may have been good, but her skills were lacking, and both were necessary to anyone who deigned to stealth around where they were not meant to be. "Did you think to walk back out the front gate after you were finished digging around in the baron's chambers?"

She blushed and her fingers plucked at the blanket in her lap. "Aye. I intended to claim I fell asleep in the kitchen after helping cook and had to return to the farm to help with the chickens before sunup."

His jaw almost dropped open in disbelief. She couldn't be so foolish as to think the guards would believe that story. It was a sure way to land herself in the castle's dungeon.

"If they grew suspicious, or realized I was a woman in disguise, then I was going to first tell them a similar story I told the guards tonight: I was there for a clandestine meeting with a man who said he loved me but then never arrived."

He closed his eyes and took a deep, calming breath. "You said earlier you planned to say you were a family friend and needed the baron's advice. Neither is a good story, but which is it?"

"If I were captured or in danger, then I planned to use the connection between our families and the lie of seeking the baron's advice."

He could tell by the way she rolled her lips between her teeth and looked away from him as she spoke that she was well aware of how foolish her plan sounded. He let his arms fall to his side, looked around the small hut, then dropped down on the opposite end of the wide bench along the wall. He tipped his head back against the wall as he sprawled his legs out in front of him with a loud, frustrated sigh.

"I know it doesn't sound like a well thought out plan," she said quickly, "but I can be very persuasive when needed. I have to work within the limits of what I have available to me."

He turned his head to see her looking at him with a steady gaze. "I am available to you. All you need do is ask me and I am yours to command." It was true. He might shout at her, want to throttle her, glare at her, and grumble about her recklessness, not because he thought so little of her, but because he was afraid of losing her—even if she weren't his to lose. But he would rather see her alive and well and out of his reach than dead or harmed.

"I believe you." The features of her face softened as a sad smile shaped her lips and she slowly shook her head. "But it is not what I want from you. I must learn to think and do for myself."

"You are a headstrong and stubborn woman, Anora."

"Is that so?" Her eyes flashed, the challenge evident in the way her sleek eyebrows rose in unison. "Headstrong and stubborn? If I were a man, you'd think those qualities admirable."

She was right about that. He did think them admirable qualities, even in her. But he couldn't let her know that lest it encourage her to continue putting herself in danger. He could tolerate a man facing danger and death, but not Anora. He'd lost too many women in his life, or watched them suffer the unspeakable, all of which hardened him. But to watch Anora be harmed, that would be the death of him. He'd dive headfirst into a bed of nails before he would let anyone hurt her. He knew far too well the ways men could degrade a woman, reduce her to nothing more than a soulless shell, because he'd witnessed it more times than he could count.

He had to stop thinking on the horrors that could befall her before his imagination went to places that would turn him into the feral animal he barely kept contained just beneath the surface of his skin.

"You told me how you got into the castle, now tell me why you were there." He couldn't imagine she was a simple thief. She must have been looking for something specific. "And *don't* say curiosity."

With her legs still tucked under her, she shifted on the bench to face him. She was quiet for a long moment as she studied him intently. He could almost see the thoughts rolling around behind her eyes. Finally, she said, "I was there to prove a point."

"What point?" he prodded when she didn't elaborate.

"That I will not sit back and allow some man to take advantage of me."

His head pounded as the blood thrummed from her words. He jumped to his feet and demanded, "What did he do to you? I will make him pay with his life if he touched you."

Anora looked startled by his outburst. She held up her hands and said in a calm voice, "He didn't touch me. Please, sit back down."

Hunter did as requested but his head continued to pulse with his anger.

"You said all I need do is ask, so I'm asking." She narrowed her eyes and leveled a challenging stare at him. "Are you a man of your word, Hunter?"

The woman was shrewd, he'd give her that. He did not have much to offer anyone, save a talent for dark deeds, but he did have his own code of honor and that included being a man of his word. "I did say that," he admitted, "but I first you must tell me exactly what you are asking for and why. I am assuming there is more to this display tonight than the thrill of being where you don't belong."

"There is." She nodded slowly as she studied him with suspicion. After a moment, she nodded with what appeared to be resolution and said, "Show me how to take back from others what is mine; how to protect myself, the goldsmith shop, and my father as he gets older; teach me what I need to do to stop others from believing they can take advantage of me, rob me, or force me to their will. And don't look at me like it is impossible. There are women who are acting as matriarchs of castles, or who run alehouses, inns, and…well, brothels."

She at least had the decency to blush as she said the last. "You want to be a woman who lives by her own means? Completely without the protection of men?"

"Yes!" Her entire face glowed with excitement and hope.

It killed him to dampen her enthusiasm, but what she wanted was impossible. He did not want to mislead her, so he pointed out what she seemed to be missing about the women she listed. "I assume you are speaking about the Lady of Clun when you speak of women ruling castles." Isabella Mortimer, Lady of Clun, was the daughter of Roger Mortimer—a powerful lord who was loyal to King Edward and dominated the Welsh Marchers until his death two years prior in the final months of the king's conquest of Wales. The daughter was nearly as formidable as the father.

Anora nodded vigorously. "She rebuilt the castle on the hill above the village and readied the fortress in preparation for King Edward's battles with the Welsh. I saw her often in Oswestry. She even came to the smithy once to inspect Sumayl's work on the swords commissioned by her commander of the garrison."

Her eyes lit up when she spoke of the woman. He imagined many of the women of Oswestry revered Isabella Mortimer and were emboldened by the woman's command of a strategic fortress. But there were differences between Isabella Mortimer and Anora that could not be disregarded. "Her status as a noblewoman and widow give her rights other women do not have, and she had a garrison of men to protect her."

"I may not be noble, or a widow, but the law says that I shall inherit my father's goldsmith shop when he—" She swallowed hard. "When he is gone, regardless of my state of matrimony. There are other women who run shops and establishments, and I want to do the same."

"If they are truly alone, it is not easy for those women. And they are not selling goods as coveted as gold, silver, and gems. Once word gets out that you are alone in a goldsmith shop, you will be the victim of endless robberies." He waited for her to lift her eyes too look at him again, then added, "Or worse. You will not be given the same respect as a widow, and without a brother or father to protect you, too many men will think it is their right to take advantage of you—in business, or otherwise."

She flinched, a barely perceptible ripple of fear in her tightened jaw muscles, but she did not look away from him. "That is why I am asking you to help me. The thieving has already begun, and men already are trying to take advantage of my father's declining health. Sumayl will always do what he can for us, but I fear for him. He is one of the strongest men I know, but as a foreigner, if anything happens, it will be assumed he is at fault. And like my father, he is getting older."

"What do you mean the thieving has already begun?" Her eyes widened and he realized he'd bellowed the question.

She lifted her chin and set her lips in a thin line. "If you agree to help me, I will tell you more about it."

"No. I will not help you," Hunter said, his voice churlish. He pushed to his feet and paced the tiny room as he scrubbed a hand through his hair. "It's time you found yourself a husband to keep you in hand."

It was the cruelest thing he could think to say to her, and it sickened him. Sickened him to think of her being forced to bend to the will of another man and sickened him that he would tell her it was what she needed. But he could think of no other way to save her from herself. "Pick one of them—the butcher, or farmer, or goldsmith—and have a family. That will keep you busy and out of trouble."

Her mouth dropped open, then snapped shut, but the disgust was clear in her voice as she spoke through clenched teeth. "You don't know me very well, Hunter, if you think that is the solution. I don't have the makings of a good wife, and because of men like you, I never intend to marry."

"Of course you will marry. It can't be that hard to be a good wife." It would bring him to his knees to see her married to another man, but it was a pain he'd have to suffer.

"Is that so?" She laughed bitterly. "*I* can be a good wife?"

"Aye, you can," he said irritably.

She pushed to her feet and stomped toward him. "I've grown into womanhood without a mother to guide me. I was raised by my father, an older brother, and a blacksmith who taught me how to climb trees, wield a knife, and shoot a bow better than most boys. Any man who deigned to marry me would regret it the moment he realized I do not have the disposition to be coquettish, keep a home, coddle children, *or obey*." She visibly shuttered as she said the last.

It was true that Anora didn't have the traditional upbringing of a girl, and she was not a common woman. Many girls grew to womanhood without the guidance of a mother, but not many grew up with a father who encouraged his daughter to speak her mind so freely or express her opinions so boldly. It was apparent from the time he'd spent in their household that Frode admired his daughter's intellect and courage, and he did everything in his power to foster those traits. Others would have said placing more boundaries on her was merely teaching her the necessary limits of being a woman, but Frode would never consider stifling the light that made his only daughter shine.

In truth, it would break Hunter to see that brightness dimmed in Anora. He knew too well the wilted look of a women who had all of the light and goodness snuffed out of them. Anora's exuberance was what he loved most about her, and it would make his life easier if she were less of a force drawing him into her. But he would never wish for her to be anything other than whom she was now, even if his entire being longed for her whenever he was in her presence. And when he was away from her, he ached for her bright smile and easy laugh.

She wasn't smiling or laughing now, though.

"I will find a way, Hunter," she said calmly without looking at him. "You can either help me or get out of my way. But do *not* tell me ever again to just find a husband."

His heart twisted painfully as he watched her pick up her saddle bag and walk out the door of the hut. It was what he wanted, for her to hate him, to put a barrier between them that would protect her from him, but still he felt the loss of her far too keenly for his liking.

Chapter Twelve

Anora had no idea where she was or which direction was home, but still she walked out of the hut and closed the door behind her. The night did not appear quite so dark and the rain had thankfully eased while she'd been arguing with Hunter about whether or not she needed a husband to fix everything for her. Willow immediately nudged her with her muzzle and stomped a hoof into the soft earth.

"Aye, girl, we will be on our way soon," she muttered to her horse just as the door opened behind her. She stepped to the side as Hunter emerged with the bowls from their dinner in his hand.

From the dim light spilling through the doorway, she watched him duck between the slats of wood fencing that enclosed the far end of the horse shelter. The inky blackness from earlier had turned to an eerie gray and she could see Hunter's silhouette among the trees as he looked to the sky and turned in a circle. Appearing satisfied with the conditions, he emitted a sharp whistle.

"If you will wait for me to rinse the bowls and summon Shadow, I will guide you from here." His voice was flat, devoid of emotion. At least he'd had the decency not to command her to wait for him.

"Another truce then," she agreed with a nod, "for the sake of expedient travel."

"Aye, another truce," he said over his shoulder as he walked deeper into the trees and disappeared.

She slung her saddle bag over a slat and saddled Willow while she waited for Hunter to return. He reappeared moments later with his horse in tow. Anora took the bowls from him to return to the sideboard in the hut while he saddled Shadow.

"I put your blanket in your bag," she said as she pulled the door to the hut closed behind her. She held out Hunter's heavy saddle bags to him. "And I doused the fire with the sand from the bucket."

He nodded his thanks as he reached for the saddle bags. "Do you need a leg up?" he asked with a tilt of his head toward Willow.

Anora shook her head and loosened her mare's reins from where they were looped through a ring on the wall of the shelter. She followed Hunter through the gate of the small encloser to where Shadow stood beneath a canopy of dripping leaves. "How far to Oswestry?"

"Less than two hours." He finished tying the bags to the back of his saddle, then reached into one of them and pulled out a small bundle, which he handed to her. "Put this on, in case we encounter anyone on the journey."

Anora unrolled the leather cap, pulled it over her head, and carefully tucked her disheveled braid and any loose strands of hair beneath it. She tilted her head down toward him then turned it side to side for his inspection. He nodded his approval, then swung smoothly onto Shadow's back.

"Stay alert and as quiet as possible. Soldiers will be looking for us."

"Do you think any of them recognized us?" Anora worried that she may bring danger to her father's doorstep because of the encounter with the guards and their clumsy escape.

"I'm most concerned you may have been recognized by the guards from the woods. I didn't have time to—" He looked away from her and sighed, then faced her again. "I think the second guard will recover. He probably didn't get a good look at you in the dark, but if he did, it will be a problem."

Anora's skin prickled as an icy chill wrapped around her with a shiver.

"Are you all right?"

"I've been a fool." She swallowed hard. Fear and regret gripped her throat as reality settled into her bones. She had been stoic about the violence when they were making their escape, accepted it as necessary then dismissed it. How could she have done that? "People died because of me. When did I become so heartless? Why didn't I stop you?"

"You become single-focused when under duress. The instinct is to survive, and your senses are dulled to anything else."

"But did they have to die?"

"Aye," Hunter said gruffly. "They did. Did you really think you could breach the walls of a fortress, steal whatever you planned to take, and walk out the front gate? Baron Payne would have had those guards flogged for letting that happen. And the guards would rather see you chained up in the dungeon than have their skin flayed open with a whip. This isn't a game, Anora."

She clenched her teeth to keep her chin from quivering as she stared at him, processing everything he said. Her life wasn't a game, either, but she seemed powerless to do anything about it.

"This is not a life you want, Anora." His tone was angry, but she deserved nothing less. "This is what it takes to rely on no one but yourself." He grabbed her wrist in his firm grip and tugged her closer to him. He looked like he wanted to chastise her more, but he stopped. His shoulders dropped and the hard set of his lips softened. "Do not think on it now. Think only of getting home without further incident."

Anora bit the insides of her cheeks to focus her mind. She pulled her wrist gently from his grip and said, "Lead the way."

For the next two hours, Willow plodded along behind Shadow as Hunter led them through the woods from one trail to the next. Occasionally, they would ride a short distance on the road, but then he'd veer into the trees again and they'd continue on under the cover of the forest and the dark.

And all the while, Anora thought about the men who died while they escaped Castle Whyte. She tried to convince herself that it was because Hunter chose the difficult way out of the castle, and left to her own plan, violence would have been avoided. But the truth of the matter was the world could be an unfair and ugly place. She'd overheard Sumayl once tell her brother that men had to be prepared to kill or be killed at any given moment. Hunter was well aware of the fact, and her fate may have been far worse if he hadn't taken matters into his own hands.

Even those who didn't trespass or pursue risky endeavors could find themselves in situations that were life or death. As was the case when Baldwin was killed. Her brother had done nothing to deserve his demise, but he'd died a hero trying to save others. As sad as it was, it was not uncommon. Men and women died violently every day. She didn't know if she could take a man's life with her own hands, but did that mean she had to give up goldsmithing and give herself over to a marriage she did not want just for the protection?

And if she gave up goldsmithing, what did she have left that mattered?

It was exhausting to think about, but it was something she had to sort out. And she would. But later, when she wasn't tired, cold, and hungry.

The high walls of Oswestry came into view and relief like she'd never known coursed through Anora's body. She could hardly wait to get home to crawl into her bed and sleep for days. "I can make my way from here."

"I'm not leaving your side until I know you are safely home and under the protection of your father and Sumayl."

"Fine." She expected nothing less from Hunter, and as much

as it irked her, she didn't have the will to argue with him about it. "But there is no need to come into the house. That will just upset my father."

Hunter stayed silent as Anora nudged Willow to quicken her pace toward the village. She was eager to get home before her father sent someone to Widow Griswold's cottage to check on her. When she could, she lent a hand to the kindly woman who was left with five children to raise on her own after her husband's death the previous winter. With that many children and the wet autumn weather, it seemed at least one of them always had a cough or ran a fever.

As they approached the gate, Anora saw a familiar figure walking toward the village from the direction of the meadow where Willow was often turned out to graze. The man turned to see who approached and stopped when he recognized Anora.

"What are you doing here, Sumayl?" she asked the blacksmith. The worry on his face fueled the regret that churned in her stomach. If he was looking for her, then her father must know she wasn't where she said she would be.

"It isn't what you think, Sumayl," Hunter said.

"It's Frode you owe the explanation to, not me." Sumayl said as he glared at Hunter. He looked Anora over from the tips of her toes to the top of her head, then leveled a disapproving look at her that made her feel like an errant child. He turned his back to her and started toward the gate as he said over his shoulder. "Your father is pacing a rut in the floor planks with worry."

Anora's heart sank. "I said I would return by morning." It was a feeble answer, and she wished she had just kept her mouth closed.

Sumayl stopped at the gate and turned to face them both, the disappointment clear in his dark eyes. He crossed his arms over his chest in a stance Anora knew well. It was how he always stood, even when he was relaxed, but his strong arms and broad build made him look intimidating no matter what his mood. "The widow Griswold sent her eldest to request your assistance last night." Sumayl said, his tone hard. Anora felt a sharp stab of guilt that must have shone on her face because Sumayl nodded in agreement as if she'd spoken her regret aloud. "I searched every lane looking for you before I realized Willow was missing. Your father was at least comforted by the thought that you had likely left of your own volition."

Anora opened her mouth to speak, but Sumayl held up a hand to stop her. "Save it for your father." He dropped his arms back to his sides, turned on his heel, and led them through the gate as he grumbled, "I should have known you two were up to something."

She looked at Hunter as they followed Sumayl to the paddock and dismounted. He looked stoic, but she knew him well enough to see the subtle ticking of his jaw that belied his calm demeanor. Her father was not the type of man to assume the worst and he would believe Anora if she said nothing happened between them, but Hunter probably thought he was in for a tongue-lashing, and worse still, that he might be pressured to marry her if her father thought her virtue compromised.

They dismounted when they reached the tiny paddock beyond the forge. Hunter reached for Willow's reins and said, "You can take her from here, Sumayl. Frode will want to know immediately that she has been found. I will see to the horses."

Anora did not like being treated like a child, handed off from one guardian to another, but at this moment, she felt she deserved it. She had lied to her father and Sumayl, something she had not done since she was a girl, and it filled her with shame.

Sumayl dropped a meaty hand on Hunter's shoulder. "You will be joining us as soon as the horses are tended to." It wasn't a question, but Hunter nodded anyway, to which the blacksmith responded with a grunt that seemed to be part of the secret language of men.

Anora fell into step at Sumayl's side for the short walk home to the goldsmith shop. "I am sorry for the duress I caused, Sumayl. And sorry you had to search for me. Were you out all night?"

"It matters not," he said, his voice gentle, which only made Anora feel worse. "Your father will be relieved you are home."

It pained her to think of her father up all night, pacing the floor with worry, and feeling helpless to do anything about it. "Is he in a terrible state?"

"I will not lie to you; I have not seen him this upset since your brother's death."

"Oh, hell and damnation," she muttered between clenched teeth, as she clutched at her heart, the pain of hurting her father like a knife to her chest.

"His worry abated somewhat at the discovery that Willow was also missing. Once we knew nothing had happened to you on the way to the widow's house, but rather that you had fabricated the story of going to see her, he felt more hopeful that you were not harmed." A low mirthless chuckle rumbled in his throat. "Bad fortune for you that the part about the widow needing assistance came to fruition. Had she not sent her eldest to request your presence, we may not have discovered your ruse."

"It was a poor decision on my part not to tell both of you the truth about where I was going and why," Anora admitted. She should have thought more about the consequences if her lie was discovered before she returned.

"May I assume you will be telling us the truth now?"

Anora's shoulders slumped. Even if she had a choice in the matter, they deserved better from her than lies. "Yes, Sumayl, I will be. And I will need the guidance of both you and my father to know what to do next after you hear my story."

"This sounds to be of grave importance," Sumayl said, turning to look down at her as they walked. "So grave that you felt it necessary to dress as your brother?"

She nodded as she ran her hand over Baldwin's tunic. Her plan had been to return home under cover of the night when no one could get a close look at her face. She patted at her hair to be sure it was still tucked into the cap Hunter loaned her as she scanned the lane to see how many people had noticed them.

Fortunately, because it was Sunday, there were very few people on this side of the village. She imagined most were gathering outside the church to attend mass, and for that she was grateful. Many in Oswestry knew her well and would not be fooled by her disguise. Added to the fact that Sumayl was just as well known and even more noticeable with his dark skin, towering height, and wide shoulders, there was no chance of them going unnoticed or unrecognized on this lane. People with skin the same rich brown as his were not entirely uncommon in the streets of London, but there was no one else who looked like him in Oswestry.

"Men are fortunate to get to wear breeches," she said with a small smile. "Gowns are not always easy to contend with, especially when having an…adventure."

"An adventure? I am intrigued," Sumayl said as he opened the back door to the goldsmith shop.

As they entered, Anora looked longingly up the stairwell that led to the upper floors and their private chambers. What she wanted more than anything was to crawl into her bed and sleep.

"Anora?" Her father appeared in the doorway between the back room and the shop front.

"Yes, Papa. I am here."

"My heart cannot take this," he said as she walked into his outstretched arms to hug him. "When I discovered you were gone, my mind went immediately to all the terrible thoughts of what might have happened to you."

"Hunter was with her," Sumayl said. He was leaning against the hearth, massaging his thick hands, which he complained of aching more often than not these days. "He is seeing to the horses."

"I did not mean to scare you, Papa," Anora said, her heart breaking at her father's worry.

"Are you wearing your brother's clothing?" He plucked at the fabric of her breeches.

"I am." She stepped out of her father's embrace. "Sit down,

Papa, and I will tell you about it while I prepare the stew."

"Why is Hunter with you?" her father asked as he settled heavily onto his bench by the table. "What does he have to do with your story?"

"It is not what you think, Papa," Anora said as she grabbed a knife off the sideboard and pulled a few turnips toward her.

"It must not be good," he said in a low voice. "You always find something to do with your hands when you are forced to discuss something difficult."

It comforted Anora to be reminded of how well her father knew her. "You have always been observant, Papa."

"Where is Hunter, Sumayl?" her father asked, turning toward the blacksmith. "I sense his presence is important for this conversation."

"If he doesn't walk through that door shortly, I will personally find him and drag him through it myself." Sumayl leaned against the hearth with his eye on the door.

"Papa," she said slowly, "are you expecting me to tell you that Hunter and I are…" She couldn't say the word out loud.

"Lovers?" he provided, lifting his eyebrows. "I'll kill him with my own two hands if he doesn't do right by you, but aye, I am expecting that. And if Hunter proves as honorable as I expect him to be, I will be happy for it."

Anora's mouth dropped open as she groped for what to say.

"As your father, I cannot condone clandestine meetings with your lover," he tipped his head to the side and smiled wistfully, "but as a man who knows what it is like to be in love, I cannot fault you. Your mother and I—"

"Papa!" Anora held up her hands to stop him from saying more. "I encountered Hunter by coincidence, and he insisted he accompany me home to ensure my safety. His behavior was above reproach and honorable at all times. We are *not* lovers."

She heard the snick of the door as it closed and turned to see Hunter. All the color drained from his face as he stared at them wide-eyed.

Anora felt her jaw drop open as she looked from Hunter to her father and back to Hunter. "Did you hear all of that?"

Hunter nodded slowly while Sumayl let out a deep, rumbling chuckle.

She snapped her mouth shut and pressed her lip together. With a nod, she turned back to the sideboard, poured four tankards of ale, and brought them to the table. "Please sit down. You, too, Sumayl."

Hunter straddled a bench and leaned his arm on the table while Sumayl sat across from him next to her father. Anora took a hefty swig from her tankard of ale, then set it back on the table and returned to the sideboard to continue chopping vegetables for the stew.

"As I was saying,"—the knife thwacked against the wood of the sideboard as she cut the stems from turnips and set them to the side—"I encountered Hunter by coincidence, and it is only part of what I need to tell you."

"Where is this place that you met Hunter, *by coincidence?*" her father asked.

"Castle Whyte." Anora turned to face the table, knife still in hand. "I just realized I've not asked you why *you* were there, Hunter. Why *were* you there?"

He waved his hand dismissively. "Tell your story first, and then I'll decide if I'm going to reveal my reasons for being there."

She continued to cut the turnips into chunks for the stew as she spoke. "Madam Ruby brought jewels to the shop to sell last week, as she's done before. You were in the smithy with Sumayl, so I completed the transaction."

"Aye," her father said suspiciously. "You told me about the transaction."

Anora set down the knife and sat across from her father at the table. She reached to take her father's hands in her own. "What I didn't tell you, Papa, was that there were two pendants in with the other pieces that I set aside because...they are similar in design to mine."

She reached into the neckline of the tunic she was wearing and pulled out a leather thong hanging around her neck that was strung through a pendant about the size of a coin. She rubbed a finger reverently over the design as Hunter leaned closer to get a better look. It was engraved with vines decorated with tiny gems as blossoms on the oval plate of gold. The intertwined vines were each in the shape of an *S*. "You told me yourself that until mama died, your favorite design to make was of the intertwined *S*'s, for Sapphira Smith, because it pleased Mama so very much."

Frode let out a soft sigh. "It was like a secret shared between us. After she died, I could not bring myself to make them anymore." He touched a finger to the pendant Anora still held out on the stretched leather thong. "You have the last remaining pendant. At least, the last in my possession after the theft." He lifted his milky eyes to her face. "Where are the pendants from Madam Ruby?"

"I hid them in my room," Anora admitted.

"Why did you not bring them to me directly?"

"I know I should have told you, Papa," Anora said sheepishly, "but I wanted to bring you more evidence than just two pendants and Madam Ruby's word she got them from Baron Payne. I thought if I could find the other stolen pieces, then there would be enough evidence to prove...to prove Edmund had knowledge of the theft."

Anora hated to bring this information to her father about Edmund. She'd hoped to have solid proof of the baron's involvement when they had this discussion. For her father to accept that Edmund Payne had any involvement in the theft that left his wife dead would be devastating considering the history he shared with Edmund's father.

"Fetch the pendants, Anora." Her father's voice was quiet and stiff with anger.

Anora did as her father asked and put them in his hand when she returned. She watched as he rubbed his fingers over the pendants. "Hunter, do you know the story of how my wife died?"

"I do not," Hunter said respectfully.

"Mama was killed by thief," Anora said when her father couldn't seem to find the words to recount the events of that horrible day. "Papa and I went to the market in Ellesmere that day, and Baldwin had stayed behind with Mama to mind the shop. Baldwin was in the front of the shop and Mama was polishing and packing two fine pieces commissioned by the old Baron Payne—Eustace—for the newly appointed abbot to Shrewsbury at the time." She stopped, as a wave of grief hit her harder than it had in a very long time. Her eyes watered and it felt like someone was pushing their thumbs into them as the pressure of her tears built.

Hunter had the grace to look away from her in that moment, and her father picked up where she left off, his voice cold and clipped. "Sapphira or Baldwin must have let the intruder in through the back door, and since they unbarred it to let the person enter, it was likely someone familiar to them. Baldwin was hit with a stone on the side of his head and knocked unconscious. From the state of the room, it seems Sapphira tried to fight off the intruder. When we arrived, she was lying next to the fireplace with a gash in her head. I think she was pushed backwards and hit her head on the stones as she fell. She lingered for nearly a fortnight, but never again awakened."

"I am sorry," Hunter murmured with a nod of deference. He looked truly mournful, and Anora wondered about his mother. He'd never mentioned any family, but there was a haunted look to him that suggested he'd suffered his share of painful losses.

"The thief took the chalice and platter commissioned by the old baron," Anora continued, "these pendants, and he took an emerald ring my father had made especially for her."

"She didn't typically wear it when working in the shop," her father said, "but she had brought it down, along with these pendants, from our private chambers earlier in the day to show to Lord Godfrey of Whitchurch. He wanted to commission a gift to give his bride on the day of their wedding and Sapphira thought he might like to commission something similar for his new wife. When I left for Ellesmere, she had put the ring on her finger and planned to return it and the pendants to the locked chest in our chamber after she gave them a good polishing along with the pieces for the abbot."

"Did Baldwin not get a look at the intruder?" Hunter asked.

"He recovered quickly and fully from the blow to the head with the exception of his memory," Anora explained. "He recalled nothing of that day, not even from the morning hours before the intruder hit him. He had no recollection of anyone entering the shop, or even that he was in the shop with our mother that day."

"Lord Godfrey?" Hunter pressed, "I assume you suspected he might be involved and investigated him."

Frode nodded. "Lord Godfrey commissions pieces frequently and has for more than twenty years. There was nothing to indicate he had anything to do with the robbery."

"There are rumors that Baron Payne is overspent," Hunter said, "and evidence is mounting that he is making alliances that would displease the king."

"Baldwin always harbored suspicions about Edmund," Anora said carefully. It felt like a betrayal to her father to speak unfavorably about the only son of his esteemed friend. Her brother had brought up his concerns about Edmund once after the robbery, but Frode had refused to believe he could do something so heartless and cruel to a woman who'd known him since he was an infant.

"He is not his father's son in any way that matters. Eustace was a man of integrity, but I've heard the reports, of Edmund's shortcoming since taking his father's place," Frode murmured with a sad shake of his head. "I've given up hoping that Edmund would become a baron worthy of his father's name."

"You've always believed that if we found the pendants, then we'd have found Mama's killer." She'd yet to say the words aloud, but now that she had, she was even more determined to prove Edmund's guilt.

"It is a dangerous endeavor to accuse of nobleman of theft," Sumayl said, "and worse yet to accuse him of murder."

"Did you tell Madam Ruby you recognized the pendants?" Hunter asked.

Anora shook her head. "I commented on the lovely design and asked if she knew where they came from. She said Baron Payne used them as payment for services at her establishment."

"And you are certain they are the stolen pendants?"

"This one has four flowers," Frode said, holding up one of the pendants. Then as he lifted the other. "And five on this one."

"Is there a significance to that?" Hunter asked.

"I gave my wife a pendant every summer to mark our years together, adding a flower for each year." Frode's voice grew thick as he spoke. "For our tenth year, I made her the pendant Anora is wearing, and an emerald ring with vines engraved on the band. The pendants got larger each year. The last one I made had sixteen gems encrusted flowers on it."

"If the commissioned items were the target, then logic would say the thief knew the baron's business," Hunter said. His eyes were narrowed to slits and his mouth was pursed in concentration.

"Aye, that is exactly what Baldwin thought as well," Anora said. "But why would Edmund steal pieces commissioned by his own father? And why would he want to embarrass his father by leaving him empty handed for the welcome of the abbot?"

"He wouldn't be the first son of a wealthy lord to spend more than his father allotted to him monthly," Hunter said. "It's not uncommon for young nobles to accumulate debt in anticipation of the incomes they will earn and the inheritances they will receive. If their fathers are unaware, or unwilling to finance the excesses, they can find themselves in a dangerous bind."

Frode set the pendants on the table and lifted his milky eyes to Anora, and asked in a shaky voice, "You went to Castle Whyte looking for the other pieces?"

"Yes, Papa," Anora said quietly.

Her father's face paled. "If he were the thief, then he is also the killer, and he could have killed you had you been discovered."

Anora nodded. "It was risky, but I wanted to find the proof and show Edmund that we are not as helpless as he thinks us to be. Otherwise, he will continue to torment us."

"But you are not the one to do that," Frode said angrily. "I will not let him take you from me, as well. It is better that you stay out of his sight and let us deal with this. If he thinks you are a threat to him, then he will become a threat to you."

"He is already a threat to me."

"What do you mean?" Her father was nearly shouting at her now. "Has something happened?"

"That is the other part of this story that I have not told you yet." Anora braced herself for the repercussions that would come from her next confession. "We were robbed again during the Lammas Day festival. "The brooch I made for the merchant's daughter in Shrewsbury was taken, but nothing else. And just days prior, Baron Payne found me at the market and proposi-tioned me to be his mistress again. He insinuated that if I refused, I would come to regret it."

"What?" her father and Sumayl bellowed in unison. Sumayl pushed to his feet so suddenly that his bench toppled backwards onto the floor.

Hunter was silent after her confession, but when Anora looked at his face, she could see the muscles clenching in his jaw. When he spoke, it sounded like a feral growl and sent chills down Anora's spine.

"I am going to kill him."

Chapter Thirteen

Hawk had specifically instructed Hunter not to kill Baron Edmund Payne. He was to get in Castle Whyte, find something incriminating against the man, and get out.

Leave nothing unturned.

Leave nothing behind.

Leave no trace.

It was what he did best. And why he *was* the best. Nothing and no one could deter him from the objective. Many men had tried to bring Hunter low, and none had succeeded. Until the past night, and then everything had gone to hell faster than the devil could hunt down a damned soul. And all it took was Anora in breeches with her hair tucked into a cap to abandon his mission and leave a trail of bodies on his way out.

Killing the baron would mean defying Hawk and risking severe punishment by the crown if he could not prove a justification. Hawk, of all people, would understand defying a direct command for the sake of a woman, but the king was not so forgiving—Hawk had the scars on his back as proof. But even if he couldn't have Anora, he would never let the baron have her.

The red veil of anger slowly cleared from Hunter's eyes as he lifted his gaze to look at the others around the table. Sumayl, Frode, and Anora stared at him in varying degrees of disbelief.

"I meant no disrespect." Hunter combed his hand through his hair, disgusted with his lack of control.

Sumayl stooped to right the toppled bench and Anora pushed to her feet to return to the sideboard and continue chopping.

Frode studied Hunter warily for a long moment, as though assessing how danger of a man he really was and whether he wanted him anywhere near his daughter. Then he dropped his forehead onto his fingertips and rubbed at his temples as he asked, "How could the brooch have been stolen, Anora? I was here when Callow came for it. He said the design was exactly as hoped and he was certain his daughter would be pleased with it."

"The brooch I presented was the second I made," Anora admitted as she absently chopped a turnip into chunks. "When the first was stolen, it seemed a direct attempt to undermine me, to make me feel vulnerable. If I failed to deliver the piece after it had been paid for, it would damage my reputation and likely end my chances to be a goldsmith in my own right. I couldn't let that happen."

"I would have helped you. I wouldn't have let you fail," Frode insisted. Hunter could see the defeat on the older man's face from his daughter's lack of faith in him, whether perceived or real.

"I know, Papa," she said in a sympathetic tone as she stopped the stew preparations to look at her father, "but if I went to you to remedy the situation, then I was giving the thief what he wanted, which was for *me* to fail. And if Edmund had aught to do with it, going to you only reinforced his assertion that I need a man to protect me."

Anora was an expressive speaker, but it made Hunter nervous to see her emphasizing her words with her hands when she was waving a large knife in one of them. He went to her and carefully reached for the knife handle. "Sit and talk to your father. I'll ready the stew."

She still wore her brother's clothing, but she'd removed the cap he'd given to her and a rope of pale-yellow hair was draped over her shoulder. He smelled the dampness of the forest on her, but also the scent of something brighter that was uniquely her and he involuntarily drew closer to her as he gently tugged the knife handle from her grip. He suspected she was just as affected as he by the light touch of their hands because the expression on her face changed from resistant to mildly confused. The length of his body brushed against hers as he stepped around her to the sideboard in a motion that felt oddly intimate and familiar.

"This is still my shop, Anora," Frode said gruffly. "And my home. You were not right to keep this from me. Sumayl should have crafted new locks immediately after it happened."

"I thought about the locks," Anora said. She settled onto the short bench he had just vacated so that her back was not to him at the sideboard. "But the thief obviously has a quality set of pass keys to so easily open both locks. Changing them would not be a deterrent. Since the day of the thefts, we've not all been gone from the shop at the same time, and the doors are barred from the inside when we are here."

Frode turned toward Sumayl. "I have the pass keys you made for Baldwin still in the chest upstairs. Have you made any others?"

"Of course not," Sumayl said firmly. Hunter knew the blacksmith was one of the most talented in the region and his work making locks was some of the finest he'd seen. "And I made those only to better understand how to create the most secure locks."

"Baron Payne would have access to smiths willing to make him the keys," Hunter said. Smiths skilled in the art of locks were hard to come by, but besides Sumayl, there were several others in the realm. The penalty for making illicit keys was steep, but for a good price, it was possible to get them.

"*If* it was the baron," Frode said, shaking his head as though he could not fathom him capable of such a deed. "He was here only six or seven days ago to inquire after our well-being."

"He is not a good man, Papa," Anora said earnestly. Hunter agreed with her assessment, but he would keep that bit of information to himself for the time being. "Nothing was taken other than the brooch I had made for Callow's daughter. The other gems and metals were not touched."

"Where did you have brooch?" Hunter asked. He didn't like the idea that nothing else stolen. The brooch would be the most recognizable and hardest to sell. If the thief was after money, they would have taken the metal and gems, which could easily be sold.

"I had locked it in the chest per usual while we were at the festival." She pointed to the heavy chest attached to the wall, secured with metal straps and heavy lock. "The only people who knew about the brooch were you, Sumayl, Callow, and Edmund. Callow had nothing to gain from having the piece he commissioned for his daughter stolen. But Edmund would benefit if I were frightened into agreeing to his proposition. And after Madam Ruby told me it was the baron who paid her with the pendants, I had no doubt he was the thief, or someone he hired."

Hunter's stomach clenched like he'd just been punched. If he hadn't stayed away because of his inability to keep a clear head when near Anora, he may have known about the theft and the baron's threats. "When did Baron Payne start to press you into becoming his…mistress?" He nearly choked on the word.

"The first time was after I again refused his proposal to be his wife more than a twelvemonth past."

Hunter pushed the knife through a fat onion. "You didn't mention him as one of your suitors last night." It was not unheard of for lesser barons to marry the daughters of wealthy merchants, and Hunter knew well why Edmund, or any man, would want a prize like Anora for wife and bedmate. She was stunningly beautiful with her elegant stature and striking features. Hunter was not immune to her beauty, but it had been radiance of her smile when she laughed that had first caught his attention and made his heart pound like a drum in his chest.

"You're right, I did not. I didn't think it necessary," Anora said, obviously peeved again.

"Not necessary?" He slammed the blade through the onion

again as he blinked back the water pooling in his eyes from the pungent aroma. "Not necessary when I found you sneaking around the castle of a man who has requested your hand in marriage? *And* has pressed you to become his mistress? This is information I need to know if I am going to help you."

"I didn't ask for your help," Anora snapped.

"You're getting it anyway." He'd sleep on the floor of the shop with his back to the door for the rest of his days if that's what it took to keep her safe from Edmund Payne. Even before Hawk had sent him on his mission to find out who the baron was aligning with and what he was planning, Hunter knew Baron Payne was a despicable man with sadistic tastes. They suspected Edmund was meeting with Marcher lords conspiring against the crown. And like many men, he had a penchant for frequenting brothels on his journeys, but he had little care for what shape he left the women in when he departed. The thought of him putting his hands on Anora in *any* capacity made Hunter want to return to his old ways of killing men in the dead of night just because they were brutes deserving of nothing better.

"I didn't ask for it last night, either, and look how that turned out." Anora threw her hands up in the air in frustration and glared at him. He had picked up the onions to bring to the pot hanging over the low flame in the hearth but stopped midstride to meet her angry glare. Before he could respond, Frode interjected.

"Stop, both of you."

Hunter dropped the onions in the pot then returned to the sideboard feeling duly chastised.

"Anora," Frode commanded. "Tell me what happened yesterday and last night."

"I went to Castle Whyte, knowing the baron was not there, to see if I could find the brooch or any more of stolen pendants."

"He could have come by the pendants without having stolen them himself," Frode said. "And how did you know he was not at the castle?"

"Before he let me fetch you from above stairs, he told me he had business to attend to in the south of Wales but would return by Michaelmas at the end of the month. He said I had until then to consider his proposition and after that he would not be responsible for anything that happened to me or the shop."

A red veil of anger clouded Hunter's vision again, but before he could protest, both Frode and Sumayl voiced their outrage.

"How dare he!" Frode nearly bellowed.

"The snake!" Sumayl exclaimed slamming his fist down on the table.

"If I could prove he had the first brooch I made, or if he had any more of the items stolen so many years ago, I could use that against him somehow."

"Anora," her father said on a heavy sigh full of warning as he shook his head side to side. "You could have gotten yourself killed. How did you even get into the castle?"

Hunter was grateful for the distraction of chopping as she recounted entering through the front gate under the guise of having a delivery for the kitchen. She explained how she waited until dark and then used the keys she had taken from the chest in Baldwin's room to enter the baron's bedchamber. When she didn't find what she was looking for there, she searched his private solar. "He had a cask of jewels in his bedchamber, but the brooch wasn't there, and I did not recognize any of the others. The chests in his solar only contained coins. That's where I encountered Hunter."

"How did you know Anora was in the castle?" Frode asked. "Or were you there on business of your own?"

Hunter dumped the last of the chopped vegetables into the pot over the fire, then sat down across from Frode. The man may be advancing in age and his eyes failing, but he was still as shrewd as the day he met him two years prior. "I was gathering information for Hawk and stumbled on Anora when I saw her creeping up the stairwell to the baron's chamber."

Frode visibly paled and Sumayl groaned, no doubt from the

same surge of fear that stabbed at him when he thought about what could have happened to her if he had not been there.

"I followed him from the castle," Anora said, her voice deceptively light.

Hunter leveled a warning glare at her as she took a swig of her ale. Her father and Sumayl deserved to know that they were nearly caught in case soldiers started nosing around in Oswestry looking for them.

Anora set her tankard on the table but continued to clutch it with both hands. "We encountered some guards during our escape. I had to distract two of them until Hunter could...attend to the situation." Before Frode or Sumayl could say anything, she added hastily. "But we evaded them. And the others—"

"Others?"

"Aye," Hunter wasn't sure how much more Frode could take before the shock killed him. "I don't think they got a good look at us, but they are likely looking for a woman dressed in breeches and her traveling companion."

"Lord, help us," Frode muttered.

"Hunter led us to a hut in the forest and we hid there until the rain subsided. We've not encountered anyone since making our escape from the castle. Not even after we left the hut and made our way here."

Frode heaved a heavy sigh. "That is not the explanation I expected." He let out a mirthless laugh. "I'd rather deal with a clandestine tryst than this fiasco."

"I am sorry, Papa. I did not mean to make things worse."

Frode reached across the table and took his daughter's hands in his own. "I am sorry that you have been shouldering this burden alone."

"I know it sounds absurd, but I wanted to prove Edmund wrong. If he had stolen the brooch from me, then I wanted to steal it back, and let him see that I am not as incapable as he thinks me to be."

"He is not the man his father was," Frode said with a sad

shake of his head. "Eustace would be ashamed of what has become of his son for the disrespectful way he has tried to shame you and our family."

Hunter felt the heat of shame as it crept up his neck and into his cheeks. He'd wanted to seduce Anora himself, and had nearly given into his desires, which made him no better than the baron. He'd spent hours at this same table, listening to tales of when Frode served King Henry as a code decipherer, of his determination to become a goldsmith despite coming from a long line of blacksmiths, and of the way he loved his wife and children. Frode was a man of integrity and Hunter admired him for it. To have the privilege of being a trusted friend and then seduce his daughter would be an affront that would not be forgiven.

To clear his head of thoughts of Anora, Hunter asked. "Do you think he had anything to do with what happened to your wife?" If he did, it was one more reason for Hunter to kill him.

"Baldwin suspected him from the beginning," Anora said. "He never liked him, even when they were boys. He said Edmund was often jealous and cruel."

"I didn't want to believe him," Frode admitted. "I thought it was the natural rivalry between boys."

"From what I have discovered of him in the last months," Hunter said, "Edmund Payne is a man who lacks in scruples and is needlessly cruel to people who are weaker than him." The baron had journeyed to the holding of Gilbert de Clare—a man known for causing strife among his fellow Marcher lords—with increasing frequency in recent months and sampled nearly every bawdy house along the way. The stories told by the harlots about him of degradation and a penchant for inflicting pain were all the same, and reason enough to want to see the baron dead. He hardly remembered his mother, but he imagined it was a man much like Edmund Payne who had deemed her life worthless because she was a whore in one of the cheapest bawdy houses in London.

"What can you tell us about why you are investigating Edmund?" Frode asked.

"Someone has been killing livestock and ransacking tenant holdings on land under the protection of Hawkspur. Hawk suspects Baron Payne is behind the attacks." He trusted Frode and Sumayl to be discreet, and for the sake of convincing them of the dangers of being associated with the baron, he added, "From what I've uncovered thus far, Payne is getting himself in deep with dangerous men with questionable loyalty to the king. He is not a man you want your family associated with."

Frode cursed quietly, then said, "I should be the man to protect my daughter and avenge my wife, but I am no longer a young man." He lifted his unfocused gaze in Hunter's direction. "I understand that your loyalty to Lord Hawk means that you are required to put his mission above all others, but I would ask that if you find any evidence that proves—or disproves—Edmund's involvement in the thefts or the death of my beloved Sapphira, that you share that information with me."

"Of course," Hunter readily agreed. He'd already decided he would do everything in his power to ensure the baron was never again a threat to Anora or Frode.

"Until then, Sumayl and I will do all that we can to shield Anora from him."

"I will not hide," Anora insisted. She put her hand over Hunter's forearm as if to keep him from leaving, and he felt like he'd just been singed. "Nor will I be left behind to idly await my fate. Let me help you bring him down."

"No." It was instinct and self-preservation that brought the abrupt answer to his lips before he'd even thought about it. Every time they touched, another measure of his self-control slipped through his fingers.

Her grip on his arm tightened. "Don't you understand? If I let you do this while I stay here, hidden behind barred doors, and wait until you tell me the situation has been remedied, then I will have surrendered to the notion that my life is not my own."

"Anora," he growled, though he couldn't be certain if it was in warning or out of desperation. Or both.

"No, Hunter. I will not let you deny me this, because if you do, what happens to me? If the proof of Edmund's duplicity is not found before he returns at the end of the month, what recourse will I have? It is only a fortnight until Michaelmas, which means I have only a fortnight to determine the course of my future. I will not sit idly by and let others manipulate the outcome of my life. If I do, that will be my lot for the rest of my days. And that is no life."

He wanted to argue with her, to tell her it was foolish to try to stand up to a man like Payne, or any man for that matter, but he couldn't find the words. He knew what it was to feel helpless, the utter frustration of having no options, the humility of being forced to bend the will of others, and he would not wish that upon her.

The desperation on her face melted away and was replaced with a look of sheer satisfaction. He shook his head in defeat because she knew him well enough to see that she had won, that he would not deny her the need at the core of every man—and woman—to live free of the bonds imposed by others.

God help him, but he was about to make the worst decision of his life.

Chapter Fourteen

NORA WAS TERRIFIED.

And exhilarated.

She had won the argument and here she was, on the open road to Shrewsbury with Hunter as her escort. They were to meet with Madam Ruby to discover if she'd sold jewels to other goldsmiths that matched the description of the brooch she made, or the pieces her father made that were stolen more than a decade past. Then they would continue on to Hawkspur, where Hunter would report what he'd discovered about the baron, and together they would decide on a plan to bring the baron low.

It had not taken nearly the amount of convincing she expected for her father to agree to let her accompany Hunter and continue her quest.

Or for Hunter to acquiesce to her presence on his mission.

Granted, she'd had to compromise. She'd wanted to find the brooch on her own and show Edmund Payne that she did not need to depend on him for her protection, nor was she afraid of him. The harrowing escape from the castle had shown her exactly how vulnerable a woman alone could be, and she no longer believed Edmund would be tolerant of her exploits if he caught her trespassing. She'd had to accept the protection of Hunter and reap the benefits of his skills and knowledge in order to partake in the mission, but it was a small sacrifice if it meant she would not wait helplessly at the shop with her father while Hunter fixed her problems for her.

Anora slid a sidelong glance at Hunter. He rode with a rigid posture and stared straight down the road ahead. He'd not spoken to her since they'd left Oswestry, but she hadn't let that bother her. She knew Hunter didn't want her with him and that he would travel faster without her.

"We do not have to travel at a walk," she said after they'd been plodding along for an hour. "I know how to sit a horse."

"Not necessary." His gaze continually swept from the trees to the road. Sometimes, he looked behind them to be sure they weren't being followed, but he'd yet to look at her. She'd been concerned that fighting her attraction to Hunter in order to stay focused on the mission would make the journey together difficult. Based on his current disposition and blatant disregard of her presence, that would not be an issue.

"You do not appear very happy," Anora said, unable to tolerate the silence any longer. She smiled as she spoke because she sincerely did not want to provoke Hunter. She merely wanted to converse. "I mean, you appear more unhappy than usual. Are you ever *not* unhappy?"

She felt the familiar zing of triumph when she saw him close his eyes and clench his teeth until the muscles in his jaws rippled. Banter and teasing, she'd learned, were the best way to draw him out of whatever dark place he went to when he was silent. She suspected he feigned his annoyance with her because the longer they bantered, the more the tension eased from his shoulders.

"Yes."

Anora waited, and when he said nothing more, she prodded, "When are you happy?"

"When I'm alone, unhindered by others." He slid a narrow-eyed gaze her direction.

She laughed at his grumpy tone and furrowed brow, but she'd made him look at her. "If I am a hindrance, you can be on your way," Anora said with a light shrug. "I won't tell my father. After I meet with Madam Ruby, I will continue on my way to Hawkspur to present my case to Lord Hawk and visit Galiena." She'd not seen her dear friend since she'd given birth to twins six months prior. "If I join a group of travelers and keep my face hidden," she pulled up the hood of her brother's mantle as she spoke, "everyone one will think I am a moody traveler, like you, and leave me alone. I shall be safe enough."

"We have an agreement," Hunter grumbled after huffing out a frustrated breath.

She really should quit teasing Hunter, but the tedium of the ride was making her restless. "In truth, I did not expect you to agree to this arrangement."

"You left me with no choice," he said with a glare. "You've already proven yourself to be reckless. I fully believed you when you said you planned to find the brooch with or without my help, and your father would never forgive me if I let you go alone and something happened to you."

"As I said before, I can be very persuasive when needed," she said with a smirk.

He grunted in response, but Anora couldn't tell if it was because he agreed, or because he disapproved.

"Have I told you how much I like wearing breeches? It is so much easier to ride a horse when you don't have a kirtle and chemise getting twisted and pulled in every direction while trying to sit in the saddle." When he didn't say anything, she continued on, "I am much better prepared should we get confronted by bandits and have to fight them off."

"You won't be fighting anyone. If anything, I will be fighting *because* you are wearing those damn breeches."

"Do I look so threatening?" She pushed her hood back as Hunter's eyes raked from her head, where her hair was tucked into another of Baldwin's caps, down the length of her trousered leg to her booted foot resting in the stirrup. The perusal was thorough and completely unsettling. Her skin tingled with awareness as if she had been touched.

"You are far too shapely and graceful to be a man," Hunter said, his eyes narrowed in disapproval.

"You think me graceful?" She laughed at the obvious blush that colored Hunter's cheeks.

"I think you do not move like a man."

"What do I need to do to move like man?" She was genuinely curious.

He flitted a quick glance her direction. "Straighten your legs more and don't stick your…your…"

"My what?" She could guess what he was trying to say, but she enjoyed his discomfort.

"Your backside," he said quickly. "Tuck it under more. It will reduce the curve from your back to your…hips."

She ignored the obvious strain in his voice and did as he said as she settled into the saddle with her new posture. "Is this better?"

He turned his head, his eyes flitting quickly down her back, then just as quickly turned his attention back to the road again. "Better."

"Thank you, Hunter," she said, with a satisfied smile.

"Also, quit smiling."

She pressed her lips together in a thin line and scowled in her best impression of Hunter. "Is this better?"

He looked at her briefly then shook his head. "Your nose is too fine, your lips too pink, and line of your jaw too elegant. You will never pass for a man. At best, and from a distance, you might be mistaken for a boy."

She waved her hand dismissively at him, though she couldn't help but be flattered by his assessment of her. "It is only because you know me that you cannot envision me as a man. Anyone else will just see a thin, unthreatening man."

"You talk too much to be a man," he drawled.

"Not all men are as tight-lipped as you, Hunter," she said, crinkling her nose at him to soften the rebuke. "I think you get as much satisfaction from our verbal swordplay as I do. In fact," she continued, holding up a finger to stop the response that was forming on his lips, "I think we make a good pair, you and I, and I'll wager when this mission is over, you will see the value in our continued partnership."

His eyes widened in shock, and he looked like he'd swallowed a lump of coal.

"Hear me out," she said with enthusiasm as she warmed to the idea. "I could do the talking, and you could do the strong-arming. You hate talking to most people, but often the best way to gather information is by asking the direct question. You'd be amazed how much people open up to me and say much more than they ever intended just because of a simple question and a welcoming smile."

He scowled. "What about the shop? I thought goldsmithing was your dream."

"It is the perfect cover. We can travel anywhere without raising suspicion. It is not unusual for my father and me to go to a nobleman's home to discuss work to be commissioned. We are often traveling to make deliveries or attend markets in other regions. No one will think to question us if they believe us to be traveling merchants. And I could be your lookout while you do your business."

He sighed. "What is it you think I do?"

"I think you are Hawk's spy. You prowl around in the dead of night and steal information."

"That's not too far from the truth, but it is not the only thing I do."

"What else then?" she asked, not only from curiosity but because she knew it would annoy him, which was the only fun to be had on this journey.

He pressed his lips together as if he'd said too much. "*Not your business.*"

"Ooh, I am intrigued. Another mystery about you for me to solve." She lifted her chin, "But not to worry. I will learn all of your secrets while we are working together."

"I work alone," he grumbled.

Anora was not deterred. "Do you not work with your liege, Lord Hawk? Or Red? You were with Red when Galiena sought refuge from my father after being chased through the streets of the village by an assassin."

"That is different. I am duty bound to my liege. And Red? His ass just requires saving at times."

She laughed at that. "You are his keeper, then? He will be so pleased to hear that is how he rates."

"He may not be pleased," Hunter said, with a tip of his head as though seriously considering the situation. "But he will not be shocked."

"That I believe. I imagine he knows as well as any that your arrogance knows no bounds."

He completed the scan of the road ahead and behind, and the forest on either side, then leveled a steady gaze at her. "It is another trait of men."

"Arrogance?"

He nodded.

She squared her shoulders and lifted her chin. Arrogance was more than just confidence, she decided, sneaking a sideways glance at Hunter's profile. There was an air about an arrogant man that exuded strength and power. It wasn't merely a case of acting the part; it was a belief of being infallible. The allure of a confident man was undeniable and just another reason she was intrigued with Hunter. She looked at him from the corner of her eyes and wondered what trait in a woman had a similar effect on a man.

"I can feel you looking at me."

A sudden heat flushed her cheeks at being called out once again while staring at him. She was twenty-three years of age, well beyond the age most women married and had children, but she'd never desired that for herself. Hunter was the first—and only—man who had captured her attention and invaded her thoughts when she was least expecting it. But he'd made it clear that he wasn't looking for a woman in his life. He'd confessed she was a distraction to him, but then he'd pushed her away.

She shook her head to clear the confusion in her thoughts and searched for something else to discuss. "Why would Edmund risk the ire of Hawk by ransacking his land and tormenting his tenants? Isn't Hawk a powerful lord with close connections to the king?"

"Edmund doesn't care about ire," Hunter said, "and aye, Hawk and the king have a mutual respect."

Anora waited for him to say more, and when he didn't, she said, "Being a man of few words is one of your more annoying traits."

"I am certain I have many," Hunter said with smirk, then returned to scanning the forest and road ahead.

"Aye, there are. But we do not have the time today for me to recite them all. Besides, I am more concerned with Galiena and the babies. Are they in danger if Edmund attacks Hawkspur?"

"You need not worry. Red will kill anyone who tries to harm her or the babes."

"I want more assurance than that." Anora did not doubt Red would lay down his life protecting his wife and family, but even Red could be brought low by a marauding army if outnumbered. "Should she and the children leave Hawkspur until this situation is resolved?"

A startling sound that resembled a scoff escaped from his lips. "Red will never let them out of his sight."

"But—"

"You need not worry," he said in a bored voice. "Red will protect them from any danger. And Hawk is prepared to fight for the castle. Edmund will not be successful."

"You stole something from Edmund's solar. Is it enough to prove his nefarious deeds?" She turned her face toward him when he didn't answer immediately.

"No, it isn't. And if I hadn't been forced to abort my mission,

I may have found what I needed."

She shrunk down in her saddle, her cheeks heating at the accusing glare he turned her direction. "You should not have aborted your mission on my account. I would have found my way out of the castle."

"No, you wouldn't have," he bit out through clenched teeth.

She dismissed his irritation and returned to their original topic. "You still haven't explained why Edmund would risk the wrath of another Marcher lord, and one with far more power."

Hunter let out an exasperated sigh before he relented and answered her question. "Payne and his men were instrumental during the conflict with the Welsh, and he believes he deserved a larger boon from the king than the just the coin he was awarded. He wanted Hawkspur and petitioned the king for it when it was revealed that the former lord of the castle—Lady Alyce's brother—was a traitor to the crown."

"Four years have passed since King Edward's fight with the prince of Wales ended. Why would Edmund risk the wrath of the king now?"

"The king does not typically get involved with the conflicts between Marcher lords and expects them to resolve their own issues. If a lord is too weak to defend himself, then he doesn't belong in the Marches."

"Would it not take a significant force to take Hawkspur Castle from Hawk and Lady Alyce? I would not think Edmund strong enough for that."

"He is aligning himself with lords who are rumored to be creating an alliance as a show of power against the king. They know Hawk and Lady Alyce do not support them and they would prefer Hawkspur to be under the rule of someone sympathetic to their cause—like Baron Payne."

"Baldwin never liked Edmund, and I have seen him for the deplorable man he truly is, but it is still hard to believe that someone who knew my family intimately could be so callous as to attack my mother and steal from us while she was bleeding on the floor."

"It is a cowardly deed," Hunter said, combing his hand through his hair. It had become a familiar gesture to Anora, since he did it whenever he was annoyed, irritated, or angry.

"If he was responsible for my mother's death, whether by his own hand or by someone loyal to him, I want him to pay." Her voice shook with her anger. She didn't often show the depths of her bitterness over what had happened to her mother, but it was always with her, like a thorn buried deep under her skin. Most of the time it was a dull throb, but at other times it felt like a finely honed blade slicing her to ribbons. "As my father said, he is not in a position to avenge my mother's death, and Baldwin is gone. That leaves me." She turned her head toward Hunter and waited for him to look at her. "That is why I went into Castle Whyte, despite the risks."

Hunter released a long breath, but for once, he didn't look like he was about to chastise her. "Now *that* I can understand."

Chapter Fifteen

A NORA VIBRATED WITH curiosity and excitement as they walked along the busy lane toward Madam Ruby's brothel. The anticipation of seeing something typically forbidden to her thrilled her, but she needed to stay calm and not attract attention. She took long strides, as instructed by Hunter, and enjoyed the sensation of being unhindered by the swishing fabric of a gown.

Hunter had told her the best approach was the direct approach. Two men walking through the front door of a brothel in the middle of the day would garner less attention than two men trying to sneak in the back door of said brothel.

"Heavier steps. Slouch a bit," Hunter instructed in a low voice. He'd also smudged her cheeks with dirt before they rode through the town gates after informing her that her skin was too perfect for a man's.

It was a new experience to walk in the light of day in a crowded lane and go unnoticed. Nobody gave her any attention, other than stepping to the side to get out of her way, which she attributed to her menacing-looking companion. What was most remarkable was that she didn't have to endure the leers and unnerving stares from men that always made her feel self-conscious and vulnerable. She was tall for a woman, taller than some men, and she often garnered unwanted attention because of it. But as man, she was no one special, and she loved it! Loved the anonymity of being inconspicuous and the idea that she could do whatever she pleased because no one watched and judged her every move.

Except for Hunter.

"We should have gone in the back," he grumbled at her.

"Why?" She'd done nothing to disguise her voice, so she coughed and tried again in a lower pitch. "Why?"

"Men don't move that gracefully. People are looking at us."

"No, they are not. And if they do, they will be looking at you. You are quite intimidating, you know." She lifted her head just enough to peer out from under the hood of the mantle she wore to look at the people walking in the lane.

"Thank you for the praise."

"What praise?"

"That I'm intimidating."

She almost laughed but held it in so as not to attract additional attention. "It wasn't meant as praise."

Hunter nudged her with his shoulder and nearly knocked her off balance. She tipped her head down to hide the smile that pulled at her lips. She'd seen men nudge each other in the same way before, as if to bump the other man's shoulder was a signal of appreciation. Barbaric as it was, it seemed to be a gesture of acceptance, a sign of approval, and Hunter had just bestowed the honor of it upon her. She felt her chest expand with pride, only to be deflated in the next instant.

Hunter bumped her in the shoulder again. She looked up to acknowledge his gesture only to see him point toward the door of a tavern on the other side of the lane, saying, "This way."

Not a gesture of comradery, then. It was a prod to get her moving in the right direction. And a reminder that she did not understand men as well as she thought.

She surveyed the front of the building, which looked like any other tavern with an inn on the upper floors, heavy timber framing, and shuttered windows. She couldn't say what she expected a brothel to look like, but it wasn't this. She expected something more…momentous.

They entered the tavern and hesitated while their eyes adjusted to the dimly lit room after being in the midday sun. She reached her hand up to push her hood back, then ran her fingers under the edge of the coif to ensure no stray hairs had come loose.

"Quit fidgeting," Hawk warned. He scanned the room as he walked toward the long sideboard of tankards in front of a row of kegs. He pointed at a table in the corner. "Sit. I'll bring ale. Don't forget to slouch and God's teeth, don't fidget."

Perplexed, she did as instructed. She hadn't expected to linger in the tavern, but did not question why as she slipped onto a wooden stool behind a table pressed into a dark corner near a large hearth with a steaming cauldron hanging over the flames. Several heavy, soot-coated beams supported the ceiling, hanging low enough that Hunter had to dip his head to avoid hitting it against them.

The rich scent of a roast simmering in juices reached her nose and set her stomach to rumbling. They'd not eaten on the journey to Oswestry, and the hunk of bread she'd eaten before they left her home in the morning was long gone.

Hunter slid a tankard across the table to her, then sat on another stool with his back to the wall. From their vantage point, they could see everyone in the main room as well as into the room that extended toward the back of the building. Only a handful of tables in each room had people sitting at them. Evening was still some hours away and she expected the tavern would fill up as the night wore on.

"Is that your stomach I hear?" Hunter asked after a particularly loud growl emanated from Anora.

"It has been hours since we've last eaten," she said defensively. "Are you not hungry?"

He shook his head.

"How can you thrive on so little sleep or food? I rarely see you rest or eat."

Instead of answering her question, he rose and retrieved two wooden bowls and a loaf of bread from the sideboard, then set another coin on the edge of the board. The proprietor nodded and grunted his acknowledgment as he lifted an empty keg and started toward the back door with it.

Returning, Hunter set a bowl on the table and slid it to her with a chunk of the bread. His own bowl he filled from the cauldron hanging in the hearth, then sat down and dipped his bread into the steaming gravy. He stabbed a piece of the meat and brought it to his mouth but stopped chewing mid-bite.

"Don't look at me that way," he said between gritted teeth, his lips barely moved as his gaze darted around the tavern. "Get your own roast. It would look odd if I served you."

The blush that covered her cheeks was not very manly when she realized her blunder. Of course, she must serve herself.

They did not speak as they ate their meal and drank the ale, which was an unexpectedly good brew. Anora was still not sure about the reason for the delay, but she didn't ask questions as she watched Hunter and waited. He must have good reason for his actions. They finished eating, and still Hunter did not make a move to go upstairs.

Leaning closer to Hunter, she asked in a low voice, "Are we waiting for something? Is there a reason we are not going to Madam Ruby yet?"

He glanced at her from the corner of his narrowed eyes. "I am debating the wisdom of bringing you to this place." Hunter's eyes continuously scanned the room as he spoke. "I have a mind to leave you here while I go speak to Madam Ruby." He turned to look at her directly. "But I fear you will find more trouble if left alone."

"I've come this far; I will not be deterred." She tired of this argument. Hunter had to know by now that it was a fruitless endeavor to try to sway her. "I have questions to ask Madam Ruby about the baron. And I want to know if she's seen similar pendants in the past thirteen years that she may have sold to another goldsmith."

"She does not pry, and she doesn't like questions," Hunter said. "She listens and she remembers. As do all of the women who work for her."

Anora tipped her head to the side and studied Hunter. "You are quite well-versed in Madam Ruby and her women." She'd meant for her tone to be nonchalant, as though just making an observation, but even she could hear the snide undertone. Jealousy was an ugly thing, and she had thought herself immune to it, but obviously she was not. At least not when it came to Hunter.

Before he could respond, a door creaked open at the far end of the back room and a man stumbled out, walked unsteadily across the tavern, and crossed near their table. His clothes were filthy, and he stank of ale, onions, and sweat. Anora held her breath to minimize the sickly stench as he passed by. He flashed a gap-toothed leer at her and Hunter, the few teeth he had black with rot, then mumbled something about a conquest before proceeding out the front door of the tavern.

"Did he come from above stairs? Did one of the women have to…" She didn't even know how to finish the question. It sickened her to think of anyone having to endure the man's stench for any length of time at an even closer proximity than what she just experienced.

"Aye." Hunter's tone was flat. "Did you think all the men handsome and pleasing to the eyes and nose?"

Anora hadn't allowed much thought about the men who would visit a brothel. She supposed some men would not be very appealing, and she knew some could be violent, but she'd not thought in detail about what that would be like for the women until this moment. A shudder shivered through her body as she realized the women likely did not have the option to say no to servicing any of those men.

"You don't have to do this," Hunter muttered. He studied her intently with a deep crease of concern between his brows. "I can ask your questions for you."

A torrent of doubt flooded her. She had been excited and enthralled, but now she felt sick with dread. Yet, there was too much to lose if she did not see this through. "I cannot turn back now."

Hunter held her gaze for a long breath then nodded once. A welcomed sensation of calm washed through her and she was grateful Hunter was here with her.

He downed the last of the ale in his tankard and set it to the side. "Let's go."

She took one last large gulp of her own ale then pushed to her feet and followed him to the creaky door at the back of the tavern. The only light in the enclosed stairwell came from a room at the top, but Hunter's frame as he climbed the stairs in front of her blocked her from seeing what awaited them.

"One of my favorite men," a woman's voice sang cheerily from above them.

Hunter grunted in acknowledgment as he cleared the top step and moved to the side for Anora. They were in a moderately sized salon with plush but shabby chairs and low tables arranged throughout. Madam Ruby stood in front of them, flanked on either side by two large men. She was dressed in a demure gown of black that made her look as though she were in mourning. When Anora had seen her at the goldsmith shop, she'd been dressed similarly in dark colors, but she'd assumed it was what the woman wore when outside of the brothel. She didn't know what she expected Madam Ruby to be wearing inside the brothel, but it wasn't this.

"I'd ask if you want your usual arrangement, but I see you've brought company," Madam Ruby said in her smooth, melodic voice.

Another twinge of unwanted jealousy pulled at her heart when the madam referred to Hunter's "usual arrangement" and she struggled to keep her face from showing her distaste. She was not naïve to the ways of men, and she was sure Hunter was no different from other men, but to think of him in a brothel, in the arms of a nameless woman as they shared their pleasure together, made her gut twist.

Madam Ruby smiled serenely as she assessed Anora from her capped head down to her booted feet. When her gaze returned to Anora's face, her eyes narrowed as she studied her features. "Who do we have here?" she asked, but her tone had a knowing air as one slim, black eyebrow arched high over her sparkling green eyes.

"We would speak with you privately," Hunter murmured, "if you will be so kind, and then I can explain."

With a flick of her wrist the two men flanking her moved away and sat at a table in the corner laden with tankards and trenchers of food. Both men, intimidating in size and demeanor, kept a constant eye on all that transpired.

The door at the bottom of the stairs opened and closed just as the creaking of another door could be heard somewhere behind Madam Ruby. Hunter tipped his head in the direction of the corridor behind her. "Is there a room available?"

Madam Ruby nodded and turned to let them pass as she said. "Rose is in her usual room and unaccompanied at the moment."

Hunter waved his hand at Anora as a signal to follow him, then started down the corridor. The sounds of tinkling laughter, seductive murmurs, and moans of satisfaction reached Anora's ears, all if it making her feel uncomfortable, unsettled, and…curious.

They passed by several doors on either side of the corridor, and more again when they turned first one corner and then another. As they reached the far end of the last corridor, Hunter stopped and knocked lightly on a door. As they waited, Anora tried not to think about how Hunter was at ease finding Rose's "usual room" as she looked to the end of the passageway where a door was blocked by a man dozing in a chair. He opened his eyes and lifted his head to look at them, then, seemingly satisfied they did not pose a threat, dropped his head back against his fisted hand to doze again.

A feminine voice beckoned them to enter from within the chamber and Hunter pushed open the door. A woman of about Anora's age was stretched out on the bed, clad in nothing but a thin white chemise, cut very low and loosely tied. Her eyes went wide when she saw two people enter, but then she jumped to her feet and practically ran to get to Hunter. She stretched up on her bared tiptoes and pressed a kiss to his cheek. Irritated, Anora huffed out a breath and gazed around the room to avoid looking at them.

The woman turned to Anora and asked, "Who is this?" She didn't step away from Hunter as she spoke but merely turned her head as she clung possessively to his biceps. Her honey-colored hair floating around her shoulders in loose waves. Her face was pretty, with high cheekbones that glowed pink, and with pouty lips, but there were dark circles under her faded-blue eyes and a wariness in her gaze.

"An acquaintance," Hunter answered, his hands resting lightly on the woman's elbows. "We need to speak to Madam Ruby alone. Is there somewhere for you to go?"

The woman nodded, gave Anora one more assessing look, then released Hunter and slipped out the door. A scant moment later, there was a sharp knock, and another woman entered the room. This one was dressed similarly to the first woman in a thin chemise, but she was taller and had chestnut hair plaited loosely down her back. She smiled affectionately at Hunter. "Madam Ruby will be here shortly. She is…negotiating with a patron."

"Is all well?" Hunter asked, the concern apparent in his eyes as he looked at the woman.

"Oh, aye," she said with a seductive smile. "Nothing she has not faced before."

Hunter nodded, then said, "And all of you are well?"

She shrugged. "Well enough. Eliza is moving to a room above stairs and will soon birth her babe."

Anora watched Hunter open the coin pouch hanging from his belt, pull out a handful of coins and hand them to the woman. "See that she gets what she needs for the next month and give Madam Ruby the rest to keep her off the floor for some time."

An unwelcome surge of jealousy coursed through Anora's body as the woman took the coins and pushed up on her toes to press her lips to Hunter's cheek. She turned gracefully on the ball of her foot, gave Anora a curious look, and left. Anora didn't have the right, but she seethed pondering about how many women Hunter had to support because of what she assumed were his indiscretions.

Anora raised her eyebrows at Hunter and widened her eyes in mock appreciation. "You are certainly well-known and well-liked here."

Hunter obviously heard the judgment in her tone, which was sharper than Anora intended, because his head snapped in her direction. His eyes narrowed at her in disapproval, but he didn't respond, his reaction chastisement enough to put a blush in her cheeks.

"If you have something you want to know, ask me plainly. If you have something to say about the women, I suggest you swallow it."

Embarrassed, she turned away from Hunter and crossed the room to stand next to a cushioned chair. It wasn't the women she was judging, though she was curious about them—especially Eliza and her baby—but rather Hunter. Before coming here, if someone had told her that Hunter frequented brothels, she would have dismissed it as expected and not put too much thought into it. Now that she stood in the brothel with him and witnessed his familiarity with the women as they expressed their affection for him, the knowledge felt far too vivid and personal. Her stomach felt like she'd swallowed bitter berries and her entire being felt itchy and...dirty. She pushed thoughts about the women, and speculations of just how familiar they were with Hunter, from her mind, and focused instead on her purpose for being here.

Hunter stood by the shuttered window, which he had pushed open just a crack to let fresh autumn air and light into the dank, chilly room. He peered out onto the lane below, but stayed hidden in the shadows, out of sight. She looked around the room, which was as unexpectedly tidy, though the linen sheets were crumpled in the middle of the bed and a musky fug hung in the air that Anora could not identify. The room was sparse, with a chest along the wall, a cushioned chair, a few hooks on the wall, and a small table and one wooden chair in the corner. She wondered if this room contained the whole of Rose's belongings, or if she only used this room for…work.

The most fascinating items were a polished silver mirror propped up on the table, a neatly placed comb and brush, and several small pots that presumably contained tinctures and powders for the face and lips. Anora had seen women with their lips painted unnaturally red and the cheeks permanently blushed with powder. She'd thought most of them looked startingly garish.

The only other items in the room were placed on a low bench near the bed: two large bowls of water, a neat stack of folded rags, and slivers of soap. The water in the first bowl was still clear, but the second bowl looked like watered milk and there was a small pile of crumpled, damp-looking rags under the bench. "Did we disturb the woman before her bath?" She pointed to the water and towels.

Hunter's gaze dropped to the bench, then lifted to look directly at her. "No. They are for washing their…" he hesitated, flustered. "For washing between men."

"Oh," Anora said as the heat rose in her cheeks.

Madam Ruby entered the room and went immediately to Hunter but kept her eyes on Anora. The older woman's face was devoid of emotion as she studied her, but to Anora, it felt like the heat of a thousand candles directed at her.

Hunter cleared his throat and caught Anora's attention, then ran his gaze quickly over her body from head to toe, as though telling her to look at herself. Only then did she realize that she'd lowered herself to the chair to sit with her back ramrod straight, her hands folded neatly in her lap, and her feet flat on the floor and pressed together at the ankles. She had no idea why she'd done that, other than possibly the fact that Madam Ruby had a superior air about her that made Anora feel like she needed to be on her best behavior. She'd been fascinated by the woman the few times she'd been face-to-face with her at the shop, but to see her in her own environment was mesmerizing. She moved with so much grace, yet exuded power and commanded obedience without even saying a word.

Anora coughed to hide her embarrassment, set her feet apart, and smoothed her hands over the breeches covering her thighs, but she could tell by the knowing grin on Madam Ruby's face that it was too late.

"You look familiar," Madam Ruby said. "Please remove your cap." Anora looked to Hunter, who stayed silent, then back to Madam Ruby. She rose to her feet then as she pulled the coif from her head, letting her hair fall over her shoulders. Madam Ruby's smile broadened, but she did not look at all surprised. "Ah. We *have* met before. You are Frode's daughter, from the goldsmith shop."

"Anora," she said. "I helped you a sennight ago when you brought in some pendants and other jewels to trade for coin."

"Yes, I remember you well. You are quite unforgettable." Madam Ruby spoke in an even, measured way, and Anora was unsure of how to interpret the comment. It seemed she choose every word deliberately and controlled with precision every feature in her face and every movement of her body as she spoke. It made Anora feel completely unsettled and unnerved.

Madam Ruby, Anora concluded, was a woman to study and emulate.

She tried to affect the same commanding countenance as she responded to Madam Ruby in an equally serene voice. "Then you will remember the pendants I purchased from you—the pendants you said were given to you by Baron Payne to pay his debt." She surmised that the other woman preferred the direct approach.

"Though I do not make it a habit to reveal the names of the men serviced here, I answered you because you are Frode's daughter." The words were said in a polite tone, but the thin set to her lips and the squared shoulders indicated Madam Ruby would not give up more information quite so readily.

Anora swallowed her nerves and stepped closer the older woman and Hunter, who had remained silent but observant to this point. Madam Ruby was not as old as her father but looked to be a woman in her later years. She was nearly as tall as Anora, but with a more robust and appealing figure. Her hair was so dark as to be almost black with strands of silver-gray weaving throughout the thick braids wound about the top of her head. This was not a woman to be trifled with, and she would quickly see through any pretense. "I understand that you have been an acquaintance of my father's for some time." Anora blushed as she realized what she said sounded like an insinuation. "I mean you have conducted business together." She closed her lips and shook her head. Her confidence and poise collapsed with her clumsiness.

Madam Ruby let out a little laugh. "I understand what you are trying to say. Your father has always treated me with respect, and I trust his conduct, which is why I have conducted business with him for many years. He is one of the few goldsmiths who pays me a fair price for the jewels." Her lips curved slightly. "As did you."

"Then you may recall my mother."

"I regret I did not know her," Madam Ruby said with a tip of her head. "I did not make the acquaintance of your father until after your mother was gone."

"Are you aware she was murdered?" Anora asked. Her voice shook slightly, but she pressed forward. "A thief came to our shop thirteen years ago, attacked her and my brother and stole pendants, an emerald ring, and two commissioned altar pieces.

My brother recovered from his injuries, but my mother never woke again."

"I remember hearing of it, and I am sorry for your loss," Madam Ruby responded, gently. "The thief was never found, as I recall."

"Nor were the stolen treasures," Anora confirmed. "There has been no sign of them in all these years…until you brought two of the pendants to my father's shop to sell."

Madam Ruby looked from Anora to Hunter. "I noticed you took special interest in them, but I knew nothing of their history. Are you certain they are the same?"

Hunter nodded. "Frode has confirmed they are two of stolen pieces."

Madam Ruby lifted her chin and took a deep breath. "You are here to ask if Baron Payne has paid me with more jewels. He has not. He has always paid with coin up until recent months. The only jewels I have accepted from him were those two pendants."

"I have to ask, though I can guess the answer, did he indicate anything about where he got the pendants, or if he had more of them?"

"He did not," Madam Ruby said. "I do not ask questions, and no explanations are given by the men who frequent my establishment."

Anora nodded her understanding, though she was disappointed. "Is there anything you can tell us about Baron Payne that may be of use?"

"I do not care for him, but he is a frequent customer. He is indulgent, self-serving, impetuous, and impulsive," Madam Ruby said, her contempt clear. "The rumors are that he has been spending his coins on vices and foolish endeavors faster than he can earn them. He is not the baron his father was."

Anora's eyes widened. "That is my father's sentiment."

"I cannot say how the pendants came to be in the baron's possession, but I can say I do not trust him, and I would believe even the most shocking stories about him."

Hunter rubbed his knuckles along his jawline. "Castle Whyte is not a large estate, but it was always a prosperous one. How could he possibly have drained the coffers in the two years since his father died?"

Madam Ruby let out a mirthless chuckle. "I've seen many a man lose fortunes overnight. Baron Payne spends much of his time and wealth in brothels, and not just mine. He's also got a penchant for games of chance—has since he was just a young colt."

"When was the last time the baron was here?" Hunter asked.

"Seven nights ago," Madam Ruby said, "but he paid with coin on that occasion."

Anora was not the only one surprised by this news; Hunter's brows shot up as he asked, "When did he pay with the pendants?"

"The early part of summer." Madam Ruby shrugged. "I thought they were exceptionally beautiful, so I kept them awhile. But with winter approaching and Eliza's baby on the way, it was time to turn them to coin."

"Even when he was younger, did he ever pay with anything other than coins? Perhaps he paid some of his gambling debts with jewels." Anora was desperate to find something that would answer the question as to whether Edmund had acquired the pendants recently, or if he'd had them all along.

"I don't recall him ever paying me in anything other than coin, but if he did, I would have sold any jewels to your father. As far as gambling debts, I cannot speak to that."

"How often do you see him?" Hunter asked.

"Once or twice a month, and often for two or three nights. He always brings companions with him. They are rowdy and demanding, but they make for a prosperous few days."

"What companions?" Hunter asked.

Madam Ruby slanted her eyes at Hunter and said, "I owe you much because of your kindness to me and my ladies so I will tell you what I know." It was clear she did not appreciate his questions.

Hunter looked away from Madam Ruby as though embarrassed by what she'd said. Anora didn't want to dwell on what those kindnesses were, or how much kindness it took to gain such respect from Madam Ruby. She had so many questions that she didn't want to know the answers to, like did *all* men visit brothels? And how often? She couldn't imagine her father in a place like this, but perhaps she fooled herself in thinking only disreputable men frequented houses like Madam Ruby's.

"The baron is usually accompanied by his commander and handful of guards, but occasionally, he will have a man of some import with him. After he used the pendants to pay for his entertainment, I did not see him for nigh on a month. Then he returned with a man he called Gilbert. He was obviously a man of some wealth and power because Payne pandered to him like he was royalty. They left after two days, and he readily paid what he owed in coin, plus more as a generous gift to the ladies who'd served them. Edmund's been back twice since, but only with his men, and he's paid in coin each time."

Hunter scratched his knuckles back and forth over the trimmed whiskers on his jawline, his brow creased in concentration. "Did he say where Gilbert was from?"

Madam Ruby thought a moment. "Not that I recall."

"Can you tell me what he looks like?"

"He is a fit man. Not tall, but broad and strong. Older than you," Madam Ruby said tipping her head toward Hunter, "but not as old as me. He had hair like fire and a temperament to match. He scared away the younger girls and even made one of the more seasoned ladies cry. Beatrice was the only one to appeal to him, experienced enough to stroke his ego and still manage his gruff demeanor."

The man sounded horrible, and Anora cringed at the thought of what Beatrice had to endure with the brute. What sickened her even more was the casual way Madam Ruby spoke about it, as though it was nothing unusual for them.

Hunter made a noise of disapproval deep in his throat that

sounded like a growled grunt.

"Do you know who he is?" Anora asked Hunter.

He was silent a moment, then said, "I know men like him."

"They are abundant." Madam Ruby lowered her gaze, and her dark lashes fanned over the top of her cheeks in a rare show of vulnerability. It made Anora even more curious about the woman who ran this brothel and who was in charge of so many women and in control—more or less—of the men they serviced. She tried to guess Madam Ruby's age but could not be certain. Her hair was streaked with gray but was otherwise still dark. Her hands were marked with dark spots and her fingers were knobby, but her face was smooth, and her cheeks were naturally bright. Whatever her age, she was a woman wise, as well as hardened, by experience.

"Baron Payne has always been one of those men, but of late, his tastes have progressed to new heights." A look of disgust came over Madam Ruby's face. "When he was last here, he spent much time instructing Beatrice on his newly acquired…tastes. Some of them quite depraved." She stopped and tipped her head to the side. "Beatrice can tell you if either Payne or Gilbert said anything that may be of use to you. I shall fetch her." She moved silently and fluidly to the door, like a shadow—another impressive skill of the commanding woman that did not go unnoticed by Anora.

"Put your cap back on before Madam Ruby returns with Beatrice." Hunter looked furtively at the door. "She does not trust women and will speak more freely if she believes you a man. If you stay in the shadows and don't speak, she may not pay you much mind."

Anora looked down at the forgotten coif hanging from her fingers, then pulled it over her head and quickly started pushing the loose strands of her hair under it. When she was finished, she looked at Hunter with eyebrows raised in question and turned her head from one side to the other for his inspection.

She hadn't expected the jolt of heat that pricked her skin when he moved close, his gaze meeting hers, as he ran the rough pads of his fingers along the sensitive skin behind her ear. She stood perfectly still as he pushed a tendril of hair under the cap. His warm breath whispered over her cheeks. She closed her eyes then, as her own breath caught in her throat. His fingers stilled for a heartbeat, then brushed gently down the column of her neck before he broke the contact. She felt the coldness of the space between them even as she heard him step away from her.

It was the most intimate thing she had ever experienced, and it left her heart beating furiously. She opened her eyes to look at Hunter and wondered if the brief touch had affected him as much as it did her, but—as usual—his face was an expressionless slate.

The door to the room opened and Anora feigned a cough as she turned away from Madam Ruby and another woman who followed behind her. Hunter stepped toward the other women, obstructing their view of Anora and she took the moment to catch her breath and steady her pounding heart.

"Who did that that to you, Bea?" Hunter asked in a low tone, his voice deceptively calm. Anora turned to see the tense set to his shoulders and his fists clenched at his side. His back was to her, and she could not clearly see the woman standing next to Madam Ruby.

She took a careful step to the side to get a look at what had caused Hunter's anger and cringed to see the bruised face of the woman at Madam Ruby's side. Madam Ruby gently pulled back the corner of the woman's thin chemise to reveal an array of yellow and purple bruises around her neck, then lifted the billowing sleeve to reveal more discolored marks on her arm.

The woman stood still and did not resist as Madam Ruby cupped her chin to turn her head side to side and held out her arm to display the damage. The sense of proprietorship on the part of Madam Ruby and the lack of resistance on the part of the woman reminded Anora of a breeder picking up the legs of a horse to show the state of the creature's health to a potential buyer.

Beatrice turned toward Anora as Madam Ruby released her

arm and locked eyes with her. She couldn't look away from the woman as they stood staring each other. Beatrice looked at her with curiosity and stoicism, as though she waited for Anora to pass judgment upon her as she stood on display in her chemise and covered in bruises. Anora looked at Beatrice in awe, confusion, and something akin to pity. How could she tolerate allowing others to possess her, to handle her body as though it was a thing to be manipulated, to have no say over who touched her and how?

Madam Ruby's voice broke through the moment and severed the odd connection between Anora and Beatrice. "The patrons sometimes get overzealous, but if they get violent, my men intervene and escort them to the door. Unfortunately, Beatrice was not able to alert anyone to the extent of Lord Payne's demands as he had bound her hands, stuffed a scarf between her teeth, and tied it off."

Anora felt her mouth drop open, unable to stop her shocked response and the sick roll of her gut. The depth of Edmund's sadistic tendencies went far beyond what she could have ever imagined.

"It is not the first time he's tied my wrists," Beatrice said in a dispassionate voice and with a dismissive shrug as she turned her attention back to Hunter. "Others have done it, too. But this time he put a gag in my mouth and put his hands on my neck. He said it would make the act better for me." She snorted then and jutted a hip. "As if he's ever cared about that."

"This is from *seven* nights ago?" Hunter said through gritted teeth. "I'll kill him."

"You do enough, Hunter," Madam Ruby said. "I will not have you involving yourself in this. It will only bring more trouble for me. Now, ask your questions. Evening will be here soon, as will our patrons."

"Lord Payne did a lot of talking despite having shut me up by stuffing a scarf in my mouth," Beatrice said in a sardonic tone.

"Did he give any indication where in Wales he's been spending time?" Hunter asked.

"Carmarthen," Beatrice said without hesitation. "After tell-ing—and showing—me about all the tricks he learned from a harlot named Scarlet at a bawdy house in Carmarthen, he boasted that he would buy me from Madam Ruby. When I said he couldn't pay the price to take me from Madam Ruby, he said he was now more powerful than his father ever had been, and soon he would be the most powerful Marcher lord in the region."

"You were also with the baron's companion, Gilbert?" Hunter asked.

"Was that the red-haired donkey's ass with him this sum-mer?" Anora saw Beatrice huff out a breath of air and roll her eyes. "He's not much easier than Payne."

"Did he say where he was from or why he was in Shrews-bury?"

Beatrice shook her head. "Not much of a talker, that one. Had a lot of demands and liked it when I was loud, as long as I wasn't talking." She pursed her lips and waggled her eyebrows suggestively to emphasize her point.

Anora wanted to be away from the brothel. She wanted to crawl into a corner and hide. The excitement and exhilaration from earlier had given way to nauseous aversion. How these women lived this life was beyond her understanding and made her heart ache for them.

Hunter pulled a pouch from beneath his tunic and took out several gold coins, which he handed to Madam Ruby. "For Beatrice for this night and the next. And whatever else you may need."

Anora's confusion must have shown on her face because Hunter said to her in a low voice, "I paid for the nights to allow for her to rest and recover from her bruises."

"Oh," Anora said, feeling contrite, and very uncomfortable with everyone's eyes on her as she nodded her understanding. She'd not truly expected Hunter to be paying for Beatrice's services, but she was perplexed by the protective interest Hunter seemed to have in the women here. She knew him to be a good and caring man, but she was beginning to wonder just how much he cared for Rose and Beatrice. Was it purely out of interest for their safety and well-being? Or was it because of his affection for the women? "Obviously I am not well-versed in how all of this works," she said with a wave of her hand at the room.

"I should hope not." Hunter chuckled and shook his head. He turned on his heel and reached for the door handle. "We will be leaving now."

"Thank you for your time, Madam Ruby, Beatrice," Anora said. With a bob of her head to the women, she started to follow Hunter from the chamber, but then she stopped.

She couldn't understand the life these women led—why Madam Ruby would partake in selling the services of the women, or how Beatrice could let strangers use her so deplorably—but what she did understand is that no one enjoyed being controlled and manipulated. Anora was not trapped in a life anywhere near as difficult as these women, but she felt a kinship with them that she suspected all women shared. Whether harlot, peasant, merchant, or noblewoman, they were all subject to the whims of men.

Until today, she'd thought women like Madam Ruby and Beatrice had given over to the whims, but perhaps they merely pushed back against them in the only way they knew, and with the only resources available to them.

Anora turned back to the women, clasped each by the hand and squeezed. She mustered as much kindness and understanding as she could into her eyes. It was a small gesture, but it was too hard to say everything that was in her heart, so instead she simply said, "Thank you."

Chapter Sixteen

Hunter didn't think he could withstand another night alone in the forest with Anora.

The sun hung low in the western sky, and it would be dark long before they reached Hawkspur Castle if they were to leave now. The taverns and inns near the brothel were full of men looking for ale, women, and fights, and he had no doubt that if they tarried too long, Anora in her breeches would attract attention.

And trouble.

"Where are we going?" Anora asked as he led her through the streets of Shrewsbury to the side of town that was less rowdy.

"To find you a room for the night."

She looked up at the sky. "Are we not continuing to Hawkspur?" Her voice was flat, devoid of her usual enthusiasm. She'd been distracted and subdued since they left the bawdy house.

"It will be dark long before we can get there." He studied her, curious about *which* part of the last hour brought on her somber mood.

"But the sky is clear. It will be easier traveling than the other night." Her hood fell back as she tilted her head up to scan the horizon. The late afternoon sun lit up the delicate features of her face and the smooth column of her exposed neck. Hunter looked around the lane to see if anyone else noticed that she was far too beautiful and graceful to pass as a man.

It was true; there wasn't a cloud in the sky to be seen. But Hunter was certain the moment he was alone with Anora in the deepest stretch of the forest, the weather would turn on them and they'd be forced to take shelter in another cramped hut. Or worse yet, under an outcropping with very little to keep them warm. He didn't want a repeat of two nights ago when he'd had to endure the torment of having her within arm's reach while he fought the demons that wanted him to give in to his desires. "Is Madam Ruby good to the women?" Anora asked without preamble, catching Hunter off guard with the change of topic.

Hunter thought for a moment before answering the question, curious as to what her purpose was in asking it. "The women in her brothel are afforded more consideration than most harlots."

She turned to look at Hunter, "Is that where women who don't have a man to protect them end up?" The look on her face was a mixture of sadness, fear, defeat, and something else he couldn't discern. But the earnest look in her eye as she posed the question told him his answer was of importance.

"Aye, some do," he said carefully.

Her shoulders slumped and he stopped walking as she turned to face him. "I'd never put much thought into how women ended up as harlots. I assumed it was because they chose the way of life. That they lacked…"

He prayed she didn't say "morals." What these women did had nothing to do with what they thought to be right or wrong. It was a matter of survival. But as much as it would irritate him to hear her pass judgment on the women, it was to be expected. The society that did not approve of how these women earned their food and shelter was also the same society that condemned them with no chance of redemption because of a moment of poor judgment, a naivete that was taken advantage of, or circumstances over which they had no control.

"…the *desire* to marry," Anora finished as she looked at some invisible spot over Hunter's shoulder. "I thought these women to be like me, wanting to determine their own destinies, but with a different notion of how to do so. But what woman would choose to be beaten and demeaned and treated so horribly?" She turned her gaze back to his. The vibrant blue of her eyes had changed to the deep blue of a stormy sea. "I cannot imagine those women yearn to be harlots in a bawdy house any more than I do, yet that is the life they now have."

"It is not your fate, if that is your fear." He knew Anora would never be so destitute as to turn to prostitution to survive. Her father and Sumayl would never allow it to happen, and for as long as Hunter had breath, neither would he. It sickened him to even think of her in that situation. It had been years since he'd lived in a brothel, but the despair and heartbreak endured by the women who lived there would be with him forever.

"It is not so different from becoming the mistress to a despicable baron. Which will be my fate if I fail to prove Edmund's guilt." There was a bitterness to her voice that Hunter had never heard before, and he noticed for the first time that her face had lost all its color. "He will terrorize me until I have no choice but to relent."

"You are not going to be anyone's mistress," Hunter said, more loudly than intended. He looked around quickly to be sure they weren't being watched, then grabbed Anora by the shoulders and locked his gaze with hers. "That is not your fate."

Her eyes grew wide with panic. "My father will not be with me forever, and if something were to happen to Sumayl, I will be at the baron's mercy." She gasped for air in shallow sips, her gaze darting all around her as though looking for an escape. "Edmund will be as cruel to me as he is the harlots he frequents."

He had to get her some place private and away from the eyes of strangers. He searched the lane, and seeing an inn on the other end, he directed her toward it. The tavern on the first floor was smaller than the one below Madam Ruby's brothel, and the clientele were of a quieter sort—mostly weary travelers.

"My companion is ill and needs a room," Hunter said to the innkeeper as he slapped several coins on the bar. The woman was gray haired and stooped, but her eyes were keen and sharp as she inspected Anora leaning into Hunter's side with her hood pulled low over her forehead.

"Let's see yer face," the woman said.

Anora pushed her hood back, leaving the cap in place, and looked at the woman. She was still pale, and though her breathing was under control, her face was strained with exhaustion.

"He don' look too bad," she grumbled. "Last door at the end o' the corridor. Ye each get a bowl o' stew an' a crust o' bread. I'll send up an extra blanket. Ye won't be sharin' a blanket, judgin' by the size of ye."

"It's appreciated," Hunter said with a nod to the innkeeper.

"Don' be causin' trouble or I'll 'ave me sons drag ye out by yer scruff."

"Aye, goodwife, there will be no trouble from us." Hunter turned toward the stairs built against the side wall and motioned with his chin for Anora to walk in front of him.

The room at the end of the corridor was cramped, perhaps half the size of the chamber he'd slept in at Frode's home the prior night. The furniture in the tidy room consisted of one stuffed mattress on a low frame and one spindly wooden chair. A linen sheet was stretched over the bed with a folded blanket placed at the foot of it. It was as he'd feared, only worse. They weren't in a tiny cottage, or a cramped cave, but in an actual room with a mattress. Of sorts. Still, it couldn't be helped right now.

Hunter stepped to the side to allow Anora to enter, and the backs of his knees knocked against the chair in the corner. She turned in a half circle in the tight space, then said, "Makes the hut in the forest seem quite spacious."

He laughed out loud at her comment, relieved that she

seemed to be returning to herself, and was rewarded with a small smile. "Aye, but I'd wager the food is better here." She chuckled softly, the sound like a balm to his hardened heart. He tore his gaze away from the way her lips curved when she laughed and almost groaned when he realized the only other thing in the room to focus on was the bed.

She shifted uncomfortably, looking a bit lost, and he suspected she had come to the same awkward realization that the only other place to look, if not at each other, was the bed or the ceiling.

"Saddlebags," he blurted. When she looked at him in confusion, he added, "We left them with the stablemaster. I'll go get them." She nodded and squeezed herself against the edge of the bed so he could pass. He stopped on the other side of the door and looked back at her. "Are you all right now?"

Her entire face softened, and she beamed at him as though the simple question was a kindness beyond measure. "I am."

At her reassurance, he turned and strode down the corridor without lingering. The stable was on the other side of the village, and he used the time to remind himself that Frode had put his trust in Hunter to guard his daughter while they uncovered the truth about Payne.

He'd not squander the honor.

Which is why he'd spent the last night—while sleeping under Frode's roof in the chamber that once belonged to his deceased son—thinking of all the ways Anora was like a sister to him. He told himself that the bantering and occasional bickering were the nature of siblings. He reasoned his intense need to protect her stemmed from the shadow of danger that hung over their first introduction to each other and forced him to guard over her and her family.

But then he came down the stairs in the early morning to find Anora preparing the morning meal, and she signaled for him to take a seat at the table as naturally as if he'd always been part of her mornings. The ease and comfort of the simple gesture struck him with an unexpectedly strong pull of longing. Longing for family. Longing for calm. Longing for the dependability of a home. Longing for acceptance. But especially, longing for her.

He wasn't surprised by the longing for her, but he was taken aback by the flood of longing for things that had never been a part of his life. Things he hadn't even known that he wanted until that moment.

Things that were not meant for a man like him.

It would only be a matter of time before he got restless and needed to escape the confines of a home and the pressures of pretending to be a man he wasn't. He could feign civility in the presence of others for some days, maybe even weeks, but then the demons started to claw at his insides, and he had to withdraw until he had them under control again. His was not a life meant to be shared.

By the time he retrieved the bags and returned to the inn, his head was clearer, and his focus was sharp. Until Anora opened the door at his knock and all the sense he'd talked himself into his head disappeared like smoke. After two years, he knew her face, her smile, her voice better than anyone else's; yet she could still cause his breath to catch in his throat at the most unexpected of times. She'd removed her cap and the hair that worked loose from her braid framed her face in soft waves of white gold. Heaven was another place not meant for a man like him, but he couldn't imagine the angels in heaven could be any more breathtaking than Anora was in this moment.

He stepped into the room and set the saddlebags against the wall. "Next time, bar the door," he said, his voice gruff with irritation that he directed at her but that was meant purely for himself. "And don't open it for anyone but me."

"I didn't think anyone with nefarious intentions would knock first," she said cynically with a tip of her head as she raised her eyebrows at him.

"Are you hungry?" he asked, knowing it was best to feed her before she got any crankier. But to be fair, he could be the reason for her brusqueness considering he barged in and immediately started giving her commands—which he knew she hated.

"Yes, I am hungry." She reached for the cap she'd discarded on the bed, but he stopped her.

"I'll bring food to the room," he said with a shake of his head. "You draw too much attention. You might look like a tall, lanky lad at first glance, but it's only a matter of time before someone gets suspicious and causes trouble."

She jutted a hip to the side and flopped the hat down on the bed. "Are we to be trapped in this little room until we leave?"

Hunter winked at her and gave her his best smirk. "Not *we*, angel. You."

Her mouth gaped open to respond, but then she snapped her lips closed and looked at him with wary confusion.

"And please tell me you packed something else to wear in your saddlebag. You're not much less of a distraction in a gown, but I've taken all I can of you wearing breeches." *Hell's demons!* He hadn't meant to wink, or to sound so…flirtatious. But it was done, and the best thing for him to do was to leave before she had asked him what he meant by his witless comments. He turned on his heel and left, then waited after pulling the door shut until he heard the sound of the bar being dropped in place.

He took his time in the tavern, drinking a large tankard of ale to clear the wayward thoughts of the woman upstairs from his mind before collecting the plate of cold meat, cheeses, and bread, along with a flask of wine on a tray to carry up to the room. He felt like a battered fighter heading back into the fray of a battle that he was quickly losing as he went back to face Anora again.

"It's me," he called as he pounded lightly on the door of the room with the toe of his boot.

The satisfying sound of the wood bar scraping along the door frame reached his ears as he waited for Anora to let him in. She pulled the door open then squeezed herself into the corner between the door and the bed to allow him to enter with the food.

"It would appear the bed is the only place to set the tray." She closed the door and put the bar back into the place.

He set the tray in the center of the bed, then pulled the only chair near and motioned to Anora to sit while he perched on the edge of the mattress, stretching his legs out in front of him. "Eat," he suggested as he poured wine into one of the wooden cups.

She broke off a piece of cheese and popped it into her mouth. "Do you know Rose and Beatrice…well?"

The abruptness of her questions with no warning as to what she might say still caught him off guard after all this time—which was surprising considering he did not care for the meaningless talk most people engaged in for the sake of politeness. "Well enough," he answered hesitantly.

"Intimately well?"

She certainly was not afraid to pry into matters most would think too personal in nature to discuss. He chewed on a hunk of cheese as he looked at her trying to discern what her purpose was in asking this question. Her face was serene and her eyes curious as she patiently waited for his answer. He shifted uncomfortably anyway. "No."

She brought the cup of wine to her lips and took a sip, seeming to let the liquid sit on her tongue before finally swallowing it. He tried not to focus on the slow, deliberate act but he couldn't tear his eyes away from the way her lips pursed as she savored the taste. He clenched his teeth and turned his attention back to his own food.

"Your sudden discomfort would say otherwise, Hunter," she said in a soft voice. He looked at her to see if she was mocking him, but the slight tip of her head and the earnest set to her eyes appeared sincere. "I am merely curious. I know I should not pry, but there is so much I do not understand about you. And…about *things*."

Hunter nearly choked on the bread in his mouth when she said the last. Surely, she was not asking him about the intimacies that happen between a man and a woman. He liked it better when she was irritated and combative, and he wished they could return to that instead of this quiet, easy way of conversing. He cleared his throat. "I do not think you are expected to understand."

"That is the problem, is it not?" She let out a long sigh. "Why is everything meant to be such a mystery for women? We would be much better prepared for…" She circled her hand in the air as she looked for the right words. "For men and children and *life*. If only men didn't think they should keep secrets."

"I believe that is the duty of a husband, to educate his wife on those…matters." It felt like he was chewing on sawdust as he said the last because he didn't completely disagree with her statement. Much heartache and pain would be avoided if women were less naïve and vulnerable.

"But what if a woman doesn't want a husband? Is she to remain in the dark about these things?"

He couldn't imagine many things more tortuous than having to explain to her the intimacies shared between men and women because it would mean voicing all the things he wanted to do with her without being able to touch her. "If you do not desire a husband, then all you need know is that men are brutes and to never let them get you alone."

Her lips quirked into a coy grin. "And if a person should fail in following that rule?" She looked around the small, barred chamber as she asked the question, and the irony of his words, considering her current situation, became abundantly clear.

"You think me a brute?" He arched an eyebrow but kept his tone light to match hers.

She shook her head then took a drink of the wine. "I think you try to pass yourself as a brute but at your core you are a kind and honorable man."

He nearly choked on the bread he was swallowing. No one had ever referred to him as either *kind* or *honorable* and her assessment shook him to his core—firstly, because there was a slew of dead men who would not agree with that description of him, and secondly, because he did not agree with it, either. He was sullen, cynical, and mistrustful, and truthfully did not like most people. Beyond that, he was a killer—through acts of war or necessity arising from loyalty to others, not because he enjoyed it—but even so. He was not a good man and his soul, he was sure, was blackened and singed by Hell's fire. As much as it swelled his chest with pride to hear her say it, and as much as he wanted to be what she believed him to be, he was neither honorable nor kind.

"You overestimate me," he said in a low voice, unable to look at her face as he spoke for fear the inevitable disappointment would crush him.

"I think there is much more to you than you want people to know," Anora said. "The women at the brothel genuinely like you. They went out of their way to speak to you, and they did not seem to be flirting. They have true affection for you, and I would wager they do not have affection for most of the men they"—she blushed yet straightened her shoulders and forged ahead—"service."

Hunter stared at her for a long moment, wanting to tell her the truth, that he didn't go for the services they offered, but rather to offer them respite. He could not save them, just as he could not save his mother, or any of the other women who'd tried to protect him as a child born to a harlot and raised in a brothel. But he could provide food, clothing, and coin to buy them a night of rest. And when men were habitually cruel in their sadistic demands, he could stop them from ever bothering the women again.

Dead men could do no harm.

As much as he wanted to save the women from the life they were forced to live, he knew that without the coin they earned, they would be forced to beg in the streets and be subjected to far worse. At least in a brothel, they had shelter, food, and a family— of sorts. "I don't go to the brothel for the reasons you think."

She tipped her head and gave him a puzzled look. "Not for…"

He shook his head. Occasionally, he took his ease with a willing widow, but he knew that was hardly different and little better than patronizing brothels. Still, it was better than visiting a bawdy house where the wary uneasiness of him once being a boy trying to survive in a place not meant for children returned and gnawed at his gut.

"I look after them like a brother would a sister," he explained. "If they need something, I do what I can to provide it. And if they need protection, I provide that, as well."

"Brothers are good to have," she said with a wistful smile. "Baldwin was always my greatest champion. He was the first one to tell me never to settle for a husband who would expect me to give up what I love. He said I should look for a man like our father who would treat me the same way our father treated our mother." She laughed, the sound like wind rustling through the leaves of the forest trees. "He also said the man who married me would need the same patience and understanding of our father to put up with me."

"I am certain if Baldwin were here, he would tell you that any man who marries you would be fortunate." It was the truth. She was magnificent, bold, and witty, and he couldn't imagine any man not thinking her perfect already.

She looked at him and gave him a dazzling smile, her blue eyes mesmerizing him with their brilliance. "The women are fortunate to have *you* as their *brother.*"

He was not typically the one to back down from anything, but he was the first to break his eyes away from their locked gaze. The intensity of her stare, the promise and hope that he saw there, was more than he could endure. His resolve was dangerously close to being quashed as his longing to touch her grew.

"Are the men who were at the doors of the brothel Madam Ruby's hired guards?" Her ability to change topics in the blink of an eye was astounding. He should be more prepared for it, but she managed throw him off kilter every time.

"Aye," he said cautiously. "They are in her employ."

"I could do the same," she said, her face brightening. "My reputation as a goldsmith is growing and if I can continue to sell commissioned pieces, I could afford to hire guards as protection. They would be my hired brothers." Her eyes became wide with excitement and her jaw had dropped open as though the sudden idea was the solution to all of her problems. "Who needs a husband when a man can be *hired* for all the same purposes?"

"*All* the same purposes?"

She let out a little embarrassed laugh. "Well, not *all*, but for the ones that are important."

There were so many responses he wanted to give to her ludicrous statement, but none of them were appropriate, so he kept his mouth shut.

"I think it is a perfectly reasonable idea," she continued, her enthusiasm growing. "More women who are not in a position to marry should do the same. No one would fault me for taking measures to ensure my safekeeping when my profession means that there will always be gold, silver, and gems, and jewelry of considerable value on the premises." She paused, and lifted her hand to her face to tap at her cheek in thought. "Of course, it would need to be someone I could trust."

The woman's determination was as boundless as it was tiresome. "Anora, I—"

"You could do it, Hunter," she said, cutting him off. "You could take Baldwin's place as my brother."

"No." He didn't like the idea of being paid to protect her, and he certainly didn't want to be a brother to her.

"You have not taken the time to consider the idea," she insisted.

He opened his mouth to respond, then closed it. She was staring at him wide-eyed, as though daring him to disappoint her, but her lips were twitching with amusement. He was rarely surprised by anyone, and even less frequently fooled.

"You are jesting with me," he said with a shake of his head. He laughed at his own gullibility, something he hadn't experienced since he was a child, before he'd become hardened by the cruelty and callousness he'd come to expect from people.

Her smile broadened and her nose wrinkled as the pink tip of her tongue peeked out between her white teeth. She was enchanting in her triumph. So much so that he started to reach for her before he realized what he was doing. He quickly lowered his hand, pretending that he was reaching for his cup instead, which he lifted and drained in one long gulp.

Most people in this world were a nuisance and not worth his time, and those that were worth his time were better off without him. He'd never been loved, he didn't know how to love, and he wasn't worthy of love. He knew how to be cold, how to kill, and how to shut out the rest of the world. To be within arm's reach of the one woman he was not able to shut out of his mind was about to break him.

He stood abruptly and reached for the door, but her hand was on his arm before he could lift the bar, the warmth of her touch burning through the linen of his shirtsleeve.

"Where are you going?" The question wasn't harsh, but he could hear the disappointment in her tone.

Shame flooded him, making his shoulders heavy and his feet feel like stones. The fault was not hers that he could not control his thoughts around her, that she made him feel things that were unfamiliar and unwelcome. "I merely meant to give you some privacy."

"I think you are lying," she said, her voice steady and soothing.

He turned to her. "I cannot be your hired guard or take Baldwin's place as your brother."

She stepped closer to him, until the length of her body nearly touched his and he could smell the sweetness of her skin. "Tell me why you cannot, Hunter."

He stared into her face. His eyes moved over the curve of her cheek to the dimple in her cheek, then he lifted his gaze to the pink bow of her lips, which parted with a soft intake of breath.

Before he was aware of what he was doing, his thumb was caressing gently over the plumpness of her bottom lip, and he looked into her eyes to see her response to his touch. She was staring directly at him, her gaze unwavering. Sliding his thumb over the cleft below her lip until it rested under her chin, he tilted her face so that their lips were a mere breath apart. He stayed there for a long moment, looking into her eyes, watching them darken with excitement and desire.

It was what he wanted, for her to desire him, but it would only lead to her ruin because he was not capable of being the man she needed. He hardened his heart and said in a low voice, "Because when I am with you, what I feel is far from brotherly."

"Then kiss me," she whispered against his mouth, her lips brushing his as she spoke.

It would be so easy to give in, to take her lips with his and plunder her mouth until she gasped and sighed with pleasure. He put his hands on her shoulders and gently pushed her away from him. "You would come to regret it."

It was worse than a knife to the gut to see the hurt in her eyes as he turned back to the door. He slid the bar from the brackets and said, "Bar the door behind me."

"Where will you go?" Her voice was controlled, the hurt he'd seen evidence of just a moment before tamped down and extinguished.

"I will be here, outside your door. We will leave for Hawkspur in the morning," he said as he pulled the door closed. He waited until he heard the scrape of wood as the bar slid into place, then lowered himself to the floor and leaned his back against the door.

He'd not been there long when a young lad appeared carrying a blanket. "Mum said ye needed this." The scrawny boy dropped the blanket at his feet and started to scurry back down the corridor, but Hunter called to him to stay his feet. When the boy turned back to him, he said, "It's worth a halfpenny to you if you bring me two of the largest tankards of ale you can carry."

He pulled two coins from his pouch and held one of them out to the boy. "Give this to the goodwife for the ale, and when you return with them, I'll give you the half-penny."

The boy took the penny in his grubby hand, then looked at the half-penny Hunter held up in the boy's view pinched between two fingers. He nodded at Hunter then ran down the corridor, his feet pounding on the stairs as he hurried to do Hunter's bidding.

When the boy returned, he was carrying one large tankard clutched in both of his hands, which he set down on the floor next to Hunter, then turned on his heel and ran back the way he came. A moment later, he returned with the second tankard of ale, which he set carefully on the floor next to the first one, then extended his hand to Hunter expectantly.

With a chuckle of approval, Hunter placed the coin in the boy's outstretched palm and asked, "Do you sleep in the tavern at night?"

"Why do ye wanna' know?" the boy answered, slanting his eyes suspiciously.

"I mean no harm," Hunter assured him, recognizing the knowing look of a boy who had witnessed much in his short life. "I will need to fetch our horses from the stable across town in the morn and could use the assistance of a strong lad. If you are below stairs when I come down and ready to go to the stables with me, it's worth another half-penny for you."

The boy smiled broadly, revealing deep dimples. "I'll be there."

"Good," Hunter said then dismissed the boy with the flick of his chin as he brought a tankard to his lips to take a swig of the yeasty ale. He expected it would be long, sleepless night with images of Anora invading his thoughts. The lingering scent of her skin and feel of her soft lips against his would make it impossible to close his eyes without seeing her parted mouth and desire-darkened eyes.

He heard her moving about the room on the other side of the door as she picked up the tray from the bed. After a bit more rustling, he heard her climbing into the bed, then the room went quiet.

Did Frode have any idea of the torture it was putting him through to serve as Anora's escort on this damnable mission?

He drained what was left of the first tankard of ale, then picked up the second as a bitter chuckle escaped his throat. In a low voice he grumbled to the empty corridor, "I think you knew exactly what you were doing, old man."

✦ ——— ·◦◦◆◦◦· ——— ✦

Chapter Seventeen

O THER THAN A quick smirk and a rolling of his eyes when he saw the bottom of the breeches sticking out from under her gown as she mounted the horse, Hunter had hardly looked at her or spoken to her since leaving Shrewsbury. He'd convinced her that the longer she tried to pull the ruse, the more likely someone would find her out and then question her, which could prove dangerous. She knew he was right: It was considered an affront to God's law and punishment could be severe should she be caught. Though many people would pay no mind to them, if anyone did decide to make a fuss about it and attract attention, the consequences could be grave.

"Until you've tried riding a horse astride in a gown with nothing beneath, I will not listen to your rebuke for the breeches," she'd said in defense of her actions. She almost laughed at the thin line formed by his lips as he turned away from her to mount his own horse. It didn't occur to her until later in the day that perhaps it was the suggestive nature of what she'd said rather than the fact that she was wearing the breeches that riled him.

In truth, she was not put off by his silence because she had enough thoughts of her own to sort through. A restless night of going over every touch and every word before he'd stomped out of the room the evening before still hadn't been enough for her to make sense of her feelings. His response to her suggestion that she hire him to be the protector her brother would have been, coupled with the confession in the hut that he was always aware of her even when he ignored her, seemed proof that he was fighting an attraction to her.

"Because when I am with you, what I feel is far from brotherly."

But then when she'd tried to kiss him, he'd humiliated her by pushing her away and leaving the room. She tried to remember his tone when he said the words. Did he say them with regret? Or was it scorn? Perhaps he meant he did not even hold the affection of a sibling for her, or that he felt nothing when he looked at her.

It was so frustratingly confusing!

She stole a glance at him. He'd kept his horse a pace or two ahead of her the entire day, constantly scanning the road ahead and behind, and the surrounding forest. She didn't think he'd looked at her even once during that time. The realization that she'd made a fool of herself by thinking he wanted to kiss her as much as she had wanted to kiss him last night made the heat rise in her cheeks, which only angered her more. How dare he pretend he was just as unsettled by her touch as she was by his, and then push her aside?

He probably knew that with his handsome face, and those piercing eyes of rich emerald, and sensual lips that begged to be tasted, that he could convince any woman to disregard her virtue and have his way with her.

But he had refused her.

She supposed it was because of her lack of experience. It was true that she had only been kissed by one man in a moment of passion, even if it had been fleeting. The kiss had been with the son of a merchant from Hereford whom she saw frequently at the market there. He'd been more of a boy than a man, and it had been terrible—clumsy, too wet, and horrible tasting. She'd never told anyone of the kiss, not even Baldwin. But she had been young and curious, and no one else had ever tried to kiss her in that way.

Hunter's breath had been sweet and smelled of the wine they'd just drunk when she tried to kiss him last night, and…

Stop! She shook her head to rid it of the memory. It was futile to dwell on one moment from the prior night and better to push any thoughts of kissing Hunter far from her mind.

She stared at his back as he rode on his horse ahead of her. He'd warned her the journey would be longer today than the prior day's ride, but she wondered how much longer she would have to endure sitting in the stiff saddle with Hunter stoically pretending that being alert to the surroundings required all of his attention. Even when they'd stopped for a quick respite and to rest their mounts, he'd hardly spoken to her, choosing instead to busy himself with inspecting the horses' hooves and adjusting the saddles.

They must be getting close, she reasoned, because the sky was glowing a brilliant orange through the dark clouds in the horizon, and soon it would be dusk.

Just as it registered in her mind that that wasn't the sunset she was seeing, she heard Hunter mutter, "God's blood!"

He bolted forward on his horse, then stopped and turned his mount back toward Anora as though just remembering she was still with him, his features strained as he ran a hand through his hair in frustration. "Follow me," he ordered and turned his mount in the direction of the distant fire.

They rode at a brutal pace for a short distance along the road, then turned into the forest, breaking branches as they went until a narrow trail appeared in front of them. They followed the trail up a hill until it turned and continued just below the ridge line for some distance. Finally, Hunter halted Shadow, but he signaled to Anora to remain quiet and stay where she was as he dismounted and climbed up the steep incline to the crest of the ridge to peer over the precipice.

Anora slid from her Willow's back and started up the hill, wanting to know what was happening. He turned as soon as he heard her approach from behind him, shooting her a stern glare, then motioned her to stay low and come forward quietly. When she reached the crest of the ridge, she crouched next to him among the low shrubs. A small settlement was nestled into the side of the hill not far below them in a valley with pastures of sheep extending out from the handful of buildings.

It would be a tranquil sight if not for the fact that the buildings were ablaze with bright flames. The structures were collapsing as they were consumed by the fire while the voices of desperate people screaming and wailing carried on the wind to Anora's ears. She covered her mouth with her hand to stop herself from crying out in desperate alarm, though she did not expect anyone would hear her over the shrill howl created by the flames, wind, and mournful shouts of the people below.

"We must go to them," Anora said in a strangled whisper. "We have to help them." Her heart broke at the sight of people trying in vain to extinguish the flames while others huddled together in groups. Dead sheep dotted the pastures, and those that were left were standing on the far ends of the fields, away from the chaos, bleating in fear and confusion.

Hunter scanned the valley and hillsides below, then pointed to a group of riders kicking up dust on the road cutting through the valley and into the forest. "Stay here!" he commanded as he pushed to his feet and sprinted down the hill toward the horses. He leapt onto Shadow's back before Anora could muster the breath to protest and she watched as he disappeared into the thick of the trees at a full gallop.

She turned back to watch the riders, but they soon disappeared into the cover of the trees once the road reached the forest. Her gaze flicked between the road and the village for what seemed an eternity with no sign of Hunter in either place.

What she did see was a path that led from the village up toward the ridge where she huddled. She couldn't see exactly where it ended on the ridge, but she was certain if she followed the ridgeline, she would find the trail and could then make her way down the village. A twinge of guilt niggled at her for defying

Hunter's order to stay where she was, but a quick look to the horizon confirmed that the night was descending, and darkness would be upon her soon. And since she had no idea where Hunter went or when he would return, she decided it was safer to make her way to the village than to stay in the forest for the night with no means of protecting herself. Besides, she reasoned, the attackers had left the village, and she could be of use to those who still battled the fires.

It took longer than she anticipated to find the trail leading to the village, and it was almost completely dark by the time she and Willow were making their way downhill. With a pat to her horse's neck, she murmured, "I am trusting your superior eyes to find our way, Willow."

She tried not to think about Hunter's fury when he discovered she was not where he left her, but she was sure the village would be the first place he would go to look for her, and he would see the rightness of her decision once she explained her reasoning.

Her worries and guilt were immediately forgotten as she got closer to the settlement and saw up close the devastation wrought by the fires. At the edge of the hamlet, she came upon a small child kneeling over the body of a woman. She dismounted and went to the child, but the little girl did not even acknowledge her presence.

"Mama! Mama!" She repeated the cry as she rocked over the body of her mother, her little hands pulling at the woman's ripped tunic as she tried to wake her. Anora crouched and pressed a hand to the woman's chest to feel for any sign of life, but the pool of blood beneath her head did not bode well. When she could not feel a breath moving her lungs or the beat of her heart, she gently pulled the little girl away from her mother's body and into her arms.

"What is your name?" she whispered into the child's ear as she turned her away from the horrible sight of her mother only to find that they were surrounded by the evidence of the violence that had befallen the village. The little girl continued to whimper against her shoulder and weakly call for her mama as Anora walked farther down the lane toward the commotion and looked for anyone who might be able to comfort the child.

In the center of the village men, women, and the older children worked to contain flames that looked to Anora beyond hope of being extinguished, while others broke down the doors of any buildings not yet completely consumed by fire. There was a small group of people huddled against one of the few buildings not touched by fire, but they looked to be more small children, elders too old or feeble to fight the fires, and a few adults with grave injuries.

As she approached the group, a woman came running toward her with her arms outstretched. "Mair!"

Anora relinquished the girl when the child turned and put out her arms to the woman, obviously recognizing her. The woman brushed a hand over the child's hair and peered into her face as though she looked for confirmation Mair was truly safe and whole. When she seemed satisfied the girl was hale, she hugged her tightly to her chest and lifted her eyes to Anora. "Her mother? My sister?" The words were spoken frantically and in Welsh.

Anora felt the weight of the world on her shoulders. "I am sorry," she replied in her limited Welsh and shook her head so the woman would understand. The woman's face contorted painfully as she pressed her cheek to the little girl's head. Tears ran down her sooty cheeks, but she fought to regain what she could of her composure.

"I do not know you," the woman said in English, narrowing her eyes at Anora inquisitively.

"I am Anora. I came with—" She turned to look over her shoulder despite knowing Hunter would not be there as she tried to think of how to explain her presence. "I was on my way to Hawkspur and saw the smoke. I want to help in any way I can."

"Follow me." The woman handed Mair to an older woman sitting on the ground with other children, then took Anora by the arm as she hurried toward the homesteads where the wind was blowing sparks onto the thatched rooftops of cottages and other structures. "If anyone is inside, we must get them out. The doors were barricaded after people tried to hide in them," the woman said frantically as she pointed to a row of cottages engulfed in smoke but not yet on fire, though the flames were getting dangerously near. "Help me open the doors." With that, she was gone, already running to the closest building and kicking and pulling away the pitchforks, hoes, and scraps of wood levered against the door to hold it closed. She pushed it open before quickly moving onto the next door, clearing the barricade and pulling open the door to call out to anyone who may be inside.

Anora followed her, helping to clear the doors, hearing people coughing and yelling as she drew closer to the smoke-filled cottages. She couldn't even begin to comprehend how anyone could be so heartless and cruel to hard working, innocent people. People poured from each cottage the moment the door was opened.

Wind began to catch the flames, blowing them and embers from one cottage roof to the next in the row of structures. Anora realized that soon the entire row would be aflame.

"Is there anyone else inside?" she yelled toward the people who were gathered a short distance from the burning buildings, many of them kneeling on the ground as they coughed and tried to clear the smoke from their watering eyes. Realizing they could not see to know if anyone was left behind, she went to each door to call out while she peered through the thickening smoke for any sign of people still trapped inside.

As the people recovered from their coughing and their eyes cleared, they returned with blackened and soot-streaked faces to look for anyone else still in the cottages. Anora took a breath and looked around at the chaos and destruction only to notice a flame start to shimmer and grow on the roof of a single cottage next to a small wooden pen near the edge of the settlement. She could see something jammed against the door and thought she heard yelling from the vicinity. As she ran toward the building, sparks and ash landed on her, some burning through the material of her clothing to blister her skin, but she ignored the pain.

She kicked away the wooden staff wedged against the door and flung it open. A gray-haired man fell through the opening and into her arms. His hands were covered in blood, and he was hoarse from yelling. She helped him to his feet, and he immediately stumbled toward the pen at the side of the cottage.

"My lambs!" he wailed in Welsh. "My lambs!"

Anora put a hand on the man's shoulder as she looked down into the enclosure. There were three little lambs lying in a wide puddle of blood in the pen, their throats slit.

"We heard them crying," he said, tears streaming down his face. "I tried to break the door down. They tortured them. My wife had to listen to them kill her little loves."

Anora looked over her shoulder at the cottage; the flames were dancing along the rooftop had not yet burned through the thatch. "Your wife? Is she in there?"

The old man turned, the light from the growing flames illuminating his horrified expression. They both started toward the door of the cottage, holding their arms up to shield them from the smoke beginning to fill the one room structure as they entered. Against the far wall, Anora could see a woman lying on a bed with her arms over her head as if trying to hide from the horror around her.

"She cannot walk without help," the man said in a scratchy voice as they both moved to her bedside. Anora watched as a gap formed in the roof and the flames jumped to the beams inside the cottage. The man spoke to his wife in Welsh, coaxing her from the bed as he slid his arm under her shoulders to help her sit. When she was upright, he slid his other arm under her knees and tried to lift her, but the strain was too much. Anora quickly moved to the other side of the woman to slide an arm under the woman's legs and the other around the woman's back to help support her. She clasped her hands over the man's forearms in each place and together they were able to lift the woman and shuffle toward the door.

They were halfway there when a beam fell and hit the man in the shoulder, knocking him to the ground. Anora was unable to bear the weight of the woman alone and they both toppled down to the floor as Anora cried out in dismay. She pushed to her knees, overwhelmed by defeat as she looked at the scene in front of her. The old woman was sobbing while she reached for her husband. The old man was not moving, likely knocked unconscious from the heavy piece of wood slamming into him. The beam that had felled him glowed red on its edges as the embers curled through it and more burning thatch from the roof and slats of wood from the walls were falling into the room. It was only a matter of time before the entire structure would be engulfed in flames, and collapse. Panic took hold of Anora as she tried to pick up the woman in her arms once more.

"We cannot leave him," the woman sobbed in Welsh.

Anora coughed, watching through watering eyes as the flames raced across the walls, moving closer to the door. In moments they would be cut off from escape and the entire cottage would come crashing down on their heads. She wanted to run for the door, get out while she could, but she could not bring herself to leave the couple to die.

She could barely keep her stinging eyes open, and her lungs burned like they, too, were on fire, but she reached for the woman one last time, determined to save her.

Or die trying.

✦ ⎯⎯⎯ ⋅∞◆∞⋅ ⎯⎯⎯ ✦

Chapter Eighteen

"ANORA!"

Hunter heard a bellow rend the air and his throat felt like it was being ripped apart. In his panic, he didn't realize the frantic shout came from him as he ran down the hill toward the burning cottage he'd just seen Anora disappear into with an elderly man. He watched her struggling under the weight of the body she was trying to drag from the cottage. She had hooked her hands under the arms of the person and was pulling the body backwards through the door and out to the path in front of the cottage. His heart had already been pounding nearly out of his chest when he saw her emerge from the cottage, but when he saw her go back into the burning building, he was sure it stopped beating. What the hell was she doing? He ran as fast as his legs would carry him toward the collapsing structure, praying the entire time to a god he was certain had already forsaken him.

Everything he'd ever learned went right out of his head as he ran straight into the inferno to get to Anora. He'd learned from a young age that the only person who cared about him was himself, and living to fight another day was more important than anything else. He'd found nothing and no one worth the sacrifice of his own life.

Until Anora.

Smoke poured out the door and roof of the cottage and he could hear timbers falling, but that did not stop him from charging headlong into the blazing hell.

This will be how I die. He heedlessly searched through the smoke for Anora inside the cottage. Through the haze, he saw her bending over another body, pulling at its arms and trying to tug the lifeless form toward the door. He reached her in two steps, grabbed a fistful of the tunic covering the man's chest to lift him off the floor, then grabbed Anora's arm and pushed her ahead of him toward the door with a bellowed command. "Go!"

The trio cleared the frame of the opening and were only a few steps away when the cottage collapsed completely, shooting flames high into the sky as ash and sparks rained down on them. Hunter did not let go of Anora or the man he dragged by his tunic until they were a good distance from the burning structure. To his relief, someone had picked up the woman Anora had pulled from the cottage and moved her out of harm's way as well. He lowered the man completely to the ground and released his tunic, then spun Anora to face him.

"What the hell were you thinking?" His voice sounded feral and angry, even to his own ears.

"Stop shouting at me," she huffed in a hoarse voice, "and quit shaking me."

Hunter realized then that he had a death grip on her arms and was shaking her in his desperation to assure himself she was truly safe. "You could have been killed!"

"I couldn't let them die," she said defensively, trying to break free from his grip. The anguish visible on her face nearly broke him. "Please, let go."

Hunter did let go, but only long enough to pull her into his chest and wrap his arms tightly around her with his cheek pressed to her hair. She smelled of smoke, but he inhaled gratefully. She was alive and—at this very moment—safe. "I thought I was going to lose you." He suddenly felt like he couldn't get a breath into his lungs past the lump in his throat. He gasped, his head spun, and he fought to keep his legs from buckling. He'd never felt anything like this before and he wasn't sure what was happening to him. All he knew was that he had to keep holding her as tightly as he could.

"Hunter," he heard Anora say in a gentle tone in his ear. It was the most beautiful sound he'd ever heard, like the voice of an angel. "Please, let go. You're hurting me."

He released her and ran a hand through his hair, cursing himself for losing his mind and his inability to piece what little sense he had back together. She held her arms out at her sides, and it was then that he noticed the sleeves of her chemise were in shreds from the many places that sparks had landed on the fabric and burned through to her skin. Gently, so as not to hurt her, he took her hands and carefully rotated them until her palms faced up so he could see the extent of any damage.

"Anora," he groaned as he released her hands and circled around her to assess the full extent of her injuries. To his immense relief, he did not see any significant burns or scrapes anywhere else on her body other than the scattering of burns on her arms. Her face was streaked gray from the smoke and ash, and the stray hairs that had escaped from her plait were singed. "How much does it hurt?"

"Not enough to be of concern," she said, her head cocked to the side as she studied him. Before he could think too long on why she was looking at him that way, she averted her gaze and said, "We cannot just stand here. There is more to be done."

"Burns can be serious. You need tending to as soon as possible." His experience with injured soldiers had taught him that the sooner the wound was tended to, the better the chances of healing without infection. Especially burns. He'd seen too many men perish from an injury thought to be inconsequential.

She shook her head as she looked at the burning village around them. "There are others hurt far worse who need attention first."

The earth shook as a thunderous pounding drew near. *Riders.*

Instinctively, Hunter shoved Anora behind him as he turned to face them. A contingent of men wearing the familiar regalia of the Hawkspur Castle guard rode into the village with swords drawn as they scoured the lanes of the village from atop their horses to ensure the enemy was gone before dismounting to appraise the situation.

"They are gone," Hunter called out to the men. He recognized the leader of the group as Bard, another one of Hawk's elite force.

He relaxed his grip on Anora, and she immediately scurried out from behind him and went to the old couple, now being tended to by another woman who looked just as bedraggled and soot smudged as she did. He reluctantly watched her go, then turned back to Bard, tamping down the beast inside him who wanted to carry her away from here and hide her away somewhere for the rest of their lives to keep her safe from the dangers of the world.

Bard shouted orders to the men, directing some to assist the injured and others to put out the fires. Two soldiers were sent back to Hawkspur to fetch more men and wagons for transporting people to the castle. After he'd dispensed all the men to their duties, he turned to Hunter and clasped arms with him.

"What happened here?" Bard asked Hunter, walking briskly toward the largest fire in the center of the village.

"I saw the glow of flames on the horizon and went up on the ridge to see what was afoot," Hunter explained, scrubbing a hand over his face. "A band of men was riding away from the village on the south road. I tried to intercept, but they were too far gone."

"With no insignias or hint of who they were," Bard said through gritted teeth. It wasn't a question, but a statement. Bard was rarely without a smile on his face or a jest on his lips, but he was also a realist with razor-sharp instincts. There were only a handful of men that Hunter fully trusted to fight as his side in a battle, and Bard was one of them.

"They're getting more deadly," Hunter said with disgust. For months, bandits had been causing disturbances, destroying property, and harassing the tenants of Hawkspur, but this was far and beyond the mischief of prior incidents. "Hawkspur needs more men if they are to stand guard at the castle and also at every settlement."

Bard grunted in agreement. "Hawk will want to hear about what you saw. Let's get this done and the villagers back to Hawkspur, then you can meet with him." Bard clapped him on the shoulder then returned to directing the efforts of his soldiers and the able villagers.

By the time the fires were extinguished, or at least reduced to smoldering piles of ash, the dead buried, and the injured loaded onto wagons, Anora looked like she was ready to topple over from exhaustion. She practically swayed on her feet as they watched the last of the villagers leave for Hawkspur Castle under the escort of Bard and three of his soldiers and did not protest when he offered her horse to a man with a heavily pregnant wife. The journey to the castle was short, less than four miles, but still daunting for a woman who looked on the verge of giving birth. Hunter settled Anora on Shadow's back, then swung up in the saddle behind her, nudging his horse into an easy walk once she was settled in his arms.

She was covered in soot and ash and smelled of smoke and sweat, and he never wanted to let her go. Her bravery in the face of danger had been magnificent. She'd not hesitated for even a breath before risking her life to save others, and she'd refused to leave before making sure everyone else was cared for.

Hell and damnation, but it was getting more difficult to pretend that he wasn't completely and hopelessly enamored with her. Now, she leaned her weight against his chest as she rested her head on his shoulder and a cold, hard part of his heart softened. He knew he'd regret it later, but he wrapped his arm around her and breathed in, searching for the lingering scent of the honeyed soap she favored under the stench of the smoke, as she cuddled into him.

"Where are we going?" she asked sleepily when he identified himself to the guards patrolling the perimeter of Hawkspur village before he turned the horse away from the main road and onto a narrow path.

"I'm bringing you to Galiena."

"Now?" she asked, suddenly alert as she wiped her hands over her cheeks. "I'm filthy. I need to bathe before I see Galiena and her little ones."

"You can bathe there. Red will fetch a tub and water for you."

"No!" She put her hand on his chest and pulled on his tunic to make her point. "Stop, Hunter. It is the middle of the night, and they will be sleeping. We cannot barge in now and wake them. Is there not somewhere else we can go?"

He had a small cottage on the edge of the Hawkspur village, but no way in hell was he going to take her there. It wasn't much larger than the forest hut they'd stayed in only a couple nights earlier and was just as sparsely furnished. Worse, it had a much more comfortable bed. Visions of her in it and what would inevitably happen if he brought her there made him shift uncomfortably in the saddle.

"They have two wee, finicky babes. They don't sleep much these days." Galiena had given birth to twins only six months hence and even Red was exhausted from the demands of having two babes in need of constant care.

"We cannot disturb them and then request they wait on me by preparing a bath." She crossed her arms over her chest and fixed him with a stern look, which didn't look threatening at all with the light of the moon giving her face an angelic glow. "There must be some place I can go to wash this stink and filth from me first."

With an exaggerated sigh, he admitted, "There is a stream on the far side of the paddocks below Red and Galiena's home. We can stop there." He cringed and silently chided himself for his stupidity because the only thing worse than having Anora alone in his cottage with the big, comfortable bed was being alone with her while she bathed in a stream in the moonlight.

They rode along the paddock fencing until they reached the end, then he veered into the trees and halted Shadow a short distance from the stream. He helped Anora from the saddle then untied her saddlebag where it hung over Shadow's rump. He was a large horse and easily tolerated four miles at walk with an extra rider and bags. In truth, the horse could have easily covered the ground at a trot or a gallop with the added weight, but Hunter wasn't in a hurry to reach Hawkspur while holding Anora close to him.

Anora immediately went to the stream and knelt at the edge, cupping her hands to capture the water and splash a few handfuls over her face, then said, "I think I'm just making the smell worse. A full wash and change of clothing are the only way to rid myself of the smoke and ash." She stood and peered downstream. "It looks like the stream is wider there. Is the water deep enough for me to bathe?"

"Aye, it is. A natural pool forms there." He almost groaned aloud at the thought of enduring her stripping out of her clothing and easing her naked body into the water while he stood sentinel. Even if he gave her the privacy she deserved, he'd be imagining what she looked like standing wet and naked in the moonlight the entire time. Reluctantly, he joined her at the side of the stream and held out her saddlebag for her. "Can you swim?"

"Is it so deep?"

"It's up to my chest, but the rocks can be slick. Your head will go under the water if you lose your footing."

"You've used this pool often," she said as she took the satchel. "If the water is no deeper than my shoulders, I will be fine."

"So, you cannot swim," he said, untying his own satchel from the saddle. He wasn't surprised by her admission; most people never had reason nor opportunity to learn the skill. "Then I'd best be prepared to go in the water after you." He untied his saddle bag and turned in the direction of the pool.

"You should have more faith in me," she said to his back as

she followed him to the edge of the pool. He couldn't see her face, but he could hear the hint of teasing in her voice.

"Oh, I do," he said, matching her tone. "I have complete faith in your ability to do whatever it is that will fray my nerves. I think you like mischief, Anora. And I think you very much like testing me."

When he got to the edge of the pool, he set his satchel on the trunk of a felled tree and signaled for Anora to do the same.

She placed her bags next to his, then looked at the pool before returning her gaze to him. Her eyes sparkled in the moonlight and her lips curved into a wicked grin that made his breath catch in his throat. "I do like to fray your nerves, Hunter. It is the only way I can get your attention."

For a woman who claimed to have little experience with men she was proving quite adept at being coquettish. The only problem was, she was too innocent to realize how she was affecting him, how much he wanted her, and how difficult it was going to be for him to stop when she became overwhelmed by the reality of what it really meant to be lovers.

But he would stop when she asked him to, no matter how close it came to killing him.

"You have my attention," he drawled as he pulled his tunic over his head and dropped it on the ground as he stepped closer to her. "But I don't think you really want it."

His intention was to scare her off, certain that once she saw him stripping off his clothes, her embarrassment would send her fleeing from him as fast as her long legs could carry her.

"I don't think you know what I really want," she said, her eyes riveted on him, which only made him burn hotter.

"I don't think *you* know what you really want." He loosened the ties at the neck of his shirt and tugged it over his head, fully expecting that by the time he had it off, she'd be mortified and turning away from him.

She wasn't mortified and she hadn't turned away.

Instead, she explored his chest with her eyes, taking her time as she perused every inch of his bared shoulders and stomach. *Hell!* Now he wanted to turn and run. He was becoming painfully hard and the only remedy available to him in the foreseeable future was a dousing in the cold water of the pool.

"Anora," he growled in warning.

She lifted her gaze to his and licked her lips. The sight of the tip of her tongue gliding over her perfectly plump mouth nearly broke him, but he gritted his teeth and concentrated on calming the rapid pounding of his heart in his chest while he cleared his head.

Nothing good can come of this. You will end up hurting her, tainting everything that is good about her. Walk away now, fool! He had just about regained his control and was willing himself to turn away from her when her soft, low voice called to him like a siren's song.

"I want you, Hunter."

Fuck!

Chapter Nineteen

"I WANT YOU, Hunter."

The way his eyes bulged would have been comical if it didn't hurt so much. She was certain she could have shot Hunter with an arrow, and he would have looked less horrified than he did after hearing her confession.

"No," he choked out in a raspy voice, then turned away from her and stalked to the pool. She thought she heard a groan on the wind, and she strained to determine if it was coming from something hiding in the trees, or from Hunter.

She turned away in frustration and paced the small patch of grass in front of the felled tree trunk. How dare he walk away from her when she had laid herself bare in front of him? At least emotionally, even if she hadn't done it physically. Though, if he'd given her any other response, anything to show he wanted her the way she wanted him, she would have bared everything to him.

But he did want her, and she knew it. She might not be worldly when it came to matters of men or the heart, but she knew the way Hunter held her in his arms on the horse was not just to keep her from falling to the ground. He'd *clutched* her to him like he was afraid of dropping something fragile. She may have dozed much of the way from the burned hamlet to

Hawkspur, but she'd been very aware of the way his thumb rubbed gently against her ribs where his hand rested, and she'd counted at least seven different times that he'd pressed his lips to the top of her head or nuzzled her hair.

The water sloshed as Hunter stepped into the pool and Anora turned her head in the direction of the sound. His boots and breeches were in a pile by the shore, and he waded into the water with his back to her. She couldn't tear her gaze away as the water slowly rose higher on his muscular calves and thighs as he walked deeper into the pool. His entire body was limned in silver moonlight, accenting the broad expanse of his shoulders, the muscular planes of his back, and a very firm bum. She swallowed hard and flexed her fingers that itched to touch him.

He dove under the water sending ripples over the surface as he skimmed along beneath it. When he did emerge, he shot up like a jumping fish, then flung his head back so that his hair sprayed water in a high arc above him.

"Hunter!" She sounded like a mother chiding a petulant child, but she didn't care because he deserved the rebuke.

He turned slowly, the lithesome movement of his body mesmerizing as her eyes stayed riveted on the expanse of his chest and the ripple of muscles on his stomach. Everything about him exuded lethal strength and carnal allure.

She most definitely wanted him.

"Why won't you touch me?"

He opened his mouth to respond, then snapped it shut. In the light of the moon, she could see his chest rise and fall as he took a deep breath. His eyes were trained on her, but he stayed silent.

She was long past the age when most women married, and she had accepted that a husband and children may not be in her future. Not only had she not found a man willing to take her as she was, she'd also not found any she thought attractive or interesting enough to tolerate for a lifetime.

Until Hunter.

She felt exhilarated when she was with him. He was the only

person who ever made her stomach flutter or her heart pound as it did now, and she feared if she did not seize this moment, she may never get the chance again.

She was terrified!

Terrified of rejection, but even more so of regret.

"You wouldn't kiss me at the inn." She tugged on the leather thong tied at the bottom of her braid as she walked slowly toward the edge of the pool, then ran her fingers through her hair to loosen the strands. "But you kissed the top of my head when you thought I was asleep on your horse."

He continued to stand as still as stone as he watched her. The knowledge she had his attention emboldened her and caused her skin to tingle with excitement. It was not at all appropriate that they were alone like this. Nor was it appropriate how much she wanted to touch him. And it was vastly inappropriate how curious she was to see all of his body.

"Tell you me you don't want me, Hunter," she said as she kicked off her boots and set them aside.

Hunter's lips parted, but whatever he meant to say appeared to get stuck in his throat when she unbuckled her leather belt, pulled it off, and dropped it on the ground next to her boots. It did not escape her notice the way his gaze followed her hand as she bent and reached down to grab the hem of her gown. She enjoyed having his attention far more than she ever expected, but when she hitched up her gown to reveal breech-clad legs, his lips curved into a smirk, and she heard him huff out a small laugh.

She couldn't help but laugh along with him. Here she was, feeling powerful in her newly found confidence, and then she ruined it by stripping away her gown to reveal…more clothing! Her cheeks were suddenly hot with embarrassment, and she closed her eyes, so she didn't have to look at Hunter. She still had the hem of her gown in her hand as she straightened to her full height, feeling anything but appealing standing in her breeches.

"Anora." Her name rolled from his lips in a guttural growl.

Oh, hell! He was going to chastise her for trying to seduce him and tell her she was being a fool.

"Damned breeches," she said with a sigh of defeat. "I know you dislike them and now they've ruined the moment." A woman with more experience would know how to salvage the situation, but she was at a complete loss.

She looked to see why Hunter was not laughing at her for the disaster she'd made of the moment only to find him staring intently at her. The expression on his face was not one of mirth, or disdain, or disapproval. Instead, his eyes were sharp, and his lips were parted as his tongue slid slowly over them, like a predator eyeing his prey.

Perhaps all was not lost.

"Do you know why I dislike your breeches?" he asked in a deep drawl.

She slid her hand up higher on her leg with the hem of the gown still clutched in her fingers, then shifted on her feet to jut out her hip. Her confidence soared again when the focus of his eyes when directly to the curve of her hip and then down her leg. "Why?"

He swallowed hard then lifted his eyes to look at her face. "Because your legs look so fucking good in them, and all I can think about when you are wearing them is what you would look like without them."

The smile that curved her lips was beyond her control and only grew wider as he started moving toward her from the far side of the pool. She kept her eyes locked with his as she untied the breeches at her waist until they were loose and began to slowly slide toward her ankles. Hunter moved almost languidly across the pool as he watched the breeches fall, but when she started to pull the gown up the length of her body, he froze again. She lifted the gown over her head and added it to the pile on the ground. Wearing only her chemise, she took a deep breath to steel her nerve and walked into the pool.

The thin undergarment floated up around her legs and her skin rippled with gooseflesh as she glided deeper into the water.

Once she was submerged up to her waist, she tipped her head back and dipped beneath the surface of the pool to rinse the smoke and ash from her hair. When she surfaced again, Hunter was directly in front of her.

"Do you know what you are doing?" His voice was hoarse, the words hardly more than a raspy whisper as he scrubbed his hand over his face.

Anora reached to brush her fingers along Hunter's collarbone, tracing the ridge of it to the notch at the base of his throat, fascinated by the way goosebumps rose on his skin and she wondered if it was from her touch or the chill in the air. She lifted her gaze to his as she slid her palm down his bare chest to feel the strong, steady rhythm of his heartbeat. His skin was warm despite the coolness of the night air and of the water.

"No. I don't know what I'm doing," she said with a coy smile, "but I think I will figure it out."

He put a hand over hers where it rested on his chest and skimmed the knuckles of his other hand along the line of her jaw as she looked up into his eyes. She practically purred when he traced his fingers in a featherlight touch down the column of her neck. Her breath caught in her throat at the delicious sensation of his caress on her sensitive skin.

"We shouldn't be doing this," he said, but his tone and his face lacked conviction.

"Stop talking and kiss me," Anora said, leaning into him.

Thank God, he did as requested, because she felt like she'd combust if he didn't. He touched his lips to hers with a growl that rumbled in his chest and vibrated against her hand, still pressed over his heart. The kiss was gentle, but it set her heart to racing, the beat of it thrumming in her ears. She breathed in, the heat of his breath warming her lips, and relished the soft press of his mouth against hers. It was nothing like her first, only—and unpleasant—kiss. This kiss sent delicious waves of desire spiraling through her.

But she wanted more.

She put an arm around his lean waist and pulled herself closer to him. Hunter rewarded her by wrapping one hand around the back of her neck and the other to the small of her back as he sucked her lower lip between his. She gasped and felt her stomach flipflop. When he released her lip and slipped his tongue between her teeth to rub against hers, unexpected heat pooled low in her belly.

There was nothing clumsy about this kiss. Hunter nipped, tugged, and licked at her mouth, eliciting soft moans from the unexpected pleasure of their tongues entangled so intimately. She didn't think anything could be as wonderful as kissing Hunter, and she let out a little whimper of protest when he slid his mouth away from hers.

"Anora," he said in a slow drawl as he brushed his lips over her face and down to her neck. "I've wanted to kiss you since the first day I knew you."

She tipped her head back as an exquisite wave of sensations rolled through her body. "If I'd known it could be like this," she said, every word punctuated with a breathless pant, "I'd have coaxed you into kissing me a long time ago."

He chuckled as he trailed torturously slow kisses down her neck, stroking his tongue over the sensitive skin. With a contented sigh, she skimmed her palm up the corded muscles of his bicep and over the solid contours of his shoulder until her fingers slid into his hair at the nape of his neck. Her contentment quickly turned to a restless yearning as her body responded to his touch, tingling and tightening in anticipation. His thumb brushed against the underside of her breast, and it sent a fissure of shock straight to her core. Both of her breasts suddenly felt heavy and tight, and she let out a cry of relief when he cupped one globe in his palm and rubbed the calloused pad of a finger back and forth over the thin, wet material of the chemise covering her beaded nipple. When he gently squeezed her breast, her belly clenched as her body pulsed with an ache that longed for release.

He slid his mouth over her collarbone and down to her other

breast to take the nipple into his mouth and tease it with his teeth. Even with the added obstruction of her chemise, his breath was hot and the touch of his tongue like fire. She fisted her hand in his hair and arched her back, wanting him to take more of her into his mouth. Her hips pressed into his and she let instinct take over as her body cradled the hard bulk of his erection. Fascinated by the heavy thickness of him pressing against her, she shifted her hips slowly to rock her pelvis against him, the movement making her body clench and coil.

"Oh, God, Anora," Hunter groaned as he slipped his hand down her back and cupped her bottom to add more pressure to the rhythmic rubbing of their bodies.

She grasped at the wet chemise tangled around her legs and pulled at it until she could lift her leg and hitch it over Hunter's hip to bring him closer. He immediately hooked a hand beneath her knee and brought his mouth to her ear to suck the lobe into his mouth. She wound her arms around his neck and lifted her other leg to hook it around him.

"Hunter," she gasped. "I want…"

"I know, angel," he said in a raspy voice. His arms wrapped around her waist as he lifted her higher against his body and walked toward the shore of the pool. Anora wriggled her hips against him restlessly. "Oh, God, love. Don't do that."

The soft breeze blew against Anora's skin as Hunter emerged from the water, sending ripples of gooseflesh over her already overly sensitive skin. He had to pry her arms from his neck after he set her on her feet.

"No, Hunter," she protested as he released her. How could he push her away when her entire body was throbbing and aching for him? The sight of his lithe, muscular, naked body glimmering in the moonlight as he walked toward the tree trunk where their bags rested only made her body ache more.

When he turned back to her, he had his blanket in his hands. He shook it out with a snap and spread it out on the ground in front of her. Her breath caught in her throat as he stepped slowly across the blanket toward her, giving her a full, unhindered view of his prominent cockstand.

She'd never seen anything like it, and she couldn't take her eyes from it. "It's magnificent," she said in awe as he stopped in front of her. Fascinated, she reached her hand out to touch it, wanting to know what it would feel like in her fingers, but he grabbed her wrist to stop her. She lifted her gaze to his face, her protest ready on her lips.

"No, angel." He released her, then reached for her chemise, and pulled it over her head, baring her completely to his gaze.

She thought she'd be mortified to ever let anyone see her fully unclothed, but with Hunter, she wanted to be naked, wanted nothing to keep her from feeling his skin against hers. He took a half step backward and let his eyes blaze a slow trail down the length of her body. He didn't touch her, but his gaze set her on fire as he took his time looking at the curves of her body. Just when she thought she'd perish if he didn't touch her, he took her hand in his and pulled her to the center of the blanket, then gently laid her down and covered her body with his.

It was a new and very welcome sensation to feel the weight of him pressing her into the blanket, and she sighed contentedly as his warmth enveloped her. She wriggled against him, delighting in the feel of the coarse hair on his legs rubbing against hers. But what thrilled her most was his undeniable desire for her as evidenced by his thick erection pressing into her hip. He braced himself on his elbows as he brushed a strand of hair from her forehead and took his time looking into her face and rubbing his thumbs over her cheek bones.

"You act like you've never seen me before," she whispered after a long moment.

His lips quirked with a little chuckle. "I've not seen you like this, spread out on a blanket with the moonlight in your hair." He brushed a kiss over her lips. "You are so beautiful."

Anora had never cared whether or not she was considered beautiful. She strove to be considered clever and capable. But in this moment, the reverence in Hunter's eyes and his worshipping words made her want to be beautiful for him.

The weight of his body as it pressed down on hers was the most delicious feeling Anora had ever experienced, and she basked in the pleasure of his warm breath tickling her ear, the heat of his skin sliding over hers, and the dizzying intoxication of his long, languid kisses.

She lifted her hips and pressed into him restlessly, wanting to feel more of him. As though he understood her need, he shifted his weight onto one elbow and put his other hand over her breast to knead it gently as his mouth worked its way down her neck to the other breast. She tangled her fingers into his hair and arched up into him wanting more.

"Hunter," she pleaded. The heat coiling in her core pulsed and ached for him and she didn't want to wait any longer. "I need you."

"Where, angel?" He lifted his head and looked at her face even as he swirled his tongue slowly around one breast and flashed her a wicked grin.

Anora locked her gaze with his, unable to look away, mesmerized as he flicked the tip of his tongue against her taut nipple. The sight of him touching her, and watching her body respond, excited her in a way she couldn't explain. Never had she imagined the pleasure to be had from the touch of another.

No, not just another. From Hunter.

A cry escaped her lips when he grazed his teeth over her sensitive nipple. His eyes widened and he looked as though he wanted to devour her.

"Where?" he asked again as his fingers teased over her thigh.

"Here," she said as she lifted her hips and pressed into his heavy erection nestled between them.

With his eyes still locked on her face, he dragged his tongue between her breasts and further down her stomach. She let out a little yelp of surprise when his tongue swirled around her belly button then continued lower.

"Wh-what are you doing?" she asked as she pushed up on her forearms. She wasn't experienced in the intimacies between men and women, but she couldn't imagine this was how it happened. She felt completely vulnerable and exposed as he nudged her legs further apart with his elbows, but before she could protest, he blew gently on the apex of her thighs.

"Would you prefer I tell you what I am going to do?" He nipped her inner thigh. Anora rolled her lips between her teeth as she inhaled sharply, startled by how much she liked the little bite.

"Or should I show you?"

"Tell me." She loved the gravelly sound of his voice when it was thick with passion and the way the deep rumble vibrated through her when he spoke. Anora bit her lip to keep her focus when he chuckled and nuzzled his nose into the mound of her sex.

"I'm going to make you see stars, angel. First with my fingers..." He ran the tip of his finger over the wet folds between her legs and Anora released a shaky breath. "Then with my tongue." He flicked his tongue between the folds. It was just once, but it was enough for Anora drop her head back with a hum of satisfaction.

When he slid one long finger between her folds, caressing the ache that pulsed at her core, the strength drained from her arms, and she dropped back onto the blanket with a moan. "Oh, yes."

"Good girl," he praised, as his fingers slid in and out of her passage in an excruciatingly slow rhythm that left her gasping for air.

When he added another finger to the motion and found a particularly sensitive spot to circle with his thumb, her back arched involuntarily and she clutched at the blanket with her fingers. She didn't know what was happening, and her body was responding in ways that were completely out of her control, but she felt like she'd perish if he stopped. Exquisite pressure was coiling at her core and rippling through her body in gentle waves.

Just when she thought Hunter could not make her body feel

any more pleasure, he replaced his thrusting fingers with his tongue and her hips bucked as the pressure built inside her, threatening to explode. He cradled her hips in his hands as he suckled and licked until she was in a frenzy.

"Don't stop," she panted and buried her fingers in his hair to hold him tightly against her. "Oh, God, Hunter!" He plunged his tongue deep, putting pressure in all the right places and she felt a thousand stars of light explode through her body as wave after wave of ecstasy shot from her core out to her limbs.

When she came back down to earth and opened her eyes, Hunter was at her side, gently brushing strands of her hair from her face. She closed her eyes and started to turn her face away from him, feeling suddenly very self-conscious about the intimate way he'd touched her and her exuberant response.

"No." He gently pinched her chin between his thumb and forefinger and turned her face to his. "No regret."

The way he looked at her, like he was seeing her for the first time, melted away her awkwardness. He cradled the side of her neck in his hand and rubbed his thumb softly over her cheekbone as he leaned in toward her. When his lips hovered just above hers, he stopped, searching her eyes for approval.

"No regret," she whispered.

He kissed her then, leisurely sliding his lips over hers and gently exploring her mouth with his tongue. His kisses were warm and sweet, and she never wanted them to end. She curled onto her side and into his chest to take more of his heat as he massaged his hand over her shoulder and then down her back. He groaned, deep and guttural, when she shifted onto her side and pressed into him as she slid a leg over his thigh.

It was then that she realized he had yet to have his release. She put her hands on his chest and pushed away from him to end the kiss. "What about you? Should I not return the favor in some way?"

Anora felt his chest rumble with a low chuckle. "The favor?"

She narrowed her eyes at him and said with a playful smirk to hide her embarrassment, "What am I to call it then? This is all new to me."

A damp strand of hair blew over her face, and he brushed it away with his fingers and tucked it behind her ear as her skin shivered from his gentle touch. "'Favor' is good. And though it pains me to decline, angel, there isn't time."

Her stomach fluttered wildly every time he called her "angel." She loved the growl in his voice at the start of the endearment and the way it felt like a warm caress by the time it finished rolling off his tongue.

"The sun will be up soon and once Bard discovers we did not return to Hawkspur, he will send a search party." He stroked her ear in a thoroughly distracting manner as he spoke.

Anora pressed her cheek against Hunter's chest and sighed. She wished they could stay right here forever, sheltered from thieves, marauders, and loathsome barons. With Hunter's arms wrapped around her, she felt safe and protected from the rest of the world. She never wanted him to let go of her, and she never wanted to let go of him.

Oh, Lord above! What had happened to her? She'd gone from being contented with the future she'd laid out for herself to being willing to forsake everything and everyone if it meant staying in this moment forever. All of her hard work to learn her craft, the persistence to gain the trust of customers, and the preparations to carry on her father's business and honor his legacy would be for naught.

Hunter kissed the top of her head and effectively pulled her from the confusion of thoughts that had erupted in her head. He untangled his limbs from hers, then helped her to her feet and draped the blanket over her shoulders.

"Once you are dressed, it is but a short ride to the stable."

She busied herself with pulling a gown and chemise from her saddle bag, feeling grateful she'd packed an extra change of clothing, and shaking out the wrinkles, while Hunter dressed. As she donned her clothing, she chided herself for making more out of the situation than was warranted. As life-altering as this night had been for her, it was not that for Hunter. It was a pleasurable hour meant to be enjoyed, and even remembered, but probably nothing more.

He returned to her side with her discarded clothing from earlier, including her still-wet chemise. Smoke had permeated the items, and the smell was still so shockingly strong, she considered just disposing of the items. She wrinkled her nose.

"It will take some washing," he said, "but they should be salvageable. Just don't put them in the saddle bag with anything you don't want to smell the same."

At his advice, she repacked the few things she had into one side of the saddle bag and then stuffed the stinking clothing into the other side, focusing on her tasks all the while so as to avoid looking at Hunter. By the time she had everything stuffed back into the bags, Hunter had returned with Shadow. He secured the packs to the saddle and then held out his hand to assist her onto the horse's back.

She rode the short distance sitting in front of Hunter with her back as straight as an arrow while she tried not to let any part of her touch him. If she leaned back into him, and if he put his arm around her to hold her steady, she'd not be able to stop herself from melting into him and purring like a kitten.

As it was, she could feel her cheeks burning like a child with her hands stuffed full of stolen sweets.

Chapter Twenty

WORDS WERE NOT Hunter's strength.

He searched his brain to find the right words to say to ease Anora's discomfort, but he had no idea what to say to reassure her. He hated that she was obviously doing everything in her power not to touch him as she rode in front of him on Shadow's back. On the other hand, if she did lean back into him, he'd not be able to stop himself from wrapping his arms around her and pulling her into him as he breathed in her intoxicating scent.

As it was, he could still taste her sweetness on his tongue, and he wanted more of her.

It was said nothing was more dangerous to a warrior than a beautiful woman. He'd never understood the sentiment. Any man with a measure of sense and discipline would never be so easily overcome by a woman who sought to bring him low. But now he wondered if that vulnerability had nothing to do with the woman and everything to do with the man.

From the moment he met Anora, he'd been infatuated with her easy laugh, her sharp wit, and her glittering eyes when she smiled. He'd managed to put her from his mind when he'd been away from her for more than a day. Yet, the more time he'd spent in her presence, the harder it had become to forget all of her attributes.

Still, he'd always been able to rely on the blade sharp precision of his focus when on a mission. Until three nights ago when he'd come across Anora prowling around Castle Whyte in the dead of night dressed in her brother's clothes and thinking they hid her womanly form. He should have done a much more thorough search for the proof Hawk had requested he find linking the baron to men he suspected plotted against the crown, but once he saw Anora, his sole purpose had been to get her out of the way of danger as quickly as possible. Then, last night, when he'd given chase to the men leaving the burning hamlet, he'd turned back long before he should have because of his fear of what would happen to Anora if there were more marauders, and she unwittingly was caught in their path.

She had become his Achilles' heel. His Guinevere. His Helen. And every other woman who became the object of a warrior's obsession in the ballads sung by the bards.

Regardless of the intent of the woman, the result was always the same: She crippled the warrior by making him lax, and weak.

Orange streaks of light colored the horizon as they turned between two fenced fields and rode up the hill toward the stables and the manor beyond it where Red and Galiena lived. He halted his horse as they drew near and dismounted, hoping for a few minutes of privacy with Anora before they entered the stable, but young Wart was already eagerly running toward them.

"'Unter!"

"Wart," Hunter said in acknowledgment as the boy approached at a full run, his skinny knees and elbows churning. He'd barely helped Anora from the saddle before Wart was standing directly in front of her, staring up wide-eyed with a huge grin on his face.

"Milady." Wart said, his voice full of awe. The boy fell in love with every pretty woman who crossed his path.

"I'm not a lady," Anora said to the boy and matched his grin with one of her own. "You can call me Anora."

"Wart is Hawkspur's most capable stable hand when he's not trying to charm the women," Hunter said as he clapped a hand on the boy's shoulder. He liked Wart. The young lad was a scrapper and completely uninhibited by shyness. "Anora is here to see Galiena and the babes."

"Is she yer lady?" Wart asked Hunter, still smiling up at Anora. Her cheeks bloomed with dark splotches of color, and she shifted uncomfortably as her gaze flicked to Hunter.

"No more questions, Wart." He gave Wart a playful cuff on the side of his head. "Take my horse."

"Wait," Anora said. "I have a question for you, Wart. Has anyone brought a gray mare to the stable during the night, or this morning?"

"Aye," Wart said with a vigorous nod. "Bard brought 'er in and put 'er in a stall 'imself. Said to let 'er rest and then put 'er out to graze later. Is she yers? If so, I'll take extra special care of 'er."

"She is." She smiled so sweetly at the boy that he appeared to nearly swoon. "Her name is Willow, and I trust you will take excellent care of her."

"I'll make sure she gets a good rub down an' extra oats," Wart replied with a gallant bow before taking Shadow's reins from Hunter. "Will you be wantin' yer bags brought to Red's house?"

Hunter heard a familiar voice say, "I'll carry those, Wart," and he turned to see a big, red-haired Viking emerging from the stable.

"Red!" Anora said as she hopped with excitement and allowed her friend's husband—and Hunter's best friend and fellow warrior—to embrace her in greeting. He lifted her off the ground and she squealed happily.

An unfamiliar surge of bile burned Hunter's throat, and he had the sudden urge to break Red's arms. He bit the insides of his cheeks to clear the misplaced rage that clouded his eyes. Red was his closest friend and happily married to a woman he doted on with complete devotion. It was unreasonable to think he had anything other than friendly affection for Anora, but if he didn't remove his hands from her in the next breath, Hunter was going to break.

Anora broke off the embrace and stepped back to look up at Red with a radiant smile. "How is Galiena? Are the babies well?"

"Aye, to both questions," Red said with a jovial laugh and huge grin as he put his arm around her shoulders and fixed Hunter with a pointed glare. "But we are both bleary-eyed most of the time. Ani and Erik rarely sleep at the same time."

"I can't wait to see them," Anora said, still bouncing on her feet despite the weight of Red's arm still over her shoulder. Hunter bristled at the casual way he kept Anora tucked into his side, and he knew damn well the Viking somehow could tell it vexed him and was doing it just to bait him.

Hunter tossed Anora's saddlebags at Red with more force than necessary, and he was gratified as the Viking caught them with an "oof" and released Anora to sling the bags over his own shoulder.

"I expected you hours ago," Red said, arching an eyebrow inquisitively at Hunter as though speaking to an errant child. "Bard woke me after meeting with Hawk. Said to send you to the castle as soon as you arrived. He was surprised you weren't here already."

"Bard should mind his own affairs," Hunter said. From the corner of his eye, he saw Anora redden and bite her bottom lip.

"I stopped to bathe and change my clothes. We were reeking of soot and smoke."

"Well then," Red said. "That explains your delay." But as soon as she began walking up the path to the manor, he turned to Hunter with a smirk and a knowing nod of his head. "That is one explanation to be sure, though, I suspect it is not the only one. Out of respect for Anora's father, be sure I will be keeping a very close eye on her while she is under my roof. Even if it is already too late to save her virtue." He lifted an eyebrow at Hunter, and it was very difficult not to want to punch Red in one of his laughing blue eyes. But he desisted, as part of him appreciated his friend's concern over Anora's state.

Ahead of them, Anora said, "I am eager to see Galiena." She turned to look back at them. "Is she awake at this hour?"

"She's been awake since news arrived that you were on the way," Red said with one more warning glance at Hunter as he turned in the direction of his house.

He watched Red move past Anora to lead her to the manor and had an unexpected gut-wrenching reaction to her walking away from him. He hurried to catch up to her and once he did, he reached out and grabbed her by the wrist to stop her, then pulled her toward him as he stepped closer so that their bodies almost touched. He knew Red and everyone gathered by the stables watched them, but he didn't care. In a low voice, he said, "I will not be far if you need me."

She lifted her gaze to his and tipped her head slightly. "I should hope not. We have unfinished business with the baron."

"First, I must report to Hawk. I am obligated to do his bidding."

"You will not leave Hawkspur without me." She said it as a statement, but Hunter could hear the question in her voice.

Vulnerability was a rare thing to see in Anora, and it tugged at this heart, but he would not give her false assurances. "I make no promises."

"Then neither do I." Her eyes flared and she lifted her chin. Their faces were so close he could feel the heat of her breath.

He found it exhilarating to banter with Anora—but not in this moment. Not after he'd kissed and caressed the silky, soft skin of her most private places only a short while ago. Not when he could still feel the heat of her naked body pressed against his.

"I will promise you this, angel." He hooked a stray strand of hair with his finger and tucked it behind her ear, gently stroking the sensitive skin behind the lobe. "I'll not leave you for long."

He saw her lips part and heard the sharp intake of her breath. It took all of his willpower not to claim her mouth with his own and give her a bruising kiss that marked her as his for all to see. He was acting a lovesick fool, and he had no idea what he meant to do about it, but he sure as hell wasn't going to let anyone else pursue her while he figured it out.

There was a subtle shift of her head as she leaned her cheek almost imperceptibly into the palm of his hand lingering near her ear. She held his gaze for a breath, then turned and started up the hill to where Red waited for her.

He huffed out a long breath and had just turned to make his way to the castle when he heard Anora call his name.

"Hunter." She had stopped a short distance up the hill to stand with her hands on her hips and long tendrils of hair floating on the wind, looking every bit like a bold heroine from a ballad.

"Aye?" He looked at her suspiciously because he knew the subtle curve to her lips and the fire in her eyes meant she was about to say something brazen.

"I have a promise for you," she said with a smug grin. "I will not wait for long."

◆ ⎯⎯ ·◆◆· ⎯⎯ ◆

Chapter Twenty-One

"COME TO THE solar," Galiena said to Anora after they had spent the early afternoon cooing over the babies.

Anora had slept only a few hours since arriving at the manor belonging to her friend earlier that morning. She was too excited and exhilarated to sleep any more. Excited about being with her dear friend and cuddling with the babies. And exhilarated from the memories that kept flooding her mind of Hunter's hands on her and the amazing things he did with his mouth.

She'd not seen him since she'd left him at the stable that morning, but a smile came unbidden to her lips each time she remembered the look on his face when she told him she'd not wait for him for long if he left her at Hawkspur, despite his promise to return.

I'll promise you this, angel: I'll not leave you for long.

Her response had been flippant, but after the way he'd pulled her close with everyone watching, looked at her with those smoldering eyes, and gave her a promise that made her heart almost explode in her chest, she'd had to do something to change the mood because she'd been on the verge of throwing herself into his arms and begging him to kiss her again.

As preoccupied as she was with where those kisses would lead, she needed time away from him to clear her head and ponder what all of it meant, and what she was willing to do about it—that was assuming it did mean something to him and that he wanted her as much as she wanted him. She just didn't know for certain what *exactly* it was she wanted.

She'd wait until later, when she was alone to sort through her muddled thoughts. Right now, she had Galiena's sweet little babies to keep her attention.

Little Erik was settled in his crib, and Ani was cradled contentedly in Anora's arms. Galiena had offered to relieve her of the burden of the baby in her arms, but Anora had refused, insisting that her friend enjoy the opportunity to rest. She settled into the cushioned chair facing the hearth in the solar while Galiena plopped down tiredly in the opposite chair.

"Red said to tell you he found a messenger going to Oswestry and sent your letter with him for your father." Galiena stifled a yawn and stretched her arms above her head.

"Go take a nap," Anora offered. "I can look after Ani."

Galiena shook her head. "I'd rather spend time with you."

"And for that I am grateful," Anora said, smiling at her friend. "And I'm grateful to Red for making sure my letter finds its way to Papa. He will be worried if he doesn't hear that I've arrived at Hawkspur safely."

"You must look at the chalices on the hearth. They were commissioned by the king," Galiena said with a tired, knowing grin at Anora.

"They are beautiful," Anora said as she admired the silver cups from where she sat. They were small, sized for a child, and each was engraved with the profile of a wolf, its head thrown back as if howling as its emerald eye glittered in the light. At the feet of each wolf were the links of a broken chain. They were crafted so that the wolves faced one another when placed side by side, and the detail was intricate and finely done.

And, it was Anora's best work yet—though, the credit had gone to her father because the king assumed when he made the commission that the cups would be crafted by Frode. The opportunity to make such fine pieces for the king was too good to pass up, and she and her father had agreed it would be their secret that the design and nearly all the work had been Anora's.

"They are exquisite," Galiena continued. "I am particularly fond of the way the chain links are patterned to include the first letter of each of their names. I did not notice the letters at first, but I've stared at them for so many hours now that I have every detail memorized." Her broad smile showed her pleasure in the pieces.

"I do like the subtlety of the detail," Anora said, unable to suppress the smile that pulled at her lips.

"I know it was your hands that crafted them," Galiena finally said. "The insignia on the bottom is that of your father's goldsmith shop, but I did not miss the added embellishment on the symbol—your mark to make the insignia your own."

Anora felt a surge of pride at her friend's appreciation of the pieces, and acknowledgment of her hand in the work. "It is not often the King of England commissions a piece from anyone other than his private smith. It was a great honor. Papa insisted on giving the final inspection and would not release the chalices on behalf of the king until he gave his approval, but you're correct. The design and the crafting are mine."

"You have a special talent, Anora," Galiena said, stretching out her arm to rest a hand on Anora's shoulder.

"If only others could see the same," Anora said with a sigh. "The irony is that the first commission of any substance that I secured was because Baron Payne vouched for me to a merchant in Shrewsbury that he knew well."

"Even after you refused his proposal? That was kind of him."

Anora stayed silent on the matter, not yet wanting to burden her friend with the long, sordid tale of all that had transpired with the baron over the last year, the stolen gems, and how she'd encountered Hunter at Castle Whyte. Galiena was near to falling asleep as it was, and it was a story that could wait for another time.

"It was very generous of the king to commission the pieces from my father," Anora said, diverting the conversation back to the silver cups on the mantle. Then with a laugh, she added, "He'd probably hang us for treason if he ever found out I actually did the work and not my father."

Galiena chuckled and flipped her hand in the air dismissively. "Red and Hawk will plead for your life if it comes to that." She paused, then added, "And Hunter, it seems."

Anora ignored the comment and her friend's arched eyebrow. Instead, she turned the conversation again. "The king is now indebted to you and Red for exposing the man who tried to kill his heir."

"That seems so long ago," Galiena said, folding her hands in her lap as she leaned her head back in the chair and closed her eyes.

"Nearly two years ago, and look at you now, living in a fine home," Anora said, looking around her at the finely appointed solar of the roomy manor, "with a husband who worships you, and two beautiful little babies."

Galiena laughed. "Who could have predicted running into the arms of a big, red-headed stranger in the middle of the street and using him to escape an assassin would lead to all of this?"

Anora noticed Galiena looked at the baby sleeping in her arms when she said the last. Her friend had endured much heartbreak losing her first husband and young daughter before Red came into her life. She'd never expected to find love or be a mother again. "No one deserves this happiness more than you, Galiena."

Galiena smiled as she put her hand on Anora's arm and squeezed it. "You are a dear friend, and I owe much of this to you."

"Tell me of the emeralds," Anora said, tipping her head toward the chalices on the mantle. "The king's messenger was very insistent it was to be those exact gems and no others."

"Red's uncle made a matching set of daggers when they lived

in Norway," Galiena explained. "The handle was designed to look like a wolf from Norse legend, and the eyes were made of gems. He gave one dagger to Red, with rubies for eyes, and the uncle kept the other, which had emeralds for eyes. The very day they arrived in England, they were ambushed, and his mother and uncle were killed, and the assassin stole his uncle's dagger."

Anora gasped. "That is terrible!"

"When I overheard the men in the alley plotting to kill the king's son, who would have thought one of them would be the same man who killed Red's mother and uncle. And to think it was Red's arms I ran into in my haste to escape the men." Her lips curved into a small, humorless smile at the memory, and she was quiet for a long moment. "Whether it was fate or God, I am so grateful he was there. He saved my life." She took a deep breath and turned her gaze to Anora. "The horrible man still had the dagger and still used it." Galiena shuddered as she said the last. "The king offered to return the dagger to Red after…well, after Red executed the assassin with it at the king's behest, but he did not want it, as it was tainted with so much death and evil." Galiena sighed and turned her gaze back to the chalices. "King Edward had the silver melted down and, for the queen, fashioned a small dagger as a reminder to be careful whom she trusts in the future. And the gems he sent to you to be placed in the chalices for the twins as a reminder to Red that his family name will live on in his children."

"And what beautiful babies they are." Anora touched a fingertip to Ani's nose where she lay snuggled in the crook of her elbow. Her perfect little pink bow lips parted, and her icy-blue eyes opened as she stretched and squirmed to wake up. "She has her papa's eyes, but in all else she looks like you."

"Do you want to hear something astounding?" Galiena turned her head where it rested against the back of the chair so that she was looking at Anora. "When I was standing in the shadows in that alley behind the inn that day, I had been praying for something to take me from the mundane, lonely life I was living. I didn't want to go on feeling as I did." A smile curved her lips. "I didn't realize at the time that the big, red-headed oaf was the answer to the prayer I had sent up to the heavens, but that's exactly what he has been to me."

Anora laughed, remembering the possessive way Red had loomed over Galiena from the moment she'd burst through the back door of the smithy with him following behind her, refusing to let her out of his sight. "We could all see he was smitten with you from the very beginning."

Galiena's smile broadened, then she said with a wink in Anora's direction, "Red seems to think Hunter is smitten with you."

"He is protective out of obligation to my father," she responded, but her skin tingled at the mention of his name.

"Perhaps, but Red says he's never seen Hunter so agitated as today."

"Hunter is always agitated."

Galiena shook her head. "He is withdrawn, stoic even, but always the picture of control. I've never seen him agitated."

"Up until recently, I've rarely seen him *not* agitated," Anora said with a disbelieving bark of laughter. "Perhaps you do not see him often. Or you are distracted with Ani and Erik."

"It is true, I do not spend much time with him, but Red says Hunter has been restless and unfocused ever since you arrived this morning."

Little Ani wrapped her tiny fingers around one of Anora's and stared in fascination at it. She wiggled her finger at the baby and the little girl smiled a big, toothless grin. "You are far more pleasant a companion than that mean ogre," she said in a singsong voice to the baby.

"Do you love him?"

Anora's mouth dropped open as she scoffed at the question, but then she closed it and sighed. Galiena was her dearest friend, and the only woman in her life she could ask for advice. Truly, there was no one else she trusted to discuss her feelings about Hunter.

"The last time I saw both of you together, he could hardly take his eyes from you. And now, you blush when I say his name." There was no judgment in Galiena's tone, or in the way she looked at Anora as she patiently waited for Anora to respond.

"I do not know if it is love," she admitted. "But I am infatuated with him, and I feel like I am going to melt every time he looks at me or…"

Galiena chuckled. "Touches you?"

Anora could feel her cheeks burning as she nodded.

"You need not feel any embarrassment with me, Anora," Galiena assured her. "I understand how you feel. Once I decided I wanted Red to kiss me, and let him, I didn't want him to stop. I wanted to be in his arms every possible moment." Galiena gave Anora a knowing look, and added, "And in his bed."

"Would it have been that way even if you had not been married once before? You, at least, knew what awaited you."

"Even if I had been a virgin when I met Red, I suspect I would not have resisted sharing his bed so soon after being thrown into his company." She smiled wistfully. "He was very persuasive. Still is."

Anora was shocked Galiena spoke so openly about her attraction to Red, but she was grateful her friend was as blunt and forward as she herself was. "Do you ever find it difficult to be a wife? To live up to the expectations placed upon you?"

Galiena was silent for a long moment, then said, "It is not always easy. But then, I suspect that Red does not always find it easy to be a husband. Yet at the end of the day, I would rather be with him than without him."

Anora imagined her mother, if she were alive, would have said something very similar about marriage with her father. "Do you have disagreements? Or get angry with each other?"

"Oh, aye," she said, her eyes widening to emphasize her vehemence. "With his temper and my stubbornness, it is inevitable."

"But you find a way to get past it?"

"We do." She smiled sweetly and her gaze dropped to little Ani, still cradled in Anora's arms and tugging at her finger. "That is what the nights are for."

Anora felt the heat staining her cheeks as she thought about the wonderfully intoxicating things Hunter had done to her after he laid her down on the blanket by the stream, naked under the night sky. It was true that in those moments, nothing else seemed to matter and all of her aggravations with Hunter were forgotten. But was that love?

"What are you smiling about?"

Anora's eyes shifted to her friend. "Was I smiling?"

"Aye, you were," she said with a smirk. "Does it have anything to do with the whatever happened during the extraordinarily long time it took for you to *bathe* in the stream on your way to Hawkspur?"

Anora could not stop the wide smile she felt spread across her face. "Aye, it does. And it was wonderful, and I cannot stop thinking about it." She'd not meant to say all of that, but it felt good to blurt out her excitement with someone who would understand.

"Oh, my," Galiena said with a mocking groan. "I think you and I need to have a long talk."

"Yes," Anora agreed eagerly, "please!"

Chapter Twenty-Two

"Y OU'VE AGREED TO allow Payne to come here?" Hunter asked his commander in a low voice. It took every bit of his control not to let his anger show, but Hawk was still his lord and as such deserved his respect in this. "I am certain he is behind the attacks on your villages and farms."

"I suspect the same, but I cannot accuse him until I have proof," Hawk said. "He will have an escort for the duration of his stay."

Hunter felt his blood begin to boil. "He is staying here?"

"No. He has accepted the hospitality of *Lord* Montworth." The disdain for the man was clear in Hawk's voice. He leaned back in his chair and steepled his fingers in front of him.

It was still strange to see Hawk sitting behind a table in the solar of the castle he lorded over with his lady wife. Hunter had served Hawk for more than fifteen years, and until a few years ago, most of their meetings had taken place either on horseback or in the open air around a campfire. They were soldiers and had never stayed in one place for long. Hunter had not approved when Lady Alyce became the center of Hawk's life, certain that it would lead to his commander losing the edge that had made him the most feared knight in the realm and a highly esteemed leader of an elite force of warriors—including himself. But Lady Alyce had proven herself to be as formidable as Hawk and had earned Hunter's respect, and thus his loyalty.

"Payne is planning a stop at Montworth's estate on his journey back to Castle Whyte," Hawk continued. "He is expected there in five or six days. When he comes here, he'll be allowed two men to accompany him to the hall. The others will stay outside the wall where my soldiers can keep a watchful eye on them."

"What is the purpose of meeting with you?" Hunter asked. "He must know you would never align with anyone who opposes King Edward."

"He claims he wants to meet to forge a stronger relationship since we are nearly neighbors—his words, not mine," Hawk said. "And since it is always better to know your enemy and hear their plans from their own mouth, I am meeting with him."

Hunter still didn't like it. He already wanted to kill the baron for his brutal treatment of the women in the brothels—his small way of making amends for being too young to protect his mother from a sadist like him—but he'd restrained himself because Hawk had convinced him that they had to keep Payne alive, at least until they found proof of wrongdoing. Hawk hated men like Baron Payne almost as much as Hunter and would not ask for his life to be spared if it were not important. He'd also pointed out to Hunter that the old Baron Payne was well respected by King Edward, and that the young baron had curried the attention of the king for his contribution in conquering Wales a few short years prior. Killing him would not go unnoticed.

"You've got that look in your eye, Hunter," Hawk said, the warning clear in his voice. "I cannot afford to lose you, but if you kill a nobleman without good cause, even a low-ranking one like Payne, the king will not care how valuable are to me; he'll have your head. And we both know a harlot will not rank as a just cause, no matter how battered and horrified Payne leaves them."

Hunter flexed his fingers and focused on remaining calm. Every sinew in his body and thought in his head strained to argue with Hawk. But, if not for Hawk, Hunter would likely be dead already; he owed him much. For that reason alone, he should respect his commander's directive, and had the baron not threatened Anora, Hunter would have done just that. But not now, not after Payne had set his sadistic eye on Anora. He had no choice but to kill him. And the sooner, the better. To save Anora from a man who would humiliate her and break her, he would defy his commander and face the king's executioner with no regrets.

"If we can prove he is a threat to the crown," Hawk continued, "or if we catch him in the act of terrorizing my tenants and destroying my farms, then we can at the very least present him to the king to mete out his punishment."

Hunter didn't agree with that plan, but he kept his thoughts to himself. "If he is aligning with Montworth, that should be all the proof we need that he is up to no good." Both men were lower than vermin.

"Montworth would like nothing better than to see me brought low," Hawk agreed. "But I cannot start a battle with him, or Payne, based on speculation alone. It would be foolhardy to defy the king's edict that the Marcher lords do not wage private wars. Which is why I sent you to Castle Whyte. Did you find anything?"

"Only this." Hunter pulled a folded piece of parchment from the small leather bag attached to his belt as he ignored the uncharacteristic twist of guilt in his gut. Had he not been distracted by Anora he may have found something more substantial. "It confirms he has been communicating with Gilbert de Clare." He pushed the parchment across the table to Hawk. "But I found nothing solidly incriminating."

A knock sounded on the solar door, followed by Red's booming voice announcing himself and Bard. Hawk called for them to enter and once they did, the men pulled stools up to the table.

"I'm just discussing with Hunter what he found at Castle Whyte." Hawk unfolded the parchment and read it quickly. "This is an offering of hospitality by Clare if Payne should endeavor to journey to Gloucester. The only reason Clare would bother to extend an invitation to Payne is to discuss alliances. I have no doubt they are plotting something, but the missive on its own is not enough." He sighed and tossed the parchment onto the table. "It was a grave insult when the king stripped Clare of his role as commander of the royal army in Wales after his failure at Llandeilo Fawr. Despite almost costing Edward his victory in Wales, he still believes himself worthy of being the king's counterpart instead of his subject."

"Would he seriously consider challenging King Edward?" Bard asked with a scoff of disbelief.

"I've only met the man a couple of times, but aye, he would," Hawk said. "The rumor is he wants to expand his holdings to include the Earldom of Hereford."

Red shook his head. "The man's an idiot if he thinks Humphrey de Bohun will ever give up his earldom, the title, or the power that goes with it."

"Does Clare even have an army of any worth at his disposal?" Hunter asked.

"He has resources and more allies in the south of Wales than the king will acknowledge," Hawk said. "His landholdings are extensive, and Caerphilly Castle is said to be a fortress so exceptional, even the king was envious when he saw it."

"What does Payne stand to gain by aligning with Clare?" Bard asked.

"Hawkspur," Hunter said in a low growl.

"Aye, Hawkspur," Hawk agreed. "Baron Payne campaigned for the lordship of Hawkspur be given over to him for his role in quelling the Welsh rebellion. To say he was disgruntled when Lady Alyce was allowed to keep the castle and estate after her brother's deceitful actions toward the king would be an understatement. His rage was enflamed even more when she married me and granted me the lordship at her side."

"In my inquiries of Payne," Hunter added, "it has become

clear that he has not forgiven King Edward of the insult, and no longer feels his loyalty is due to the crown. He is a man who craves power but lack scruples and exactly what Clare needs for his own purposes."

Red swore an oath and slammed his fist on the table. "Clare needs an ally to the north of Hereford if he is going to be successful in taking Bohun's earldom. Hawkspur borders Hereford, and Payne wants Hawkspur." Red pushed to his feet and nearly tipped over the stool behind him. "I'll not see my wife and children in danger, Hawk. Let's kill them both."

Hawk held up his hands to calm Red. "I already had to explain to Hunter that we cannot just kill nobleman without *provable* just cause. And we do Lady Alyce and Galiena a disservice if we get ourselves imprisoned or executed for defying the king's edict. His retribution will be swift and painful if we defy his edict and cause a war among the Marcher lords. It makes him look weak."

"Let me kill Payne, then," Red said, balling his hands into tight fists. "I'll leave you out of it if you give me your word you will take care of Galiena and the babes."

"No, Red. Sit down." Hawk insisted. "Where will I be if I lose my best men? I cannot allow you or Hunter to take matters into your own hands and leave me to pick up the slack. Besides, I don't want your children. I have enough of my own and it seems like every time I turn my back, Alyce finds another."

That was another reason Hunter admired Lady Alyce. Unable to bear children herself, she took in children who would have otherwise been destined to become street urchins and raised them as her own.

"Hawkspur will be protected at all costs," Hawk assured Red. "I have given Bard the directive to train more men and increase the patrols as soon as they are ready." He turned to Hunter. "Which brings me to the other reason for our meeting. Tell me about the men you saw riding away from the hamlet that was burned last night."

"There were five of them," Hunter said. "They wore plain, dark tunics and bore no marking or insignia anywhere that I could see, but all the tunics were the same. I was on the ridge overlooking the hamlet when I saw the fire and saw the riders escaping on the road below. I followed, but they had too much of a lead on me and I lost them."

Lost them because I didn't follow their trail to their destination but turned back to check on Anora. Guilt twisted Hunter's gut again. Twice he'd failed Hawk, and both times it had been because he'd let his emotions overtake his sense. The fault was not Anora's, but his own. He'd let her get into his head and it impaired his judgment.

"That is not like you, Hunter," Hawk said, his voice thick with…skepticism? Concern? Doubt? It didn't matter which, all of them were a blow to Hunter's pride. "You have better tracking instincts than my hounds."

"I—" Hunter stopped talking and clenched his jaw until his teeth were nearly cracking. That's how much he dreaded disappointing Hawk. Or admitting his failure aloud. He could see Bard and Red looking at him with expectant smirks and he wanted to wipe the smug looks off their faces with his fists. "I was not alone on the ridge. I escorted Galiena's friend Anora from Oswestry, at her father's request, and I failed in my duty because of… an obligation to protect her." *Christ and all his saints! Why is it so hard to speak the truth?* Because even with his most trusted companions, he was not willing to reveal the depths to which Anora had shaken his foundation.

"Anora, you say?" Hawk's sharp, black eyebrows rose slowly on his face. "*Hmm.*"

It was one short, hummed sound, but it felt like the heavy weight of judgment passed on Hunter. He had to stop himself from shifting on his seat like a chastised boy. "I made the wrong choice." Even his tone sounded like that of a petulant child. "I should have hunted the men down. It is a mistake that will not be repeated."

"Don't fail me again, Hunter," Hawk warned. "Our families and all of Hawkspur are in danger if we do not put an end to the bandits ravishing my tenants' farms."

Hunter gritted his teeth again and nodded. "I will find them."

"I do not have enough men trained yet to station guards at every hamlet and tenant farm," Hawk lamented, rubbing his knuckles across the short, dark beard covering his chin. "Bard, I want you to recruit every able man you can find. Hunter, you will lead one of the patrols. And if you catch sight of one of the marauders, you are not to stop until you have run them down or followed them to the ends of the earth. We must catch at least one of them if we are to prove who is behind this."

"It has to be Payne," Red growled, "I would wager Montworth is part of it, too."

"I don't trust either of them," Hawk said, "but until we can prove their involvement, we cannot retaliate, or we risk losing the trust of the other lords. We need proof of their duplicity."

"The worthless arse brutalizes his tenants almost as badly as he does harlots," Hunter said, his voice rising with his anger. "That should be enough to gain the backing of the other Marcher lords. He is taxing his tenants to the point of breaking. They are suffering and will likely not have food for the winter. How do noblemen not realize their prosperity depends on their tenants? They deserve at least a measure of the respect they give their horses. Payne is a danger to many, and even if he is not behind the marauding at Hawkspur, he has done more than his share of despicable deeds."

Hunter scrubbed a hand through his hair, realizing he'd let his anger get the better of him. When the chamber remained quiet, he lifted his gaze to see all three men staring at him with their brows arched high over wide eyes. They looked like they had just seen one of the Welsh fairy folk fly across the chamber.

"I've known you for a lot of years," Red said, with feigned shock, "and that is the most I've ever heard you say in one breath."

"What do you make of this strange behavior?" Hawk's question was directed at Red and Bard, but he kept his eye on Hunter as though he expected him to dart off like a skittish horse.

"He's been afflicted with it since at least this morning," Red drawled. "I was on the verge of dragging Anora away from him when he seemed unable to stop talking to her."

"Is she the disheveled but *very* lovely lady who was with you at the hamlet?" Bard asked, his overly handsome face breaking into a broad smile that showed his too-white teeth.

"Stay away from her," Hunter growled. He definitely didn't want Bard taking notice of Anora. Women swooned over him wherever he went, and for good reason, but if he smiled even once in Anora's direction, Hunter would have to break his nose and ruin his perfect face.

"I didn't want to question your methods," Bard added cheerfully, "but even the wagon managed to make the journey from the hamlet to Hawkspur in an about an hour. Rumor has it you did not arrive until the sun was rising. Did you get lost?"

Hunter glared at both of the men. He opened his mouth to respond to their baiting, but snapped it shut again because every excuse that came to mind was only going to earn him more ridicule.

"Thor's thunder, he's in love," Red said with a stupid grin.

"Shut your gobs, the two of you." He didn't need Red goading him to say out loud what he wasn't ready to admit, even to himself.

Hawk leveled an even gaze at him, his face serious. "Are you in love, Hunter?"

Hunter sighed heavily and buried his hands in his hair as he tipped his head back to stare at the wood planks of the ceiling. "It matters not if I am. She deserves better than the likes of me."

He snapped his head upright as booming laughter rang through the room from both Hawk and Red. Hawk and Red were his closest friends, but right now he despised them both.

"Do not look so angry," Hawk chided. "It is what we all say."

Red nodded. "It's the telltale sign the affliction really is love. And aye, she does deserve better," the big Viking continued, with a smirk that Hunter wanted to knock right off his face.

"No sense in fighting it," Hawk said with a shake of his head.

Hawk and Red knew what it was to fall in love with a woman, but that did not mean they knew what Hunter was going through. Like him, they were born bastards, and like him, they had learned to make their own way in a world that would dismiss them as unworthy. But Hawk and Red had found redemption for themselves. They'd proven their worth to the world. And to themselves. Hawk was a protector, a leader of men, and a favored knight of the king for his valiant deeds. Red had saved the life of the king's son, saved his wife from the clutches of an assassin, and was a breeder and trainer of the most coveted war horses in the realm.

Hunter was beyond redemption; of that he was certain. He'd been a boy of no more than nine or ten years the first time he'd killed a man for beating a harlot in the bawdy house in which he grew up. He'd jumped on the man's back and stuck a blade clean through his neck. It had taken every bit of his strength to drive it through the sinew and bone. He'd hung on to the man with one arm around his neck and his long, thin legs wrapped around his waist as the man writhed and lurched to dislodge the dagger and Hunter. But he'd clung on and twisted the blade until the man slumped to the floor to take his last breath in a thick pool of his own blood.

He'd felt no remorse. By that time in his life, he'd witnessed enough violence, most of it committed against the women, but some of it against him, and he'd vowed he would tolerate it no more. He couldn't kill every man who hurt the harlots in the house—the madam had convinced him that would cause more harm than help—but when they crossed the line he'd set in his mind, he would strike.

After the first killing, he had learned to be more discreet, often luring them outside or following them when they'd left, to slit their throats in a dark alley or along a deserted road. And every time, he'd told himself it was justified because the man dying in his hands could have been the same man who killed his mother when he was only four. He remembered the event well because he'd been sleeping in the corner of the room on a pile of old blankets. When the sounds became unfamiliar and frantic, he'd awoken. He'd tried to stop the man from hurting his mama, but he'd failed. Hunter could still feel the sting of the back of the man's hand smashing into his cheek. His head had felt like it had exploded and then everything had gone black.

In the more than two decades since he'd killed the first man, he'd been judge and executioner without remorse to perhaps a dozen more sadistic and irredeemable men. For countless others, he'd been their punisher, finding them in the night, bringing them to the edge of death, and while the fear was still in their eyes, convincing them the next time they lifted their hand against a harlot, they would die by *his* hand.

As a selected warrior in Hawk's elite army, he'd killed men in battle and assassinated others when summoned by Hawk on behalf of the king to do so, which he did without question or guilt. It was what he knew how to do, and it had come to define him. He was skilled at being lethal because he'd sacrificed his soul to the devil all those years ago when it had become apparent God was not meant for men like him and was not present in the world in which he lived.

He was tainted and Anora was perfect. If he had a soul and a conscience, he'd stay as far away from her as possible. The tiny bit of his heart that had not yet turned to stone had tried to protect her from him.

But then she'd touched him, and it was like a balm to his scorched heart. The beast that raged inside him, that was always clawing to get out, and that he fought with constantly to stay caged had calmed for just a little while. The part of his brain that told him to run, to hide, to not let anyone near had quieted while she was in his arms.

He didn't deserve her, but the selfish part of his hardened heart that had started to beat again because of her wasn't willing to let her go.

"Since you don't deserve her," Hawk drawled, "then I trust you will not object to putting some distance between the two of you. I have a job I need done."

"Of course," Hunter said evenly, though his stomach curdled at the thought of leaving Anora.

"I want you to go to Gloucester and find out what you can about what Payne was doing there," Hawk said. "Find out who he met with and what they discussed. And bring back anything you can about Gilbert de Clare and his latest activities. I want to know everything, even the rumors. I expect you will be gone a few days but try to be back here before the meeting with Payne. I don't trust him, and I want all of you here to be my eyes and ears."

Hunter nodded, then cleared his throat. "There's one more thing about Payne you should know."

"What?" Hawk asked warily.

"He is a threat to Anora."

"How so?"

Hunter explained the relationship between Frode and the old baron, and the current baron's insistence that Anora become his mistress since she'd refused to become his wife. "That does complicate matters," Hawk said with a disapproving stare.

"Aye. Payne cannot know that Anora is here."

"She will be protected," Hawk assured him. "But I expect you to remember the purpose of your mission and not let your judgment get clouded by your hatred of Payne. If you kill him before we get proof of his duplicity, it will not bode well for you."

Hunter pinched his lips together to keep himself from saying something regretful.

"I know you are aware of what will happen if you defy me and put your personal vendetta with the baron ahead of my directives." Hawk narrowed his eyes and glared at Hunter.

"I am," Hunter acknowledged in a flat tone, meeting his commander's gaze.

Hawk let out a long sigh. "But it matters not to you, does it?"

Hunter shook his head. "I'll find out what his business is with Clare, and I'll not interfere with your meeting as long as he comes nowhere near Anora."

Hawk pinched the bridge of his nose, obviously frustrated with him. "And after the meeting?"

"He's a dead man."

Chapter Twenty-Three

ANORA HAD BECOME very attached to her little namesake. She had her arm wrapped around Ani's pudgy belly as she sat perched on her forearm while they took a turn about the castle yard. Ani was facing forward with her back pressed to Anora, kicking her legs and flapping her arms as she squealed and cooed at all the sights and sounds. Galiena walked at her side with little Erik perched in her arms as he looked, wide-eyed, at everything and everyone.

The castle yard was filled with the merriment of people celebrating a successful second harvest in preparation for the winter ahead. An abundant banquet was on display for the lord, lady, villagers, and farmers to celebrate the successful bounty. And bonfires blazed to ward away evil spirits and misfortune for the winter ahead.

Trestle tables were heaped with breads, sizzling meats from the spit, roasted vegetables, savory and sweet pies, fresh apples, blackberries, and honey. Tankards and cups were filled again and again from jugs of wine or kegs of ale. Children ran and played games while the villagers and farmers talked, laughed, ate, and drank. Musicians and entertainers performed in the center of the castle yard and revelers gathered around the fires to sing and dance. The crisp tang of autumn hung in the air, which was cooling noticeably as the sun went down. Anora hugged Ani closer, but the little girl did not feel the cold with all of her excited squirming.

"Lady Alyce is waving us over," Galiena said, tipping her head in the direction of a long table set along the castle wall.

Anora had met the lady of the castle once before, the day after arriving at Hawkspur. Alyce had insisted that Galiena bring her up to the castle to share a meal and get acquainted. They had supped in a private solar while two of Lady Alyce's older children played with Galiena's twin babes on a blanket spread before the hearth. Lord Hawk stopped by for an introduction to Anora but then left the women to dine alone.

Anora had been curious to meet both Lady Alyce and Lord Hawk. Hawk was a large, gruff man with piercing black eyes and black hair giving way to streaks of silver at the temples. He reminded her of Hunter with his serious expressions and abrupt way of speaking. He was not an unpleasant man, and she imagined he could be just as intimidating as Hunter when he wanted to be, but when he turned his attention to his wife everything about him softened, from his eyes to the set of his shoulders to the tone of his voice.

Lady Alyce was no less impressive. Her genuine smile was warm and welcoming as she listened intently to everything Anora or Galiena had to say. She did not miss any detail, asking questions when she wanted to know more, and laughing easily at anything amusing. Anora felt they had become fast friends by the time the evening was over.

She liked Lord Hawk and Lady Alyce immensely and was fascinated by the sparkle in his eyes and the blush in her cheeks when they were near each other. Their love story was known throughout the realm, including how Hawk had endured punishing lashes ordered by the king rather than betray Lady Alyce's trust. It was an enviable love, their devotion to each other as romantic as any ballad sung by the bards.

As Galiena and Anora approached the lord and lady in the

castle yard, Lady Alyce's face lit up. She immediately tickled the bellies of each baby before extending greetings to Galiena or Anora.

"Are you the prettiest girl here tonight?" Lady Alyce asked Ani in a singsong voice as she pinched at her wriggling toes. She squeezed Erik's pudgy cheek, and said, "And you are going to be as burly as your papa."

"That he is," Galiena agreed. "He'll have to start walking soon because I don't think my back can withstand him getting any bigger if I have to keep carrying him."

"Here," Lady Alyce said, indicating a row of armed chairs with sturdy backs that had been set up along the table for the use of the lord and lady and their chosen guests. "You must join me and sit. And let me hold Erik while you eat something."

"Thank you, Lady Alyce," Galiena gushed and reached for a small meat pie stacked on a platter in the middle of the table. Even with Anora's help, Galiena still couldn't seem to get enough to eat or time to sleep.

The women sat and Alyce bounced Erik on her lap as she made faces at him to get him to giggle. Anora was seated between the Lady of Hawkspur and Galiena. She tried to stay focused on the conversation, but she was too distracted by Hunter's absence to truly enjoy the festivities. She smiled and answered Lady Alyce's questions, even asked a few of her own, but then she was contented to listen as Galiena regaled Lady Alyce with stories of the twins' accomplishments and antics.

"I must do my duty as Lady of Hawkspur," Alyce said after Galiena had finished eating. "As much as I'd like nothing better than to spend the evening with this handsome little man, I must greet everyone." She handed little Erik back to his mother and took her leave.

Anora and Galiena strolled among the festivities, watching the dancing and games and stopping often to exchange pleasantries with the many villagers who knew Galiena and wanted to coo over the babies. It warmed Anora's heart to see her dear friend happy and surrounded by so many loving people. Only two years prior, she had been alone, lonely, mourning the loss of her husband and daughter, and convinced that she was doomed never to be happy again. And now she had an adoring husband, a family, and an abundance of friends and people who cared for her.

Despite all the activity and new people to meet, Anora had spent the evening watching and waiting for Hunter to appear. Four days had passed since the morning they'd arrived at Hawkspur. She'd expected to see him before the sun set the first day, but he didn't show. When he still did not come to see her the next day, Anora had asked Red where she might find him. If he wouldn't come to her, then she would seek him out—and give him a good tongue lashing for abandoning her. But Red informed her Hawk had dispatched him for a mission and that he would be gone for a few days.

That was four days previous, and still he had not returned. The more she thought about him leaving without even telling her, the more frustrated she became. She was anxious to continue the search for the stolen jewels and still felt the best option was to hire Hunter as her guide and protector whether he wanted her to or not. Madam Ruby's idea to hire men as protection was brilliant, and she decided there was nothing stopping her from doing the same. She knew Hunter reported to Hawk, but perhaps his commander could be persuaded to allow him some time to accompany her for the right price. Anora had been paid handsomely for the brooch she made for the merchant in Shrewsbury, and was certain she could afford the cost.

Her plan would require journeying to goldsmith shops and likely some brothels throughout the region to inquire after anyone trying to sell the stolen pendants and altar pieces. As much as she would like to believe she could do it on her own, she realized she'd have a much harder time avoiding danger alone. With Hunter, together they were quite capable of handling dangerous situations.

She scoffed quietly and ridiculed herself for trying to deny that the true reason she looked for Hunter was because she'd not felt like she could take a deep breath since he'd left. When she closed her eyes in her bed at night, she could feel his hands on her skin and remember the taste of his kisses. She missed the way his eyes smoldered when he looked at her, and the sounds of his deep, grumbly voice, even when he growled at her in frustration.

"He'll be back for you," Galiena said in a low voice at her side.

Anora looked at her friend and tried to smile. "Is it that obvious?"

"Aye, it is."

"It is an infatuation. Once I am back at the goldsmith shop and focused on my work, I will move beyond it." At least, that was what Anora hoped. But what would happen when Hunter came to share a meal and stories with her father and Sumayl? Was she to pretend nothing had ever happened between them? Or would they come together for a night of passion and then go back to their separate lives again? As much as she wished to have him as her lover, the risks were too great for a woman. If she were to become with child, or if they were discovered, it would put an abrupt end to her career as a goldsmith and many in the village would shun her. The shame upon her family would ruin her father's business.

"It's an infatuation that is reciprocated, if Red is to be believed," Galiena said, the twinkle in her eye matching her smile.

"Even if it is, there is naught to be done about it. He may be more tolerant of my desire to be a goldsmith, but he would never be contented living in Oswestry over the shop. And my entire life is there; I cannot imagine ever leaving it."

"How do you know what Hunter wants? Other than you," Galiena asked, stopping to watch a juggler entertaining a gaggle of mesmerized children. Even little Ari and Erik kicked their feet and bounced their arms in excitement as the colorful balls arced through the air in a continuous rhythm.

"I don't know," Anora admitted.

Galiena let out a soft snort of laughter. "That, I believe. I rarely hear more than a few mumbled words from him. But from all you've told me of him during his visits to the shop and the events of the last sennight, he actually speaks to you."

She had told Galiena everything about Hunter, from his visits to the shop over the last two years to the events that brought them together at Castle Whyte, the night in the hut, going to Madam Ruby's brothel, and the journey to Hawkspur. She'd left out the intimate details of what happened by the stream, but her friend had immediately understood without explanation that something had taken place and the confusing emotions that still swirled inside her.

"I know how hard you have worked to establish yourself as a goldsmith," Galiena said, "and Hunter must know as well for the time he's spent with you and Frode and Sumayl in the last years."

"But when I told him I did not want to marry because everyone who offered for me also expected me to give up goldsmithing, he scoffed." Anora still felt the sting of it, not because he had dismissed her objections to a husband, but because she'd hoped that if anyone would understand, it would be him. He wasn't orthodox in his views of society, and he'd always laughed in appreciation when her father regaled him with stories of her obstinate independence as a child. It was a misguided notion, but she thought he might even offer her guidance on how to live as an independent woman. She'd already concluded that she needed to hire a protector after her father and Sumayl were gone, but with good fortune, it would be some time before that was a concern.

"You have to look deeper than what men say," Galiena said, "especially with a man who rarely speaks about anything, like Hunter. Saying what they truly feel does not come easy."

Anora resituated Ani to lay against her shoulder after she yawned and rubbed at her eyes. She gently patted the baby's back to soothe her, enjoying the little coos she made as she snuggled into Anora's neck.

"Even if he does feel something for me," Anora argued, "there is nothing for him in Oswestry, and everything I have is there."

"From my experience, obstacles do not stop the heart from yearning, and if the last few days are any indication, he has already worked his way into your heart." Galiena slid her a knowing look and a wicked grin as she bounced little Erik on her hip. "If you can't keep your hands off each other, which I would wager is the way of it, the rest will sort itself."

"Mayhaps we will become secret lovers," Anora said with a grin that matched Galiena's. "Is that not what the wealthy widows do, take a lover and continue about their lives? I will do the same."

"Anora!" Galiena laughed out loud at her boldness. "You are an outrageous woman. I'm not sure if I need to protect my daughter from the likes of you, or if I want her to be every bit as fearless as you."

Anora hugged the little girl in her arms. "As her auntie, I plan to corrupt her in all the best ways."

"That is what I'm afraid of," Galiena said with a roll of her eyes.

"What are you afraid of?" The women turned to find Red standing behind them with a wooden tankard in hand.

"Anora's influence on Ani." Galiena turned a radiant smile toward her big, burly husband. He planted a kiss on the top of her head and scooped up Erik on one arm.

"And with good reason," Red said with a booming laugh and a wink in her direction. He held out the tankard to her. "I brought you some wine, Anora, and I hope it will ease the sting a little when I say I want to steal my wife, son, and daughter away from you for a dance around the fire before the babes fall asleep."

"I think I can be persuaded." She handed Ani to her mother and took the proffered cup. She inhaled the wonderfully aromatic steam coming from the tankard of fruit and spices mulled in a warm wine. "Have fun and don't worry about me."

"Someone would like to say hello," Galiena said in a low voice with a nod over Anora's shoulder. Anora turned to see Tommy Cutpurse shifting nervously from foot to foot while twisting his cap in his hand.

"Tommy," Anora said with delight. She was truly pleased to see the boy at Hawkspur. He'd been living as a street urchin in Oswestry stealing from unsuspecting patrons of the local pubs when he found himself embroiled in the same mess with Galiena that put them inadvertently in the path of an assassin. Tommy had been forced to stay in hiding at the goldsmith shop until the danger passed, and in that time, Anora came to see what a bright and inquisitive boy he was under all the grime and attitude. He had grown in the two years since then, but she guessed him to be no more than about ten years old, though he was definitely wise beyond his years from being forced to survive on his own for so long. "I am certainly pleased to see you."

Tommy smiled up at her and bobbed his head. "Pleased to see you, milady."

"Are you getting along well here at Hawkspur?"

It had been Hunter who had gained the boy's confidence and convinced him he would be of use to Lord Hawk at Hawkspur Castle.

"I am," he said proudly. "I 'elp the smithy in the forge. Clean the floors. Put away 'is tools. Git 'im what 'e needs."

"I'm sure you do a fine job of it, too," she said. It warmed her heart to see the boy thriving and taking pride in his work. He was a good lad at heart and Hunter had been right that he just needed a purpose to keep his keen mind busy and out of trouble.

"'Unter didna' say you were comin' 'ere." Tommy said perplexed.

"Do you see Hunter often?"

Tommy nodded. "'E comes by the smithy often. 'E likes to 'elp, too."

"He does, does he?" Anora said, interested in that bit of information. "He likes to help Sumayl in his smithy when he is in Oswestry, too."

"'E says 'e likes poundin' things."

"I imagine he does," Anora said with a little laugh, picturing Hunter trying to hammer away his sour moods.

"I 'afta go now," Tommy said, staring up at Anora expectantly.

"It was very good to see you, Tommy." She smiled at him as she waved him away.

Anora enjoyed the warmth of the cup of mulled wine on her hands as she inhaled the rich aroma and sipped the wine while she meandered through the bonfires, only half-heartedly listening to the bard as he sang an epic ballad of unrequited love. She'd weaved her way around another bonfire and was bringing the cup to her lips for a sip when she saw a familiar face with piercing eyes rimmed in dark lashes, the shadow of a dark beard marred by a thin scar along the jawline, and subtly curved lips. Her heart stopped beating in her chest as her gaze locked with Hunter's. He had his back to the castle wall, his arms crossed over his chest, and one leg bent with a foot pressed to the stones. He looked freshly bathed with his wet hair slicked back away from his face. How long had he been watching her? And how long had he been standing there?

She froze in place when she saw him, the cup still poised near her lips. Her skin rippled in anticipation of his touch, and she knew Galiena was right: He had already worked his way into her heart.

Without looking away from him, she brought the cup to her mouth and took a long, slow drink of the wine, deliberately licking her lips as she lowered the cup. She saw his lips part and his Adam's apple bob in the light from the dancing flames, and a flush of satisfaction washed through her at his response.

The memory of his hands and mouth on her body in the moonlight by the stream flooded her mind and she shivered. The way he watched her every move as she continued to walk among the revelers with unhurried steps was intoxicatingly delicious. The noise faded, the crowd fell away, and she felt dizzy with power as she kept his focus on her slow, deliberate progress.

His intent stare stayed with her for several more paces before he pushed off from the wall and slowly walked toward her. Her throat went dry at the hungry look in his gaze that never left her. His pace matched hers, but there was something dangerous and seductive in the way he moved, and she instinctively licked her lips.

They each intently watched the other as they moved toward an unspoken destination. Anora knew how this would end, and she would not accept any outcome other than the one that was playing through her mind of him skimming his hands over her naked body, his touch setting her aflame. And she wanted him naked to run her hands down the broad chest and chiseled abdomen that had haunted her dreams since the night by the pool when he stood with the water gently rippling at his hips.

All of her resolve, all of the sense that she'd reasoned through in the last days, flew from her head and only he mattered in this moment. She would not think about after, or what was to come of them, or of her. Already, she was well past the age of marriage and was likely to spend her life as a spinster. She wanted to experience passion at least once in her life, to have a love affair to remember.

As he came closer, her heart pounded in her chest, the beat of it pulsating in her ears. He stepped in front of her, and she stopped. Neither of them spoke. Anora held his gaze but was determined not be the first to break the silence. She brought the cup to her lips again and took a slow drink while she studied his face. His eyes dropped to her lips when she pulled the cup away and she licked a drop of wine from her lower lip, elated at the way his eyes homed in on the movement as she heard his breath hitch in his chest.

When finally he lifted his eyes to hers, he closed his own fingers over the cup, the warmth of his skin sliding slowly over her fingers as he took it from her hand. She watched as he brought the cup to his mouth and drained it in one swig. It was her turn to swallow hard as his tongue slowly wiped across his lips to capture the droplets there.

The rest of the world faded away as they stood staring at each other, neither of them moving, and neither of them in a hurry to look away. He had mesmerizing hazel eyes, fringed with dark lashes that added to the intensity of his gaze. They were truly arresting eyes, every bit as beautiful as the rest of his face.

"You have neglected your beard," she said, feeling her lips curve into a small smile that did not match the excitement thrumming through her body. She ran the tip of a finger along the hair-covered line of his jaw. The texture of his beard against the pad of her finger sent a prickle of awareness along her skin. Meeting his eyes again, she said in a near whisper, "I like the way it feels."

His eyes flared and his lips parted slightly, and she knew he was remembering, as she did, the way his beard had brushed against the sensitive skin of her inner thighs four nights ago. The memory made her skin tingle as though it had just happened, but the four days since had been the longest of her life as she waited to see him again.

"I fear I will have to remove you from consideration for the position of my protector if you insist on disappearing for days at a time," she said with a smirk, turning away from him to watch as his friend Bard took his place by the bonfire with his lute.

She felt Hunter move to stand behind her, his voice a low rumble near her ear as he said, "But I brought something to tempt you."

She wondered what he could possibly have to tempt her beyond the way his voice made her entire being vibrate, or the sweet anticipation tingling her skin at the thought of him touching her.

He reached around her, presenting a petite pie on a bit of cloth in his outstretched hand. She picked up the dainty pie between her fingers and studied it in the light. It was smaller than the palm of her hand and mounded with honey-soaked berries that looked heavenly.

She gasped and touched her finger to the mound of berries piled on top of the dessert, glistening in the light of the bonfires. The honey was sweet on her tongue when she licked it from her finger, but not nearly as sweet as the sharp sound of Hunter's breath catching in his throat.

She turned to face him, delighted with the gift. "Is this one of the famed berry pies from the Hawkspur kitchens? Galiena told me all about them, but we were not quick enough to get one."

"They are almost as valuable as gold in these parts.

"How is it you were able to get one, then?"

"I have an arrangement with Cook." The triumphant smile on his face warmed her heart.

"You have a very nice smile, Hunter. You should show it more often."

He scrubbed his hand down his face, obviously embarrassed by her observation. She took pity on him and returned her attention to the pie, taking a small bite. "Oh," she hummed with appreciation as the sweet mixture of tart berries, currants, and honey in an impossibly thin pastry crust melted in her mouth. "This is wonderful!"

She turned the pie and held it up in offering for him to take a bite, but he shook his head. "It is for you." When she gave him a questioning look, he said, "A hungry Anora is not a happy Anora."

"Am I really as bad as that?"

He nodded as another smile flitted across his face. "Aye, I prefer you fed and happy, like my horse."

She gasped with mock indignation. "You compare me to your horse?" She picked a plump berry from the pie and popped it into her mouth, sucking on the tips of her fingers in a deliberately slow motion as she held Hunter's gaze with her own.

The muscles in his jaw flexed as his focus dropped to her

mouth, but he managed to say in a low voice. "It is the highest of honors."

Anora liked this side of Hunter, easy and teasing. But she liked the way he watched her every move even more. "You should smile more often."

"You said that already." He narrowed his eyes and scowled at her with suspicion, though she could see there was no sincerity behind it.

"It is very becoming on you." She reached up and ran her thumb along the bottom edge of his lip, the urge to run her tongue along the same path making her dizzy with desire. Remembering where they were, she dropped her hand to her side and forced her gaze away from his mouth. But when she looked in his eyes, she could see the same desire reflected there.

He licked his lips as his Adam's apple bobbed. "You bring out the devil in me, angel."

"A smile is not the worst." She popped the rest of the little pie into her mouth and tried to focus on the tang of the berries instead of the heat coursing through her body from his smoldering stare.

"People will think I am growing soft." he said, as he turned away from her and attempted to school his face into a serious expression.

"They wouldn't dare," she said, smiling when she saw the corner of his lips twitch while he scanned the crowd. Her eyes followed the direction of his, but all she could see were the backs of the people focused on Bard as he strummed the last chords of the ballad. Tipping her head toward the warrior-turned-singer, she said, "He is a man of many talents. A warrior and a musician."

"He is the man with a smile the ladies love. And a voice."

"And yet no one would dare call him soft," she teased as she wiped her hands together to brush off the last of the pie crumbs and then ran her tongue over the corner of her lip where some stickiness remained.

"I would," he growled, the sound catching in his throat as he turned his face toward her again.

She finished licking her lips as she studied his face for any sign that he was sincere. "I thought you liked him."

"I do not dislike him."

The arrogant arch to one raised eyebrow and the slight curve to his mouth told her he wasn't serious. "High praise, indeed."

He nodded. "He is one of the people I dislike the least, right behind Red."

She laughed and shook her head at his indifference—which she no longer believed to be real. "And where do I rate on your scale of people you dislike the least?"

His face grew serious as his gaze locked with hers, but before he could answer, Bard stuck a loud chord on his lute and started into a raucous song that got everyone to their feet. People started clapping and dancing in circles around Bard and the bonfires, and the sudden burst of merriment from the revelers drowned out Hunter's response to her question.

"Will you dance?" she asked, leaning closer for him to hear. "Or are you afraid that, too, will make you appear too soft?" She thought she heard a growl rumble in his throat, but she couldn't be sure. Regardless, he took her by the hand and stalked toward the nearest circle of people kicking their feet and skipping as they circled the fire together. Hunter didn't smile as they danced, but she could feel the heat of his eyes smoldering every time she came into his arms to spin in circles.

As much as she wanted to deny it, her heart already belonged to Hunter.

And one day, he would break it into a thousand pieces, of that she was certain.

Chapter Twenty-Four

HUNTER HATED DANCING.
He'd never understood the allure of it.

Until now.

He still didn't like it, but the radiant smile lighting Anora's face made up for the discomfort as he stiffly bounced on his feet to mimic the other dancers. He liked it decidedly better when everyone released hands, and clasped elbows with a partner to spin in a circle. Anora was laughing, her cheeks flushed with merriment, and he thought he'd never seen her looking more beautiful than at this moment. He didn't want the dance to end and almost protested aloud when she released him to join the dancers as they weaved in and out of each other in opposite directions. He forced himself to move along with them until he was back in front of Anora and could touch her again.

The instant she put her hands back in his, he took advantage of the moment to spin her away from the rest of the dancers. He had no desire to dance with anyone other than Anora, and he loathed having to share her with anyone. Her smile broadened as he led her away from the crowd, but the fleeting reminder niggled at him that he did not deserve her, that he was a selfish man for letting his desire for her overrule his sense.

And then she leaned into him, and what was left of his self-control went up in flames. He inhaled the scent of her skin, fresh and sweet like fields of flowers coming to life in the morning sun. Or maybe it was her hair. Whichever it was, he wanted to bury his face in the crook of her neck and lose himself in it.

He quieted the voice in his head telling him to walk away from Anora before he did something that would only lead to regret and tamped down the nagging guilt that he was a selfish bastard for wanting her too much to save her from him.

Then her voice, unwavering as her gaze, asserted itself to chase that voice away. "Take me away from here, Hunter," she said. "I want to go somewhere we can be alone."

Without hesitation, he took her by the hand and led her away from the revelers and merriment. Mercifully, the singing and dancing kept the attention of most of the people, so it was easier to escape the castle yard unnoticed. And those who did see them leaving together were sneaking away for their own clandestine rendezvous and kept their eyes diverted. They passed through the castle gates and walked a short distance down the main lane before Hunter turned off on the narrow path that led to the edge of the village.

"Is this your home?" Anora asked as they entered the small cottage at the end of the lane.

"When I am at Hawkspur, aye." He'd left a small fire in the hearth when he went up to the festival. It still smoldered. Now he released her hand to add some sticks to the embers. They quickly caught fire enough for him to add another log, then use another stick to light the candles on the hearth, and the table.

Anora stood, watching him, but saying nothing as he secured the door then scanned the inside of the cottage—which consisted of a bed, one wooden chest, a table and chair, a small hearth, and very little else. He wondered how it looked in Anora's eyes. She lived in a respectable home above the goldsmith shop, with private bedrooms and a comfortably appointed salon for the family to gather. In comparison, his cottage hardly ranked higher than the rough hut in the woods where they took shelter from the rain.

She appeared emboldened, and began to roam the room, first touching the cloak and tunics hanging on the hooks next to the door, then proceeding to the mantle above the hearth where he had placed a stack of palm-size blocks of wood, a scattering of tiny swords, and the small contingent of freshly carved wooden soldiers. An unfamiliar surge of warmth spread across his chest as she studied the way the handles of the toy swords fit snugly into the outstretched chiseled fist of a warrior, and he realized it was pride.

Hell's fire! He was losing himself to Anora.

"Did you say something?" Anora said as she picked up one of the little soldiers, turning it over in her hand as she took in every detail.

He shook his head and scrubbed his hand over his face. He'd not meant to mutter the oath aloud, but he was in trouble when it came to this woman. All the defenses he'd spent a lifetime honing, the walls he'd spent nearly three decades building, were crumbling around him, leaving him far too vulnerable for his liking.

"I didn't know about this talent of yours," she said with a smile as she slanted her eyes at him. "What do you do with them?"

"They are…for the.…" Why did he feel so awkward admitting he made the toys to give to orphans, street urchins, and any other children who looked like they needed something to bring them a modicum of lightheartedness in their lives? "They're for children who might need a diversion. I make them when I have nothing else to do with my hands."

"How do you make the little metal swords?" She squinted her eyes as she held one closer to look at the detail.

"Sumayl makes them from the scraps in the smithy when he has time."

"*Ah*," she said with a nod. "I should not be surprised."

She set down the armed warrior in her hand and let out a

pleased exclamation as she picked up the figurine leaning against the back of the mantle. His breath caught in his throat as he waited to see if recognition registered when she looked closer at the carving.

"This looks like a fine lady. Perhaps Lady Alyce?" she asked with a smile. "Are these for her daughters?"

It wasn't the lady of the castle he modeled the figurine after, but if she didn't recognize herself in the carving, he wasn't going to tell her. "I just started carving that, and need more practice, but I thought the girls might like something different than a warrior to play with."

"Girls will think it lovely," she agreed. Then she shrugged, her nose crinkling in that way he loved so much as she smirked at him. "They might like it more if you fashion her to hold a sword, like the ones you give the boys. Or, better yet, a bow and a quiver!"

Her excitement was contagious, and he couldn't stop the laughter that escaped his own lips. "I will take your advice into consideration."

"Do you always carry them with you to give to children?" She seemed genuinely delighted with the little figures.

"Aye, I always have a few in my saddlebag. But this batch is going to Lady Alyce for her children. Her brood has increased dramatically over the past months."

"Galiena told me about the orphans they take in to raise as their own," Anora said as she set the figurine back on the mantle. "She said there seems to be an abundance of orphaned children that find their way to Hawkspur of late."

"She is not wrong," Hunter said, stepping in front of the table to perch on the edge of it. He was itching to touch Anora, but sensing she was nervous and needing time, he curled his fingers around the edge of the table as he leaned on it, instead. "Lady Alyce has a soft heart."

She tipped her head and gave him a quizzical look. "Usually that would not be a compliment coming from you, but your voice does not have the usual ring of disdain. Am I to believe Lady Alyce is tolerably respectable in your eyes?"

He laughed again and nodded once. "I have come to appreciate her."

Her smile widened and she let out a throaty laugh. "High praise, indeed. Does she know that she has made it onto the very short list of people you like?"

"I didn't say I *like* her," he teased. He couldn't remember the last time he'd felt so contented. As much as he wanted to be near her, to touch her, he also didn't want this easy banter to end.

She pointed a finger at the row of carved toys on the hearth. "I think this is proof enough of your esteem for her. You are not a man who uses his words to let people know how you feel. But you make it clear in other ways."

He felt like the floor had fallen away under his feet, and he was grateful he was perched against the table, or he may have crumpled to the ground. He couldn't remember the last time he'd felt so laid bare. He should be hating this moment, putting up his walls to hide what she could apparently see so clearly, but he didn't want to do any of that. With anyone else, he would have been horrified by this show of vulnerability. With anyone else, he would have told them they were wrong.

But this was Anora.

Anora who had felt like an old friend from the first time he saw her that day so many months ago when he followed Red into her father's goldsmith shop. She spoke to him like they'd known each other forever and that it was perfectly natural for them to join together to poke fun at Red and Galiena. She'd been the perfect combination of charming, witty, mischievous, and conspirator as they teased and prodded their friends about the obvious attraction between the two. He was like a moth to a flame as far as she was concerned, constantly trying to get closer to her warmth no matter the consequences.

Anora, who always saw him for who he was and never looked past him like he was invisible.

Anora, who didn't shrink from his foul temperament or believe him to be the heartless beast that he was.

She crossed the room to stand between his outstretched legs where he sat perched on the table, a soft smile on her angelic face. Two thin braids of white-gold hair wrapped from her temples to her crown like a halo, and tiny translucent wisps floated around her face. The rest of her hair was woven into thick plait that hung down her back and nearly touched her hips. He'd watched the gentle sway of the braid when she was walking through festival and dreamed of loosening it to run his fingers through the silken mass.

"Are you going to tell me where you disappeared to for the last four days?" Her voice was whisper soft, the question gentle instead of accusing.

"Aye, later," he responded as he spread his knees wider and reached for her. He caught her around the waist and pulled her toward him, relieved when she didn't resist but moved eagerly into his arms. "I can't think about anything else when you're this close."

Her smile was radiant and blinded him with its honesty. She wrapped one arm around his neck and placed her other hand on his shoulder. "Did you think about me at all while you were gone?"

"More than I should have been," he admitted. She'd been a constant distraction, and the only reason he'd been able to focus at all was because anything incriminating he found against Baron Payne for Hawk's purposes would also serve his purposes to keep Anora safe from the brute. "Every time I closed my eyes, I was on the blanket by the stream with you in my arms, remembering the feel of your silken skin under my fingers and the sweet taste of you on my tongue."

The tempo of her breathing increased, and her eyes turned a deeper shade of blue. "For a man of few words, you can certainly create an image."

He nuzzled her neck, breathing in her scent, then kissed along her neck to her ear, relishing the way she couldn't seem to catch her breath. He scraped his teeth over the lobe of her ear and said in a low voice, "What did you see when you closed your eyes?"

"You," she gasped as she leaned into him. "You standing in the pool with water running over your chest and arms."

"Mmm," he hummed against her delicate skin as he kissed along her jaw line. He skimmed his hands around her back and pressed her to him, the feel of her in his arms again felt like balm to his soul.

"Hunter?" she asked breathlessly.

"Aye?" He pulled back to look her in the face, certain she was going to ask him to stop. It would be torture, but it would save them both from where they were headed. If she didn't stop him, and she let him love her, he would never be the same. He would be ruined.

She put a hand on either side of his face and looked into his eyes. "I don't want to leave here tonight with regrets."

He took a deep breath and loosened his grip on her, grateful at least one of them had the sense to let reason prevail over passion. "You are right."

"No," she said as he started to withdraw from her. She turned his face toward her again, her expression earnest. "I mean, I do not want to leave here without knowing what it is to be a woman in a lover's bed. Whatever my future holds, I want to have this night to carry with me always. I want this night with you."

"Anora—" She put a finger to his lips before he could tell her that he would never be satisfied with just this night.

"Just love me, please." She replaced her finger with her lips against his, the touch so gentle and tender, it nearly broke him. "No questions. At least not yet."

He traced the curve of her cheek with his fingertips, then skimmed them lightly down to her throat. He brushed his thumb under her chin and wrapped his fingers around the back of her neck. "I am yours to command, Anora."

Her eyes widened and a grin curved her lips just before she

pressed them to his for a kiss that was not nearly as deep or as long as Hunter desired. "Then I command you to remove your surcoat."

"As you wish." He leaned back to remove his belt then pulled the garment over his head and dropped it on the floor.

She smoothed her hands over the shirt covering his shoulders, then pulled the ties free at his neck and loosened them. His skin rippled like gooseflesh when she brushed her fingers along his collarbones as she pulled the neck of his shirt wide. He liked the way her eyes drank in the sight of him, pleased that she was taking her time to look at him, but he had to clench his hands at his side to keep from touching her and pulling her to him to bury his face in the crook of the neck.

When she tugged at the front of his shirt to pull it up over his chest, he impatiently reached behind him and pulled it off in one smooth move, tossing it in the pile with his surcoat. She took a step back to get a better view of him as her fingers traced over the contours and planes of his chest and abdomen. Her touch was like molten fire on his skin as she tormented him with her excruciatingly slow inspection of him.

"How did you get this?" she asked as her finger slid along the thin line of a white scar on his ribs.

"I got arrogant," he rasped. "Thought I was invincible and tried to fight more men than I could handle."

She lifted her gaze to his face, her eyes wide. "How did you escape?"

"I can be fast on my feet when needed." He smiled sheepishly. "I was young and stupid, but I learned a valuable lesson."

"Not to take on so many men at once?"

He laughed. "I learned to be stealthier and attack from the shadows instead of running straight into the fray."

"That sounds dangerous," she said as she continued her perusal of his torso.

He gritted his teeth as her fingers brushed across his navel, then dropped to the ties at his breeches. His cock was already hard and twitching in anticipation as she loosened the draws and pulled the waist open. When she looked up at him with wide eyes and a wicked grin, he couldn't take it any longer. He wrapped his arms around her waist, picked her up off her feet and brought her to the bed to flop her down on her back.

She laughed, the melodic sound the most beautiful thing he'd ever heard, and he couldn't help but laugh with her. He came down on top of her and kissed her. She sighed into his mouth as she arched into him and purred in contentment. After a long, intoxicating kiss, she pushed on his chest until he rolled off her and onto his back.

"You are meant to be mine to command, remember?"

He groaned. "I do."

She pushed off the bed, then scooped up his leg and tugged one boot off, then the next. He dug his fingers into the blanket spread over the mattress as he looked up at Anora standing over him like the goddess she was in his fantasies.

"Anora," he growled when she tugged his breeches over his hips and down his legs. When he was stripped completely naked, she stood between his splayed knees where they hung over the edge of the mattress and looked her fill at him. His cock throbbed painfully, and he feared that if she touched him even once, he'd be done.

She dropped to her knees on the floor and ran her hands up his legs, her touch the sweetest torment as she glided her fingers over the fine hairs on his thighs. He gritted his teeth as he lifted his head and watched her studying him in fascination. He'd hold still if it killed him to appease her innocent curiosity.

He almost came apart when she wrapped her fingers around him and rubbed her thumb over the bulging head of his cock. She released him when he groaned, asking, "Did I hurt you?"

"Only in the best possible way," he growled. He sat up and grabbed her under the arms to pull her up on the bed, then flipped her onto her back and looked down at her. "If you continue that torment, I'll be spent in an embarrassingly short time."

"But I want to touch you and taste you the way you did me." She was looking up at him so earnestly, he almost laughed, if only because she had no idea how much he wanted exactly that.

"Another time, angel. Tonight is for you."

"I want it to be for both of us." She brushed a lock of his hair from his forehead, the tiny gesture overwhelmingly in its tenderness. "It should not be just me who has all the pleasure."

He did laugh at that. "Did you think I didn't get any pleasure from the other night?"

She shrugged and her cheeks reddened. "You didn't…"

Her embarrassment was endearing, and a reminder of just how inexperienced she was with men. "Until tonight, that night was the most pleasure I've known. There will never be anything sweeter than seeing your pleasure." It was the truth. He'd had other women, though not as many as most men, but never had he experienced anything like the taste of Anora as she came apart in his arms.

"I want to see your pleasure."

He sat back on his knees and reached for one of her legs. As he pulled the boot from her foot, he said, "Oh, you will." He pulled the other boot off, then ran his hands up her legs under her gown, relishing the way her tongue darted out to wet her lips at his touch. "If you want to see my pleasure, command me to ravish you."

She tipped her head back with a deep-throated laugh. "Ravish me, Hunter. I command it."

Chapter Twenty-Five

ANORA WAS HELPLESS in Hunter's hands.

Her entire body felt boneless, and she melted the moment he touched her. She had every intention of exploring his body the same way he had explored hers the night by the stream. Every part of him was magnificent from his smoldering eyes to his broad shoulders, narrow hips, and especially his jutting manhood. She'd gotten a glimpse of him in the moonlight the other night, but to see him in all his glory was breathtaking.

She'd wanted to do a slow exploration of his entire body, but wasn't disappointed when he forced her to relinquish control and told her she could touch him even more, but later. In truth, she started burning for him the moment he was naked and laid out before her, her core pulsed in anticipation of what was to come, and her body ached to be touched by him.

He lifted one of her arms to loosen the ties that pulled the sleeve tight from her elbow to her wrist, then did the same with the other. She watched in fascination as he carefully and methodically loosened all of the ties on her gown and slid it up her body. She sat up to help pull it over her head, emboldened when she heard the hiss of his indrawn breath when she was fully bared to him.

"My God, you're beautiful," he said in awe. He reached for

her plait, gently pulled it over her shoulder and tugged on the bit of ribbon tied at the end. When she reached up to comb her fingers through the braid to loosen it, he stopped her. "Let me. I've imagined this for so long."

He treated her with as much care as a precious piece of jewelry as he freed her hair from the braid, slowly running his fingers through the strands until it hung loose and cascaded over her shoulders in long waves. When he was done, he sat back and looked at her, his eyes roving slowly from her head down to her legs, setting fire to her skin with the intensity of his gaze.

"You said you were at my command," she said with a grin, "and if I recall, I commanded you to ravish me." She reached for him, and he settled his body over her hers, every part of him pressing deliciously against her.

"As you wish, my demanding angel." He nuzzled her neck, and she let out a long sigh of contentment.

The four days since he'd touched her last seemed like an eternity ago, and her body had been wound tight since, waiting for him to touch her again. She buried her fingers in his hair and laughed unexpectedly when he nibbled a ticklish spot under her chin.

"Kiss me," she commanded when he hovered his face over hers, smiling as she laughed. He obeyed and licked softly along the contour of her upper lip, then covered her mouth with his as their tongues tangled.

She was breathless by the time his lips left hers to track kisses down her neck as his hand slid over her hip and up her ribs to cup her breast. Her back arched and she gasped as his mouth closed over her nipple and the rough pad of his tongue laved the sensitive skin. She squirmed under his touch as her entire body ached to feel his hands on every part of her.

He didn't make her wait. He brushed his hand lightly over her belly then lower as she parted her thighs. A sigh escaped her lips as cupped the center of her, applying pressure to her mound with his palm as his fingers caressed along the slick folds of her sex. She pressed into his hand and was rewarded when he slid the pad of his finger over the throbbing bud that demanded his attention. She slowly rolled her hips as ripples of pleasure pulsed through her core. He slid a finger deep inside her and she gasped as her body pulsed around it. When he slid a second finger inside her, stretching and massaging, she arched her back a let out a rapturous moan. He pumped his hand in a steady rhythm as his thumb rubbed circles at the hard nub hidden in the folds. Delicious currents of pleasure radiated from her center as he continued the sweet torment.

A protest parted her lips when he pulled his hand away from her until his mouth covered her center and his tongue pressed into her, swirling deliciously until she cried out as the friction exploded into waves of white-hot pleasure radiating through her body.

He lifted his head to look at her, a wicked grin on his face and she laughed with delight. He kissed her belly, then the valley between her breasts, each of her nipples, her neck and finally her lips as he covered her body with his. The thick ridge of his cock was nestled against her, the heat of it radiating as it pulsed against her stomach.

"I want more of you, Hunter," she gasped. "I can't get enough of you."

He leaned his weight on to his elbows as he smoothed his hands over her head to pull her hair away from her face. "I am yours, angel," he said as he looked into her eyes.

Emotion overwhelmed her and she felt her eyes begin to well. She'd heard women whisper and giggle about the pleasures to be found in the arms of a lover, but she'd not been prepared for the way her heart swelled, and her soul ached for him. She couldn't seem to get close enough to him, and even with every part of him touching every part of her, it wasn't enough.

"Love me, Hunter," she whispered. "Love me before I perish with need."

"As you command," he said and lowered his mouth over

hers. He pulled at her lip with his teeth, then swept his tongue against hers as he slid a hand over her hip and down to her thigh. He clasped her leg under the knee and pulled it up to his waist so he could settle deeper between her parted thighs.

He lifted his hips and guided the tip of his cock into the slick folds, and she sighed her contentment at the wondrous feel of him slowly stretching her. She flinched at the slight stinging sensation, and he immediately lifted his hips as he continued to nip at her lips with his teeth and caress her tongue with his own.

She didn't want him to retreat. She wanted him inside her, but he hovered his hips just above her. She slid her hands over his back and down to his muscular backside and pressed to let him know what she wanted. His lips kissed a path from her mouth to her neck as he slid inside her and pumped his hips slowly and carefully up and down. Her body adapted to the fullness of his thick shaft filling her as he pushed a little farther with each thrust.

"Oh, God, Hunter, that's good," she said in a hoarse whisper as he thrust deep and buried himself inside her. She bent her knees and lifted her legs high around his waist, loving the feel of his body interlocked with hers.

He skimmed one hand over her ribs and hooked her arm to stretch it up over her head. Then he did the same with his other hand so that her arms were bent around her head. Then he put his hands over hers and intertwined their fingers.

She was trapped beneath him, caged in by his arms with his hands pinning hers to the mattress, and his face hovered above hers. She tipped her head back and gasped her pleasure.

"Look at me, Anora," he growled above her.

She did as he commanded, and their eyes met as he rocked into her faster and harder. Her lips parted with sounds of pleasure, her back arched, and her body tightened and pulsed around him as he brought her closer and closer to ecstasy, the intensity of their lovemaking increased by the intimate connection of their locked gazes.

He was beautiful. His hazel eyes glittered between his dark

lashes, his expression was hungry, and his lips were parted as he watched her. His hands tightened around hers as the muscles in his neck strained, but still he didn't look away.

Her eyelids fluttered as the pleasure coiled and swirled low in her belly and her head tipped back as she started to lose herself to the exquisiteness of it all. His mouth dropped to her neck as her head fell to the side and he sucked hard at the sensitive skin below her ear. She gasped with how wonderful it felt, and her cries increased as he moved in her, increasing the tempo until shards of light exploded inside her and radiated through her body, down her legs to her toes and up her arms to her fingers, still intertwined with Hunter's.

She let out a long, lusty sigh of pleasure as Hunter groaned and buried himself deep inside her, then slowly collapsed on top of her. His cock pulsed slowly inside her and the waves of pleasure became gentler as her body melted into the mattress.

"Am I hurting you?" Hunter asked, the words muffled against her neck.

"No." She arched and wriggled below him. "I don't ever want you to move."

"Good," he said as he nuzzled her ear with his nose. "Because I don't think I can move."

Chapter Twenty-Six

WHEN HUNTER COULD move again, he rolled to Anora's side and kissed her on the nose, then got up from the bed to fetch a linen cloth. He dipped it in the basin of water then returned to the bed and gently pushed her legs apart. She sat up and reached for the cloth, but he shook his head and smiled at her cheeks, and the way they were flushed with embarrassment.

"Let me, angel," he murmured and laughed when she flopped back on the bed with a huffed sigh. He finished his ministrations, then returned to the basin to rinse the linen and clean himself. He climbed back onto the bed and pulled the heavy blanket over them, then scooped her into his arms to hold her against his chest.

"Where did you learn to be so gentle with a woman?" she asked in a sleepy voice as she snuggled into the crook of his arm. Then her eyes popped open, and her cheeks flushed again. "Never mind. I don't want to know."

He rubbed a hand slowly up and down the silky-smooth skin of her back. "What I learned is how *not* to treat a woman."

She turned in his arms and rested her chin on his chest so she could look up at him. If there was a heaven, he didn't think it could be any more beautiful than her face. He combed his fingers through the fine threads of her hair and tried to slow the thoughts that raced around in his head.

"Where did you learn how not to treat a woman?" Anora asked in a whisper-soft voice.

He didn't know why he even said what he did. He'd never spoken to anyone about his mother or his life as a boy in a brothel. Hawk knew where he came from because he'd been the one to take him from that life and give him a purpose. But even he didn't know the details.

"I was raised in a brothel," he said evenly and waited for the horrified expression to transform her angelic face. It would kill him to see her repulsed by him, by where he came from, by what he became because of it, but something in him wanted to tell her. If she rejected him, then it was better to have it done with. But if she didn't…

"Was your mother a…" She couldn't say the word but there was no condemnation in her voice or judgment in her eyes.

"A harlot," he finished for her.

"Is she still alive?"

He smoothed his hand over her scalp in long, slow strokes, as though he were soothing a cat, but he did it to soothe himself just as much as her. "She was killed when I was four. I don't remember very much about her. After she died, the other women took care of me the best they knew how."

Anora shifted to fold one arm over his chest to rest her chin on to bring her face closer to his. With her other hand, she rubbed slow, distracting circles on his chest. "How was she killed?"

"A man who paid for her services got angry—I don't know why," he shrugged, "it doesn't matter why—and beat her to death."

A tear fell onto her cheek as she squeezed her eyes shut as though trying to block out the horror of what he'd just said. When she opened them again, they were watery and bright with unshed tears. "I am so sorry, Hunter. No child should have to go through that."

He agreed, but it didn't change anything. "I stayed in that brothel until I was nine." The gentle touch of her fingers skimming softly over his chest was too much for him, and he couldn't keep his focus. He caught her hand in his and held it still over his heart. "I had to leave because I killed a man." Her eyes widened, but not in fear. "He was hurting one of the harlots and would have killed her if I hadn't intervened."

"You did the right thing," Anora said gently.

"Is it the right thing if you keep doing it?" he asked and a nervous, mirthless chuckle escaped his lips.

She was silent for a long moment, and he felt himself start to sweat under her scrutiny. Finally, she said, "Only you can know that."

"I moved from brothel to brothel after that, staying until some man had hurt the women too many times or beaten a harlot until she was nearly dead." A pit formed in his stomach. He didn't want to admit to any more. "You will think me the devil if I tell you the rest."

She shook her head. "I know you are not a demon, Hunter. I want to know. I want to know everything about you."

He sighed heavily. His mouth was dry and ashy, but he decided it was better to be honest with her. "It was too dangerous for the woman and the brothel owners if I killed a man in the bawdy house. It attracted the wrong kind of attention. When I decided a man was not treating the women well enough, that he was too dangerous to be with them, I followed them from the brothel and killed them in some dark, remote part of the road, then returned to the brothel with no one any wiser to what I had done. It doesn't justify what I did, but at the time, it felt like some sort of retribution for not being able to protect my mother."

He saw the way her eyelids fluttered before she blinked several times to hide her distress. "I understand that, Hunter. Vengeance is a powerful motivator. Especially for a mother taken too soon."

She was right, but her need for vengeance hadn't tainted her beyond redemption. "When Hawk found me and chose me to become one of his elite warriors, not much changed. I am still a killer of men. It's what I do and what I am good at." He felt hollow inside. "It's what I am."

He wanted to lose himself in the depths of her sapphire eyes. When he looked at her, he felt there was still hope to heal his soul, but at what price to her? She stared at him for a long while and studied his face. Finally, she said, "You are so much more than a killer, Hunter."

He dropped his gaze away from hers. He'd never been one to back down, but he couldn't stand to look at her as she tried to convince herself that he was redeemable.

"Hunter, look at me," she said gently. He lifted his gaze to hers, and his heart cracked in his chest. She was so pure and so beautiful, and he would ruin her. "When I look at you I see a man who is a protector. A man who is loyal to his friends and willing to do anything for them. A man who mentored a young boy because he recognized himself in him. A man who cares about women the rest of the world wants to forget and tries to make their lives more bearable. You have a huge heart, Hunter, and I'll never believe otherwise."

He lifted her hand to his lips and pressed a kiss in the center of her palm. "If I were half the man you believe me to be, angel, I would be better than most men, but I'd still not be worthy of you."

Chapter Twenty-Seven

"IF WE DO not want to wake them, we will have to wait until sunrise to gain entrance," Anora said with dismay as Hunter walked her toward the manor of Red and Galiena in the early morning hours. She did not regret her actions of the previous night, or spending it in Hunter's arms, but she felt sheepish sneaking up to the door in the wee hours before the sunrise. Still, it was far less conspicuous than emerging from Hunter's cottage in the morning when the entire village would be awake and alert.

"You will not have to wait," Hunter predicted in a low grumble as they rounded the corner of manor stand before the door leading to the kitchen.

Anora jumped and a yelp escaped her lips as the door flew open and Red emerged like an angry giant. His face looked like thunder, his eyes were flashed with anger, and his fists were balled at his side.

"Get inside, Anora," Red said in a voice sharper than steel.

She stood frozen with shock, staring at her friend's husband. The Red she knew was jovial, always jesting, kind, and easy in manner. She didn't know what to do, or why he was so angry. He was not her father, and Hunter was his trusted friend. Whatever this was seemed to be an overreaction.

"Anora," Red bellowed again as he pointed into the house. Then, as if he had heard the thoughts in her head, he said by way of explanation, "You are a guest in my home. It is my duty to protect your virtue as your father would."

She didn't know whether to huff with indignation or laugh at the absurdity of the situation. Beside the fact that she was a woman grown, she didn't think even her father would have reacted so harshly to her returning in the hours before dawn with Hunter as escort. He had hardly protested when they returned to the shop together the morning after she'd snuck into Castle Whyte. Before she could state that point, Red came to a halt in front of Hunter, their chests nearly touching.

"Do I need to beat sense into you?" Red growled through gritted teeth, staring his friend in the eye. Anora opened her mouth to offer a defense, but before she could say anything, Red said, "Get inside now, Anora." He'd not looked away from Hunter as he sharply enunciated each word.

"Go, Anora," Hunter said with a gentle nudge from his hand against her lower back. He, too, did not look away from Red as he spoke.

She backed away from the two men, squaring off as though they wanted to rip each other from limb to limb. "He did nothing wrong," she said in an attempt to diffuse whatever was happening between them.

Galiena was suddenly at her side. She looped an arm through Anora's and pulled her away from Hunter and Red. "Leave them be," she urged as she dragged her into the kitchen.

Anora heard a loud thump behind her and turned just in time to see Red shove Hunter hard in the chest a second time as another thump resonated from his palms connecting with Hunter's chest. He reeled backwards several steps, and her stomach clenched with fear as she tried to pull free of Galiena's grasp. It hurt her to see Hunter harmed and humiliated, and she wanted to stop Red before he pushed him too far.

"Red is being unreasonable," Anora hissed at Galiena when

her friend tightened her hold on her arm.

"He won't hurt him," Galiena insisted. She pulled her further into the kitchen and closed the door behind them.

"He already was hurting him," Anora said, her voice shrill with panic. Galiena chuckled, which only spiked her ire. "How can you laugh at this?"

"Red is not truly that angry. He's just following through with what he thinks is his duty. To your father and to Hunter." Galiena rolled her eyes and set a reassuring hand on Anora's forearm. "Red would never hurt Hunter, and Hunter knows that."

"Then what is happening?" She was somewhat reassured by Galiena's calm demeanor but still puzzled by the absurdity of the situation. "Why is he doing this?"

"Because he likes you." Galiena said with a smile and a yawn as she turned on her heel and started up the stairs. "Come up to the solar so I can hear if the babies awaken."

Anora looked at the door for a long moment, contemplating whether she should go back and try to reason with Red, but decided against it as she did not wish to embarrass Hunter. They would draw a curious crowd as it was, which would only add to her embarrassment if she interfered because then everyone would know the argument was about her.

She followed Galiena up the stairs and flopped down in a chair facing the hearth, feeling very sorry for herself. But when she looked at her friend, guilt overwhelmed her. "You should go back to sleep, Galiena. I do not want you up on my account when the babies will awaken soon enough."

Galiena shrugged, then narrowed her eyes and flashed a wicked grin. "I want to hear all about your night, first."

"No," Anora said with a shake of her head, but she couldn't stop her lips from curving into a smile. She reached across the short distance between the chairs facing the hearth and took her friend's hand. "Are you disappointed in me?"

"Absolutely not." Galiena turned her body in the chair so she could curl her legs under her and look directly at Anora. "I knew Hunter was in love with you the first time I saw him at your shop. He wouldn't stop staring at you," Galiena said, her voice sleepy and soft.

Anora laughed. "How could you remember that. You were completely distracted by what had happened that day. And you only had eyes for Red."

"Even Red noticed. But when he asked Hunter about it later, he just shrugged and refused to say anything more about it. Which isn't surprising, considering Hunter doesn't say very much about anything to anybody."

Anora laughed softly at the truth of Galiena's words.

They heard the door on the lower level open and close and then heavy footsteps pounded up the stairs.

"Quick," Galiena whispered, squeezing Anora's hand, "before Red gets here. Was it wonderful?"

Anora felt the heat in her cheeks as color rushed to her face, and knew she was grinning again. "Aye," she conceded, "it was."

Red entered the solar, lumbered across the room, and stopped in front of the hearth to face her with his arms crossed over his chest. He leveled his icy-blue gaze at Anora, which only made her blood boil. She would not be judged by this man who put his whole heart into seducing Galiena from the first day he knew her. He wasn't concerned about virtue then!

Still, she took a deep breath as she reminded herself that Red was the husband of her dear friend, and she was a guest in their home. An outburst would be inappropriate and ill-mannered, and she would not do anything to upset Galiena.

The outburst escaped Anora's mouth before she could stop herself. "What was that, you gigantic oaf?" Red continued to glare at her and shook his head as though he couldn't believe what he was looking at. She'd not meant to yell, or to jump to her feet, but his nonchalant demeanor after what had just happened was too much.

Red continued to stare at her for several breaths, and Anora feared she may have crossed the mark in the sand that she had just tried to convince herself to avoid. She was about to apologize when his booming laugh filled the room.

"Red," Galiena hissed, pointing a tiny finger at her huge husband. "If you wake those babies up, they are yours for the day." She turned her finger in the direction of Anora next. "I say the same to you."

Feeling duly chastised, and rightfully so, Anora whispered a sheepish apology.

"I like you, Anora," Red said through a toothy grin, his voice only slightly softer than his normal boisterous level.

She sighed, feeling even more sheepish than a moment before. "I like you, Red, but I'm not happy with you right now."

He arched his auburn eyebrows in genuine surprise. "Because of that?" he asked, hitching a thumb toward the yard outside.

"Yes. I am a grown woman. I do not need you to protect my virtue."

The big Viking smirked at her in his lop-sided way that made him look like a charming but mischievous boy. "If I had wanted to do that, I would have broken down his door hours ago and dragged you both from his cottage."

Anora's mouth dropped open. That wasn't the response she was expecting. "Then…then why were you harsh with Hunter?"

He sighed heavily. "Because Hunter is an idiot."

"I do not expect anything from Hunter." Embarrassment and a twinge of sorrow twisted her gut as she circled the chair to lean her arm against the high back as she faced Red. "I am not trying to force him into anything."

"I know that," Red said with a dismissive snort as he strode to the big chair behind the table in the center of the room and sat, stretching his legs as he leaned back. "I also know how Hunter feels about you. But the fool has been trying to deny it, even to himself, for far too long."

"Trying to beat sense into him is not the answer," Anora said, rolling her eyes toward the ceiling. Why did men think a good pummeling was the way to get through to another man? Besides, she didn't even know what she expected after what happened last night, but whatever it was, she and Hunter had to come to that determination themselves. "I will not have him guilted into being with me, Red. I haven't even figured out how he can possibly fit into my life and still be happy."

He studied her for a long moment, then stole a glance at his wife and let out another heavy sigh. Anora shifted her eyes to Galiena, but the serene expression on her friend's face gave no hint as to what the silent exchange between husband and wife meant.

"Is Hunter too coarse of a man for you?"

The question from Red startled Anora. "Of course not!"

"Is it because he's had an undesirable upbringing?"

"His upbringing has nothing to do with how I feel about him." Anora felt a flare of indignation at the offensive question.

"Is he unworthy of being your husband because he is from the lower class?"

"Do you really think me so arrogant and lofty? Even if I wanted him for a husband, no one would dare say he is not worthy. If anything, as the daughter of a merchant, I would be considered too lowly for a warrior in Lord Hawk's elite army. He's most certainly done enough to earn the respect of the Crown and would not be denied if he asked for a noble wife." Her chest heaved with her anger and indignation on behalf of Hunter, and her face felt flushed and overly warm. She crossed the room to the window and pushed back the shutter to breathe in a deep breath of cool air, the damp tang of wet grass clearing her head.

"We are in agreement, Anora," Red said, brooking no argument.

"Who is not in agreement, then?" she asked, leaning her head against the window casement as she looked out at the sun beginning to rise over the valley, silhouetting horses as they grazed lazily in the expanse of pasture below them. The tranquility of the scene was in direct contrast to her unsettled nerves.

"Lord Hawk? The king? I do not believe my father would feel that way."

"I cannot fathom any of them thinking Hunter unworthy," Red agreed. "But there is one person who does think that."

She did not turn to face him, but something in his tone made her heart ache. Hunter had always been one to fade into the landscape, always disappearing like smoke in the night so that one was never certain he had truly been there.

Before the night started, she'd told Hunter she didn't expect anything from him—and she didn't—but she knew her life had been changed unequivocally. His life was not one that fit well around a wife, and she wasn't even sure hers fit around *being* a wife, but she couldn't imagine ever giving herself to anyone else after Hunter.

When she turned around, Red was gone from the room, but Galiena was still curled in the chair, watching her intently. "Are you all right?"

Anora nodded and crossed back to the other chair in front of the unlit hearth to sit. She turned to look at her friend and laughed softly at Galiena's wide, questioning eyes and sharp, arched eyebrows. "Maybe I'm not all right." She sighed and dropped her head against the high back of the chair and stared at the wood planks of the ceiling. "But I will be."

"I know you will," Galiena said in her soft, soothing voice that always made Anora think this was what it must be like to have a sister, to have a confidant who never judged, who understood even when no words were spoken, who accepted all the pieces of the whole, even the broken ones.

Anora dropped her head to the side to look at her friend and smiled, grateful that she was with Galiena during this very confusing time when she needed a friend more than anything. "I'm so happy I have you in my life."

Galiena winked at her in response, then said. "Do you love him?"

Anora huffed out a long breath, then admitted, "Hopelessly."

Chapter Twenty-Eight

"BARON PAYNE IS not as cunning as Earl de Clare," Hunter reported to Hawk about his information-gathering sojourn to the south. He'd been successful on Hawk's mission, but he'd not found anything solid to link Payne to the jewelry thefts.

It didn't matter to Hunter whether he found the evidence or not. The fact that he threatened Anora was all he needed to justify killing the baron. But for Anora, it would give her some sense of peace to know whether or not he was the thief or involved in the robberies.

"Clare has been the most powerful lord of the Welsh Marches since before you sprouted hair on your ballocks," Hawk said, leaning a hip against the parapet as he scratched his chin. "He didn't get there, and stay there for more than two decades, by playing the fool. As much as I don't trust the man, I can't help but admire him."

"Aye, he is not to be underestimated, but from what I'm hearing, he is playing a dangerous game, as you suspected. He is building an alliance among the lords to challenge the king's power in the Marches. With the rebellion over and relative peace in the Welshes, they fear they will be relegated to the same position of the lords of the realm and lose their exceptional power."

Hawk grunted his agreement. "They are not wrong in their fears. The crown gave the Marcher lords autonomy because it was needed to effectively contain the Welsh borders, but with the rebellion quelled and the Statute of Rhuddlan being enforced as the law of the land, the need is not the same." Hawk rubbed his knuckles back and forth along his bearded jawline, a sure sign of his tension. "The king will have no choice but to rein in the privileges of the Marcher lords and Clare knows that."

"Despite all my contacts having the same information, they are still hearing it from someone else, and none of them were witness to any of the conversations. And I could find nothing in Clare's chambers to incriminate him," Hunter said, huffing out a breath of resignation. "He does not communicate anything via missives and insists on face-to-face meetings for anything of importance."

"He is a wise old dog who does not leave a trail," Hawk said with a mirthless chuckle. "What about Payne? Did you find out anything more about him?"

"Payne is a braggart," Hunter said with disdain. "He doesn't know when to keep his mouth closed. He's boasting to anyone who will listen about his alignment with Clare and dropping veiled threats about Humphrey de Bohun. He's making it clear that he thinks Bohun is losing his hold in the Marches and should be careful if he wants to keep his lordship."

Hawk narrowed his eyes, and his face clouded with disgust. "What is he saying of me?"

Hunter did not temper his words. "He says the same of you."

A heavy sigh of frustration escaped Hawk's lips. "It is as I expected. He knows I am aligned with Bohun and loyal to King Edward."

"From what I've learned of Payne, if you apply even minimal pressure, he will admit his alliance with Clare to inflate his own ego," Hunter advised.

"Payne brought a man with him to the bawdy house in Shrewsbury earlier in the summer who fit Clare's description. It proves nothing, but we know they've been meeting."

Hawk nodded his agreement. "Baron Payne will be here on the morrow. I would ask you to lead an extra patrol to guard over the hamlets and farmsteads tonight. I do not trust Payne will not try to do something he will regret, and I have no desire to be caught with our ballocks in our hands again. I just wish we could catch him in the act."

"That would solve a lot of problems," Hunter agreed. "I would like nothing more than to come upon him with a torch in hand. The king could not naysay a sword through the baron's belly for burning your farms. Bard said this morning you have ordered the patrols increased for those living outside the village."

"And each hamlet is to assign a lookout during the night," Hawk said. "Someone who can sound an alarm for the inhabitants. The attackers do not want to be seen or caught, and a handful of farmers wielding hoes and axes is likely to deter them. The cowards prefer to ambush the hamlets when everyone is asleep and defenseless. Locks and barricades do not protect against fire set to the thatch roofs."

Hunter was silent for a long moment as he stared out over the castle wall watching Anora. His entire being ached for her. He'd been fool enough to think that because he cherished her happiness above all else that he would be able to stay away from her when this ordeal was over. He'd planned to step aside and let her find a man worthy of her love. But after last night, after making love to her and holding her in his arms as she slept, he'd become a selfish bastard because he no longer cared if he wasn't good enough. He couldn't breathe without her. He'd never feared death, and he still didn't, but for the first time in his life, he would not welcome death. He'd die to protect Anora, but with his dying breath, his only regret would be that he did not get to have another day with her.

"Did you find anything to connect him to the robberies at Frode's shop?" Hawk's question pulled Hunter back into the present.

He shook his head as the bile churned in his stomach. "No sign of the stolen jewels. Only a trail of beaten and battered harlots forced to cater to Payne's sadistic tastes."

Hawk nodded. "How long do I have before you take the matter into your hands?"

Hunter looked down from the parapets at a long clearing at the bottom of the valley to where Anora was helping Hawk's daughters practice shooting arrows at targets of straw. As long as Anora stayed at Hawkspur, he trusted she would remain safe, but as long as Payne was alive, she would always be in danger. "A sennight."

"I remind you again that my protection only extends so far with the king. If he is not a direct threat to Hawkspur, the king will have your hide for causing a war over a personal vendetta."

Hunter grunted his acknowledgment but was not swayed. Anora was not safe as long as Payne was alive.

"The girls are never that interested when I encourage them to practice with the bow," Hawk lamented to Hunter as he turned the subject to lighter matters.

"How many daughters do you have now?" Hunter asked with a quirk of his lips. He noticed Lady Alyce was standing behind the girls making sure no other children wandered into the area.

"At last count, we have four."

"And sons?"

"Three," Hawk said, clapping a hand on Hunter's shoulder. "But in another month, I suspect we will have more of each."

"You are very tolerant," Hunter said, watching Anora as she helped one of the girls nock an arrow and position the bow to shoot.

"Aye, well, we know what it is to be motherless. How am I to say no?"

There was truth in Hawk's words. The first scraggly hints of a beard had been starting to show on his jaw when he met Hawk, but the man had changed the course of his life, and he would be forever grateful. Hawk had seen something in Hunter that was redeemable and showed him what it was like to be someone other than a thief and beggar raised in brothel.

"They are fortunate to have a home with you and Lady Alyce," Hunter said, genuine in his praise.

"Lady Alyce is a kind woman," Hawk said, his voice gentle. "I did not think to ever be a father, or have a family, but I am glad for it."

Hunter studied his commander as he watched the women and girls below, their laughter and excited voices floating up on the breeze. Hawk continued to train and lead an elite force of warriors, though he assigned the duty of leading patrols and missions to his more experienced men, Bard being one of them. He rarely ventured beyond Hawkspur's borders save for when required for diplomacy. He no longer experienced the exhilaration of riding out to face danger, sleeping in the forest under the night sky while not knowing when he would return. Yet, he seemed contented with this turn in his life. There were strands of gray visible in his black hair, but his face did not look as haggard as it once had.

Granted, it was a time of relative peace in the Welsh Marchers. Other than a few flare ups by rebels, the rebellion was over, at least for the time being, and King Edward had turned his attention toward Scotland. But there were Marcher lords with their own political ambitions and Hawk was constantly trying to discern who were his true allies and who aspired above their stations.

"Do you have any regrets?" Hunter asked the words out of his mouth before he could stop them.

Hawk glanced in Hunter's direction. "No. It was time to focus my talents elsewhere. I am not as fast as I once was, and it was only a matter of time before I paid dearly for my vanity if I continued. There are days that I am struggling to keep ahead of the more experienced trainees. If I met one of them on a battlefield now, my pride says I could still best them, but the reality is I would leave Lady Alyce a widow again."

Hunter was shocked by Hawk's confession, but he understood it well. He was not as old as his commander, but he felt the toll years of fighting and living hard were taking on his body. Touching a finger to the scar along the edge of his chin, he thought about his own future, and when he would have to admit he was not as strong or quick as he needed to be. To be fair, he had taken a blade to the face because he had been caught off guard, distracted with thoughts of Anora years earlier. It had been his first indication that she was a detriment to him.

"If you are asking about being a husband," Hawk continued, "I have no regrets on that front either." He smiled and chuckled low in his chest. "Bard sings of men who fall victim to the wiles of enchanting women and put her above all else. There was a time when I scoffed at such romantic notions." His gaze dropped as he looked upon his wife standing with his daughters in the field below. "I would give my life before I would let anyone harm one hair on her head. Hell, if anyone even hurts her feelings it takes everything in me not to rip them from limb to limb."

Hunter let his own gaze drift to Anora. From her actions, he could see that she was demonstrating to the girls on how to stand properly and take aim. She released the arrow, and it stuck cleanly into the straw target, just on the edge of the square of cloth attached to the center. He had no reason to feel a surge of pride in her abilities, but he felt it anyway.

Perhaps what he was mistaking as pride was actually admiration for a woman who refused to be deterred from what she wanted. She had found her way through sheer determination in a world that did not favor women. It was how she became a goldsmith and what drove her to right the wrongs committed against her.

He turned his attention back to Hawk. "Does Lady Alyce ever push you to the brink of madness, worrying to the point of distraction when she insists on doing things herself?"

"Almost daily," Hawk answered with a laugh and clap to Hunter's back. "But if I quash her fearlessness, then she will not be the woman I fell in love with."

Hunter shook his head, trying to sound indifferent. "You and Red are better suited to having a wife than I ever will be. I may have to leave women and families to the two of you."

"As if it is ever a choice, my friend."

✧ ⎯⎯ ·⌘· ⎯⎯ ✧

Chapter Twenty-Nine

ANORA'S HEART RACED when Hunter stepped through the doorway to Galiena's kitchen, and her breath caught in her throat when his gaze connected with hers. His lips had the faintest upward curve, as if it was a secret smile only for her, and it sent warmth swirling in her chest.

"May I speak with Anora?" he asked Galiena.

Her friend looked to her for approval before answering. When Anora nodded, unable to keep the smile from her face, Galiena said, "Of course." Little Ani was already sound asleep in a basket at Galiena's feet, and she was rocking Erik, whose eyes were drooping as he sucked on one of Galiena's knuckles. She gestured up the stairs with her chin. "The solar is the most private."

Hunter took Anora by the hand, his calloused fingers closing over hers possessively, and tugged her along behind him. She had to nearly skip up the stairs to keep up with him as he led her to the solar, then shut the door behind her. Before she could ask what this was about, he backed her into the door and caged her in with his arms. Her breath caught in her throat as he pressed close to her.

"God, I've been thinking about you since the moment I left you this morning." He nuzzled her hair, inhaling deeply. "I said I wasn't going to do this, but the moment I'm near you I lose all reason."

She melted into his arms with a long sigh. It felt like she'd not truly been able to fully breathe since he left her this morning, but now he was here, and she could breathe again. Her skin tingled and her core throbbed. She put her hands on his biceps and leaned into him, her lips seeking his. He breathed in sharply as their mouths met and his eyes closed. Emboldened, she traced his lower lip with her tongue, eliciting a low growl in the back of his throat that she'd come to love.

He pressed her entire body against the door with the length of his own as his hands sliding up her back and curled over her shoulders as though to hold her in place. She almost laughed at that thought because she had no intention of going anywhere unless it was with him. He kissed her thoroughly, lifting his hands higher to bury his fingers in her hair and angle her head to his advantage. His kisses were almost frantic as he explored her mouth with the warmth of his tongue. Her heart raced as he overwhelmed her with his passion.

She slid her hands up his arms, then wrapped her arms around his neck and pressed her body closer to his. One of his hands skimmed down her back and encircled her waist to hold her tightly against him, the hard planes and ridges of his body deliciously snug against hers. She knew, as she molded perfectly into him there would never be anyone else for her but Hunter. She buried her fingers in the hair at the nape of his neck and tugged on his lower lip with her teeth, unable to imagine wanting anyone else the way she wanted him.

Hunter pulled his mouth from hers to trail kisses over her jaw and down her neck, his teeth nipping at the sensitive skin below her ear and above the curve into her shoulder. A sigh escaped her lips as ripples of pleasure coursed over her skin, a luxurious heat pooling at her core.

"Hunter," she said on a gasp, "can we not go to your cottage?"

He growled low in his throat, making her knees wobble as he nipped her earlobe, then pressed his forehead to hers, his breath as rapid as her own. He closed his eyes as he let out a long sigh. "I must be away, angel."

"Why?" She wrapped her hands around the back of his biceps as if to keep him from leaving. "Is this because of Red? Is he making you leave because of me?"

"No," he said with a scoff, his brow creasing to show how absurd he though the notion. "What made you think that?"

"He was not very happy with you when we returned this morning. He pushed you and was berating you."

"That was nothing. And he did it because he respects you. I expected no less from him."

"Galiena said much the same," she conceded. Though she understood that Red felt obligated to be her guardian while she was in his home, it still irked her that she was not considered able, at the age of twenty-four, to stand for herself. "He didn't try to forbid you from seeing me, did he?"

Hunter laughed as he backed away from where he had Anora pressed to the door, but he took her with him with his arms still wrapped around her. "No. That would have resulted in a true fight."

Anora rested her hands on his shoulders and drummed her fingers against him as she waited for him to explain what Red was angry about. When he offered nothing more, she decided it was not her place to pry. "Tell me then, where are you going? When do you leave? And does this have anything to do with Payne?"

He laughed. "You can interrogate with the best of them. I leave in an hour. I am to lead a night patrol and will be back on the morrow." He squeezed her a little tighter as he added, "Payne will be here at midday tomorrow to meet with Hawk, and I would ask that you stay out of sight."

"He wins if I let him dictate my actions, Hunter." Anora dropped her arms and gently pulled out of his embrace. She paced in frustration, hating how helpless Baron Payne made her feel. "I am beginning to doubt we will ever find the proof we need. I'd rather confront him and force him to explain why he had the pendants, and here, with witnesses, may be the safest place to do that."

"Now is not the time to confront him about anything, Anora," Hunter crossed his arms over his chest as he watched her pace. "If we accuse him of anything or reveal we even know about the pendants, he will bury any evidence he might have, and we will never find it."

Anora stopped in front of Hunter and matched his stance with her arms crossed in front of her. "Surely, he cannot be so witless as to carry the jewels with him, but they were not at Castle Whyte, either. Where is he keeping them?"

"There is more of Castle Whyte to search. I will find them or…"

"Or what?" she asked, narrowing her eyes suspiciously at him.

He took a couple backward strides and perched on the edge of the table, bracing his hands on either side of him as he studied her. She bit into her lip to keep her mind off of the urge to stand between his outstretched legs and wrap her arms around his neck, knowing where it would lead. He was far too alluring, and from the slow, arrogant smile that spread across his face, he knew it.

She cleared her throat to keep from stammering. "You haven't answered my question."

"I was watching you look at me, angel."

She narrowed his eyes at him. "Arrogance is not as attractive as you think."

He laughed. It was a deep, rich sound that she rarely heard coming from him, and she wanted more of it. "You should laugh more often. Even if at my expense."

"I'd say that one was at mine. You have a way of drawing blood with your words before your victim realizes they've been cut."

She dropped her arms to her sides and took a step closer to

him. "Is that a compliment to my wit or an insult to my character?"

"Always a compliment." His demeaner softened, but his words were serious. "If I ever deign to insult your character, then my soul has been truly and fully reduced to ash because I will have doused the only light in my life." He scrubbed a hand over his face and dropped his gaze to the side for a moment, then looked at her again. "Whatever you do, angel, don't let me douse that light."

She took another step closer to him. "You would never do that. I've seen what is hidden beneath the glaring and growling. You don't dislike people as much as you want others to think. You're a protector and you have a bigger heart than I think even you know."

He stared at her a long moment, dropped his gaze again and cleared his throat, his discomfort obvious. "I didn't want to leave without telling you. I will return on the morrow."

"I will be here," she responded simply, clasping her hands in front of her. She longed to reach out and touch him, to caress her thumb over the crease between his brows, to cup his face with her hands and make him believe he was everything she said he was, everything she saw in him. Her gut told her he was not ready to believe her, wouldn't even hear what she was saying, and wouldn't recognize the adoration in her eyes.

"I would ask that you stay out of sight while Edmund is here," Hunter said. "If he gets skittish, it will make our job more difficult."

Our job. She couldn't stop the smile that curved her lips as she agreed in a soft voice, "Yes, it will." She closed the short distance between them to stand between his knees and put her hand on his cheek. "This will be the only time I will hide away from him. Can we agree on that?"

Hunter pressed his lips together but relented after a moment. "Aye. We are agreed."

"Galiena and I are invited to Lady Alyce's private chambers

on the morrow, but in the morning. Her girls like to dote on the babies, and it gives Galiena some respite from constantly trying to entertain them. We will be back here before the noon meal, and I will stay here until I receive word he is gone from Hawkspur. Will that be satisfactory?"

"It will," he conceded, but she could tell by the tight set to his mouth that he was not happy about it.

She buried her hands in the hair at the base of his neck and pressed her lips to his for a soft kiss. "Be safe and come back to me, Hunter."

His hands rested on her hips, and he pulled her closer. "Don't worry about me, angel."

"I know it is a simple mission for you," she rubbed her thumb over the scar along his jawline, "but I will not rest easy until I see you again, with my own eyes."

Hunter's throat bobbed as he swallowed uncomfortably. "I do not expect you to always be waiting for me. It is not a life you should want."

The pressure on her hips from his hands shifted as he tried to push her away again, but she resisted. She refused to give him the space for the stones of the wall he tried to build between him and every person in his life. She'd come to know that wall well over the last couple of years, watched helplessly so often when he added layers of protection, and rejoiced when he lowered it and rested his defenses, even if only for a short while.

"You can try to push me away, but I am not so easily put off." she said in a soft, soothing voice, as she leaned into him again. "I have no expectations of you, and I do not expect you to change who you are." She felt his grip tighten on her hips again and his mouth opened to speak, but she stopped him with a finger over his lips, and a shake of her head. She could see in his eyes he was going to protest, and she would not let him ruin this moment. She wanted him to take her words with him and think about them. If he still wanted to protest after he returned, then so be it. "I want you to kiss me, then go do your duty as Hawk has requested."

She melted into him as one of his arms snaked around her back to pull her tightly against him. His other hand cupped the back of her neck as he gave her a long, thorough kiss.

After he left, she stared out the window trying to ease her unsettled nerves. She did not want anyone to force her to change to fit into their lives, and she could not expect anyone else to change to fit into hers. But the ache in her heart and the fear in her gut as she watched Hunter leave was crushing. She couldn't let him see her distress because it would only distract him, and distractions were dangerous. Could she tolerate a lifetime of feeling this way every time he left?

She couldn't deny she loved Hunter. And she was certain he loved her.

But she feared it may not be enough.

Chapter Thirty

THE NIGHT HAD been arduous, and the patrol far from a success as far as Hunter was concerned. In a sharp turn of events, he rode at the side of Baron Payne toward Hawkspur Castle.

A contingent of two dozen soldiers accompanied Payne, as well as the small band of six men who accompanied Hunter, and tenants from two small settlements near the border of Hawk's land that had been attacked and set on fire during the night. Wagons were loaded with women, children, and a few injured men, one severely so. Two more of Hunter's soldiers were absent. They'd seen a man on horseback in the distance as they'd ridden toward the second fire and gave chase. They'd yet to return, and Hunter was hopeful that meant they'd been able to stay on the man's trail and would eventually return with a captive.

Hawk was not going to be happy in the least. Two hamlets had been attacked during the night. Even with the added patrols of Hawk's soldiers disbursed around the countryside looking for marauders, they'd still managed to slip through. It galled Hunter that the raiders were able to hit two locations right under their noses.

Hawk had instructed Hunter to patrol the border between

Hawkspur and Montworth's holding where Payne was staying as a guest of the minor baron. Montworth's small fortress was near to the border with Hawkspur and clearly visible from the southernmost hills of Hawk's landholding. They'd seen nothing and no one suspicious from the fortress, but when the two fires started, Payne and a contingent of the soldiers rode out from the gates to lend their assistance with conspicuously good timing.

"You will not convince me they were anything but Welsh outlaws," Payne said now as he rode at Hunter's side.

"What reason would Welsh rebels have for burning the cottages and farms of their own people?" Hunter bit out through gritted teeth. The two tenant settlements had been small and not far from one another, but they both consisted of mostly Welshmen. It was not uncommon in Marches to have Welsh and English living side by side, and Hawk welcomed any tenants willing to work if they remained peaceful. His reputation in this part of the Marches as a fair and generous lord had been instrumental in maintaining unprecedented peace in the area. These strikes were unusual in that the sole intent was to demoralize the tenants. Nothing was stolen and no gain was had by the marauders—other than making the Lord and Lady of Hawkspur look incompetent.

"Who can say what goes through their heads?" Payne's arrogant tone grated on Hunter's nerves, along with the arrogant arch to his brow as he slid Hunter a sidelong glance. It was taking every bit of Hunter's self-control not to reach across and throttle his last breath from the worthless brute. "You saw them. They didn't even know how to help themselves. My men had to do everything: stop the fires, gather the tenants, and tend the injured while those peasants watched in useless shock."

Hunter gave a noncommittal grunt from low in his throat as he scanned the terrain. That was not what Hunter had observed, and his own men confirmed it. Payne's soldiers had created confusion and, in his opinion, been purposely more of a hindrance than a help. Soon after they arrived on the scene, fights were brewing between Payne's soldiers and those from Hawkspur. In a tense moment, he'd been forced to remind Payne he was on Hawkspur soil and to bring his men to heel before the hostility erupted into a full battle.

The sun was rising in the distance, but the trees were still silhouettes shrouded in gray. He was watching the horizon with one eye, but his other was on Payne and his men. They posed a greater threat than anything that may be hiding in the forest.

If Hunter had not made his promise to Hawk to give him a sennight to determine if Payne was responsible for the vandals and the purpose for his deeds, he would have already killed the man. As it was, he was adhering to his duty, though it was a constant battle with the demon raging inside of him, desperate to protect Anora.

"It was rather fortuitous for the peasants that we were near, considering the small band of men with you was not enough to control the fires, let alone prevent them." Payne's voice was an irritating drone in Hunter's ear, and he wasn't sure how much more of him he could take. "I can only imagine Hawk's displeasure when he learns of the loss of nearly all the structures in two hamlets from fires that should not have happened under your watch."

Hunter stayed silent and kept his focus on the road ahead. This journey could not be over soon enough for his liking.

"I heard the men call you 'Hunter.' I've heard about you, but I don't remember meeting you face to face." When Hunter did not turn to acknowledge the man, he said in a nasally, superior tone, "You do not seem to know who I am."

Hunter slowly turned his head to face the baron and leveled a steady stare at him. Payne was not a particularly large man and there was nothing intimidating about him—definitely repulsive but not intimidating. He had beady eyes and sharp, protruding features that made him resemble a rodent in Hunter's mind. All he needed was long whiskers and a naked pink tail. "I know who you are."

"And I know who you are," Payne sneered. "You are nothing but a lackey hired to do Hawk's dirty work. Little more than an indentured servant, really. *I* am a baron, a nobleman with the ear of powerful men. I expect you to treat me with the respect due to me owing to my station."

Hunter continued to look at Payne with an intentionally bored expression on his face before turning his gaze ahead of them again, with a slow sigh of exasperation. Hunter's teeth were near to breaking from the force of his clenched jaw. He wanted to knock the cocksure cur from his mount and beat him into the dirt.

Baron Payne edged his horse closer to Hunter and Shadow so that their knees grazed together. "Because of my respect for Hawk, and the dread I am certain you are feeling having to tell him of your failures, I will overlook your insolence this time. But if you disrespect me again, know that I will have you licking my boots like the worthless piece of shit you are."

He'd meant to keep his mouth shut. He'd tried really hard not to let Payne prick his temper. But a man could only take so much.

His hand shot out and grabbed the worthless baron by the neck of his tunic, twisting it tight and pulling his ugly face close to his own. He looked into the baron's wide, terrified eyes, as their noses almost touched, and the stench of the man's breath wafted into his nostrils. "You may be a baron, but I am a man who has taken the lives of so many men I have nothing left of my soul but the blackened ashes. I know you for who you really are, and I know all about your sadistic fantasies. You are a coward, and you prey on those weaker than you. You belong in Hell, and I will gladly put you there, even if it means I have to take you with me to do it."

They were surrounded by soldiers now, both the baron's and his, but Hunter didn't care. He'd already overstepped the bounds of propriety. No one had interfered, but they were at the ready, awaiting a signal from either man, yet the men from Hawkspur were vastly outnumbered and Hunter was not a fool. He released the baron's tunic and settled back in his saddle.

Payne glared at him for a long moment, not moving, no doubt calculating how to save face in front of his men without causing a bloodbath, though Hunter knew he was itching for the latter. "I will overlook this…indiscretion," he said through gritted teeth, his eyes bulging, "and leave your commander to determine your punishment. But if you ever place your hands on me again, I will have them detached from your arms as is my right as a nobleman, and no one—not Hawk, not even the king—will condemn me."

Hunter wanted to wrap his hands around Payne's neck and squeeze until his little, darting eyes popped from his head. Instead, he nudged his horse to walk on. "Let us get these people to Hawkspur."

The men who had spurred their horses forward to gather around them reined to the side and let them pass, before returning to their positions in the procession.

Hawkspur came into sight as the road turned into the next valley, the castle sitting as sentinel on the top of a high hill with the village spilling down the slope from the castle walls. A patchwork of pastures and fields ringed the bottom of the hillsides, stretching all the way to the edge of the forest surrounding the hills. Hawk had done much to improve the defenses of the castle, clearing the forest back far enough to see any raiders trying to get close to the fortress. Another wall was being constructed at the base of the hill, completely enclosing the village and structures dotting the hillsides—a sure indication that Hawkspur had prospered under the combined governance of Hawk and Lady Alyce.

The morning sun was becoming brighter as the gates to Hawkspur opened and a contingent of soldiers emerged, riding hard in their direction. They were soon surrounded by Hawkspur soldiers, who quickly assessed the situation with the injured tenants.

"Again?" Bard asked angrily, scanning the wagons loaded with the men, women, and children, all of them smudged and dirty with soot and ash, and some injured. He noticed a man lying on the floor of one of the carts, a severed shaft of an arrow protruding from his shoulder.

When Hunter and his men had come upon the man at the second hamlet to be pillaged during the night, the man had been barking orders and organizing the inhabitants of his tiny settlement, his expression stern and focused despite the sweat dripping from his pale face and the weight of the arrow protruding from his upper chest. When the fires were under control and he had finally collapsed, three of Baron Payne's soldiers held him down while another quickly cut through the shaft so that only a short piece protruded from his shoulder, but they left enough of the arrow to grasp for the removal. The man had growled and gnashed his teeth like an injured wolf, but as soon as the initial burst of pain from having the arrow manipulated subsided, he told the men to push it the rest of the way through his chest to dislodge it. Unfortunately, the valiant man had passed out when the head of the arrow struck bone.

Bard pointed at one of the soldiers from Hawkspur. "Go back and tell the healer to prepare for this man." Then turning to Hunter he asked, "Are there any more serious injuries?"

Hunter shook his head. "Nay. Only minor. But the damage to the settlements is extensive."

"Everything is gone," a young woman sitting in the cart said. Her eyes were misty, her hair disheveled, and her clothes torn. Hunter had noticed her sitting in the dirt, looking forlornly at the farmstead that had been burned to ashes as they loaded the cart with the injured man. He'd asked her then if she'd been harmed by the marauders and she'd said she hadn't, but her voice had remained flat and lackluster.

As the group rode through the castle gates into the bailey of Hawkspur Castle, Hunter saw Hawk standing above the portcullis, surveying the group as they entered. When he saw

Hunter, one eyebrow twitched questioningly, but he gave no other indication of his reaction to seeing him riding into Hawkspur in the company of Payne.

The healer, barn hands, Lady Alyce and her maids, and several women from the village were awaiting them in the castle yard and rushed forward to assist as soon as the party came to a halt. The horses were led away after the men dismounted, people were helped down from the carts and ushered to trestle tables scattered in the yard. Tubs of water for cleaning were being hauled over and placed where people could get to them, linen cloths were stacked on the tables, and the kitchen helpers were bringing out loaves of bread, jugs, cups, and platters with cheese, meats, and whatever else was readily available.

Several of the soldiers, including Hunter, assisted the injured man with an arrow in his chest up the stairs and through the door to the hall at Lady Alyce's direction. He'd lost a fair amount of blood and was weak in the knees and near to collapsing.

"Bring him there, under the window." Lady Alyce pointed the men in the direction of a table draped with a linen sheet and positioned directly in the ray of light shining in through the window opening.

The healer already had his instruments spread on the end of the table. He looked up at the men as they approached the table. "Help him lie back on the table."

"What is your name?" Lady Alyce asked the injured man after he was set on the table. His face was sickly gray and covered in a sheen of sweat. Hunter feared he would soon lose consciousness.

"Dylan, my lady," the man said with a gasp. He didn't look at Alyce but rather turned his head to the side and scanned the room as though looking for someone.

"Do you have family with you, Dylan?" she asked and followed his gaze.

"I believe she is his family," Hunter said, tipping his head toward the young woman from the cart who now stood in the doorway of the hall, wringing her hands and looking near to toppling over from exhaustion.

Alyce went to her immediately and put an arm around her shoulder to lead her to the table. "Come, let him see you. Is he your husband?"

"He is," the woman said in a shaky voice. She put her hand on her husband's cheek, and he gave her a weak smile.

"I'll be fine, Cati," he said in a bare whisper.

If the wound did not fester, then he would recover, of that Hunter was certain. But the threat of infection was real, and he'd seen many men brought low by it. Fortunately, Hawkspur had one of the most competent healers in the region, and his chances of surviving were greatly increased now that he was in the care of Lady Alyce's household.

"Brandy is being fetched for you," Lady Alyce said, glancing from Dylan to his wife. "Both of you." To the healer she said, "Water is being heated in the kitchen and will be here soon."

At that moment, a group of women rushed in with buckets of water and more linens. When Hunter realized Anora was among the women, he quickly glanced around the hall to be sure Payne had not come into the hall. Last he'd seen of him, he and his men were following their horses toward the stables with Hawk as escort.

Anora set a bucket of steaming water next to the table with the other buckets then immediately came to Hunter where he stood along the wall a short distance away to give the healer and those assisting room to work. She stopped just short of touching him, her eyes misted as she stared at him, and her jaw flexing as though she was struggling to maintain her composure.

"What is the matter?" he asked, his chest tightening at the look of fear on her face.

"I am just so relieved it is not you on the table," she whispered. "We didn't know who was hurt, only that we were to fetch water and prepare for a man shot through by an arrow. I was terrified it might be you. I know it is irrational to be so upset, but I had a sick feeling in the pit of my stomach that would not go away."

He held out his arms to her and she immediately came into them. "I'm here and I'm whole," he whispered as he buried his face in her hair and squeezed her to his chest. He felt her arms wrap around his middle as she nodded her head.

"I thought I would be better at this. That I could be stoic and accept the risks that come with loving a man like you." The words were said in a quiet whisper, and Hunter could hear the anguish in them, and it tore at his heart. But what pierced his heart even sharper was the rush of satisfaction from hearing her say she loved him.

He wanted to tell her he loved her in return, but the knowledge of the pain that he caused her stopped him. Every time he left on a mission, she would be forced to deal with this same torment. It was killing him to see her in distress. And worse yet, to be the reason for it.

Hunter had just released his hold on her and was about to tell her about Payne's arrival at Hawkspur when the door to the hall opened and Hawk entered with the baron on his heels. The gaze of both men quickly settled on Hunter where he stood along the wall with Anora just stepping out of his embrace. With his hands still on Anora's arms, he turned her toward the back of the hall in the futile hope that Payne would not recognize her from just the back of her head.

"Payne just entered," he warned in a low voice, but he was not quick enough. Anora had already turned her head to look over her shoulder at the newcomers. He heard her indrawn breath at the sight of the baron. For his part, Payne's expression changed from one of thunderous rage in flash, and then just as quickly back into a mask of indifference.

"I've come to see about the man with the arrow in his shoulder," Hawk said as he walked toward the table. "How does he fare?"

Hunter moved to stand in front of Anora to block her from Payne's view as he silently cursed himself for his stupidity. He should have warned Anora of the baron's presence before he said anything else. But once again, his feelings for her had clouded his judgment.

"I am inspecting the wound now, my lord," the healer said as he wiped at the bloodied shoulder with a wet linen while Dylan grunted in pain. "It will need to be cut out, I'm afraid. It cannot be pushed through."

Lady Alyce eyed Hunter with a knowing look as he searched for a way to get Anora discreetly away from the hall. She was a very perceptive woman, and one of the few people who knew him well. In the four years since Lady Alyce had won the heart of Hawk, Hunter had developed a deep respect for her leadership, fairness, and genuine kindness. Never had he involved himself in romantic affairs of anyone, but when Hawk and Alyce were at a crossroads, he'd broken his own rule and meddled when he couldn't stand to see the obstinate fools suffer any longer.

"Cati," Lady Alyce said, gaining the attention of Dylan's wife where she stood at her husband's feet, her face contorted in misery as she helplessly watched her husband enduring the pain of the healer's prodding. "Your husband will require a clean bed to rest once the healer is finished. I suggested a room above stairs be prepared. This way he can be close, and it will be easier for us to assist you with his care. Is this acceptable?"

Cati nodded but did not take her eyes from her husband. If she stayed, Hunter knew the pain her husband would endure as the arrow was cut from his shoulder would be her undoing. And when the healer cauterized the wound, she'd probably faint dead away.

Lady Alyce grabbed Anora by the hand, then turned to Cati. "I would appreciate your assistance to prepare his room." Hunter breathed easier and was grateful to Lady Alyce for deftly removing Anora from the room at the same time as Dylan's wife.

Cati tore her gaze from her husband to stare at the lady, her eyes wide and panicky as she continued to look back and forth between the two. It was obvious she wanted to stay with her husband. Hunter surmised if he were lying on that table and about to go through what Dylan was set to endure, he would not want the woman he loved witnessing his pain.

"Go, Cati," Dylan grunted. "I will be there soon."

The young woman hesitated, then patted her husband's leg in a gesture of reassurance and followed Lady Alyce and Anora from the hall. Hunter wanted nothing more than to leave behind them. Instead, he clasped forearms with Dylan and squatted at his side to look the man in the face.

"There was poppy in the brandy," the healer told Dylan, "To help with the pain."

Hunter saw the strap of leather sitting on the table and reached for it. He knew from experience the poppy was questionable as to its effectiveness. Some men seemed to feel nothing after having it administered to them, and for others, it did nothing to dull the pain.

As the healer cut into the wound to get to the flared head of the arrow, Dylan's eyes flew open wide, and he roared in pain. Hunter slipped the leather between his teeth and Dylan bit down with a groan as his eyes watered. His strong fingers dug into Hunter's forearm and Hunter hung on to him to keep him from flailing inadvertently at the healer. The young farmer had hands as strong as a blacksmith's, and the pressure he was applying to Hunter's forearm was intense. Despite his arm feeling near to snapping, he smiled at Dylan and asked, "Is that all you've got?"

Dylan roared in response and clamped his big hand like a vise on Hunter as he bucked again in response to the healer pulling the arrow loose from his shoulder. The surgeon pressed a linen into the wound to staunch the flow of blood, then held out his hand for the glowing iron that would be used to cauterize the wound.

Before Dylan could turn his head to see what was coming, Hunter said, "You could be a warrior with the grip and power you have in your hand. Should you ever want to give up farming, I'll train you to join us."

Dylan's face twisted with pain, and he let out a long, low growl as the acrid stench of burning skin filled Hunter's nostrils.

"The worst of it is over, mate." Hunter kept his forearm locked with Dylan's while a salve was applied to the burn. The farmer's grip slowly relaxed and he spit the leather strap out from between his teeth and took several deep breaths.

"I'll train with you," Dylan said through panting breaths and a weak smile, "but I won't leave Cati or the farm. Train me how to lodge an arrow in the arse of the coward who did this."

"Aye," Hunter agreed. "I will. When you are healed, we will begin the training."

Hawk approached and set a hand on Dylan's good shoulder. "Now you must rest and heal. We will discuss rebuilding your farm soon. Hunter, help him to the chamber above stairs before he passes out."

Hunter had kept his eyes on Payne during Dylan's ordeal. He feared the baron would try to sneak away and find Anora, but he'd stayed put to watch the entire ordeal with arms crossed over his chest and a bored expression on his face.

Assisting Dylan by his good arm, Hunter got the man to his feet and up the stairs to the chamber where his wife awaited him, along with Anora and several of Lady Alyce's maids.

Cati greeted him with her hands on his cheeks and a kiss to his lips, but pulled away embarrassed when she realized her husband was leaning on Hunter for support. "Forgive me, my lord. I was overcome with relief."

"I am not a lord," Hunter corrected her. "And do not apologize."

"Kiss me again, *cariad*," Dylan said drowsily, still leaning on Hunter. "It helps me forget the pain."

Cati blushed, but the smile that came to her lips when her husband called her "sweetheart" was radiant. She pushed up on her toes and kissed him quickly on the lips, her face as red as a beet. "Let us get you off your feet, *fy nghalon*." The Welsh words for *my heart* were soft and melodic, and tugged at Hunter's heart because it was a phrase his mother had used with him when he was a child.

"Over here," the maid called Gertie ordered. She was the younger of the two women who served Lady Alyce.

"Set him on the stool so we may bathe him before we put him in the bed," Edna, the older of the maids, ordered. "We've just cleaned the bedding, and I do not want it soiled with blood and soot."

Hunter helped him to sit, then stepped back as the women took over. The maids and Cati had him stripped of what was left of his filthy clothing, washed him from head to foot, and dried him. Hunter helped the women move him to the bed while Anora gathered his ragged clothing and set it outside the door of the chamber.

Dylan's eyes closed the moment his head was cradled on a pillow. He was in good hands with his wife and the maids to see to his every need.

Hunter looked at Anora and tipped his head toward the door. When they were in the corridor with the door to the chamber closed, he took her by the hand and led her to the window opening at the end of the passageway. Her face glowed and her hair looked ethereal, shimmering in the sunlight streaming in. Hers was the face he would see each time he closed his eyes for the rest of his days, and he would awaken each day remembering that she once admitted to loving him.

But right now, he needed to remember how tormented she was when she admitted to loving him, her fear when she thought he had been hurt, and the knowledge that he would cause her heartache every time he rode away from her. Most importantly, he needed to remember that the last two days had been a catastrophe of errors because he had let his discipline slip, had let his own longing for her dull his focus. Because of his failing, homes and farms were burned, Dylan was nearly killed, and he'd exposed Anora's presence to the baron, putting her in the path of danger. These were mistakes that never would have happened on his watch before he'd allowed himself to love Anora.

"What are we going to do now about Payne?" Anora asked

while he was still trying to figure out how to tell her what she didn't want to hear.

There was a flush in her cheeks from her excitement, and he had to resist the urge to brush a thumb over the blush on her cheekbone. Instead, he sighed, rolled his lips between his teeth, then said, "If I thought you'd be safe in Oswestry, I'd bring you there, but it's too late for that. The safest place for you is here, in Hawkspur Castle."

"What are you saying?" she asked, confusion in her eyes.

He would not be deterred. "I will make the request of Hawk and Lady Alyce to host and protect you until our business with him is settled. Now that Payne knows you are here, you are not safe."

Anora pressed her lips into a thin line, her glare cutting him to the core. "You say *our* business, but you do not mean to include me."

Hunter took a step back, needing some distance from her as he shook his head. "I'm at my best when I work alone."

Anger flashed in her eyes as she spoke through tight lips. "I am a hindrance. Is that what you are telling me?"

He scrubbed a hand over his face, knowing that any way he said it, she was going to be angry with him. "Aye. You are."

Her mouth dropped open and she gasped. Then she snapped it shut, narrowed her eyes, and planted her hands on her hips. "Tell me, Hunter, how many of the stolen jewels have you found? It is my family who has been wronged by him. Do you have any idea the depth of his betrayal if he was responsible for killing my mother?"

Hunter flinched because everything she said was true. He'd found nothing, and though he understood the pain of losing a mother, he'd never had any of the handful of people he let close to him betray him as the baron had done to Frode and Anora. Edmund Payne had been a trusted friend and had been treated as family by the kindest, most generous people Hunter had ever known, yet he'd heartlessly taken advantage of that trust. Even if

Payne were not responsible for killing Anora's mother, robbing them and pressing Anora to become his mistress were nearly as despicable.

"Forgive me," Anora said, laying a hand over Hunter's chest. "I was cruel and thoughtless, speaking from anger and desperation."

"Do not apologize to me," he said, covering her hand with his own where it was radiating heat against his chest. "I am the one who must ask for forgiveness and make things right. These last days, I have been blundering everything because you are all I think about. The desire to hear your voice, to make you laugh, to see the light reflected in your eyes, to watch your every move, to touch you, is consuming me. I'm worthless to do anything else." Gently, he lifted her hand away from him and released it. "But I am nothing if I am not a warrior, and you deserve better."

She made a choking sound in her throat. "First you say the words I want to hear, but then you turn them against me."

"I am not turning them against you," Hunter argued in frustration. Expressing what was on his mind had never been his strength. Hell, having anything to express had rarely been an issue until he gave into his desires and seduced Anora. He wanted to tell himself it was a mistake, but he would never regret Anora. "I cannot accept failure in myself, and I will not let you, either."

"You do not get to determine what I will or will not do," she said, her voice sharp with displeasure.

"Your obstinance is going to get people killed. I am not trying to have a power struggle with you. Payne will use you against me and I will be powerless to it." He wanted to shake some sense into her but instead shook his head in frustration. "Your fearlessness is making you foolish."

"Your *fear* is making you foolish." He winced when she cupped his cheek in her hand but said nothing as she held his gaze. After a long moment, she dropped her hand and stepped away from him with her arms crossed protectively in front of her. "What is it you plan to do?"

"Payne is expected to remain at Montworth's holding for another couple days. If I leave now, I can get to Castle Whyte before nightfall. If the jewels are there, I will find them."

"And then what?" she asked impatiently.

"Then you appeal to Hawk to use his power as a nobleman to have the baron arrested." It was a baldfaced lie, but he didn't want to tell her the truth. She would have her answers if he found the jewels, but the baron would be dead before the king's justice could be imposed. Hunter had already judged the baron irredeemable and only his death would keep Anora safe from him.

He waited as Anora studied his face, and was relieved when she finally said, "I will do as you ask. I will stay at Hawkspur until you have returned, and the baron is gone from here. And to keep Galiena and the babes safe, I will stay in the castle if Lady Alyce and Hawk permit. But I am only giving you two days, Hunter."

"And if I'm not back in two days?"

She lifted her chin. "Then I return home to Oswestry. And pray that I find some other solution to keep Payne away from me and the shop."

"I will not let it come to that."

She stared at him evenly, her lips set in a thin line.

He knew he should leave and let her stay angry with him. It would be easier for both of them that way. But he couldn't do it. He reached for her and pulled her into a crushing embrace. She only hesitated for a breath before she wrapped her arms around his middle and held him to her. After a long moment, he kissed the top of her on the forehead then released her and turned to leave. He had no intention of looking back and wanted to be away from her as quickly as possible before he lost his determination.

As he reached the end of the corridor and started his descent of the stairs, he heard her call after him.

"Two days, Hunter! And then I take matters into my own hands."

✵ ⸻ ·◌◈◌· ⸻ ✵

Chapter Thirty-One

"YOU KEEP INTERESTING company, Lord Hawk," Baron Payne said with an arrogant sneer as he looked from Red on Hawk's right to Hunter who sat on his left.

It was fortunate for the baron that a wide plank table separated them because Hunter had the overwhelming urge to wrap his hands around Payne's neck and squeeze until his beady eyes bulged from their sockets.

They were sitting under a tent in the field beyond the stables. Hawk had wisely chosen to have the meeting out in the open where they could see who was listening to the conversation. He apparently didn't want the untrustworthy baron in or near his castle any more than was necessary either.

Baron Payne sat on a chair across the table from Hawk. He was flanked by two of his soldiers, but Hunter doubted they were actually men of any consequence. Neither of them looked like they were comfortable sitting at the table, and they'd not said a word since they sat down to face Lord Hawk at their commander's side.

"I understand you've met Hunter," Hawk drawled.

Payne nodded. "I wouldn't recommend him as your representative in the future as he's not very diplomatic."

Hunter narrowed his eyes at the arrogant cur as Hawk said,

"He's not meant to be diplomatic."

"What is he meant to be, then?"

"None of your business," Hunter growled.

"And this one?" Payne asked with an arrogant flip of his hand toward Red.

Red bared his teeth and growled low in his throat. Hunter had to bite his cheek to keep from laughing. The rugged Viking could be as wild and dangerous as he looked, but in truth he was big-hearted and jovial.

"Why are you here, Payne," Hawk demanded.

"I come with either an offering or a warning. Which one is dependent upon you," Payne said with a smugness that belied his standing in the realm when compared to Hawk.

"Get to the point," Hawk said, his irritation obvious.

"As Marcher lords, we hold power other lords in the realm only dream about. If the king tries to harness that power, it will start a war. With Wales conquered and the Welsh rebels tamed, there is talk that the king no longer wishes to recognize our autonomy."

"We are autonomous," Hawk agreed, "but I've heard no declaration from King Edward that he is going to change anything."

"He does not need to make a declaration. It is only a matter of time before he feels threatened by us. We must be prepared."

Hunter watched Hawk from the corner of his eye as he leaned forward to brace his forearms on the table. "And how do you suggest we prepare?" His voice was deceptively cool and even.

"An alliance," Payne stated simply, but a bead of sweat rolled down his temple and he shifted in his chair.

"With you?" Hawk's tone was thick with sarcasm.

"Aye," he said, indignant. "And others."

"Which others?" Hawk asked as he leaned back in his chair.

"I am not at liberty to say, but if you agree to an alliance and prove your worthiness to me, you will learn who the others are."

The corner of Payne's lip curled up as though he had just bested Hawk in some way, but his face fell, and his cheeks reddened when Hawk's booming laughter rang out.

"*You* will determine my worthiness?"

Payne nodded his head. His confidence had slipped, and his ears appeared to burn with his anger. "I don't think you know who you are dealing with. My family has held Castle Whyte for longer than you've been alive."

"I know very well who I am dealing with," Hawk said. "I know you are meeting with Gilbert de Clare, Earl of Gloucester, who is lacking in loyalty to the King Edward. I know you petitioned the king to be rewarded Hawkspur Castle as payment for your part in quelling the Welsh rebels and tried to take the demesne from my lady wife and me. And I know I don't like you, Payne."

Payne's lips were pressed into a hard line and his eyes blazed with hatred. "If that is the way of it, then there is no reason to continue this meeting."

"Finally," Hawk said in a flat voice. "Something we agree on."

Hunter stood, along with the other men in the tent, and it took all of his restraint not to lunge across the table at Payne for the torment he'd inflicted on Anora and her father. He didn't even try to hide his contempt for the deplorable man as they faced each other across the table.

Now his gaze locked with Hunter's. "The woman, Anora. You tried to conceal her from me this morning, but I knew it was her." Payne said. "Has she told you we have a history together? Her father has begged me to marry her as a favor to—"

Hunter's restraint snapped and he lunged across the table at Payne, and both men tumbled to the ground as chairs toppled around them. His fingers were closing around the baron's neck and the coward's face was turning purple by the time Red pulled him off the odious man.

As Payne was being helped to his feet by his men, Hunter

snarled through clenched teeth, "You fucking stay away from her and her family."

"You will regret this," Payne whined as he rubbed his neck.

Hunter made to lunge at him again, and the baron and his men practically ran from the tent.

"Escort them back to Montworth's border," Hawk ordered his men as Payne and his soldiers were mounting their horses. As they rode away, he turned to Hunter and said, "You may have started a war with the baron."

"Do you care?" Hunter asked in a low, angry voice.

"No," Hawk admitted.

Bard entered the tent, his typically handsome face as dark as thunder.

"What is it?" Hawk asked.

"The man we captured this morning leaving the fires confirmed what you expected."

"Hired by Payne," Hawk said.

"Aye," Bard answered, though Hawk hadn't stated it as a question. "He's part of a larger band of hired thugs. They were told to do whatever it takes to make it seem you are not strong enough to hold a castle in the Marches."

"Just the excuse Payne and Clare need to justify taking Hawkspur by force." Hawk gritted his teeth then slammed his fist down on the table. He turned to Hunter. "Get the evidence you need, then do with him as you will."

$$\text{·} \diamond \text{·}$$

Chapter Thirty-Two

"I RECOGNIZE A kindred soul in you."

Anora turned to see Lady Alyce standing a short distance away on the wall walk with a gentle look of understanding on her kind face. She'd been leaning on her elbows on the stone parapet, watching the village life below the castle wall as she racked her brain for what she could do to protect herself, her father, and the goldsmith shop from Baron Payne.

Folding her hands demurely in front of her, she nodded respectfully to the lady of the castle. "Pardon, my lady?"

"I prefer my friends call me Alyce," she said with a smile that helped to put Anora's restless nerves at ease. "I think you and I have something in common. This is my preferred place for when I have much on my mind that needs to be sorted."

Anora laughed lightly. "Is it so very obvious?"

Alyce moved to Anora's side and leaned against the parapet, resting her folded her hands on the stone as she looked out over the village. "It is. But even more apparent was Hunter's distress when he requested your protection here."

Anora's stomach was a roiling mess of conflicting emotions. Her heart ached for Hunter, but her pride still stung from his lack of faith in her. She feared for his safety knowing he was distressed, but much to her shame, felt perversely satisfied that he was as conflicted and tormented as she was over the situation.

"How can I be so angry with someone I love so much?" Anora felt the blood rush to her cheeks, embarrassed for blurting the question before she thought about what she was about to say.

"I believe it is *because* you love him so much." Alyce's lips curved in a small smile of understanding. "If it were not so, his actions would not be of such import. It is why I still get angry with Hawk."

"He causes you anger, even now? You have yet to come to an understanding?" Anora had hoped that if there was a future with Hunter, it would not involve so much conflict.

It was lady Alyce's turn to laugh. "Yes, he still angers me, as I do him, at times. Two strong-minded people will not always be of the same mind. But at the end of the day, I know Hawk to be good and kind, and I know he loves me and wants what is best for me." She leaned against the parapet and looked out over the village. "But he also knows I can be stubborn—too stubborn at times—and often when he challenges me it is because I am pushing for the sake of pushing instead of being honest with myself that my reasoning is not sound."

Anora felt her cheeks redden as she stood next to Alyce looking out over the village and admitted, "Another thing we have in common."

"Having said all that," Alyce arched a sleek auburn eyebrow as she spoke, "it did take time and training on my part to make him realize the full extent of my capabilities."

"That is the current struggle I am having," Anora conceded. "He does not think me capable of anything that involves risk."

"It is because of his fear of not being in control and not being able to protect you. For me, the struggle became easier when I admitted that I can be a hindrance to Hawk if he is more focused on keeping me safe than on dealing with the threat. Certain situations Hawk is more adept at handling, and in others I am more adept. Learn his strengths and learn yours. Remember that it is a game of giving and taking. There will be times for you to be bold, and there will be times for you to let Hunter do what he does best. With time, he will learn the same lesson."

"I've been determined for so long that I would not let a man force me to change," Anora lamented. "I want to be accepted for who I am."

"There is a difference between giving up who you are and realizing when to compromise. I am a better judge of that now. As is Hawk."

Anora sighed as she digested Lady Alyce's wisdom. "In truth, I understand Hunter's fear. Yesterday, when we did not know who had been shot with the arrow, I was sick with worry that it might be him. And when I saw him returned, whole and hale, I nearly collapsed with relief. It was the worst heartache I've ever experienced, and I do not know if I can live that way, wondering every time he leaves if he will be returning."

"I understand," Alyce said, her voice sympathetic. "Remember that the man you fell in love with is the man before you now—as he is now. If you ask him to stop being a protector, to stop being the prideful warrior he has been for most of his life, then he will no longer be the man you fell in love with. I think some measure of why we love them is because they are dangerous, untamable men who show their vulnerabilities and true heart only to us, and if we ask them to no longer be dangerous and untamable, then we are asking them to stop being the very thing we love."

Anora's heart twisted because there was truth in what she said. "Is it worth the pain and dread every time they leave?"

Alyce set her hand on top of Anora's where it rested on the stone wall. "Aye. It is."

✦ ⸺ ·◇· ⸺ ✦

Chapter Thirty-Three

ANORA WAS SITTING by the window in the hall sewing rag dolls for little Ani and Erik from scraps of fabric and ribbons provided by Lady Alyce. She planned to spend the afternoon with Galiena and the babies and wanted to finish the toys before she went.

"Milady," a polite voice said from behind Anora. She turned to see Tommy staring up at her, his expression more serious than usual. He wrung his hands, and his large brown eyes were wide with worry.

"What is it, Tommy?" She set down the rag doll, trying to quell the surge of panic that was clogging her throat. Hunter had ridden out the previous afternoon, after Hawk's meeting with Baron Payne concluded, to sneak into Castle Whyte in the dead of night again and search for the stolen jewels. "Has something happened to Hunter?"

As he shook his head, a lock of dark hair fell in front of his eyes and he stuck out his lower lip, huffing a breath to blow the lock to the side of his face. "'E's fine. At least, I think 'e's fine. I don' know nothin' 'bout 'im."

"Forgive me for interrupting, Tommy," Anora said, taking mercy on the poor boy. "Please, what is it you came to tell me."

"There's a lady at the gate," he said and pointed toward the back of the hall.

"At the front gate?" she asked as she pointed in the opposite direction toward the large front gate to Hawkspur Castle.

He shook his head again, and again the lock of hair fell in front of his eyes. This time he swiped at the hair with his hand. "The back gate."

Anora was immediately suspicious. She did not have any acquaintance here who would not feel comfortable coming through the front gate and directly to the hall if they wished to speak to her. "Did she say her name?"

Tommy nodded. "She said to tell you she is Beatrice, maid to Lady Ruby."

Anora felt the skin on her arms ripple with gooseflesh as she processed what the boy said. Beatrice was the woman from Madam Ruby's brothel who endured Baron Payne's perverse attention. If Madam Ruby had sent her to Hawkspur, perhaps that meant more of the stolen pendants and jewels had surfaced. "What else did she say? Did she give you anything to give to me?"

"She looked scared. Said to tell you she 'ad a message from 'er lady, but she couldn't wait too long for you. If she is gone when you get to the gate, she said you should go to Lady Ruby's to find 'er."

Anora looked around the hall, but the only other person there was the maid cleaning and stocking the buttery. When Baron Payne and his men left Hawkspur the prior afternoon with a contingent of Hawk's soldiers as escort, it was agreed she would stay within the confines of the castle and walled yard where the guards monitored anyone who entered through the gates. At least until Hunter's return.

"Is there a guard at the back gate?" Anora asked Tommy.

"Aye. 'U the 'uge."

It took a moment for Anora to understand. "Ah! Hugh the Huge?"

Tommy nodded, his brows pinching together in confusion. "'Tis what I said."

"A huge guard is good," Anora said, feeling better about the situation. "I will go now to see her." She would not have to step outside the guarded gate for Beatrice to deliver her message from Madam Ruby.

"Oh, e's not 'uge, milady. It's a jest. They call 'im that cuz 'e's not."

Anora sighed at that discouraging bit of news but decided he would not be assigned as guard if he were not competent.

Tommy scurried along beside her. Her unusual height and his lack of height forced him to run every other step to keep up with her. If the situation weren't urgent, she would have slowed her pace, but she wanted to get to Beatrice before she decided to leave. She was likely fearful of the baron or one of his men recognizing her, and unaware that they had already left Hawkspur.

The gate was nothing more than a narrow door in the wall that was secured with heavy bars at night, but it allowed easier access to those who brought food and supplies for the nearby kitchen.

"Where's 'U?" Tommy muttered as they drew nearer to the narrow door. "'E's supposed to be on this side of the door."

Beatrice was standing just beyond the door, wringing her hands and looking very uncomfortable to be away from the brothel.

"Is 'U there?" Tommy called to her, running in front of Anora.

"Aye," Beatrice answered, looking over her shoulder and pointing down the path. "He's helping a woman with her baskets." Turning back, she said to Anora, "Thank you for seeing me, milady."

"I am not a lady, Beatrice. You may call me Anora." The last time Beatrice had seen her, she was dressed in men's clothing, but she doubted the astute woman was fooled by her disguise. "What news have you?"

Tommy was still standing in front of Anora, as though trying to protect her until Hugh returned to his post. He rocked side to side trying to see around Beatrice.

Beatrice looked nervously around the castle yard, then stepped back to the other side of the door, out of sight of any passersby. Anora stopped just shy of the gate threshold and put her hands on Tommy's shoulders to keep him from bobbing like an eager ferret in front of her.

"Mad—" Beatrice pressed her lips together when she realized her near blunder. "*Lady* Ruby wanted you to know that she has received more pendants."

Anora released her hold on Tommy and took a step toward Beatrice. "Are you certain? Baron Payne has not been in Shrewsbury for some time."

Beatrice was vigorously nodding her head and backing away from Anora, but before the behavior fully registered in her brain as odd, someone reached from the side of the door and grabbed Tommy. A man in a plain tunic, like that of a farmer, stepped back to be near Beatrice, pulling Tommy with him as he held a hand over the boy's mouth and a knife to his throat. Anora opened her mouth to scream, but stopped when she saw a thin line of red dots start to form on Tommy's neck.

"Do not make a sound, and come forward now, my lovely, or I will slit the boy's throat from ear to ear," the man sneered in a low, harsh voice.

Despite being truly terrified that the man would kill Tommy anyway, Anora did as she was told, unwilling to let a child die because of her. Her heart nearly broke when she looked at the brave boy standing tensely in the man's grip, trying valiantly to shake his head *no* at her despite the hand clamped around his jaw. As she passed through the gate door, she saw from the corner of her eye a form lying prone against the outside of the castle wall. She glanced up and realized that the guards on the wall walk would not see Hugh unless they leaned out over the parapets, which meant his absence could go unnoticed for some time.

There were several men scattered along the path leading

from the back gate to the narrow road that led down to the valley below the castle, but when two turned and started walking away from the castle toward the road, and the other walked directly toward them with an ugly sneer on his face, she knew they would be of no help.

When they met up with the first man, he draped Anora in a plain brown woolen cape of a farmer with the hood up to hide her hair and mumbled a threat to Tommy that if he didn't want the lady to die, he was to stay quiet and cooperate. Tommy walked silently at her side, a scowl on his face and his lips pressed together.

Anyone looking down from the castle wall now would see what appeared to be a few tenant farmers, a woman, and a boy on their way back home after making a delivery to the castle. Until Hugh was found—Anora said a prayer that he would still be alive—there would be no reason to be suspect of the group. She turned her head just enough to see Beatrice staring straight ahead, her face set in stony, uncaring expression. Rage flared in her chest that she would take part in a ruse this cruel, but the hot surge of anger turned to pity when she saw the quiet tears flowing down Beatrice's cheeks. She was a victim in this just as much as Anora and Tommy were victims.

What this was, Anora was not yet certain, but she knew in her gut that Baron Payne was responsible for it. She should have been more afraid, but she was too angry at the coward. If Beatrice told him about her and Hunter coming to the brothel to ask questions about the pendants, then it was no longer a secret that Anora had the evidence that he was involved in the robbery from all those years ago that left her mother dead. If she'd had any doubts, the fact that he abducted her seemed just as much an admission of guilt as saying the words aloud.

Before this ordeal was over, whether it ended with her alive or dead, she would finally know the truth about Edmund Payne and whether or not he killed her mother.

A horsedrawn cart was waiting for them on the road. One of

the men grabbed Tommy, holding the knife to his throat again as he ordered Anora and Beatrice to climb into the wagon. The man then forced Tommy into the wagon, and followed behind him, seating himself between the boy and the women. Waving the knife between the two women, he said, "I don't want to hear a word from either of you, or I'll kill the boy. And if I think you are trying to signal each other," he shrugged and said nonchalantly, "I'll kill the boy for that, too."

One of the other men climbed onto the bench at the front of the cart and picked up the reins to guide the horse. The other two men walked ahead at the sides of the horse.

Anora's heart ached for the terror that Tommy must be feeling. She wished she could do something to assure him everything would be all right, but the guard was blocking him from seeing her, and she would be lying if she tried to tell him all would be well. Her heart sank with each passing moment as they trundled farther away from Hawkspur, and their chances of rescue diminished.

Closing her eyes, she said a prayer to the heavens to beg that no more harm would come to Tommy, and to plead for someone at Hawkspur to realize soon that they were missing. She still felt certain that once Hunter found out they were gone, he would stop at nothing to find her, despite the tense words they'd exchanged before he left.

Anora decided prayer alone would not be enough to escape this situation; she also needed to do her part to save them. Her small eating dagger was attached to her belt beneath her tunic. It wasn't enough to harm a man, but it could prove a useful tool. Looking around to see what else was at her disposal, she noticed a large hole in one of the floorboards of the cart where a tree knot had once been. It was near enough to her that she could slide her feet to either side of the hole so that it was covered by the cape wrapped around her. The voluminous cape was wrapped around her and hid her actions if she moved slowly. She removed the dagger from her belt and used it to tear at the threads of the chemise under her tunic. When she had a handful of little scraps of material, she started dropping them through the hole in the floorboards of the cart in the vain hope that Hunter might notice them on the road and be astute enough to realize they were a sign from her. While she ripped at her chemise and continued to drop bits of it onto the road under the cart, she also resumed praying that Hunter would find them soon.

If Baron Payne was behind this—and she was certain he was—she feared everything was going to get much worse for her and for Tommy once they were delivered into his hands.

Chapter Thirty-Four

HUNTER KNEW THE moment he saw the riders wearing surcoats with Hawk's insignia galloping toward him on the road that something had happened to Anora. And for the first time in his adult life, he felt his head spin and his limbs go slack with fear and dread. It felt like someone had knocked the breath from his lungs and drained the blood from his body.

"What news?" he called as soon as they were near, reining his mount to a halt. He recognized the two men who skidded to stop in front of him, their horses still prancing from the rush of galloping, but he could not recall their names.

"Lord Hawk has sent riders in all directions looking for you, and for Anora. She and the stableboy Tommy are missing, feared to be abducted from the castle."

Hunter roared in frustrated anguish, causing all of the horses to sidestep in circles. "Did anyone see what happened?" he asked once he'd caught his breath again.

The same guard added, "Wart saw them walking toward the back gate but was not concerned until he did not see them returning. When he went to the gate to look for them, Hugh was knocked out cold."

"When?" Hunter asked, nudging his horse into a trot, knowing the guards would keep pace.

"Three or four hours hence."

He looked to the west to judge the amount of daylight left, cursing when he realized he had maybe two hours before darkness fell. They were close to Hawkspur, only five miles, maybe less. He gave his horse his head and pushed him into a full gallop. He'd ridden one of Hawk's horses for the journey to give Shadow a rest and was grateful the horse had good legs and impressive speed.

He had no doubt Baron Payne was behind this. Hawk had sent a contingent of his soldiers to escort him and his men back to Baron Montworth's holding only a day ago and promised to keep an eye on them until they started the return journey to Castle Whyte.

The question was, where did he take her? He may have taken her to the holding of an ally, perhaps Montworth's fortress. Or was he bold enough to take her directly to Castle Whyte? His arrogance made him confident he was above reproach, and his castle was an impressive fortress that was nearly impenetrable—save for the secret escape tunnel that Payne didn't realize was not so secret anymore.

Hawk, Red, and Galiena were already awaiting him in the stables at Hawkspur Castle when he arrived. He'd left Shadow with the stablemaster in his absence and was relieved to see the stallion saddled and ready to ride when he entered the stable, as were several other horses. The leather saddlebags were bulging with supplies and tied in place on the backs of the horses.

"Tell me what you know," Hunter demanded gruffly of Hawk and Red.

"Eat this while you listen," Galiena said, handing him a chunk of warm bread drizzled with honey. Hunter shook his head, but she insisted, "You will do Anora no good if you fall from your horse because you didn't eat." A fierceness transformed her face into sharp points. "I'm counting on you to find her and bring her back. You need your strength."

He relented when she held the bread and a mug of ale up to

him again. His stomach roiled with hunger and fear, and the bread was like ashes in his mouth, but Galiena was right: He was of no use to Anora if he did not keep up his strength.

"I thank you," he said around a mouthful of bread to appease Galiena, then turned to Hawk and repeated his demand, "Tell me what you know."

"A woman came to the back gate by the kitchen," Hawk informed him, "claiming to be a maid of a Lady Ruby. Said her name was Beatrice, and that she had important news for Anora. Hugh sent Tommy to tell her of the woman, but he remembers little else after that."

"Beatrice? Maid of Lady Ruby?" Hunter was even more perplexed now. He found it hard to believe that Madam Ruby would betray Hunter to Baron Payne after the coin and protection he'd provided for her over the years. "You are sure of this?"

"Aye," Hawk continued. "Hugh regained consciousness a few hours ago. And though his head is splitting at the seams and aching like someone is pounding a drumbeat on his skull, he remembers clearly the woman who came to the gate. What he doesn't remember is how he was knocked out, or who did it, but he does recall some men standing a distance behind her. He thinks one of them may have lured him over the gate threshold before hitting him over the head."

Hunter took a long swig of the ale to wash down the last of the honeyed bread. "I'm sure there is no sign of Beatrice anywhere near Hawkspur now."

"Aye, you are right," Hawk conceded. "We are not sure how she convinced Anora to come to the gate, and we are not clear on the events that transpired once Anora arrived there."

"I do not take her to be a fool, or one easily duped," Red said, smoothing his beard over his chin. "This Beatrice must have presented her with a compelling reason to come to the gate."

"She is from Madam Ruby's brothel in Shrewsbury. We met with Madam Ruby and Beatrice before coming here to find out more about the pendants they received from Payne's. If Beatrice showed up saying she had a message from Madam Ruby, Anora would have been interested."

"Do you think Madam Ruby is working with Payne?" Red asked.

Hunter shook his head. "We've had a working relationship for several years and I don't believe she would so easily betray me. Beatrice is a favored harlot of Payne's and was likely put up to this without Madam Ruby's knowledge. Edmund has mistreated Beatrice in the past and would not be above beating her until she complied." Digging into the pouch at his side, he pulled out a rolled bit of parchment and handed it to Hawk. "Payne has been overspending for too long to make himself look more important than he is. This is the current ledger he has with the money lender in Knighton, after leaving this as partial payment more than a fortnight past." He reached down into his boot and pulled out a small gold pendant with intertwining vines encrusted with a total of eight gems.

"Is it from the trove of stolen jewels?" Hawk asked, leaning over to inspect the piece in the palm of Hunter's hand.

"Yes. Frode made a similar pendant for his wife every year to commemorate their time together. Each one had as many gems as the years commemorated. It's a unique design and nearly identical to the ones Madam Ruby received from Payne as payment."

Hawk reviewed the ledger, which showed promises from Payne to provide wool to the merchant in June at a reduced price in return for payment months before the shearing season. "June has long since passed, and I presume the merchant did not get his wool."

"Correct," Hunter confirmed. "And he has since discovered he is not the only merchant Payne was borrowing money from with the promise of selling them his wool in the summer at a reduced price to match the money loaned to him during the previous year."

"It is little wonder he covets Hawkspur, then. He will soon

lose everything if he does not find a revenue stream."

Red gave a derisive snort. "He'd squander the money and ruin the land, just as he's done with his father's estate."

"There is one more piece of news," Hawk said. "The man captured from the raid on the hamlet has confessed to being a mercenary hired by Payne. I am readying a contingent of men, which Bard and I will lead to Castle Whyte in your wake. But four men are ready to ride with you now, along with Red."

"I owe you more than my thanks," Hunter said as he clasped forearms with his commander.

"Go, find Anora and bring her back. The confession of the hired marauder is enough to justify my retaliation, but abducting your woman along with the mounting proof he robbed her family and killed her mother justifies your vengeance."

⁂

Chapter Thirty-Five

T HE SUN WAS beginning to set when the cart rolled into Welshpool, and Anora prayed they would stop somewhere for the night. The longer it took them to get to wherever they were going, the more time Hunter had to catch up to them. She kept searching for ways to prolong the trip and the inevitable audience with Edmund Payne—for she had no doubt Payne was behind this despite the silence of her captors.

The men who had walked alongside the cart when they left Hawkspur were now mounted, having retrieved their horses from a clearing in the forest some miles from castle, and now flanked the cart in the front and back as they rode. There was one man driving the wagon, and one seated in the back to ensure Anora felt properly threatened every time she opened her mouth to speak or shifted positions. Tommy sat with his back straight as an arrow as he stared straight ahead in an impressive display of bravery and grit. Beatrice was huddled under her own cape, refusing to make eye contact with Anora.

Anora was stiff from sitting on the low wooden bench in the back of the wagon, cold from the heavy mist that had plagued them for the last hour or more, irritated by the particularly strong stench of the wet wool cape, and angry that her captor was quick to put the blade to Tommy's throat anytime she moved or opened her mouth to speak. Anora had asked to share her cape with Tommy, who had been shivering for the past hour, but the cruel man had refused, offering to put the boy out of his misery if the damp chill was too much for him.

From the corner of her eye, she studied the man in the cart. In her mind, she had named him Clay Face because his features were distorted from what she assumed were too many broken noses and blows to the head. His nose was flattened, as though someone had started to fashion it from clay then quit before adding any defining features other than a distinct curve where one did not belong. His brow and cheekbones were prominent but oddly shaped with flat planes in unexpected places.

He looked to be similar in age to herself, and she wondered if he had a wife somewhere, or children. If he did, he was possibly the coldest person she'd ever had the misfortune to encounter. She couldn't imagine anyone who was a father themselves being able to so callously threaten the life of a boy—and even draw blood to demonstrate his willingness to follow through with his threat. There was a line of dried blood on Tommy's throat where Clay Face had touched the blade to his skin to ensure Anora's cooperation.

When they reached the crossroads in the center of the village, they did not turn toward the east in the direction of Castle Whyte as she expected but instead turned northwest on a narrow road that was not much more than a path, leading deeper into Wales. She questioned for the first time her assumption that Baron Payne was behind her abduction. She tried not to panic, but the thought of facing an unknown foe was somehow far more terrifying than facing the enemy she knew.

She'd never cared for him, even as a young girl. He was arrogant, condescending, and spiteful as a young man, and becoming a baron had not changed him. But, until recently, she had the mistaken impression that the friendship and mutual respect their fathers shared would protect them from any real harm from Edmund. She realized how wrong she was in that assumption.

Regardless of who was behind the abduction, devising an escape for her and Tommy was paramount. And the farther they got into unfamiliar territory, the more difficult it would be for her to find her way back.

"Please, can we not stop to attend to matters of nature?" Anora asked, as she leveled an unwavering gaze at Clay Face, despite his immediate response of putting the blade to Tommy's throat. For his part, Tommy sat still with a look of pure boredom on his face, and a surge of pride in the boy's bravery emboldened her. "Unless you prefer I piss right here, which will make the entire wagon reek of it."

"We will stop soon. You will have to wait until then." Clay Face had a perpetual sneer on his face and a voice laced with contempt.

"Fine," she said succinctly, turning to look straight ahead again. "But not too long or we will all regret it." She had kept quiet to this point because she feared for Tommy, but she would not cower in front of these men. And the moment she could get Tommy away from them and to safety, she would be done cooperating.

Clay Face was true to his word; they stopped a short while later at the side of the trail next to a clearing. Dusk was turning everything pale and shrouded, but she could see a single horse hobbled and grazing while its master rested against the trunk of a tree. As the man stood and walked toward them, Anora recognized the distinctive swagger of Edmund Payne.

"I was right," Anora snapped, pushing to her feet in the cart. "It was you."

Clay Face jumped to his feet at the same time, pulling Tommy up with him, but Edmund held up a hand to stay the man before he did anything stupid, much to her relief.

Perhaps there was hope of getting out of this alive.

"Tell me, Anora, what do you think this is?" Edmund's voice was steady, and cold as ice.

She glared at him for a long moment, then perched on the

side of the wagon, swung her legs over and dropped to the ground in front of him. The action made sparks shoot up her legs, made numb by hours in the wagon, but she refused to let her discomfort show. "At the very least, it is an abduction. What right do you have to do this?" Her indignation over the matter far outweighed her fear of the situation in this moment.

"Have you forgotten?" he said with cool indifference. "I am a baron. A noble lord from a noble birth." He prowled slowly but steadily toward her. "You, Anora, are not noble. The daughter of a rich merchant? Yes. Beautiful? Yes. But not of the same class. Unless I choose to make you a noblewoman."

"That does not give you the right to abduct me by force," Anora reminded him. She had no idea what he was trying to prove with his little speech, but even a nobleman was not above the laws of the realm.

"And who is going to naysay me on your behalf?" He stepped menacingly closer to her as he spoke.

Anora noticed the fine lines that had begun to form on his face, and that the hair at his temples streaked with strands of silver, in sharp contrast to the rest of his dark hair, which he kept neatly shorn close to his skull. In every way, he was Hunter's opposite: short hair that did not touch even his ears in contrast to Hunter's hair that hung to his shoulders and curved around his face; sharp features that made Edmund appear imperious compared to Hunter's rugged handsomeness; eyes that were black and cold and so dissimilar from Hunter's warm green eyes flecked with gold and rimmed in dark lashes. Everything about Edmund was sharp, scornful, and repulsive, making Anora's skin crawl as he stalked closer to her.

"Perhaps you believe your lover will save you. He is your lover, is he not?" His tone was almost pleasant but still made her skin crawl. When he was within arm's reach of her, he tipped his head to the side and arched a thick eyebrow at her. "Hunter, is that his name?" He flicked his hand dismissively. "It is of no matter. He is nothing more than a hired sword arm. Expendable.

Worthless. Someone paid to do his lord's bidding." His upper lip curled as though he was referring to the filthy vermin that scurry around in the sewage. "Someone who will not be missed."

Anora felt her knees shake beneath her gown, and her stomach twisted in apprehension. That she would feel terrorized by this man vexed her because that was exactly what he wanted from her: fear.

She would not give it to him.

But she could give Hunter time by stalling their progress for as long as possible. She had faith he'd find her, and she planned to do everything in her power to hinder Edmund and aid Hunter. Squaring her shoulders and leveling her haughtiest stare at him, she said, practically spitting the words, "I don't need some man to naysay on my behalf. I speak for myself. Tell me your reason for this and be done with it. What is it you want?"

He laughed then, a sinister, mirthless laugh. "You, Anora. You know that. You are a fine trophy and would make me the envy of every nobleman who did not deem me noble enough to marry any of their daughters. I've decided *mistress* is no longer enough for my purposes."

"I do not want you. That was made clear the first time I refused your proposal." He was insane if he thought she would marry him after all that he had done to her family.

"That matters not to me," he said with a shrug of his shoulders. "What matters to me is that I will get you as wife and your fortune when your father dies—"

Anora gasped. "How dare you be so callous about a man who treated you like a son?"

"He tolerated me, just as my father did. Do you know how many times I had to listen to my father compare me to your brother? Baldwin could do no wrong in his eyes."

"Baldwin, unlike you, was an honorable man." Anora took a step backwards to put more distance between her and Edmund. "As was your father."

"They were weak men. Baldwin is dead, as is my father, and

your father has one foot in the grave already."

"He is still a better man than you could ever be."

"Enough," Edmund spat. "If your Hunter is on his way, then we must go now. I will best him, but I would sooner do it at Castle Whyte. Lord Hawk cannot pursue retribution if I kill the man while defending my fortress."

"You could never best Hunter," she hissed between gritted teeth.

The dusk had nearly turned to darkness, which made it harder to see the expression on Edmund's face in response to her words. It also made it harder for her to see the hand that he lifted and cracked across her face with the speed of lightning. The sound and vibration reverberated in her head as she stood in stunned confusion while she willed her knees not to buckle. Her cheek bone felt like it had shattered into a thousand pieces, the pain blurred her vision, and she could taste blood on her lip.

A chill ran down her spine as she looked at Edmund. She hadn't wanted to truly believe it before when she'd seen the beaten Beatrice, but now she was certain the man standing in front of her was capable of killing her mother. And he would not hesitate to kill her.

The buzzing in her ears subsided and the scraping sounds of a scuffle behind her penetrated her brain. She turned to see Tommy as he struggled to climb over Clay Face, who put an end to the outburst with a swift cuff to his ear.

"I am all right, Tommy," she said in a low voice.

"Get back in the wagon," Edmund ordered as he flexed the fingers of his offending hand.

"Where are you taking us?" she asked as she gingerly touched her jaw and cheek to assess the damage. Thankfully, nothing felt broken despite everything in her head feeling like it had exploded.

"Get in the wagon and you will find out." When she didn't move quick enough for Edmund's liking, he took a step toward her. "Would you like me to throw you in the wagon myself?"

Anora did not want the odious man to touch her. She turned

back to the cart and leveled a glare at Clay Face. "Move your legs so I may gain access." She waited until he bent his legs and moved them out of the way so she could clumsily climb onto the cart. She gave Tommy a small smile of reassurance, then moved to the front of the cart and plopped down on the bench.

Thunder rolled in the sky overhead and raindrops spattered on her face.

The cart jerked as the horse resumed his course on the trail. A hollow, hopeless feeling settled in her bones as the rain progressed from sprinkles to steady, solid sheets of water. It soaked her head and ran in cold streams down her neck, but she did nothing to stop it, just as she did nothing to stop the disconsolate tears that streamed down her cheeks.

Chapter Thirty-Six

A NORA DID NOT think she could sink any lower into the depths of despair, but she was wrong.

The cart had continued on the trail, despite the building storm, until they reached the yard of a small parish church surrounded by a smattering of small huts, one larger hut, and a barn. They were unloaded from the cart and brought to the door of one of the small huts by a man garbed in priest's robes. Three of the guards took the horses and cart to the barn. Anora was ushered through the door into the hut by Edmund, followed by Beatrice, Tommy, Clay Face, and finally the priest.

The hut consisted of one sparse room with two narrow beds, a table, two chairs, one chest, a few hooks on the wall, and a single shelf that held wooden cups, bowls, and a small kettle. A larger kettle was hanging from a hook over the fire in the center of the room, the smoke curling upward to a hole in the center of the roof. Her stomach growled at the scent of stew gravy as it wafted through the hut.

"Get warm, have some food," the priest offered, though not kindly. "I will be waiting in the church when you are ready, Baron Payne." He was a tall, thin man with sharp features and a bald head, which gave him an ominous look. There was nothing comforting or pious about him as he eyed both Anora and

Beatrice with disdain, then ducked through the doorway and closed the door to the little hut.

"I had expected this to be a brief stop," Edmund said. He pulled out a chair to sit at the table. "But if the rain does not end soon, we will not be able to continue to our next destination even without the cart."

"And where is that?" Anora asked, unable to hide the contempt in her voice.

"A quaint little inn, just up the road," he said with a sneer.

"Why would we go there?" she pressed.

"Donald," he said as he motioned to Clay Face. "Fetch me a bowl of stew. And one for the lady." He motioned to Anora to take the chair opposite him. "Sit."

She did so reluctantly. Her instinct was to defy him, but she needed to be smarter if she and Tommy wanted to get out of this alive. As much as it galled her, now was the time to acquiesce and save her defiance for later. Her head still throbbed from the blow to the cheek, and she did not wish to suffer another.

Edmund jutted his chin at Tommy. "Grab a bowl of stew for you and Beatrice to share. Sit on the bed there and neither of you speak or move unless told."

Donald ladled stew into a bowl, stuck a wooden spoon in it, and set it in front of Edmund. Then he did the same for Anora but included a disapproving glare as he pushed the bowl toward her. He filled a bowl for himself and sat on one of the narrow beds while Tommy and Beatrice sat on the other, passing the bowl and spoon back and forth as they ate.

Anora's stomach had been growling just a few moments before, but the thought of actually putting food in her mouth while she sat across from Edmund nauseated her. The way he watched her every move made her skin crawl. Did he enjoy looking upon the damage he had done to her face? Did it give him some sense of satisfaction? Superiority?

She turned her chair so that she did not face him directly, then picked up the spoon and forced herself to eat. If she wanted to escape—if the opportunity presented itself—then she would need the energy the food provided. She focused on the drops of rain that came in through the smoke hole in the roof and dripped down onto the fire to sizzle on the hot coals. The heat from the fire felt good on her face, and she hoped the warmth would reach Tommy where he sat on the bed. The poor child had not had the benefit of a cloak and was soaked through.

She shivered under the damp cloak and stood, aware of Edmund's eyes on her as she walked across the room, untied the cloak from around her neck, and hung it on a peg, then returned to the table to force herself to eat several more bites of the stew.

When she couldn't stomach any more of the bland concoction, she handed her bowl to Tommy. He'd been pale and shivering when they first entered the hut, but the heat from the fire and warm food in his belly had put color back in his cheeks. She didn't dare say anything to the boy for fear Edmund would find some way to use it against her. Instead, she gave his fingers a quick squeeze as he took the bowl, which he acknowledged with a small nod of his head while keeping his eyes averted from hers. He truly was a brave and intuitive boy, and when they got out of this situation—which she had to believe they would—she would let Hawk and Lady Alyce know what an amazing young man they had working in their stables.

Her nerves snapped with tension, and she felt too jumpy to sit. She stood with her hands to the fire and watched the flames dance as she tried to think of a way out of this situation. Even if they escaped, she didn't know where they were or whom to trust. The priest was obviously Payne's man and would be of no help.

Edmund pushed up from the table to stand in front of her and extended his hand, palm up toward her. Anora looked at his outstretched hand, then lifted her eyes to his face and pinched her brows together in question.

"Come with me," he said.

"Where?" she asked warily.

"To speak to the priest."

"I have no need to speak to the priest." Her stomach felt like it was weighed down with a leaden ball of dread. A ludicrous thought flit through her mind as to what Edmund Payne's intentions were for wanting her to go before the priest with him.

Edmund narrowed his eyes at her as an undeniable spark of anger flashed in his dark eyes. "Donald, bring the boy and your knife."

Anora jumped to her feet. "Leave him out of this, Edmund."

"Does this mean you will comply, sweeting?"

She hated the sound of the endearment on his lips, and it galled her to do his bidding. "I will accompany you to speak with the priest."

"Good girl." His condescending tone sent a wave of repulsion to her stomach. He turned to Donald. "Bring the boy in case she thinks to change her mind."

Anora bit into her lip to keep from panicking. She had to keep her wits about her. The chances of being rescued were thinning, but she would do everything in her power to save herself and Tommy. Hunter would find them. She *had* to believe in him, and she would do what she could to give him the time and clues he needed to get to them before something terrible happened.

Edmund took her by the elbow and tried to turn her toward the door, but she jerked her arm out of his hand, took her cloak from the hook, and yanked the door open. She didn't bother to put the cloak over her shoulders but rather held it over her head as a shield from the rain for the short walk to the church. Once outside, she waited until Donald emerged with Tommy, then stubbornly extended the edge of the cloak to cover the boy's head as well. The act earned her a scornful look from Donald, but he did not deter her.

It was a small victory, but a victory, nonetheless.

Inside the stone church, the priest paced behind an altar covered with cloth upon which sat a large, ornate Bible. He stopped and stood tall behind the altar to look at them as they approached the front of the sanctuary. In one corner behind him a candelabra held about a dozen burning tapers which emitted light over the stark interior. The other corner was draped with a curtain with one side tied back to reveal an elaborately carved chair and a wide stool. Anora assumed this was meant to be a confessional, but she shivered at the thought of being alone with the priest in that little space while sitting on the stool at his feet.

Anora draped the cloak over her folded hands and turned in a circle to assess the rest of her surroundings. Tapestries hung from the walls on either side of her—she assumed to keep the rain from coming in through the window openings—and a long bench sat against the wall below each tapestry.

"Come forward, child," the priest said, his voice devoid of caring, enthusiasm, or any hint of emotion as he crooked a finger at her.

Squaring her shoulders, Anora did as directed but stopped several paces from the altar.

"Closer." The word was sharp and loud, a sure indication of his irritation with her. She lowered her eyes and stepped closer, trying to give the impression of an obedient member of his flock. Her situation was dire, and though the priest seemed an unlikely ally, it would be foolish of her to make an enemy of him as of yet.

"What is your name?"

"Anora, Father…" She realized she did not know his name and lifted her eyes in question.

"Father Osric," he provided as he studied her face with a scowl.

She suspected the blow to her cheek had caused a nasty bruise. Already, the right side of her face felt tender and stiff, which made it uncomfortable to speak. She prayed that the priest would take pity on her and show mercy, perhaps even offer her sanctuary.

"Tell me, Anora, are you in good standing with the church?" His eyes shifted so that he was looking upon the unmarred side of her face.

Her heart sank. If Father Osric so easily ignored the proof that

Edmund had beat her, then there was no hope that she could convince him to be her savior.

"Do you attend services as you should? Are you in need of confession?" His voice was flat and monotone.

Anora cringed. She did not attend church regularly, and she could not recall exactly how long it had been since her last confession. In truth, the priest in Oswestry, Father Perry, scared her with his prophecies of doom, and with the way he harrumphed during her confessions and told her she was near-to-beyond saving. Her cheeks reddened at the thought of confessing the time spent in Hunter's arms and the deeds they'd done together of late. Father Perry would have a fit.

"Do not be afraid to tell the truth," Father Osric encouraged. He was very similar to Father Perry in his demeanor, but they looked nothing alike. Perhaps they were trained to be so stoic and cold in the same monastery.

"I am in good standing." She tried not to flinch as she lied to the priest, and she prayed God would forgive her for not trusting Father Osric and his intentions. Fortifying her courage, she continued, "I find it hard to believe Baron Payne abducted me and brought me here just for you to hear my confession. Will you tell me why I am here, Father?"

Father Osric looked from Anora to Edmund, the unease apparent in his widened eyes.

"Do not be so obtuse, my dear," Edmund said. His nearness startled her. She had not heard his approach, yet he stood almost directly at her side. His lips were contorted into a smile but there was no kindness or joy in his expression. "You are well aware why we are here. For our nuptials, of course. The priest has agreed to stand as witness."

Anora spun on her heel to face the baron. "I will *never* marry you."

He pivoted to stand in front of her, blocking her from the priest's view. In a low, menacing voice, he said, "I suggest you take some time to think about the consequences if you do not amend your response." He grabbed her upper arm in a crushing grip and led her to the back of the church. There he wrapped a hand in the front of Tommy's tunic and twisted as he lifted the boy nearly off his feet. "Do you want to see this boy have the skin peeled from his bones in slow, excruciating strokes? Donald is quite skilled with a blade."

Anora's knees wobbled and her stomach lurched so forcefully she had to swallow to keep the contents down. She tried to appeal to his vanity. "You are a lord now and your influence must surely be growing with your alliances. You are deserving of a noble woman for wife, and I am not noble."

"We discussed this already. You will make a pretty trophy, worthy of envy, and your father is wealthy, or at least wealthy enough to provide the funds I need until my other prospects come to fruition." Baron Payne released Tommy with a dismissive shove and pushed him back into the grip of Donald. "I could ask the king for a noble woman, but he has proven a disappointment in that regard. His rewards are not equal to the value of what I have done for the expansion of his realm. The daughter of a wealthy merchant is still considered a worthy bride, and I want others to be jealous of my good fortune when they see your beauty as you walk by my side. Most especially, that bastard-born, worthless peasant Hawk allows to run roughshod with disrespect." He flashed her a wicked smile. "Making you my wife, knowing you are naked in my bed, will drive him mad."

She felt his gaze like an unwanted touch as it moved slowly over her body, then back up to her face. He took her chin between his forefinger and thumb. "Now, we are going to say the words in front of the priest to make you my wife. Unless you you'd prefer to watch Donald carve up the boy."

Even in the dim light from the candelabra across the room, Anora could see the horror in Tommy's eyes and the way his lips worked as he tried to maintain his composure. She could not blame him for being afraid—Heavens above knew she was terrified out of her mind! Tommy had been threatened with bodily harm before as a cutpurse and thief, and was not easily frightened, but she suspected this was the closest to real harm he'd ever come.

"Let Tommy go first, and I will cooperate," Anora said. Her mouth felt dry and tasted of ash.

Edmund studied her for a moment, eyes narrowed, then shook his head. "I think not. I know you better than you realize, Anora. You are going to fight me every step of the way unless Donald keeps a knife to his throat."

The odious guard slid a long dagger from his boot, the candlelight glinting on the silver blade as he held it up in front of Anora's face. She didn't miss the look on Tommy's face just beyond the dagger, the way his eyes widened just slightly, and his shoulders dropped back as he came to attention. Anyone else may have mistaken his reaction as one of increased fear, but she knew it was the excitement of an opportunity that had him suddenly more alert. She gave him an almost imperceptible shake of her head, relieved when his eyes shoulders drooped with disappointment.

He'd been a talented little thief when he lived on the lanes of Oswestry, and she knew he had already calculated in his head how to steal the knife. As advantageous as it would be to them if he stole the dagger from Donald, the timing of the theft was critical. Stolen too soon, and it would cause more trouble for Tommy, but if he waited until the right moment, it could be very useful. She didn't yet know when that moment might be, but she felt certain the time was not now.

"Is there a problem, baron?" Father Osric called from the other end of the room.

"No, Father," Edmund replied over his shoulder. He turned on his heel, his eyes still on Anora, and held out his forearm. "My lady?"

She refused his arm but took a deep breath while she racked her brain for a way out of this situation as she walked back to stand in front of Father Osric. He looked down his nose at her, then looked at Baron Payne as he joined her in front of the altar.

Father Osric sighed and shifted uncomfortably, then said to Anora, "I ask again, will you require confession before saying the words that will bind you to this man in matrimony?"

"No," Baron Payne interjected before Anora could respond.

Anora was surprised to see a quick flash of discomfort in the priest's eyes. Something more than irritation. Was he afraid of the baron?

"Is there any reason this union would not be deemed legitimate in the eyes of the church?' he continued, eyeing them both.

"No, Father," Edmund said through gritted teeth.

Anora said nothing, unable to speak past the lump in her throat as an image of Donald scraping Tommy's skin with the knife filled her mind.

Father Osric hesitated but continued when the baron cleared his throat with force. "With God as your witness, do you take this woman to be your lawful wife?"

"Yes, Father," the baron said solemnly.

"And you, my lady, do you take the baron to be your lawfully wedded husband? Will you take his counsel in all things, provide him the comfort of your body, and bear his children?"

She felt the crushing weight of pain and regret on her chest. If she allowed this to happen, she would be bound to the despicable man at her side for the remainder of her life. Or his. She squeezed her eyes shut to try to shut out the pain, but the tears overflowed and rolled down her cheeks. She tried to reason with herself that she must say the words or Tommy would suffer the consequences of her actions, but she was paralyzed.

The words turned over in her head—take his counsel, provide comfort with her body, bear his children—it all sounded so horrible. She understood why some women threw themselves from the highest tower they could find rather than face a lifetime of misery and disgust with a horrible husband. How could she let him touch her when she would spend the rest of her life longing for Hunter, remembering his touch, the pleasure in his arms?

"Say the words," Edmund bit out through gritted teeth.

If she said the words, and if she…heaven help her, if she was forced to consummate the marriage with the baron, then there would be no undoing what had been done.

"Say them," he commanded again.

The priest's gaze was darting back and forth between the two of them, his discomfort increasing with each passing moment that she remained silent.

Edmund finally broke the silence, saying with a flick of his hand, "Do as you will, but the priest will attest that he heard you say the words. No one will dare question him. Or a baron."

Anora squeezed her eyes shut and hoped when she opened them again, she would wake from this nightmare.

Counsel.

Comfort.

Children.

Her eyes flew open wide as inspiration struck her like a bolt of lightning. "Children!"

Edmund looked at her like she'd just said the most absurd thing. "Aye, children. I will expect an heir."

Anora turned to him, unable to keep the excitement from her voice. "But you will want to be sure the heir is truly of your blood."

He narrowed his eyes at her and curled his lips in disgust. "Of course, it will be of my blood. I will not tolerate a whore for a wife and if you should think to make a cuckold of me, you will live to regret it."

Anora ignored the baron's outburst and blurted, "We cannot consummate this wedding."

"What?" both the baron and the priest said at the same time.

"If you want to be sure any offspring are of your loins," Anora cringed at the words and the images it conjured, "then you will need to wait until you can be certain I am not already with child."

Baron Payne studied her for a long moment, then returned his attention to the priest. "She does not know of what she speaks, Father."

"Do you understand…" The priest seemed at a loss for words. "Do you understand what must happen for you to become with child? What must happen between a man and a woman?"

"Aye, Father, I *do* understand," she said. In any other circumstances, she would be mortified by the question and the confession, but in this moment, it was her only hope to deter, or at least delay, the baron's intentions. But would it be at the cost of her life or Tommy's? It was too late now to turn back. She splayed her hands across her stomach. "I have lain with a man and may be carrying his child."

Father Osric looked stricken, unsure of how to proceed.

Edmund grabbed her by the elbow and spun her to face him. "You may be with Hunter's child?" The words were bit out in an angry staccato. His eyes looked crazed, and his chest heaved.

Anora's heart raced with the fear that she had made a grave mistake. She nodded. "Aye, Hunter."

Edmund snapped his mouth closed and his lips pinching into a thin, white line. They both stared at each other with their jaws clenched tightly and their eyes locked in confrontation. After several tense moments, the baron released her arm, took a deep breath, and turned toward the priest. "Proceed," he growled.

Anora panicked and said the first thing to come to her mind. "Are you willing to risk that the first child born into our marriage is of Hunter's blood and not yours?" She expected the baron's rage this time, and managed to duck and dodge to the side before his hand could connect with her face. He grabbed her by the arms and shook her hard so that her head snapped back and forth painfully.

"Stop," Father Osric shouted. "You will not desecrate the church."

Edmund's hands dropped his hands to his side as he looked from the priest to Anora. Hatred burned in his eyes as he said in a flat voice, "Donald, get my horse and bring it to me, saddled." His eyes narrowed into a wicked gleam that sent a chill down Anora's spine.

"Do you want anyone to ride with you?" Donald asked.

"Tell Hankin and Noll to prepare their horses to accompany me," he sneered, then added in an ominous tone, "It will not be me wondering if my first born is the spawn of a bastard, but rather the bastard wondering if his first born is of my seed instead of his."

Anora felt like she'd been punched in the stomach and was instantly nauseous. True terror washed over her as she felt the blood drain from her face.

"And the boy?" Donald asked.

"Take him and the whore in the opposite direction of Castle Whyte and dump them where their bodies will be easily found. No one will care about a harlot and an orphan being killed, but it will serve as a clear message to Hunter and Lord Hawk that if they interfere, I will kill Anora next." He cupped Anora's bruised cheek and smiled with pleasure when she winced. "But not before I've shown you what it feels like to have a real man between your thighs."

She felt the blood run into her mouth as she bit her cheeks to keep from screaming. Tommy did not deserve to die because of her. Nor did Beatrice. "I will marry you now," she said, her voice scratchy and hoarse with disgust and defeat, "if you spare the lives of Tommy and Beatrice."

Edmund's eyebrows shot up. "The time for bargaining is past, love."

Anora nearly cringed at the endearment but stopped herself lest she anger him more. "I will marry you, you will get the benefit of my father's fortune, and I will do what I can to advance your political ambitions." She could tell by the look on his face that he considered what she offered. "My acquaintance with the Lord and Lady of Hawkspur, and my familiarity of their holdings can be of use to you."

"You do realize I am not seeking an alliance with Hawkspur? I have every intention of taking it."

She swallowed uncomfortably as she nodded. "I do."

He studied her for a long moment. "If you prove you can be trustworthy, Anora, you and I can accomplish much together. With your cunning as Lady of Castle Whyte and my strength as Lord, we can become a barony of importance."

Anora felt the tears prick at her eyes, but she held them back. "Aye, Edmund"—his name felt like a curse on her tongue— "perhaps I was hasty in my refusal of you."

"I do not trust that you are not lying to me to save yourself," he said as he dug under his tunic for something attached to his belt, "but with time, I think you will see the wisdom of your words. And in the meantime, I will keep Tommy as hostage to guarantee your cooperation."

Another small victory.

He turned to Father Osric and ordered, "She is ready to say the words, Father."

Anora's body felt numb, and her ears buzzed as she repeated the words given to her by the priest to bind their union. She didn't resist when Edmund lifted her hand and held it in his own, and his words hardly registered as she stared blankly at his face. He muttered something about a memento to represent his devotion to her, he even referenced the happiness and love shared by her parents, though she didn't want to hear it. But then he slipped something on her finger and her entire world turned upside down.

She splayed her hand and looked down at the ring he'd placed on her right hand. It was an intricately carved gold ring with a brilliant emerald set into the band. It was the most beautiful ring she'd ever seen but now wasn't the first time seeing it, for she already knew every tiny detail of the ring, every curve of the ornate design around the band, every shade of green in the gem as it was turned in the light.

She knew everything about it because it had been her mother's ring.

Chapter Thirty-Seven

H UNTER WALKED UP to the portcullis gate of Castle Whyte soaked through from the cold rain and flanked by two of Payne's guards.

"What have we got here?" a guard behind the gate asked as they approached.

"Found him nosing around in the forest just beyond the clearing," one of Payne's guards responded.

"Is that so?" the gate guard responded as he motioned for the portcullis to be lifted. "What business did you have in the forest, boy?"

Hunter did not respond.

The guard to the right of him cuffed him on the back of the head. "You were asked a question."

Hunter bit down on his lip to keep himself from killing the man. "I was looking for fairy folk."

The guards looked at him quizzically, and the guard who cuffed him said, "Same shite he told us."

The portcullis was lifted and the gate guard stepped forward. "Little thick in the head, aren't you?"

Hunter shrugged.

"Bring him to the hall," the gate guard ordered. "Payne is there and will decide what to do with him."

The portcullis clanged behind Hunter as it lowered back into place to secure the castle. As they walked across the bailey toward the hall, Hunter scanned the castle walls, assessing the amount of security Payne had in place. Four guards walked each section of the wall, which was more than he typically had, but the fortress was not as fortified as he would have expected considering the baron had kidnapped a woman and a child from the holding of a rival lord and that retaliation was inevitable.

Red and the four Hawkspur soldiers who rode with Hunter to Castle Whyte were hidden in the forest near to where Hunter had created enough of scene to attract the guards and get captured. The day was early, and despite the rain and heavy cloud cover, it was still not dark enough for them to access the secret tunnel that would bring them into the chapel within the castle walls. Cover of night was required to cross the clearing at the base of the castle hill to get to the camouflaged entrance of the tunnel.

But Hunter wouldn't wait until nightfall. He needed to know that Anora was alive and well, and he intended to create the diversion that would allow Red and the others to gain entrance to the tunnel without being detected.

As they entered the hall, Hunter scanned the room for Anora or Tommy, but neither of them was there. Payne sat at the table on the dais with several other men and chewed on a hunk of meat while he listened to one of the men. He was about to take a drink from his tankard when he turned his attention to the guards. He slammed his drink down on the table and glared when he recognized Hunter standing between the guards.

"Baron," one of the guards said as they approached. "We found this man lurking in the forest. He claimed to be looking for fairy folk." He said the last with a derisive snort of laughter.

Baron Payne stared at him for a long moment, then said, "I didn't expect you so soon, Hunter."

"You know this man?" one of the guards asked.

"Aye, I do," Payne drawled. "Was he carrying anything on

him?"

"Just this." The guard handed Hunter's leather belt with his pouch to Payne and the baron immediately emptied the contents onto the table. He picked up a rolled bit of parchment and the pendant Hunter had obtained from the money lender.

"What is this?" Payne sneered.

"Your debt," Hunter said in an even tone. "A debt you now owe to me."

Payne opened the parchment and peered at the information written there, including the signature of the lender that transferred the debt holding to Hunter. The baron's lips went white as he pressed them into a straight line and slid his gaze to Hunter. He pushed to his feet, walked slowly to the hearth, and threw the parchment onto the flames.

"The lender signed more than one copy of the debt transfer," Hunter said quietly as Payne swaggered back to his chair and sat down. The other men watched in stunned silence. "Lord Hawk has the other copy, as well as another letter with my signature signing the debt holding over to him should anything happen to me."

"It is nothing," Payne said with a flip of his hand. "It is a legitimate business transaction. What did you expect to gain by purchasing the debt? Did you think to collect on it today?"

"Aye, I do." Hunter glared at Payne. He wanted to kill the man here and now, but first he had to find Anora and get her out of the castle.

Payne narrowed his gaze at Hunter and tipped his head to the side as he studied him. "Let me guess. You think to use this to bargain for Anora."

"Give her and the boy to me, let us leave unscathed, and the debt will be forgiven." He didn't really expect the baron to agree to the terms, but it mattered not. Before the day was over, the baron would be dead, and Anora would be safe in his arms where she belonged and had always belonged.

If the baron hadn't already killed her.

He tamped down the bile that rose in his throat at that thought, but calmed himself with the knowledge that Payne's pride would keep Anora alive. The baron wanted to possess Anora, and she was of no use to him dead.

Payne laughed, low and mirthless. "You think I would hand over my wife to you?"

A kick in the gut would have been less painful than the shock of the baron's words.

"Perhaps you were not aware that I've known Anora since we were children. Our fathers were well-acquainted, and it has always been their desire we marry." Payne popped a piece of meat in his mouth and chewed as he smiled triumphantly at Hunter.

"I would wager that once Frode is aware it was you who robbed his shop and killed his wife, he will not be so agreeable to the union."

"My new father-in-law would never believe you over me," he said with a sarcastic grin. "After all, we are old family friends."

"I want to see Anora." Hunter's gut twisted with dread. If the sadistic brute touched her against her will or harmed her in any way, he would still kill him, even if what he said was true.

"I'll not let you see her, but I will let her see you." He nodded to the guards and they each grabbed Hunter by an arm before he had time to resist, not that it would have made any difference. "Bring him to the yard and tie him to the post."

It could be worse, Hunter decided as the guards dragged him back into the bailey in Payne's wake. He could have been thrown in the dungeon or run through with a blade on the spot by one of the guards.

His back was pushed up against a thick wooden pole that stood half again as high as a man and his hands were tied behind him on the other side of the pole. Once he was secured, Payne waved off the guards.

He dangled the pendant between his fingers in front of Hunter's face. "You think this is enough to prove my guilt?" He laughed as he closed his fist over it. "I could have gotten this anywhere. After all these years, those pendants could have been bought and sold multiple times."

"*Could* have been," Hunter said through gritted teeth, "but they haven't. You kept them until recently."

"You think you are so clever." Payne drew back his fist and punched Hunter in the gut.

He'd been expecting the blow, but it still enraged him. *Good!* The angrier he got, the less he noticed the pain and the more focused he became. "It wasn't as easy to turn them into coin as you thought, was it," Hunter taunted. "Not when your own father put up the reward for the thief. Every money lender and goldsmith in the land would have been on the lookout for the stolen goods." He clenched his jaw and tightened his neck muscles in preparation for the blow to his face. It stung but irritated him more than it hurt him.

"You know nothing about my father or what happened," Payne sneered.

"True. But I've known many men like you," Hunter said in a deliberately flat voice. "You're a tiresome disappointment who can never live up to your father's expectations, so you demean those who are weaker than you to make yourself feel better."

The upper cut to his chin was more effective than the last punch as it knocked the back of his head against the pole. He shook his head to clear it and stretched his jaw from side to side to ease the pain as he looked at the darkening clouds above. The sky sporadically spit rain down and the wind whirled through the castle yard.

"Hawk is going to be disappointed when I kill you." Payne's eyes burned with hatred as he pulled a knife from the sheath on his belt.

"Aye, he will. But if I die, the marauder who set fire to the homes and farms of the tenants—the one now in Hawk's custody—will testify to the Crown that he was hired by you, which is in direct conflict with the king's edict that the Marcher lords are not to engage in war with each other." That got Payne's attention, and Hunter saw the fear that flashed briefly in his eyes. "It's no secret you didn't like the king's decision to make Hawk lord of Hawkspur. King Edward is not likely to intervene with Hawk's retribution once he knows what you've done, especially if you add killing me to the list of grievances."

Payne clenched his jaw and the muscles in his neck bulged as he held the knife in front of Hunter's face. They locked gazes over the tip of the blade in a silent stand-off. Hunter didn't blink when the baron lowered the knife to his neck, then even lower, to the notch in his throat above the neckline of his tunic. He pricked the skin there with his blade and Hunter felt the light trickle of blood that rolled down the front of his neck, but he did not flinch.

"I think it will do my wife good to see her old lover," Payne jeered through a twisted grin. The rain was coming down harder now, and the baron looked like a madman with his wet hair sticking to his contorted face as he bared his teeth at Hunter. "To see with her own eyes that you will not be rescuing her."

He grabbed the neck of Hawk's tunic, pulled it taut, then cut through it with his blade all the way down to the bottom seam at his hips. Then he cut through his shirt in the same way and pulled it to the side to expose Hunter's chest to the cold rain and wind. He felt his skin ripple into gooseflesh as he stood with as stoic an expression as he could muster on his face.

Payne saw the reaction of his skin to the cold air and his face lit up like a child given a toy. He continued to cut Hunter's tunic and shirt until he was left with completely bare shoulders, chest, and back. It didn't take long for the wind and rain to chill his skin so that each icy raindrop felt like a pin prick. He had to strain to keep his body from shivering, his pride refusing to give Payne the satisfaction.

"Let us see how you fare after a few hours tied to this pole," Payne said as he lightly scraped the tip of the blade across Hunter's chest, not enough to break the skin but just enough to make it sting. "I think you may be more willing to negotiate the debt you think I owe you."

Hunter watched the baron turn on his heel in the slick mud and stomp through the puddles back into the castle. He gritted his teeth together and blocked out the cold that numbed his skin and stiffened his muscles. Payne would be back, of that he was certain, but the longer he stayed away, the closer Hawk and his men would be to arriving at Castle Whyte, and the sooner Red and his men could gain entrance through the tunnel.

They'd ridden hard through the night to get to Castle Whyte, but each time they slowed to allow the horses some rest, Hunter would go over with Red the details of the tunnel, where it opened into the chapel, and the layout of the castle. Red's priority was to get to Anora and get her out of the castle before trying to help Hunter.

A shiver racked Hunter's body as the rain came down harder. He tested the ropes at his wrist, but they were too snug to escape. His muscles started to ache and burn from his arms being stretched behind him. He picked a window on the tower wall that he calculated belonged to Payne's private chamber and focused his attention on it to block out the discomfort.

What he couldn't block out was the fact that Payne had called Anora his *wife*.

Chapter Thirty-Eight

NORA PACED FROM one end of Edmund Payne's private bedchamber to the other. It made her skin crawl to be in the room where the despicable man slept.

The man who had killed her mother for the few coins he thought to fetch from the stolen jewels.

She'd long suspected it had been him, but in the deepest part of her heart, she had hoped it wasn't true. When he put the ring on her finger—the ring her father had lovingly made for her mother—she'd wanted to rail and scream. Edmund had tainted it when he tried to make it into a symbol of their union, but she would not let him. She touched the place under her tunic where the ring hung on a leather thong. She refused to wear it on her finger where it constantly reminded her of the man who killed her mother. Instead, she wore it close to her heart where she could remember the strong, willful, beautiful woman her mother had been.

She stopped in front of the hearth and held her hands out toward the flames to warm them, then turned to put her back to the heat. Her gown was smeared with mud, but it was nearly dry, and she'd stopped shivering from the cold and wet that had penetrated to her skin during the midnight ride from the priest's hovel to Castle Whyte. They'd been closer than she realized to the baron's fortress, and had arrived just before the sun rose.

Unable to stand still, she started walking back and forth across the room again. She was going to wear a hole through the floor with her pacing, but she was too angry and restless to stop. Each time she turned, she looked down at Tommy asleep on the rug in front of the hearth. He was only a boy of ten, but his presence made her feel less alone or afraid. The need to protect him fueled her bravery. Without him here, she feared she may have given in to her despair.

Baron Payne had tried to separate them, but both Anora and Tommy had clung to each other and put up such a fuss that he finally shoved them both inside his chamber and locked the door. From the moment they arrived at Castle Whyte, his men forced him to perform his duty as commander—there were preparations to be made to fend off any attempts of a rescue.

Thankfully, the demands on Edmund meant he did not get any time alone with Anora to consummate the sham of a marriage.

Her stomach grumbled but there was nothing to eat in the room—she'd looked. To her amazement, Tommy didn't complain once about being hungry. Though to be fair, the boy was still so skinny that she thought he must only eat once every other day.

He must have felt her looking at him where he slept on the floor because he suddenly opened his eyes and sat straight up. He looked around the room in confusion, but then his face cleared when he saw Anora.

"We are safe for now," Anora assured him. "But the baron will be back eventually."

Tommy reached under his threadbare tunic and drew out a dagger that looked huge in his scrawny hand. She recognized it as the one Donald had held against his neck and pulled from its sheath to threaten Tommy each time Anora did not comply with the baron's demands.

"I'm ready for 'im," he said boldly. And a little too cheerfully.

"Where did you get that?" Anora hissed in a loud whisper. "*How* did you get that?"

Tommy beamed with pride. "Pretended to trip and fall into the ugly one. 'E ne'er noticed that it was gone."

Anora sighed but couldn't stop the smile of appreciation that curved her lips. He was called *Tommy Cutpurse* for good reason: He'd been a thief living in the streets of Oswestry, stealing from unsuspecting strangers in order to survive for far too long before Hunter took him under his wing and brought him to Hawkspur to put him to work with the blacksmith there.

"Put that away before anyone sees it," she chided gently. "And don't show it to anyone. Keep it hidden until you absolutely need it."

"I wanna' stick the baron wit' it." His expression was so earnest and serious that Anora wanted to wrap him in her arms and hug him for his determination and bravery.

"No, Tommy." She hated to disappoint him, but Edmund would fend off scrawny little Tommy like he was nothing more than a pesky fly. "That won't work. I'll let you know when you should take it out."

He squished his face in annoyance but returned the knife to its hiding place under his tunic. "I hafta piss."

Anora pointed to the chamber pot on the floor. "You can use that."

Tommy started to open his breeches but then looked up at Anora, suddenly shy and embarrassed. "I'm not s'posed to piss in front o' ladies anymore."

"I can turn my back," Anora said, but Tommy had already picked up the porcelain pot. He crossed the room and tucked himself behind the tall wardrobe chest against the opposite wall, neatly out of sight.

A moment later, the door rattled as the key was placed in the lock and turned, then Edmund pushed it open and took one step inside the door. "Come with me," he said to Anora, his voice gruff with irritation.

She hurried toward him and followed him from the room, silently astounded that he seemed to have forgotten about Tommy as he grabbed her by the wrist and dragged her down the spiral staircase. He hadn't even shut the door to his chamber behind them when they left. She said a silent prayer that Tommy would have the good sense to get out of the room and find a hiding place until help arrived.

Payne's chamber was on the top floor of the tower, with three more below it, but he only descended to the next floor down before turning and dragging her out onto the wall walk and into the rain. She cursed him for being an oaf because it had taken her hours to dry, and now she would be soaked through again.

He stopped and tugged her roughly toward the inner wall to look down into the castle yard. "Tell your lover that you are a married woman."

Excitement prickled over Anora's skin as she searched the bailey for Hunter, but the bile rose in her gullet when she saw him. She squinted through the rain to better make sense of what was before her eyes. "Good Lord," she exclaimed on an indrawn breath as she realized he was bound and stripped naked from the torso up.

"Does this cause you distress, lady wife?" Edmund asked with a sarcastic drawl. "He means to bargain for you. But as you can see, he doesn't have much to bargain with."

Anora's heart was in her throat as she tried to inspect Hunter for injuries, but she was too far away to see clearly through the downpour. From what she could see, he stood with his back ramrod straight and his chin high. His legs were braced apart, and he stared at some spot high on the tower wall. She turned to see what he looked at and realized it was the narrow window of Edmund's chamber—the chamber she had just escaped.

"I haven't decided what to do with him," the baron said. "Perhaps I'll leave him there as a fixture in the castle yard." From the corner of her eye, Anora saw him turn his head and look directly at her. "It will be a constant reminder that any man who touches your or even looks at you in a way I do not like will suffer the same fate."

Anora could not take her eyes from Hunter, though it pained her to look at him in distress. He must have felt her gaze because suddenly he turned his head and looked directly at her; her breath caught in her throat.

His mouth opened and she saw his chest heave as he yelled, but whatever he said was lost on the wind. She watched his chest expand as he breathed deep again, but this time she heard the baron's name carried on the wind in an angry bellow.

"Let's get a closer look, shall we?" Payne taunted as he grabbed Anora's hand and dragged her back into the tower stairwell and down to the lower level. He pulled open the door to the bailey and dragged her out into the yard. A guard stood sentry next to the outer wall of the tower and Payne ordered him to follow as they stalked toward Hunter.

A pathetic whimper escaped Anora's lips as they drew closer to him, her heart aching at the sight of him bound and shivering even as he stood tall, his face a mask of indifference. His gaze darted to her when she reacted to seeing him this way and she saw the flash of concern etched across his face. She quickly composed herself and put on a brave face. She knew her distress would be Hunter's weakness and detrimental to either of them leaving there alive.

"You fucking cur!" Hunter bellowed when he saw Anora's face. "I'll kill you!"

She lifted her fingers to her cheek, touching the tender skin. She'd forgotten about the bruise Payne had left on her cheek when he'd struck her the night before, and she imagined it had gotten especially dark and angry looking in the time that had passed since it happened.

Payne shook his head and tsked mockingly. "I can't have another man pining over my wife, Hunter." He released her hand and took a step toward Hunter, but before Anora could follow him, she felt a meaty hand clamp down on her shoulder. She'd forgotten about the guard behind her. "You will never have her."

"Only a coward feels threatened by a woman, Payne," Hunter said. "That's why you like to torment harlots and subject them to your twisted games, isn't it?"

Anora yelped when Payne raised his hand and swung it in a wide arc. The back of his hand smacked against Hunter's face with a resounding clap. Tears stung her eyes as she watched Hunter shake his head and move his jaw back and forth. He spit blood out onto the ground, then looked Payne in the eye in a show of defiance.

"No," Anora screamed as she saw the flash of a blade as Payne drew his dagger. She tried to pull free of her captor, but he only clamped his hands tighter on her shoulders to keep her in place.

"If you kill me like this," Hunter growled, "everyone will know that you could only best me with my hands tied behind my back. Look at the disgust on your guard's face. Even he knows this is the way of a worthless craven."

Anora feared that Hunter expedited his demise with his taunts, but then she saw the mistrustful look on Payne's face as his gaze darted to the man behind Anora to assess his response.

"Fight me like a real man, Payne," Hunter continued. "Untie me and let's settle this, man to man."

Payne laughed, the sound wicked and ominous. "If that is what you want, I am not afraid. God favors noble blood, not fatherless bastards."

Anora couldn't believe that Payne would acquiesce to Hunter's request. That was too easy. He had to be playing at something. Her eyes were on Hunter to gage his reaction, and from the slight narrowing of his eyes, she assumed he didn't believe it either. Her mind raced frantically for a way to help Hunter, for what she could say to Payne to redirect his ire.

Hunter's eyes widened suddenly, and she heard a low grunt as his jaw clenched, but Payne blocked her view of him, and she couldn't see the cause of his distress. As she jerked to break free of the guard a clamoring broke out near the main gate, but the commotion only caused the guard's grip to tighten painfully on her arms. Payne spun to assess the commotion, and Anora saw the blade of his dagger dripped with blood.

"No," Anora cried out in a strained voice. The breeches stretched over Hunter's thigh were red with his blood and the stain grew as she watched in horror.

"Anora," he growled, his clear gaze locked with hers. "Get out."

"Get her inside and lock her in my chamber," Payne ordered the guard as he strode across the bailey toward the gate house.

Anora squirmed and lashed out with a kick to the guard's shin and managed to break free of the man. She ran to Hunter and slid her hands over his as she inspected him for other injuries.

"Get to the tunnel, Anora," Hunter urged. "Leave me."

Anora ignored him and circled around the heavy wooden pole to work on the ropes at his wrist. Her fingers had barely skimmed over the knots before she was picked up by a strong arm around her waist and dragged away from Hunter.

"Let me go," she said through gritted teeth as she kicked, squirmed, flailed her arms, and swung her head trying to inflict damage on the man in any way possible. Her reward was a hard cuff to the ear, but it did not dampen her fight.

Her protests echoed in the stone stairwell of the tower as the guard tried to push her up the winding stairs. She braced her feet against every step and forced him to lift her by the waist to get her over each one. By the time they reached the first level, her stomach felt like it had been pummeled from how many times the guard had to squeeze his forearm into her to hoist her up the stairs.

"I don't have time for this," he grumbled in her ear. He shoved open the door to Payne's solar and threw her into the room. He closed the door behind him and paced back and forth in front of it as he glared at her.

Anora went to stand in front of the blazing fire, holding out her hands to the heat as she glanced sidelong at the tapestry hanging on the back wall that covered the entry to into the passageway behind the great hall. The guard had to know about the corridor, but she realized that he would have no reason to think that she knew about it. She decided her best chance at escape was to get the guard to leave her alone in the room. But how?

Shouts and some screams could be heard through the narrow window opening out onto the yard below. She saw the guard's head jerk in that direction as he balled his fists, likely restless to join the fight.

Inspiration struck. She pressed herself against the wall next to the hearth as though she wanted to hide from the fight and crossed her arms protectively over herself. "Are we safe in here?" she asked in an exaggerated, shaky voice.

"Aye," the guard grunted, but he'd stopped pacing and faced the door to listen for anyone in the tower stairwell.

"It doesn't sound good," she said with feigned fear.

The guard went to the narrow window to look out over the castle yard, then stalked restlessly back to the door again. He did this a few times before he finally turned to Anora and pointed a finger at her. "Stay here and don't come out."

Anora nodded vigorously with wide-eyed innocence and pretended to cower in the nook between the wall and the hearth.

"You leave this room, and I will personally wring your pretty neck," he warned, then turned on his heel and took his leave.

Anora waited a few moments until she was sure he was gone, then ran to the window to see what was happening. The opening was narrow, but she could see men fighting on the castle wall. She scanned the castle yard. Guards ran across the bailey, but they ignored Hunter who was still tied to the post.

Hunter had instructed her to get to the tunnel below the castle, but she couldn't leave him vulnerable and defenseless. She went to the door and opened it a crack to assess if she could get to the lower floor undetected, but the first thing she heard was

Payne's voice as he berated the guard. "I told you to bring her to my chamber, not my solar." The volume of his voice grew as he ascended the stairs in the direction of the solar.

Anora didn't hesitate. She ran to the tapestry and slipped behind. it, bounded up the couple of steps into the passageway, and scurried as quietly she could toward the first alcove. The corridor was mostly dark, but pools of dim light shone where the small openings into the hall below were built into the wall. The alcoves were embrasures with arrows slits in them along the passageway, but they did not afford any light through the narrow openings due to the rain and overcast skies.

As she slipped into the first embrasure, she thought she heard the whoosh of the tapestry being pulled back with some force, and the scuff of boots on the stairs. She pressed herself as deep into the alcove as she could and willed her heart and breath to slow down. The sound of three soft footsteps reached her ears in the quiet of the corridor, then it was silent. She put her hands over her mouth to muffle the sound of her breathing and waited. After a long moment that seemed to last an eternity, she heard the footsteps retreat back into the solar, and then heard Payne shout her name. The sound faded as he continued to call her name and Anora assumed he had left the solar and was ascending the stairs to search the upper levels for her.

With her heart in her throat, Anora hurried along the passageway to the next embrasure, then stopped to listen again. The tower stairs were around the next bend, and one floor below that, access to the castle yard. Men were running down the tower stairs as they shouted commands, but Anora couldn't discern what they said. She waited until it seemed the last man passed by, then hurried from her hiding spot and followed the men down the stairs. It was risky, but she prayed she would go unnoticed in the confusion once outside.

When she reached the bottom of the stairs, a cacophony of shouts and screams reached her ears. She stuck her head out the door to see men running to the gates with swords and bows in hand. It did not escape Anora's notice that this was the same place where less than a fortnight prior she and Hunter had snuck along the castle wall in the darkness to get to the chapel across the way. It seemed a lifetime had passed since then.

There was a small outcropping of a stone wall that she had to get around but then she would be able to see clearly into the bailey. She looked in all directions, including above her, then flattened herself against the wall and scuttled to the corner. Everyone's attention was on the wall above where men were fighting and the clash of swords rang out, the sound only slightly dampened by the steady rain.

A thud next to her made Anora jump and she spun around with the expectation she was about to be captured, but no one was behind her. Something from the wall caught her attention and she looked up in time to see a body fall from the parapets to the ground below. The man landed in a heap of oddly angled limbs, his sword still in his outstretched hand.

She did her best to ignore the dead and dying men falling from the castle wall into the bailey and returned her attention to Hunter. As she rounded the corner and looked out over the wide expanse of the bailey, she saw men emerge from the chapel doors but then quickly retreat back in as a hail of arrows rained down on them.

Her heart leapt at the hope that the men were Hawk's soldiers. If they had gained entrance to Castle Whyte through the tunnel and attacked the castle guard unexpectedly from within the walls, they might have a chance of overpowering Payne's soldiers, even if outnumbered.

Across from the chapel, and in the center of the yard, Hunter was still tied to the pole. He didn't see her as she started across the bailey toward him because his attention was focused on the melee around him. At first, she didn't see the figure behind him, but when he turned his head to say something over his shoulder and shifted slightly, she thought she saw Tommy's wet mop of dark hair. He was working diligently on the ropes at Hunter's wrist with the knife, and Anora broke into a run to get to them and assist.

A scream broke from her throat when she was knocked to the ground and the breath was knocked from her lungs. Something—or someone—heavy had her legs pinned down. She pushed against the ground with her arms to lift her head and chest as she tried to pull her legs free, but she couldn't get out from under the dead weight on top of her.

"Anora!"

She heard the angry shout and squirmed frantically to roll out from under the body splayed across her lower half. Payne yelled again from the direction of the gate and ran toward her, his face contorted in a menacing sneer. She saw him glance toward Hunter as he barreled down on her, but when he realized that Tommy was cutting the ropes to free his captive, he stopped. He looked back and forth between Hunter and Anora, then let out a roar of frustration and turned toward Hunter.

Anora saw the blade in Payne's hand as he stalked angrily toward Hunter and Tommy and panic ripped through her with sharp talons of fear. "Hunter," she screamed in warning as she tried to roll onto her back and push the man off her. He had a quiver still on his back and arrows were strewn around him where they scattered as he fell from the wall. As an archer, he was thankfully not as large as many warriors, but it still took effort for Anora to roll and squirm out from beneath him.

"No!" she screamed as she pushed to her feet in time to see Payne drawing back his arm in preparation to stab Hunter where he was still tied to the pole.

Oh, God! No!

Chapter Thirty-Nine

HUNTER'S LEG BURNED like it was on fire where Payne had stabbed him. His shoulders throbbed from being tied behind him for hours, and he couldn't feel the tips of his fingers.

"Keep working, Tommy," he said through gritted teeth as he tried to look over his shoulder at him. The resourceful lad had gotten his hands on a dagger somewhere and sawed with determination at the ropes around Hunter's wrists.

"Almost there," Tommy said as he grunted and worked the dagger back and forth over the ropes.

"Good work, mate," Hunter said in encouragement as the intensity of the commotion grew around them. "When you're done, put the dagger in my hand, then hide until this is over."

He'd seen some of Hawk's soldiers open the door from the chapel where they had gained access through the tunnel, but they'd retreated when archers spotted them and shot a volley of arrows down.

As he surveyed the action, he caught glimpses of Red's fiery hair and Bard's chiseled face as they slashed their way along the castle wall with a small army of Hawk's men behind them. As long as Payne's soldiers were distracted with the fight and kept their attention away from him, Hunter would be safe. Another couple moments, and he'd be free and then he'd find Anora and get her the hell out of here.

Just then her voice rent the air as clear as a bell above the rain, shouts, and clanging metal. He turned to see her pinned beneath a man, her face full of fear as she screamed at him.

"Hurry, Tommy," he ordered in an anguished voice.

"Anora!"

"No!" Hunter roared as he watched Payne run in the direction of Anora. When the baron had yelled her name, it was full of venom. He wasn't concerned for Anora; he wanted to hurt her.

Payne stopped then and turned his attention to Hunter.

Good! "Come get me you, fucking prick." He could feel that his wrists were nearly free, and he was certain if he jerked hard enough, he'd break the remaining strands of the rope.

Payne was only a few strides away from him, his blade poised to strike as soon as he reached Hunter.

"Dagger, Tommy," Hunter ordered, and felt the blade slap into his palm just as the ropes fell away from his wrists. His limbs felt like they were held down with lead weights, and he moved with the pace and dexterity of a snail. His mind and body would not work in harmony, and he felt like he was caught in a dream, a nightmare from which he could not awaken.

He saw Anora rise up from the ground like an angel ascending to the heavens. She held something in her hand and her mouth was open as she yelled, but he could not hear her. Her arms swung forward like wings as she came to her full height, and he realized she had a bow in her hand as she nocked an arrow.

He was mesmerized by her. Then a surge of warmth spread through his body, and it caught up to the rush of commands in his brain. He leaned to the side and swung his arm forward as Payne brought his knife down toward Hunter's neck. The blade scraped over his shoulder, and it felt like molten fire had been poured over his ice-cold skin.

He felt his own blade lodge in Payne's body, then felt the weight of him slump forward. He tried to pull his knife free to strike again, determined to end the baron once and for all, but

Hunter stumbled under the weight of him as he lurched forward. It was then that Hunter saw the arrow protruding from the man's back. He lifted his gaze and saw Anora looking back at him.

He'd never seen anything so beautiful. Her hair, still silvery white when wet, was wrapped around her face and neck as she stood tall, like the most majestic and ethereal archer he'd ever witnessed. Her back was straight, and her head held high like the women warriors of lore.

She was a goddess.

A fucking goddess.

And she was his if he were brave enough to be the man she deserved.

Chapter Forty

A NORA COULD NOT take her eyes from Hunter.
Her heart was in her throat as she watched him and waited for him to slump to the ground just as Payne had done. She'd seen Payne raise the blade in the air and bring it down viciously on Hunter's neck. It was a killing blow, and Hunter shouldn't still be on his feet. She was afraid if she even blinked, he would fall to the ground, and she'd realize it was all a dream.

Hunter stumbled backwards but he stayed upright, his gaze still locked with hers. She dropped the bow in the mud and ran to him. He limped toward her and held his arms out to her as she came into his embrace.

"Angel," he murmured in her ear as his arms tightened around her back. "You're my angel."

"You're so cold," she said as she slid her hands over his icy skin. "And you're hurt," she exclaimed as her fingers touched the slick blood that streamed down his back. She tried to pull out of his embrace to look at it, but he wouldn't release her.

"It's just a scratch. I'll be fine."

"We have to get out of here. There are archers on the wall." She turned and put her shoulder under his arm for him to lean on her.

"It's over, angel."

Anora felt a pit form in her stomach. "What do you mean?"

"I mean the fighting," he said as he tipped his head in the direction of the bailey as his gaze stayed on her face.

Men still yelled commands, but the chaos was over. Hawk and Bard, wet and bloody, directed Hawkspur's soldiers as they rounded up the castle guard and helped the wounded men.

"Let's get you inside and dry. Your wounds need to be dressed, and you need to rest." Anora tried to nudge Hunter in the direction of the great hall.

"Stop, Anora," Hunter said, his voice gentle. He pulled her into his arms again and wrapped a hand around the back of her neck as he looked intently at her face, as though he needed to reassure himself she was real.

"You came for me," she said as she looked into his eyes. She'd been certain he would, but she'd feared it would be too late.

"I did," he agreed with a small smile.

"And you almost got yourself killed," she scolded as she tightened her grip on him.

"Aye, I did."

"Why?" she asked. Her stomach lurched at the thought of how close she came to losing him.

"I couldn't come through the tunnel and storm the castle with Red and only a few men. We'd have been outnumbered and dead before Hawk and his army arrived. But I was going out of my mind knowing you were in his hands. I had to take his attention away from you."

"You obstinate fool," she said as tears streamed down her face. "If you'd been killed, I wouldn't have been able to breathe again."

"But I wasn't," he said smiled at him, "because of you."

She'd killed a man, and she should feel worse than she did for the horrible deed, but she couldn't bring herself to regret her actions.

"I'm more capable than you realize," she said with a smirk. It was what she'd been trying to prove to Hunter since the beginning of this ordeal, but it seemed unimportant now.

He chuckled weakly. "I knew you were capable, but I've been constantly terrified of what you might do next that would drive me to madness. Now tell me again."

"Tell you what?"

"Tell me you love me?"

She quirked a smile at him. "I didn't say I love you."

He leaned his forehead against hers. "You said you couldn't breathe without me."

She laughed and closed her eyes. "I did say that."

"That sounds like you love me."

"And you said you are constantly aware of me." She would remember his confession in the forest hut for as long as she had breath.

"I did."

"That sounds like you love me."

He pressed his lips to hers in an achingly gentle kiss. "I love you, Anora. I've loved you since the first day I saw you."

"I love you, Hunter," she whispered. "I'll love you until I take my last breath."

She kissed him deeply then and held him tightly as the rain and ruin around them faded away until nothing else existed but Hunter in her arms with his lips pressed to hers.

Epilogue

"COME HERE, ANGEL."

Anora flashed him a grin over her shoulder that made the blood thrum through his veins. She was sitting on the edge of the bed, stretching her arms to the ceiling as she did every morning as she wriggled her back from side to side. It was the strangest and most endearing thing he'd ever seen anyone do when they first woke up.

It was also incredibly alluring.

Her white-gold hair hung in a thick mass down her naked back—he'd divested her of her sleeping chemise last night and thrown it somewhere on the floor—and brushed against the mesmerizing curve of her hip. She turned to look at him over her shoulder. Her cheeks were rosy from sleep, her eyelids still a bit heavy, and her movements slow and languid.

"I have work to do this morn," she said, but he could tell by the curve to her lips that she was open to being persuaded to come back to bed. "And so do you."

"Sumayl will wait. He'd be disappointed in me if I showed up too early when I have a new wife and a new bed, both of which need attention." He sat up, caught her around the waist with his arms, and pulled her over him.

"I think it is you, husband, who needs attention."

"You are right," he nuzzled the side of her neck and nipped at the skin under her ear. "I do need attention," He groaned in anticipation as she wriggled her body so that she was stretched out completely on top of him. He loved the way her soft breasts felt as they pillowed against his chest. He looked down at the perfect globes as he stroked his hands up her backside to her waist.

"Yes, angel," he said, the sound rumbling in his chest as she pulled her knees in by his hips and sat up, so she straddled him. Her hair floated around her like a cloud of silvery gold, her pink nipples peeking out from between the strands that hung in front of her. She leaned forward and let the hair tickle along his chest in a feather-light touch.

He grasped the firm mounds of her perfect butt in his hands and pushed his hips up to grind his painfully hard cock and ballocks against her in invitation. He was rewarded with her little moan of pleasure as her head fell back and her hips circled so that the hot, wet folds of the place he wanted to be more than anywhere else in the world rubbed against his throbbing cock. He slid his hands up to cup her breasts, another groan of satisfaction coming from his throat when she put her hands over his and arched her back into his palms.

When he couldn't take the exquisite torture any longer, he grasped her by the hips and lifted her high, then shifted so his jutting cock was poised beneath her. She lowered onto him with a long, contented sigh and took him inside her as her warm sheath and tight muscles wrapped around him and pulsed. He let her set the rhythm and watched in fascination as his beautiful wife undulated on top of him in the most sensual dance he'd ever seen.

He bit his lower lip as the tempo increased, determined she would have her pleasure before he took his, but God, it was fucking torture. He couldn't stop staring at her as her lips fell open and she turned her head to the side as her breathy pants came quicker.

Every time they made love, his chest ached with his need for her. She'd told him once that she couldn't breathe without him. He felt the same. If anything happened to her, his heart would stop beating, his lungs would stop breathing, and his soul would return to the blackened mound of ash it had been before she came into his life.

He sat up with Anora still straddling him and wrapped his arms around her. "God, I love you," he rasped as he kissed the length of her collarbone, and she wrapped her arms around his neck.

She rocked against him, then put her hands on either side of his head and lifted his face so he was looking directly into her eyes. "I love you, Hunter," she between deep, sensual kisses. Her body tightened and he covered her mouth with his to muffle the sound of her satisfied cries and his deeply satisfied groans as their bodies rippled with wave after wave of pleasure.

When it was over, Anora was draped over him with her head on his shoulder. He lay back down on the bed and took her with him, not quite ready to let her go. They lay contented in each other's arms for a long while before either of them spoke.

"I think we've gone from too early to embarrassingly late to be emerging from our bedchamber," Anora said against his chest, and he laughed.

He looked around the chamber that Frode had insisted he and Anora make their own now that they were married, and Hunter was part of the family. It was roomy and bright with large, shuttered windows that let in the light. The room was on the uppermost floor of the shop and had once belonged to Frode and his wife. But with his advancing age and failing knees, he preferred to stay in a smaller bedchamber only one story up from the shop.

Hunter had never had a true home. The closest he'd come was the cottage that he stayed at when he was at Hawkspur. But even with that he spent more time away from Hawkspur and sleeping under the stars to really consider the cottage home.

Now, he'd have to adapt to staying in one place for long periods of time, but he was ready for it.

"I wouldn't want to embarrass you," he murmured in her ear. "I think it best we just hide up here all day and not show our faces."

Anora gave him a teasing slap on the chest and scrambled out of bed before he could catch her again. "You are not a very good apprentice, and Sumayl will have to find another if you do not start behaving."

"Sumayl wouldn't dare."

"Hunter," a deep voice called from the bottom of the stairs. "Your blacksmith shop awaits, and I am not getting any younger, man."

"Aye," Hunter called back. "On my way."

He got out of bed and went to the basin to wash, then put on his work tunic and breeches.

"When does Hawk expect you at Hawkspur?" Anora asked as she pulled her gown over her head.

"We decided the first week of each month was best. I'll work with the trainees on hand-to-hand combat and teach the fine art of being *sneaky*."

"Oh, be quiet, you." Anora chided with a playful grin. "I am perfectly sneaky when I want to be."

"*Mm hm*," he said as he pulled on his boots. "You still plan to come to Hawkspur with me, right?"

She nodded as she plaited her hair. "Aye. It will be wonderful to spend time with Galiena and the babies. And Lady Alyce says she has a list of items she wants to commission for me to craft while I am there. In her last letter she said Hawk is setting up a workspace for me and has already procured the tools and supplies I need."

"Does Hawk know how much you charge for your work? Or how many pieces his lady wife thinks to commission?" he asked in mock disapproval.

"You worry about your job and let me worry about mine."

Anora pulled on her boots and reached for the door.

"Wait!"

She stopped and turned toward Hunter. He looped his hand in the front of her belt and pulled her toward him. "Just one more kiss…"

About the Author

Lois dreamed of becoming a writer since she was a child making up her own bedtime stories. She started writing after getting her master's degree in English literature, though the road to becoming a published author has been long and fraught with many of life's interruptions.

Medieval history, Great Britain, knights, and castles have been a passion of hers for as long as she can remember, but it wasn't until she was in her thirties that she became an avid reader of romances. After reading The Wedding by Julie Garwood, she was hooked on medieval romances and soon started writing her own. She loves writing about bold women, broody knights, and vexing Vikings.

She currently lives on the US West Coast with her husband and dog. They love traveling, visiting their son (also a writer!) in Los Angeles, and dreaming of living abroad.

Website – www.loistemplin.com
Instagram – instagram.com/lois.templin
TikTok – tiktok.com/@loistemplinauthor